Marion Ettlinger

Sigrid Nunez is the author of four other novels, including *A Feather on the Breath of God* and *For Rouenna*. She lives in New York City.

Also by Sigrid Nunez

A Feather on the Breath of God

Naked Sleeper

Mitz: The Marmoset of Bloomsbury

For Rouenna

Additional Praise for

The Last of Her Kind

"A remarkable and disconcerting vision of a troubled time in American history."
—*The New Yorker*

"Sigrid Nunez teaches an honors-level survey course in the sexual, political, and cultural movements that shaped the thinking (and rocked the world) of so many boomer women. Nunez's voice is unflinching and intimate, her novelistic structure as invitingly informal as jottings in a journal."
—*Entertainment Weekly*

"A compelling account of the 1960s and their aftermath, a carefully written and discerning narrative with closely drawn portraits of two prototypical yet unique women trying to construct a friendship across an unbridgeable class divide."
—*The New York Times Book Review*

"[A] powerful and acute social novel, perhaps the finest yet written about that peculiar generation of young Americans who believed their destiny was to shape history. . . . Don't miss it."
—*Salon.com*

"A masterful construction of the troubled conscience of the era and its aftermath."
—*Kirkus Reviews*

"There's much to admire here: incisive analysis about class, race, and the prison system, authoritative writing about the late '60s cultural landscape and lots of recognizable cultural markers of the time."
—*The Kansas City Star*

"Rich in historical detail, this unpredictable novel zeroes in on what it means to renounce class privilege and sacrifice oneself in the service of human betterment. Stunningly powerful, it is highly recommended."
—*Library Journal*

The Last of Her Kind

Sigrid Nunez

Picador

Farrar, Straus and Giroux

NEW YORK

www.picadorusa.com

Picador® is a U.S. registered trademark and is used by Farrar, Straus and Giroux under license from Pan Books Limited.

For information on Picador Reading Group Guides, as well as ordering, please contact Picador. Phone: 646-307-5629 Fax: 212-253-9627 E-mail: readinggroupguides@picadorusa.com

Designed by Gretchen Achilles

The author is grateful to the Lannan Foundation, the Medway Institute, and the American Academy in Rome for their generous support.

Library of Congress Cataloging-in-Publication Data

Nunez, Sigrid.
    The last of her kind / Sigrid Nunez.
        p.   cm.
    ISBN-13: 978-0-312-42594-4
    ISBN-10: 0-312-42594-5
    1. Women college students—Fiction.   2. Children of the rich—Fiction.
3. Working class women—Fiction.   4. Female friendship—Fiction.   5. Women prisoners—Fiction.   6. Radicals—Fiction.   I. Title

PS3564.U475L37   2006
813'.54—dc22

                                                            2005040098

First published in the United States by Farrar, Straus and Giroux

10 9 8 7 6 5 4

Part One

We had been living together for about a week when my roommate told me she had asked specifically to be paired with a girl from a world as different as possible from her own.

She did not want a roommate from the same privileged world in which she had been raised, she said. She did not want a roommate who had been raised, as she had been (but this was my thought, not hers), to believe you could make this kind of special request and expect it would be granted. I, for example, would never have believed that I could have had any say in my choice of roommates. I did remember receiving some forms from the college housing office that summer, and answering such questions as "Do you mind rooming with a smoker?" But that I could have filled the blank half page under *Comments* with something like "I want a roommate from this or that background" would never have occurred to me. No, I wrote. I did not mind rooming with a smoker, even though I was not a smoker myself. I had no preferences of any kind. I was completely flexible. Though I had done well in high school, I had never taken it for granted that I would go to college: no one in my family had done so before me. That I had managed to get into not just any college but a good one remained a little overwhelming. I left the space under *Comments* blank. I had no comment to write unless it was to say thank you, thank you for accepting me, and when my roommate told me what she had done, it brought me up sharp. How exactly had she phrased it? What words had she used to describe me?

———

It was 1968. "Your roommate will be Dooley Drayton," someone from the school had written me later that summer. "Miss Drayton is from Connecticut." But one of the many changes she made soon after arriving on campus was her name. She would no longer go by the name Dooley, she said. It stank of bourgeois affectation. And worse. Dooley was a family name, and the part of her family that had borne the name, somewhere on her mother's side, had been from the South, she said, and were descended from plantation owners. In other words, slaveholders. So "Dooley" was out of the question. We were never to call her by that shameful name but rather by her middle name, the taintless "Ann."

Her father was the head of a firm that produced surgical instruments and equipment, a business that had been in Drayton hands for some generations (before that they were barbers, Ann told me, and this was true and not the joke I at first took it to be), and the family owned several valuable patents. Her mother did not work, she had never worked, though she'd had a good education. She, too, was from a prominent family, older and more distinguished if less prosperous than the Draytons, and she was an alumna of our school.

"She's one of those women," Ann said. "You know: she belongs to all these clubs and sits on all these boards, she goes to a lot of benefits and parties, and when she throws a party herself, it gets written up in the paper."

I did not know any woman like that.

But I had not needed to be told that my new roommate came from a family much better off than my own. I had seen the clothes she brought from home. I had watched her unpack her suitcases and fill her closet and dresser drawers (the room comes back to me: two of each—closet, dresser, desk and chair, desk lamp, armchair, mirror, bed; I would remember the room as very small, but it seems to me now it must have been a rather sizable room if it could hold all these furnishings) with her beautiful new clothes. But I had seen those clothes before. I had pored over them as they appeared in photographs in the recent "college-bound" issues of magazines like *Seventeen* and *Mademoiselle*. The same poor-boy sweaters and man-tailored shirts, the same suede jackets and maxi skirts. The same tweeds and plaids. Heather in various shades was big that season. High-heeled boots were all the rage. Over-the-knee socks were still in style, and I remember textured stockings.

Not that Ann looked like the young women in the magazines. She was as thin as a model, perhaps even thinner than those models, who were not as thin as models are now. But she was not beautiful. Her lips were thin, so thin I had trouble imagining any man wanting to kiss them, but I suppose men did want to—she always had plenty of dates. Her nose also was thin, and sharp, and her chin was sharp—a profile like a hatchet, I remember thinking, with her long, thin neck for the handle. Her eyes were a cool shade of green, but her blond eyelashes—she was very fair—were almost invisible. She had what is sometimes called blue skin, the kind of milky, near-transparent vein-revealing skin that will not ever tan, a source of anguish to her. The word *meager* came to me the first time I saw her. She was meager. She was mousy. She had poor posture and a gawky walk. Under a hundred pounds she weighed, but her step was tromping, graceless. She did not look rich or sophisticated, there was nothing elegant or chic about her, no director ever would have cast her as herself, she was not a convincing heiress or debutante. "I can't play patrician," I once heard a waiter-actor lament, and neither could Ann. On the other hand, she would not have looked out of place waiting on tables.

She would not get much use out of that perfect collegiate wardrobe. Only for a few weeks at the beginning of the semester, the same period when she also wore makeup and set her hair, did she pay attention to how she dressed. She would set her hair at night, before bed, using setting lotion and large plastic clip-on rollers. In the morning she would comb the hair out so that on one side it turned under, in a pageboy, and on the other side it turned up, in a flip, and she raked the long bangs sideways across her brow. It was a popular style then; it had been popular for a long time. But that year it went out completely—or maybe it had already gone out. Hard to say: styles (in all things) had begun changing so rapidly. At any rate, it was all wrong now, no matter which side you looked at it: the flip was out, and so was the pageboy. Bangs were still permissible, but not set and combed like that, never.

So Ann stopped setting her hair, and then she stopped cutting it. She let it grow, including the bangs, until they were all grown out, and she washed it every day with Dr. Bronner's Magic Soap and let it dry naturally, and that is how she wore it, straight and parted down the middle, her best feature by far, eye-catching in its flaxen plenty. (Those who insisted Ann Drayton secretly used bleach did not know Ann Drayton.) And she stopped wearing makeup.

One day that fall she put up signs in the dorm: she was having a closet sale. She sold everything, even some things she had never worn or had hardly worn, for much less than what she had paid, or what her mother had paid, I should say. Ann did not keep the money. She gave it away. She gave it to some charity, as I recall, or more likely to one of the political causes she had taken up by then. And after the sale, at which I myself bought nothing (she was not giving the clothes away, but to me they were still her castoffs, and I would not have been caught dead in them), she was rarely to be seen in anything other than a T-shirt and jeans.

So far, nothing remarkable. Many of us would change the way we looked that first semester. Many would change our habits as well. Half if not more of the students who had called themselves nonsmokers on those housing forms took up smoking as freshmen, including Ann and me. We could smoke anywhere on campus, there was no such thing as a smoking *section*, and in class more often than not the professor smoked, too.

Change: many new students that year were appalled to find themselves in a college for women—for, of course, they were no longer the same people they had been the winter before, when they'd applied to Barnard. They had not suspected then what they knew for certain now: women's colleges were pre-Gutenberg, and the very first thing some of these girls did was apply for a transfer to a school that was coed.

Ann's mother was furious when she learned what Ann had done. They had shopped for that college wardrobe together. Not just money, but a lot of time and effort had now been wasted. But Mrs. Drayton had little power over Ann, least of all the power to make Ann feel remorse. Ann did not care what her mother thought. She did not care what either of her parents thought. She did not care whether she made them angry or pleased them—you could tell she was happier when she had managed not to please them. She did not please them at all when she stopped answering to "Dooley," as she had not pleased them the year before when she stopped calling them Mummy and Daddy and began calling them Sophie and Turner. It was there from the day I met her, this overt disrespect, and it took my breath away to hear how she spoke about her parents and how she spoke *to* them, on the phone. (Most of us used the community dorm phones, but a private phone was one bourgeois privilege Ann would not do without.) I actually heard her tell her mother to go fuck herself. I heard her tell her father he was a prick. I had never known anyone to speak to his or her parents this way or to treat them with such contempt. I thought surely at some point her parents would draw the line, they would punish her, they would pull her out of school, stop paying her bills—something. But Ann assured me they would never do any of this. "I'm their only child," she explained. "I could murder someone and they wouldn't disown me. I could murder one of them and the other would stand by me." And yet she saw nothing in this to admire. Such loyalty could not dilute her contempt by a drop.

She clenched her fists when she spoke of them.

What had they done to her? Had they beaten or starved her? Had they kept her locked up in a dark room? Had her father perhaps done the unmentionable? Had her mother turned a blind eye?

No. I had seen girls to whom such things had happened, and they did not behave like this one. The girl I knew whose father had done the unmentionable while her mother turned a blind eye was always telling everyone that she had the best mummy and daddy in the world, long after she had been taken away from them.

Not long into that first semester, the father of one of our classmates wrote a letter to *The New York Times*. A Columbia alumnus, he had encouraged his daughter to apply to Barnard, and he had been thrilled when she was accepted. But the school to which she applied was a far cry from where she now found herself, this man wrote. Bad enough that about the same time she received her letter of acceptance, Columbia students had rioted, occupying buildings and forcing the university to shut down. Bad enough that a Barnard girl had made national news after being threatened with expulsion for cohabiting with a boy. The nightly curfew that had been in effect when his daughter applied to Barnard had been abolished almost as soon as she arrived, along with all restrictions regarding male guests. What next?: he wanted to know. Coed dorms?

In fact, the following semester, we would demonstrate for coed dorms by exchanging beds with Columbia undergraduates for a couple of nights, and this, too, made national news.

The letter from the Outraged Father was much read on campus and, of course, derided. I bit my tongue when Ann announced she was going to write a letter in response, and I had to hide how impressed I was when her letter was printed.

It was the year of Tet, the year of the highest number of American casualties in Vietnam. It was the year of the Prague Spring, the year of the assassinations of Robert Kennedy and Dr. King, the year the Democratic National Convention turned bloody (it was also the year of My Lai, but we were not yet aware of it)—and what was it that had stirred this particular American citizen to protest? (I don't think Ann wrote "citizen"; I think she wrote some other word which an editor changed.) Curfews! The relaxing of parietal rules. Ann wrote that she was reminded of all those Americans who were more upset about the use of obscenities by war protesters than they were about the war itself. But her main point, as I recall, and presumably the reason her letter was published, was the inability of the two generations to understand each other. "We seem incapable of agreeing about what is important." For this in itself was an issue of major importance in those days: how parents and children were being wedged further and further apart.

I agreed with Ann. She was right, of course. The man's letter was pre-Gutenberg. And I was glad that in her letter Ann had also pointed out that it was only Barnard students who had to obey curfews in the first place. "We get curfews, they"—our Columbia brothers—"get maid service." For some, that female students were expected to clean their own rooms was more galling than any curfew.

So I agreed with Ann. I think we almost all did. And yet my first, honest (though unexpressed) thought upon reading the father's letter had been: Hey, this man really cares about his daughter.

As it turned out, the daughter herself, a big pink-faced girl with long blond braids who always made me think of a milkmaid, had not been so touched. Her father had not consulted her before publishing his letter, and she accused him of humiliating her.

It was the first time Ann had ever shared a room with another person. (In her house in Connecticut, which would have been spacious even for a family larger than three, she had not only her own bedroom but her own floor.) To her, the idea of having a roommate was thrilling, promising a kind of intimacy that she, as an only child, had never known. Like all only children, she had suffered from not having brothers and sisters, and though she'd always had friends, her childhood came back to her as a time of piercing loneliness. I knew that piercing loneliness, too, and that you did not have to be an only child to suffer from it. She'd been sorry when her parents decided against sending her to boarding school, not only because this set her apart from her two best friends but also because it denied her a chance to live out one of her deepest fantasies. Most of us dreaded the idea of having to share a room with a stranger, but for Ann it was one of the best things about coming to Barnard.

———

What she had really wanted, she said, was a black roommate. But she had not had the courage to ask. She had hoped she might end up with a black roommate anyway. Although in 1968 there were more black students entering college than in any year before, there were still not many. At Barnard, just about all black freshmen were paired with one another. After that first year, when students were no longer required to share a room, most of them would choose to live on the floor that was for black residents only. There was a special table in the dining room reserved for BOSS (Barnard Organization of Soul Sisters), and during meals I would see first Dooley and later Ann gaze longingly in that direction. "I wish I were black" was a sentiment she had no qualms about expressing, was indeed constantly expressing—though never within black hearing, it must be said. She felt only shame and horror at being a member of the cancerous (sometimes it was *leprous*) white race.

We were lying in the dark. It was late, and we lay in our twin beds, I under an army blanket that had belonged to my father, she under a quilt that had belonged to her grandmother. It would become our habit, chatting in the dark like this before going to sleep. A Simon and Garfunkel record was playing, the volume very low. Ann loved music, and to my astonishment she had brought to school an expensive stereo set and two large boxes of LPs.

I did not say anything when she told me this—how she had wanted a black roommate. How she had not had the nerve to come straight out and ask, and so had merely requested someone from a world "as different as possible" from her own. ("I thought they would *get* it.") And when I remained silent, she remained silent, too. The music stopped. The stereo turned itself off. This late, the traffic below our windows was fairly quiet. But there was always at least some traffic, and there was always the IRT. Another astonishment, for me, and reason for envy: how quickly Ann adjusted to living on Broadway. (On the housing questionnaire, of course I'd said no, I would not mind living in a room that got lots of street noise.)

Ann waited, no doubt she was waiting for me to respond, but I only let my silence fill up the room, and after a time I began breathing so as to seem to be asleep. And then I heard a long sigh, and almost instantly Ann herself was truly asleep.

I lay awake listening to her breathing deepen and then roughen into a snore. There was some light coming in from the street, and I could see the outline of her ridiculous lumpy head (those rollers). Between our two beds stood our two desks, and on my desk was the *Merriam-Webster's Collegiate Dictionary* that had been a graduation gift from my high school English department, and beside the dictionary was the leather-handled letter opener that had been a graduation gift from my mother. I wanted to get up and seize these two things and carry them over to Ann's bed, and I wanted to drop the book on Ann's head and, having got her attention, plunge the letter opener into her chest.

Have I said that her chest was completely flat?

For some time I tossed and turned in this wicked state, until I thought of something that made me almost laugh out loud. I tried to imagine anyone writing on the housing questionnaire "I want a roommate who is white and rich."

＊

As usual when I look back at the past, I am afraid of remembering things wrong.

If I am remembering correctly that Ann had plenty of dates, for example, she was probably prettier than I have made her out to be. And what I recall as unattractively *sharp* features might be more generously described as *fine*.

And take this: "The petite, attractive blonde is the only child of Turner and Sophie Drayton." From a newspaper article—and here I am not relying on memory. I have the clipping right in front of me. Of course, for many people it is enough for a woman to be young and blond to call her attractive.

There is a photograph accompanying the article, but you cannot tell much from it, because Ann is looking down, her head is bowed, and her long blond hair has fallen forward to hide most of her face.

✳

The next morning, nothing was said. I thought it possible that Ann did not remember the conversation, or perhaps, because I had not spoken at all, she thought that I'd in fact already fallen asleep and had not even heard her remark about the black roommate. That afternoon, I called home. When I reported the conversation to my mother, she said, "I don't understand, Georgie. You mean, she's disappointed because you aren't colored? Why would a colored girl be a better roommate than you?"

This was, as I say, right at the beginning, when Ann and I had been roommates just about a week. By that time she had made it plain how much she wanted us to be friends. Of course, I knew this would never happen. To be friends, you had to share confidences, didn't you—but imagine baring your heart to a creature like Ann. On the contrary, it seemed to me I'd have to be constantly on guard. I had no choice. I was stuck with the creature for the next nine months and would have to make the best of it. But no one could force me to be friends with her. I didn't need her friendship—not in that place. Already in those early days, I was meeting scores of other girls, many of whom I liked and who clearly liked me. As for Miss Drayton of Connecticut, I would never give her what she wanted. She would have to find someone else to play out her fantasies. I would never tell her what she wanted to know ("Everything!"). I would avoid asking her about her life, and when she asked about mine, I would answer with more silence, or lies. This was my strategy. It would take a lot of discipline—the kind of discipline I was in fact famous for being without. But my mind was set. I would thwart the dream this girl was so pathetically open about: we would never be *sisters*.

Everything she had was mine, she said. I could wear any of her clothes anytime, without asking first. I could use her telephone

12

whenever I liked—if the conversation was private, I should just tell her and she'd go wait in the hall. I could use the stereo anytime, too, and play any of her records I liked.

Whatever she owned, I could borrow. Whatever she had was mine, too.

I did not touch her clothes, most of which would have been too small for me anyway. I did not use her phone, and though the records were too much temptation for me to resist, I played them only when she wasn't there, and afterward was careful to make it look as if nothing had been touched.

Her class schedule was taped to her desk. I learned by heart the hours when she would be out. Other times, if I didn't have class myself, I'd arrange to be elsewhere. Evenings, after dinner, instead of going back to our room, I would hang out in the room of some friends down the hall or in one of the common rooms. There was a TV room and a room called the Quiet Study, and both were usually empty. I would spend hours there, neither watching TV nor studying (I would do almost no studying that semester), but daydreaming (I was a champion daydreamer in those days) or reading magazines or writing letters to good old high school friends whom I missed and with whom, I could already tell—it was part of the abiding homesickness of that first year—I would soon lose touch. Or I would write in the journal I had started keeping that summer, which, when I read it years later, would be charged with the same sense of loss, itself like a letter to someone on the point of vanishing: my own adolescent self.

When, finally, I would go to our room, it was often late. And no matter how late it was, I would always find Ann awake, as if she had been waiting up for me. She was usually reading when I came in the door, and she would close her book and smile at me—shyly, but without trying to hide how glad she was to see me. She would put on some music, her beloved Simon and Garfunkel, or Billie Holiday or Bob Dylan, and we would get ready for bed. She would stand in front of her dresser mirror and set her hair. ("Oh, I *wish* I could wear an Afro!") And while she was setting her hair, we would talk. Or more precisely, she would talk, rattling on without stopping for breath, as if she had been waiting all day for this moment, for me to come home and hear every detail about her courses, her parents, and her period.

Once the lights were out, the talk would go on, even if it was well past midnight and we both had early morning classes. It might go on as long as an hour or two. It might go on till dawn. And it was not just us; all up and down those halls, roommates were awake far into the night. (*And somebody's eyes must meet the dawn*—Dylan.) And it was during these times that my guard slipped, my resistance cracked—I was tired, after all—and something about the lateness and the music and Ann's hushed voice—I would picture her thin, thin lips moving in the dark—cast a spell on me.

I say *spell* because in fact the more Ann talked, the more I wanted to hear her.

※

Something I always gave her credit for: Ann was smart. At seventeen (she'd been skipped a grade, as so many bright kids back then were) she had already had what struck me as a remarkably successful life. There were plenty of Barnard girls who'd been skipped and who'd had brilliant high school careers. But Ann was known well beyond her school for some of her achievements. In eighth grade she had won a nationwide essay contest ("What I Can Do for My Country"), which I unfortunately remembered having entered, too. She had a scrapbook filled with clippings from Connecticut newspapers, and one wall of her bedroom at home was covered with the cups and medals and ribbons and plaques she had won, either in school or on horseback. A framed letter from President Johnson, commending her efforts to organize food and clothing drives to help Bridgeport's poor. (No such commendation, needless to say, for organizing her school's branch of High School Students Against the War.) "To a born leader" was how the principal had signed her high school yearbook. People said she might just grow up to be our first woman president—and among her youthful dreams, Ann once confessed, had indeed been that "silly" one. At the very least, she would make her name in politics. (Typically, precociously, instead of running for class office herself, she chose to manage other students' campaigns, calculating she would learn more.)

But even before she got to college, Ann's thinking had begun to change. She could no longer see herself working for the system. The system was corrupt through and through, she said, and you could not be a part of it without becoming corrupt yourself. So it was goodbye to that dream, as it was goodbye to "Dooley" and goodbye to horses. Oh, she would always love horses, she said, but equestrianism was on that growing list of things (along with tennis, weddings, monogamy, and cocktail parties) that she now called bourgeois affectations. (Sometimes she said, "That is *such* a B.A.," for short.)

Why pretend I was not envious, when I was always envious of Ann, who had accomplished so much more than I, more than any other person our age I knew?

I, too, had studied French in high school, had gotten good grades, and had even belonged to the French Club. But I could never have done what Ann did: write lengthy letters in French to a pen pal in some lycée in Provence.

Even more astonishing, she had written a children's book. Now, here was one of my own grand ambitions, though I never imagined it was something that could be done before I was much older. Years later, when I was indeed much older, Ann would tell me, "You always begin by thinking it can't be done. That has always been your biggest problem, George."

I should explain. George is my surname. My parents—my mother, I should say, since this was her domain—in a moment of regrettable cuteness, forgetting that I would not always be a wittle-bitty baby, but for most of my life a grown and (judging by other members of the family) probably not so diminutive woman, named me Georgette. This might have been something peculiar to our neck of the woods. I grew up with a Clark E. Clarke, a Simone Simon, a Shane MacShane, and a Lee Annabelle Lee. I don't even want to say what my mother named the twins. (Hint: they were born Christmas Eve.) I was called Georgie when I was small, and later Gee Gee. In high school I had to put up with Georgy Girl. (Let me at them, and I will destroy every copy that exists of that dumb song.) In college it was George that stuck—partly, I guess, because of the old girls' school tradition of calling one another by surname. Ann in particular was attached to the name, maybe because of Nancy Drew. I, too, had been a Drew fan and remembered the dashing tomboy cousin whose given name was, oddly enough, George. (Once I knew who they were, I preferred to think of George Eliot and George Sand.) And when someone on our floor started dating a George—a great bruiser of a jock—we called *him* Georgette.

Ann wrote her children's book when she was fifteen. A friend of her parents' who was an artist read the book and liked it so much he decided to illustrate it, and the book was published. Another family friend, a neighbor—not in Connecticut but on Martha's Vineyard, where the Draytons summered—was a filmmaker, and he had cast Ann in one of his films. It was the smallest of roles, hardly bigger than an extra, but still. It was a film almost everyone knew.

Hollywood. Simon & Schuster. Could I be blamed for thinking that the kinds of things that happened to Ann were the kinds of things that happened only in heaven?

Yes.

My mother, who did not like the sound of this roommate one bit, or the way I could not stop talking about her, saw fit to point out that it was *connections* that had got Ann's book published, and *connections* that got her the part in the film. Without those family connections, Mama said, neither thing would ever have happened, and I was not supposed to forget this. My mother, who could not bear that I held any illusions about the world, or that I for one moment believed that I was not just as good as any other girl. For her, the lesson in all this was the old ugly one: it was always who you knew. Which might have been true, but it could not quite strip all the glamour away, not for me.

What got even deeper under Mama's skin was this: Why does she have to go bragging about all these things to you?

But Ann was not bragging. It would be wrong to suggest that she was trying to impress me or to make me feel inferior. It might have come out that way when I reported to Mama (at the time, I was reporting to her about once a week), as it might be coming out that way now, as I write—but that is the problem with memory and narrative. I should not give the impression that Ann lay there glibly ticking off her accomplishments. These and other facts about her life came out over a long period of time, and it was not conceit or boastfulness that made her include the enviable things; it was simply that they were part of the story, Ann's life story so far, and she wanted me to know everything. It was all part of her yearning for intimacy, her need to share. In fact, Ann hated anything that even smacked of evasion or secrecy. She thought there was too much of that kind of thing in the world, and it was wrong. We lived in a society where too much was hidden, covert, and she was not just talking about the government. She held the radical notion that in a truly enlightened and just society there would be no secrets, for the very need for secrecy would have withered away. It was the existence of social inequity and the evils it gave rise to that in turn gave rise to the evil of secrecy. There was the secrecy that came from guilt (this in itself a bourgeois invention), and the secrecy that came when one individual or group desired to keep hold of its power over other individuals or groups and taught them to be ashamed of things for which they were not responsible and which they could not help. (It's been a long time. I may be simplifying or distorting Ann's thought to some degree, but this was certainly the gist of it.)

People ought to be able to trust one another and to be wholly honest and open with one another, and come the revolution, that was how it would be. Glass houses for everyone.

It all sounds much crazier now than it did at the time, but even back then I wasn't sure how Ann could possibly believe all this—though I never doubted she was in earnest. She was never *not* in earnest. And there was no touch of the hypocrite about her. She worked hard to be open, honest, and trusting herself. And so when the time came and Ann found herself in trouble, I remember how shocked I was to hear her accused of lying. It was hard for me to understand how other people—people who held her fate in their hands, no less—could not know it, too: Ann always told the truth.

She believed that some of the chains in which men everywhere found themselves were those emotional ones that prevented them from giving voice to their suffering and letting others know what they needed. This was a favorite theme, a cornerstone of Ann's philosophy of life, and I could never hear it without thinking, Don't let the pack know you're wounded, which was a kind of motto where I came from.

Where I came from. Upstate: a small town way up north, near the Canadian border. Jack Frost country, winter eight months of the year. Oh, those days before the globe had warmed, what winters we had then, what snows. Drifts halfway up the telephone poles, buried fences, buried cars, roofs caving in under all that weight. Moneyless. A world of failing factories and disappearing farms, where much of the best business went to bars. People drank and drank to keep their bodies warm, their brains numb.

The people. Given the sparseness of the population, you had to ask yourself, Why so many prone to violence? Many were related, true, and a lot more closely than you liked to think. Did inbreeding lead to viciousness? Alcoholism certainly did, and alcoholism was universal. Whole families drank themselves to disgrace, to criminal mischief, to early death. Here was a place where people seemed to be forever *falling*. And talk about secrets—more skeletons in the closets than in the cemeteries. Statistically not a high-crime area, but a world of everyday brutality: bar brawls, battered wives. And not every misdeed was perpetrated under the influence.

I remember acts of violent cruelty even among children. Woe to the weak, the smaller kids, the animals (oh, the animals) that fell into those hands. And I remember blood feuds with roots going way back to before my grandparents' time, feuds that left at least one in every generation maimed or dead. The savage world of the North Country poor. I do not exaggerate. The boy next door, a teenage giant with a speech defect so severe only his mother could understand him, hanged a litter of kittens from the branches of a Christmas tree.

And yet for all this, as I say, I was homesick when I went away to school. For all this I can feel even now the keenest nostalgia, and why? Because it was mine, my youth, my home. Because I had turned my back on it. Because that is the way of the heart. And what about my own violence? My wish to stick a blade in my sleeping roommate was not something new. I had known this kind of impulse my whole life, wanting to wound or kill any one of that number (and what a number it was, in that place where it seemed every other person was either bully or predator) who made me feel helpless, humiliated, afraid.

The Duchess of Windsor. What's she got to do with anything? Well, it was she, wasn't it, who had a pillow embroidered with her favorite motto, "You can never be too rich or too thin"? My mother, who was good at needlework, should have stitched a pillow for herself: *Don't let the pack know you're wounded.* (With, say, on the reverse side: *It's always who you know.*)

My mother. Already she has interrupted this story several times. Makes sense. She was very much with me in those days. Did I miss her? I would not say so, exactly. That last year at home in particular, I had been so glad to be getting away, and it would be a lie to say she wasn't one of the things I was glad to be getting away from. Still, Mama was with me. I would have been ashamed had anyone known how much I thought about her, how I sometimes cried, thinking about her. Some of the women who worked in the college dining hall made me think of her: she had worked in a school cafeteria herself. They had her same chronic weariness and sullen temper, the same dark, loose flesh around the eyes, the same coarse skin. It was a given that their legs were veiny, their ankles puffy, and that their backs ached. Home from work, they would fling themselves down, exhausted, and yell at the eldest daughter to start making dinner. If the girl had the spirit to balk—not tonight, she had a date, she had homework, she was pooped herself, she had cramps—her mother would heave her dead weight up and with her last bit of strength deliver a good slap.

If there is one thing I can never forgive, it is the way my mother would, without hesitation or compunction, as if it were the most natural thing in the world, lift her heavy arm and slap me in the face. She did it sometimes even in public, causing people to stare, causing me a mortification that would never leave me. Even now, from time to time, just the memory of this can make me despair, and I will feel, oozing out of me like ichor from a sore, a few drops of the will to live. It might have been news to some other students who were taking the same course in Russian literature: "At every moment, somewhere, a child is being beaten"—Dostoevsky. I knew it from the time I could walk, and sometimes the child was me.

And of course she had been beaten in her turn, by *her* mother and by her father, who kept a birch hanging ever ready from a nail behind the front door. (I saw the evil thing myself, as a child; I touched it with my own hand.)

Later she would be beaten by her husband. And though she died of a blood disease, and at a time when no one had laid a finger on her in years, these words came to me then, these words lodged in my brain when she died, and would not be dislodged: *Beaten to death, my mother was beaten to death.*

O mother of the thinning hair, the mouth set always in a peevish line. O weary, battered mother of the bulging veins, the harrowing periods, the throbbing molars, and the spastic back. I do not remember a time when you did not look worn.

Yet I knew that as a child she had won a beauty contest at a local fair. A Shirley Temple look-alike, people said, and the sole photograph to survive from those days proves it: enormous dimpled cheeks and a mop of curls. Which may explain why I was able to watch those old thirties movies over and over when they played on TV. *Captain January, The Little Colonel, Poor Little Rich Girl, Rebecca of Sunnybrook Farm.* But no one was going to tell me those ringlets were real—no more than the ones on my Shirley Temple doll (always my favorite, not to be supplanted even by Barbie). I learned the words to all the songs and often sang along (*On the go-o-d ship Lol-li-pop*), until my mother ordered me to shut up. Like so much else, those movies got on her nerves. In particular she hated the inevitable scenes (and no Shirley Temple movie was without at least one) in which Shirley had to cry. Even a child could see the actress was not up to this. But she would try: she would whine and sniffle and pout, and the scene would drag on interminably, until my mother snapped, "Someone ought to give that kid a good smack!" It was not clear whether she meant the movie character or Shirley Temple herself. What was all too clear was that Mama's own palm was itching; she would have liked nothing more than to be able to reach into the old Zenith and haul the poor kid out and smack her silly herself.

Now that she is dead, when I think of her what I feel is mostly pity. She has become what memory often makes the dead: more sinned against than sinning. And when I think of her life—with its endless physical labor, its inescapable beatings and constant humiliations—that life can seem to me in many ways hardly better than a slave's.

She had never finished school (her hands were needed on the farm), and though this was not unusual and there were plenty of others in that poor rural community with no more schooling than she had, my mother suffered this like a brand. So ashamed was she of her own speech, she did not like to open her mouth outside her own house. She did not want anyone to know (and neither did I) what a slow reader she was (in fact, she hardly read at all). She could not spell. Whatever long distance might cost, she would always rather phone me than write. Knowing her, she was probably afraid that someone besides me might see one of her letters. Then they would *know*. (Believe me, I would have made sure no one saw.) Sometimes I would use a word—*skittish* was one, I recall; another was *benighted*—and she would stare at me, lips compressed, and shake her head: never heard that word. And she did not like this, either, your using words she'd never heard. She could lash out if you did that. ("Listen, Miss High and Mighty.") You were expected to be more careful.

Until I corrected her, she thought that the doctor had diagnosed her condition as *very coarse* veins.

Those veins that gave her so much trouble came of having six children, including one set of twins, in eight years. My father—where was *he*? Canada, we sometimes thought. It was where his roots were, anyway. ("You call this winter? You call this cold?" he used to tease. "You sissies don't know what real cold is." One of the few things about him I can still remember.)

Wherever he was, no one was looking for him. Whenever Solange, the only one of us who missed him and who would herself run off and disappear one day, used to pester, "Is Daddy dead? Is Daddy dead?"

"*If there is a God!*" Mama would roar.

That story goes something like this:

Another fair, this one itinerant. A fortune-teller, a gypsy who was not a Gypsy, just a former prostitute from Niagara Falls. Holding my father's hand in hers, stroking his palm with one pointed red nail, she saw a long life, she saw a long, happy life of much good fucking, she saw tragedy should he let such a chance pass him by, and before the fair had folded its tents, those two had sneaked away—across the border, some said at the time.

Soon after he was gone, my mother sent Noel and Noelle to live with her sister in Rochester, and we were on relief.

It would never happen to me. My mother's fate would never, never be mine. To begin with, I would never stay with a man who was going to be mean to me. I would walk out at the very first sign.

My best friend in high school, a tough but beautiful girl named Ina, whose homelife was very similar to mine, called me naïve. "Hey there, Georgy Girl, get real. They're all the same, all these guys. They all slap their wives around." Which was true. Okay, not Mr. Tansey who worked at the dry cleaner's; we could safely assume Tiny Tansey had never slapped anyone. But who'd ever want to be with him? Okay, then: if I could not find a big, handsome man who would not slap me around, I would live without men. "What," said Ina, blowing an ugly sound through her pretty nose. "And be like the walleyed wallflower?"

My heart shook. She was talking about that sad case, Miss Crug.

As it turned out, it was Miss Crug, who taught English and French, who really did have something very weird going on with that right eye, and who, at forty or fifty or whatever she was, still lived with her parents—it was that sad case Miss Crug who made sure that my fate would be nothing like Mama's.

Halfway through my junior year I became her special project. Miss Crug was full of plans. *Of course* I was going to college, and I could do better than a state school, she said. She was sure I could get into one of the elite private schools. My job was to keep up the grades. Good that I played basketball and sang in the chorus. Better if I also joined some academic clubs—French, for example. It was said the SAT was not a test you could study for, but at least I could go to bed early the night before and eat a good breakfast. And remember, I didn't have to score high on the SAT, I just had to do respectably. Miss Crug had sought the advice of her brother, who had gone to a state school like herself but now taught at Barnard.

She didn't have to work hard to convince me. In fact, I never understood why Miss Crug carried on the way she did, as if it might be the end of the world (for her? for me?) if I didn't follow her advice to the letter. She could get quite strangely worked up when we talked, insisting that I take this college business with the utmost seriousness and, as if no longer able to control herself, throwing her arms around me and holding me tight, stroking my back and kissing the top of my head. Then she would pull away and stare at me for a bit, her strange eyes that were never focused now focused at last—on some deep point in my soul that it would take me another twenty years or so to locate myself.

My mother didn't have much use for Miss Crug. Like everyone else, she thought Crug was a weirdo; she laughed when she heard her called the walleyed wallflower. But she was all for my going to college, Mama said. She was already proud of how well I was doing in school, turning out to have what she called "a set of brains," being a good example to the younger kids. But with colleges all over the state, and many close to home, she didn't see why I had to go so far away, and to New York City, of all places. "I didn't even know they had any colleges there." She thought—

It didn't matter what she thought. I was going. I got in, and I was going.

I had promised that when I got to Barnard, first thing, I would look up Miss Crug's brother, who taught religion, I think, but I never did. Nor did I ever write to Miss Crug, though I'd promised to do that, too—not even to answer a letter she sent me early that fall. In fact, I never saw or spoke to Miss Crug again. My mother called me *a monster of ingratitude*, a phrase she'd probably picked up from TV. Now, of course, she was all on Miss Crug's side. That sweet Miss Crug who had done so much for me. But had I kept up with Crug, had I written her every week, had I kissed her hands and washed her feet, my mother would have found this equally vexing. With Mama, I could do no right.

I took the bus to New York, a journey that would take all day. Fresh out of bed hours earlier than usual, my mother didn't bother to put shoes on to drive me to the station, and that is how I remember her, shuffling around the bus station in worn-out open-toed house slippers, her thin hair pulled back so tightly in a rubber band that patches of scalp gleamed through. (*Why*, Mama, why?)

No tears, but a squeeze I thought would snap my ribs from that woman who could do nothing gently. "Feel like I'm never going to see you again," she grumbled, and I almost said, *Mama, you have never seen me yet.*

It was still dark as the bus pulled away, and not a mile on, we hit a deer.

From that same bus station about a year later, Solange would take off herself, a runaway. And for a long time, memory linked them: Solange gone missing, the dead deer.

Two suitcases: one old, hard, battered, and heavy; the other soft and brand-new. At the bus terminal in New York, a man appeared— big, handsome, smiling, as if he'd been sent to greet me. He offered to help, and I was surprised when, after hefting each bag, he chose the lighter one. And then, as if to prove that this really was a place like no other, a city where miracles could happen, he vanished into air.

One suitcase. I lugged it to the taxi stand. Twice as heavy it felt to me now, as if everything in the other suitcase had, by a second miracle, been transferred to it.

The taxi driver looked blank when I said "Barnard," making me wonder if it could really be as famous as Miss Crug had said. But when I added "Columbia," he nodded and took off.

"There you are! I thought you'd never get here! Are you having your other clothes shipped? Me, too. It's so much easier. But you must be starving. You missed the Honey Bear welcome dinner! You also missed my *awful* parents . . ."

Blonder, thinner. But not prettier. I had been worried about that.

I didn't say anything about the lost suitcase, just as I didn't say anything about it to my mother when I called her that same night to say I'd arrived. It was only much later that it all came out—the suitcase, the man, Mama's slippers, the deer—one night when Ann jumped out of her bed to come kneel beside mine—"Oh, tell me, George, please, what is it, what's wrong"—having been woken out of a sound sleep by my sobs.

When you think about it, it wasn't such a far cry from psychoanalysis, what took place in that room. Night after night, talking endlessly, supine (vocabulary on the SAT test), to an unseen listener. So—was anything cured by all this talk? Probably as much as has ever been cured by psychoanalysis. I know that I felt cured of something once I opened up to Ann. I felt lighter, happier, after telling her things I'd not only sworn I would never tell her, but I'd thought I would never tell anyone.

Another parallel with the talking cure: our talk came watered with tears.

A girl we knew then who was actually in analysis five days a week (she was herself the child of a Freudian analyst) had been asked by her doctor to keep a journal. In this journal, next to the date for each entry, she would draw one or more tears to indicate the number of times that day she had broken down. Only now does this strike me as odd (though not as odd as being in analysis five days a week); that girl could have been any of us. The moist, blotched faces of weeping were so much a part of that life—like the unmistakable acrid smell that lingered in the dorm lavatories for an hour or so after meals.

From the journal of the poet Louise Bogan, near the end of her life:

Tuesday, 26 July
3 pills by 9:30! Sub *feelings, but no tears.*

Wednesday, 27 July
No tears! 3 pills

Thursday, 28 July
2 early pills . . . No tears!

It's the exclamation point that stabs the heart. (The pills were Librium.)

I sit and watch as tears go by was written above the toilet paper in one of our lavatory's stalls, followed by a couple of neatly drawn pear-shaped drops, and all year long, various hands would add to these drops, until the entire inside of the stall, top to bottom, was covered. Other graffiti, in three different scripts:

Women are mostly water.
You mean: The world is mostly water.
You mean: The world is mostly women.

Once, late at night, when I went to take a bath, I found a girl who did not even live on our floor, fully clothed, curled on her side in the dry tub. Crying. I bent over her. Reek of alcohol and something else, a curdled smell, familiar to me. "Is there anything I can do for you?" Without even lifting her head, she said, "Yeah. Make me a virgin."

"I'll bet they're all virgins, where you're going" (Solange). "You're going to a School for Virgins." Her goofy taunt as she watched me pack. "I bet you won't fit in with those girls," she said. (Because she would not, could not, say *Don't leave me*.) Fierce little Solange, kid sister, baby bad girl. My little runaway.

I didn't know what *supine* meant. I looked it up when I got home. (Strictly speaking, then, the declaration that had provoked such a storm should really have been: The only position for women in SNCC is *supine*, not *prone*. Stokely Carmichael.)

Matter for endless speculation: who was a virgin, who was not. A guessing game, since, each for her own reason, some who weren't claimed they were and some who were claimed they were not. The era of free love might have been upon us, but I knew plenty of girls who were saving themselves for marriage. At least, that was the plan. That's how it was in those transitional days: curfews might have been abolished, guys might have been stealing our covers every night, but early that same fall, Columbia frat boys staged an old-fashioned panty raid (not the last of them, either).

What was an orgasm? In the beginning, only one of us—Sylvia Lustman of Los Angeles—knew. When her boyfriend, Gabe, came to visit the dorm, stares followed him down the hall. So ordinary-looking, and yet!

It was called, sadly enough, the Big O. Hetty Moore, from a large Irish-Catholic family, accused us all of being naïve and shared with us her mother's warning: with most couples, it took years before the wife's orgasm could be achieved.

One thing we never guessed, and the revelation of it gave us goose-flesh: homely, keep-to-herself Kitty Hornby (painful later to recall how behind her back it was Horny Kitty)—the one we'd guessed not only to be a virgin at the time but most likely to remain one right up to graduation and even well beyond that—Kitty Hornby of Wheaton, Illinois, turned out to have been pregnant all along. Her last night back home (she confessed to her roommate, who later told all), she and her boyfriend had taken the big chance and said a proper grown-up good-bye. Her first time! She left for Thanksgiving break (not showing yet but with a face as round, jaundiced, and deadpan as the moon). And that was that. The thing most feared. The thing that could just swallow a girl whole, make her disappear without a trace.

All that year we trooped (in pairs: no one would have dared go alone) to a clinic on West 125th Street, in the shadow of the world-famous Apollo Theater. The marquee proclaiming THE GREAT JAMES BROWN, THE KING OF SOUL, was COMING SOON could just as well have proclaimed the coming of the Pill. New then, many times stronger than any contraceptive drug prescribed today, it came wrapped in rumors of irreparable damage to health and chromosomes. We were guinea pigs—and never more willing ones.

A busy place. A long wait in hard plastic chairs. The only magazines on the table issues of *Ebony*. Everyone who worked in the clinic was black, as were the other patients, none of whom were as young as we. Ann flipped through the magazines. ("I really should subscribe to this." "God, look at these women. I wish I had that skin color.") I leaned back and studied the cracks and stains in the badly water-damaged ceiling. The Catholic in me imagined that ceiling crashing down on me. I thought about Mama: "You get yourself pregnant, and you can forget you ever had a home." And: "If women were as strong as men, half the world wouldn't be here." (The wisdom of Ina.) I had a boyfriend, but I was not in love with him. I had never been in love with anyone, though I seemed to dream of little else. Love—already I had begun to fear it would never happen. My deepest fear: that I was broken.

Before you could get your prescription, you had to have an examination, and before the examination, a little lesson about sex (as if any girl wanting to go on the Pill needed to be drawn a picture) and contraception. (Nothing about the Big O.) The nurse with her life-size vividly colored plastic models of genitals, one in each hand, like puppets. She had to do this all day? How did she keep from laughing? And the doctor, who of course had to be a man, doing his thing all day—how did he keep from crying?

Afterward Ann insisted on walking over to the Apollo. Street vendors out in full force that fine day. Wigs of platinum, silver, and auburn synthetic hair catching the light.

A man in a white robe and skullcap was telling a crowd that the end of the evil race of Caucasia was near.

Ann wanted tickets to see James Brown. The woman in the

ticket booth looked truly alarmed. "You got to be twenty-one," she said. A lie.

It was supposed to have been so exciting, going to school in Manhattan. But for all the time we spent off campus, we could have been almost anywhere. That first year, I don't remember going to a single museum or concert or play. I don't remember hardly ever leaving the neighborhood except for a couple of trips down to Times Square and Greenwich Village. Going out, we kept to the same Broadway hangouts: the West End and the Gold Rail. A block east, on Amsterdam (as far east as most would go): the Viennese restaurant, the Hungarian pastry shop, V&T's Pizzeria. And that, pretty much, was our world. Rarely did we venture below 110th Street. To the west lay Riverside Park, where we were cautioned not to walk alone, not even in daylight, and of course never at all after dark. There was no movie theater in our neighborhood, and what movies we saw were usually ones that were being screened on campus, old films, foreign films like *The Battle of Algiers* and *Jules and Jim* and *Persona*. Like most city neighborhoods, that one has gone through many changes over the years, but a few of the old places remain. They are places I would not enter casually today. Even friendly ghosts can stop hearts.

At some point Ann and I were no longer talking to each other from our beds in the dark. We were staying up till all hours with the lights on or with a few large candles burning. We smoked cigarette after cigarette—just to think how much we smoked then can start a tickle in my chest. But the conversation seemed never to be done. We had to force ourselves to go to bed. Sometimes we went to bed not because we'd run out of things to say, but only out of cigarettes. As good a description as any of that time: one single, endless, smoky conversation, interrupted by classes and a little sleep.

<hr>

Here is an old Russian joke. I think it is my favorite joke.

Two women who are imprisoned together in the same cell for twenty-five years are released on the same day. Before they go their separate ways, they hang around outside the prison gate and talk for an hour.

Whatever gossip was crackling up and down those halls, and there was a lot of gossip, ours was not a romantic love. But love was its name, all right, and like most love, it was not going to last.

Like most love, it was not equal, either.

Others found much to disdain in our friendship.

"The way she courts you is so revolting."

"Does she sleep on the floor by your bed?"

No. But she cleaned our room once a week, with no help from me. She did our laundry. It was she who remembered every Monday to strip the beds and exchange the dirty sheets for fresh ones.

I'd had best friends before, of course—Ina, for example. But Ina was one of our class beauties, a queen bee, with imperious demands, unpredictable moods, and a sting, and at times she had made me suffer. All Ann seemed to want was to make me happy. That's love, isn't it?

"You could tell her to go jump out the window and she'd do it. Why don't you try it, George?"

Ann knew what was said about her, but she had no trouble dismissing it. She had less use for those girls than they had for her. Most of them came from much the same world she came from; that was enough to make her despise them. The occupations of their fathers, the social lives of their mothers, the parties they were invited to and the clubs to which they belonged, the houses they lived in down to the ashtrays and figurines, the dark-skinned maids who worked themselves to the bone keeping everything clean, the cars in their garages, the bright blue swimming pools and the bright green lawns, Ann could have described everything—what was in their closets, what was in their medicine chests, what was in their refrigerators and pantries and cupboards—down to the set of dishes bought specially and kept aside for the sole use of the maid. She knew everything about this breed, she said—what was in their hearts, on their conscience, up their asses, under their skin. The dreams they dreamed while waking and the dreams they dreamed asleep. And to Ann, capable of loving only what was completely different from herself, they had no souls, these daughters of the ruling class. No *soul*. There was only one hope for them, she said, and that was that they learn to despise themselves, too.

One night she arrived a little late for dinner, and instead of coming as usual to sit with me and other girls from our floor, she sat down at the table that was reserved for BOSS. The crowded room went momentarily still. Then conversation resumed, knives and forks went back to attacking the tough breaded veal—but it might as well have been Ann on those plates. My own tablemates were particularly savage, and I did not defend her. (She was often attacked, and I found it hard to defend her. I had grown to love her, but I did not understand her. I loved Ann—how could I not? Had anyone ever been so kind to me? But at times I thought she was mad.)

Meanwhile, at the BOSS table, Ann was not asked to leave. Everyone merely pretended she was invisible, addressing not a word to her and ignoring any word that she said.

It was a mistake none of the rest of us would ever have made, a mistake Ann herself would never make again, either.

But though she later admitted the experience had been excruciating, she had no regrets. "Now I know," she said. "And everyone should know how it feels. For me it was only an hour. Other people have to live their whole lives like that: never seen, never heard." (She was a natural teacher, Ann. In fact, it was in her future. She would be a great teacher one day. She was big on what educators call "the teachable moment," and on turning anything and everything into a lesson. She saw it as her duty to help educate people, but always beginning with herself. It was when she turned to me that she would learn truly crushing disappointment.)

Where Ann was not content to remain never seen, never heard, was in her Afro-American literature course. She was the only white student in the class, and her hand was always up. Her favorite class, her favorite professor (Ann dismissed most of the faculty as "bourgeois ineffectuals"), the first black teacher she had ever had. Among the books on the reading list were works by Langston Hughes, Richard Wright, and James Baldwin—writers already familiar to Ann but of whom I knew nothing. From time to time, as she read at her desk or in bed, coming to some particularly striking passage, she would without warning begin reading aloud. She had a clear, strong reading voice, and at these times it rang with feeling. So it happened that when I finally came to read these writers myself, they would speak to me in the voice of a seventeen-year-old girl.

At Barnard she would carry on her tradition as outstanding student, beloved of teachers, the professor of Afro-American literature no exception. For the phys ed requirement she took up archery and was soon competing brilliantly on the intercollegiate team. It was a mystery to me how she managed it: making all her classes, getting all her reading and papers done, earning high grades, and still somehow finding time for everything else. That fall, she was out there almost every day, antiwar leafleting on College Walk. She went to countless political meetings, rallies, teach-ins. She helped run a free food program she had organized with other students and a neighborhood church group, she was a tutor in the public library's anti-illiteracy center, *and* she volunteered at a homeless shelter every other weekend.

Again, no pretending I was not envious. Here was a person who seemed to be getting so much more than I, not only out of college but also out of life itself. But I had no desire to emulate her. I resisted all her attempts to enlist me in her causes. If I was going to do any work outside school, I was going to have to get paid for it. In fact, one of the first things I had done upon arriving at Barnard was to look for a job. I found one easily at one of the university bookstores and lost it just as easily after the manager figured out that I was turning a blind eye to the liberation of merchandise. So I moved on to typing; you didn't have to leave campus to find plenty of part-time office work. "Never learn to type!" progressive parents of the day advised their daughters. "That way, you'll never end up being *just a secretary*." But for me it was too late. I'd taken a typing course in high school, and I was a whiz. (I remember being puzzled by all the job ads for typists that read "Accuracy more important than speed." Was this not obvious?) I preferred the manual to the newfangled electric machine; a keyboard that offered a little resistance somehow just felt better to me. Something deeply satisfying in the clack clack clack and the cheerful *ding!*; in the swing of the carriage return and the noise like a cricket singing as you fed a clean page into the roller. Also satisfying: the odor of carbon paper, the crinkle of onionskin, the fresh, damp inkiness of a new silk ribbon, not to mention those pleasing names—feminine: Olympia, Olivetti, Corona; and masculine: Underwood, Remington, Royal. Would not Olympia Underwood make a splendid name for a heroine? *On a visit to the country estate of her beloved cousin, Corona, she encounters the handsome but dastardly Remington Royal.*

I would be the last of everyone I knew to buy a computer, and nostalgia for typewriters and other office relics, such as the mimeograph machine, would never leave me.

Full-time student, part-time secretary. To me, it seemed a lot— too much—to ask. (Not that most students I knew didn't also hold part-time jobs.) What would it have been like to have even half my roommate's energy. It was almost frightening at times, watching her go. Someone, I recall, used the word *pathological*. ("People who have to keep going like that all the time are people who are afraid to be alone with themselves.") I remember also hearing her called *manic*, and though that word didn't say much to me at the time, when I think about it now, it does not seem inaccurate. But if there was an unwholesome side to that energy, it was still impossible not to admire—not just the energy but the dedication, the *heart* Ann threw into everything she did.

I don't believe I ever saw her in a state that could have been described as *absentminded*. She was always wholly present and in the moment, to borrow the idiom of a later day. For all the criticism her behavior could provoke (*manic, pathological*), for all the potshots taken ("She's just so fucking go-to-the-head-of-the-class"), and the fun poked ("Look out now, sisters, here come the White Tornado"), Ann was someone people were going to end up taking seriously.

I marveled at the way she continued to draw attention. This was the time when the whole world had begun to be riveted on the doings of youth. Never before had so much importance been assigned to those under twenty-five. That spring, *Newsweek* did a special report on American undergraduates, and though there was nothing at all typical about the undergraduate Ann, she was one of those sought out and written about. (It may have been the letter that was published in the *Times*, Ann's response to Outraged Father, that brought her to the attention of the *Newsweek* writers.) There was a photograph, taken in our room: Ann, smoking a cigarette, arms crossed on her chest, leaning against the wall between two posters she'd hung: Ho Chi Minh and Malcolm X. Posed. Smileless. A quotation running underneath: "What we want is for America finally to face up to its crimes."

Our own dorm room, right there in the pages of *Newsweek*.

Where was I?

Who was I? Like most undergraduates, I was just some anonymous student, known only to those who were taking the same courses or who lived on the same floor. Ann Drayton, on the other hand, was known to everyone.

We had one professor in common, Ann and I, and one day in her office this professor said to me, "Someday that roommate of yours is going to do something *big*." And I just glared at her—not because I doubted her prediction, but because we were supposed to be talking about me.

And what was there to say about me?

To begin with, the good student I had once been, the one who had inspired such hopes in Miss Crug, had somehow got left behind. I was diligent enough for the first couple of weeks, but then I started skipping classes, and (when this went unnoticed) more classes. Then I started missing assignments, and every paper I handed in was late. I never studied; I took all my exams cold. By spring, it looked as though I might flunk out. In fact, I had already begun to think about dropping out, except I had no idea where to go. Certainly not home. When I did go home, first for Thanksgiving and then for Christmas, I suffered a kind of culture shock from which it took me weeks to recover. It was a bad year. (That was the Christmas the boy next door hanged the kittens.) Mama had lost her job when the nursing home where she'd been working closed down. The family was living on her unemployment checks and donations from the church. With no job to go to, some days she never even bothered to get dressed. She spent a lot of time prone or supine, and she had lost more hair and gained quite a bit of weight. She had migraines, and even when her head wasn't splitting, her eyes remained glazed and hooded as in pain. You almost never saw the woman smile. Things were different between us. For one, we had stopped talking regularly on the phone. She didn't seem particularly glad to have me home or sad when I had to leave again. She didn't ask me how I was doing in school; she didn't ask me anything about my new life at all. It was as if simply by having been away a few months, I'd been forgotten. Out of sight, out of mind.

Even more worrying to me was Solange, who'd fallen in with a high school crowd that was doing more drugs than we were in college. In fact, that was the year heroin found our little town (everyone up there called it snow), and I'd already heard about old classmates of mine who were said to be strung out. So far, Solange was only snorting. I knew that—contrary to what some would have had us believe—a person could snort without automatically progressing to skin-popping and could skin-pop without progressing to mainlining and could mainline without becoming a total, flat-out junkie and ending up in the gutter (I would be acquainted with such persons all my life: hardworking good citizens and dutiful parents who just happened to like to shoot up once in a while), but Solange was exactly the kind of troubled teen about whom you feared the worst. My mother, without even knowing about the drugs (as mothers never seem to do), was so enraged by Solange's behavior (back talk, playing hooky, staying out with her friends all night long) that she had gone from slaps to serious battery. Solange was covered with bruises that Christmas.

I was worried, too, in a different way, about little Zelma, born after Solange and before the twins. The "good" sister, the white lamb of the family, the one who always did the most to help our mother and who had been like a little mother herself to the twins once they came back from our aunt's. Never smiling, like our mother, but mild. Utterly somber and selfless, she was eerily silent, always, in the heartbreaking manner of certain children who've seen too much too soon. "Quiet as a nun," we used to say, perhaps once too often, for she is a mother superior today. We all had our ways of escaping. Our brother Guy had joined the army—to our collective sorrow, because with our father gone, Guy, the oldest and the only boy besides baby Noel, was the man of the house. Even before our father left, we had looked to Guy for protection— sometimes from our father himself. More than once Guy had stopped him from hurting Mama, and that time when my father insisted on checking to see if my first bra really fit, I knew it was not to my mother I should turn, but to Guy. And Guy straightened him out.

He was back now, Guy, back from the war, where he, too, had discovered heroin, and this was his first Christmas home. He'd only just received his discharge from the army and wasn't sure what to do next. But he had his eye on Ina.

Ina was in trade school now, studying to be a beautician. She had not changed much, except for her looks. She had straightened and dyed her black hair blacker. Punk—Goth—before her time, she looked like Morticia Addams with that dark, dripping hair. She wore black clothes, a cross made of two metal nails around her neck, metal tacks in her ears, purplish black lipstick, and sooty eye shadow. I had missed Ina and was happy to see her again, but hanging out with her was no escape from family, for she was soon to be family, and by that summer she would also be, as they used to say, in a family way. And though at the time I was crazy about my big brother, I didn't see how a girl as tough-minded and worldly-wise as Ina, who knew us so well and whose own family was as much like ours as right hand is to left, could make such a stupid mistake. Okay, so he was good-looking—very—especially now that he was out of that geeky uniform and could let his hair grow. Past his shoulders he let it grow, and his new uniform was tight jeans and cowboy boots, a cowboy shirt unsnapped halfway down, and turquoise beads adorning his smooth, hard chest. He looked like the best thing a man could look like at that time, or any time, maybe: he looked like a rock star. So I could see how he might dazzle a girl. But Ina—hard-as-the-nails-around-her-neck Ina—how could she not see what I saw, in a flash, the whole thing, family history repeating itself. He would give her babies, and he would beat her, and one day he would up and leave her, his father's son after all.

Oh Ina! At my mother's wake, the last time I saw Ina, I could not help staring at her, searching for our old class beauty in this— witch. And even though this was a wake, and that was my own mother lying there, and Father DuMaurier himself sat within hearing, Ina raised her voice: "What the hell you looking at?"

This was my family, this was my home, but no, it wasn't—not if home meant a place where you wanted to be, where you felt safe and loved and sure you belonged. But of course, school wasn't any home, either. In spite of Ann, to whom I now felt closer than to any sister, and in spite of my other friends, who were indeed like a new family to me, I could never feel at home in a place where I was always aware of being different from everyone.

Arriving back at the dorm from Christmas vacation, in the elevator, I heard one girl say to another, "The skiing was fantastic, but we decided next year we're all going to meet in Paris."

And take the war: what a big issue it was on campus, how you could not escape it. Vietnam, Vietnam, Vietnam. But no one else I knew had a brother who was actually there. And no one else I knew was so close to flunking out and thinking of quitting.

It was shocking how much I had changed as a student in so short a time. My old teachers would not have known me. The only course I really cared about was the seminar in poetry composition I had taken my first semester, and that had turned into a debacle (another SAT word).

For as long as I could remember, I had written some kind of poetry—the great happy-making activity of my childhood—and what I'd always heard from people who read it was that it was good. It was the one way in which I was said to be superior to other kids, as Guy was superior at ice hockey. In school, in almost every grade, there had been something—a teacher's praise, a prize, publication in the school magazine: proof. And so I had grown up believing I had a gift, a calling that would bend my life to a certain path. Of course I never thought too much or too specifically about what making a life as a poet might mean, assuming the thing to do was to keep writing and everything would fall into place. I had never given much thought to what I would study when I got to college, either, but I knew that I wanted to keep writing, and I looked forward to being, for the first time in my life, in a class that was devoted to poetry. I had no doubt it would be my favorite class, the one class where I would know what I was doing and where I was destined to shine. And I could not wait to shine. Those times when I had allowed myself to be caught up in Miss Crug's fantasy and to dream with her that something momentous was being prepared for me, this was how my imagination framed it: my life as a poet was about to take shape.

We were a small class, only eight students—eight girls and one girlish instructor not long out of Barnard herself. We met at a round table in a book-lined room for two hours one day a week. Students were required to write a new poem each week and to hand these poems in ahead of time so the teacher could have them copied and ready to be read and discussed when we met for class. We were instructed not to write our names on our poems. Only the teacher would know who each author was. In class, our poems would be discussed anonymously—"So that you can talk about them more honestly and without personalities getting in the way," the teacher said. But she might as well have said, *So that you can be as tactless and brutal as you wish*.

From the first class, I found myself in the grip of a delusion, hard to explain but equally hard to shake, that all these girls and the teacher—everyone, that is, except me—had known one another before. I knew this was preposterous, and yet the feeling persisted, ever more unsettling. It arose from the fact that everyone else seemed to speak the same language and to talk about poetry in a way that I had never talked about it or could talk about it. The kinds of poems the other students wrote were written in this same elusive language. I didn't understand them for the most part, either, and I didn't know what to say about them. The only thing not obscure to me was that the problem was all mine. I was the only one in the class consistently at a loss, and I was overcome by the kind of shyness and fluster you feel when you are indeed among people whose language you speak poorly or not at all. A tourist, say, or (worse) an immigrant. A stranger. After a few humiliating attempts to express myself, I clammed up, afraid—ashamed—to open my mouth.

Each time we finished talking about a poem, the teacher would ask the same question: "Would the author of the poem like to identify herself?" Sometimes the author would, sometimes she wouldn't. But there was one who always would. A sophomore with a wide masculine face and a bulging forehead who for some reason never removed her coat and sometimes sat all through class with a hat on as well. A tricorne hat à la Marianne Moore . . . She was the class star—even the teacher deferred to her—the one who always had the most to say, and of all the poetry we read in that class, hers, the best liked, the most highly praised, was to me the most impenetrable.

But if I did not understand the poems of my classmates, they had no such difficulty understanding mine, no difficulty finding them, every poem, every line, every word, wanting. Worse than wanting. Not that I was the only one whose work was criticized—far from it. The concealing of identities really did encourage everyone to be pitilessly frank. But as far as I could tell, no one else's poems were so unequivocally and unanimously disliked. Week after week, poem after poem, everything I wrote was put down. Each time the teacher asked her question—"Would the author like to identify herself?"—I froze, meanwhile writhing within, certain that everyone had to know, from my downcast eyes and crimson face, that the despised author was me.

"Those *idiots*. Those fucking *bitches*. Well, what do you expect? Here you are writing about *reality*, but of course they're all too spoiled and stupid to see it. They wouldn't know *reality* if it came up and bit them in the *face*" (Ann).

One day, after the class had left yet another bloodied poem of mine for dead and we were about to move on, the star of our class flipped a hand in the air and said, "May I add just one more comment about this poem?" And I braced myself. I was well aware of how my poems got under this particular reader's skin, and she had a look of grave displeasure on her big face.

"I just want to say, this is the kind of poem that I *hate*." She exhaled fiercely on the last word—a real dragon hiss of contempt—and because I happened to be sitting directly across from her that day, her breath blew right in my face and a fleck of saliva landed on my cheek. I jerked my head as if scalded, and then, in a little fit of compounded shock, confusion, and hurt, I half rose out of my seat. Aware of heads turning, of eyes widening all around the table, I sat back down again. I barely heard the teacher above the roar of blood in my ears. "All the more reason for us to move on, then. But first, would the person who wrote the poem like to identify herself?"

Today I ask myself the obvious question: Could those poems of mine really have been so bad? And I answer: Yes. They must have been exceedingly bad. I have no real doubts about this, though in what particular ways the poems were bad I cannot say, since I kept no copies and I have no memory of them, as I have no memory of anything written by anyone else in that class. In fact, try as I might, I cannot remember the name of a single one of those students now, or even the name of the teacher. And this is significant, because in general I have a good memory for names.

You'd think I would remember everything about an experience that changed my life. Poetry was something to be put away now, with other childish things. This was what the class had taught me. I never took another poetry class, and in all the years that followed, I never wrote another poem again or even tried to write one. And though it would be another year before I actually dropped out, that class helped set things in motion, coloring my attitude toward all my other classes, toward being in college in general, intensifying my fear of not belonging, of not speaking the same language as everyone else—a language I might be capable of learning enough to get by, but in which I would never be fluent.

What had happened to the honor student, to the "set of brains" even my mother had to admire—what had happened to my calling? Had it all been a mistake, a big lie?

These questions were a torment to me above all because I had no answers for them, and in my heart I was often hard on Crug, whom I cursed and blamed.

And if I was not going to be a poet after all, what kind of life *was* in store for me?

In those days, everyone was reading a certain book. I myself had not read the book. I did not even know for sure what it was about, but the title spoke to me, describing how I often felt: I was a *Stranger in a Strange Land*.

I did not fail out that first year, partly because the college did not want me—or any student for that matter—to fail out, and partly because I managed to pass all my finals, a feat that could not have been accomplished without the help of speed. But I was always ready to take speed, whether I had a good reason or not. By now, drugs of every kind were easy to come by, and we had the milkmaid, Outraged Father's daughter, going up and down the halls with her pails full of uppers and downers. Now was the time to put in your order for black beauties, which not only would enable you to stay up all night cramming but would also sharpen your powers of reasoning and argumentation, rhetoric and expression. (Is this really so different from an athlete using performance-enhancing drugs? Think about it.)

May. The campus magnolias in bloom. Long days in the library, long nights at my desk, typing furiously, poor Ann trying to sleep with her pillow over her head. Smoking furiously, chewing gum furiously, no appetite, but unquenchable thirst. First light and birdsong. (*And somebody's eyes must meet the dawn.*) Forty-eight hours, no food, no sleep, something like the beginning of bedsores from so much sitting. *Hundreds* of cigarettes. *Gallons* of coffee. Shakes, sweats, nausea, palpitations. Panic attack. ("This shit is strong. If you can't come down, let me know, and I'll give you a hit of Thorazine.") Crashing, sleeping fifteen, twenty hours straight, unrousable ("You were starting to scare us"). Waking at last with a splitting head, hacking cough, bleeding gums, many pounds lighter, and hungry enough to eat cockroaches.

After school closed that year, I went home only briefly (I had decided I would not spend another vacation with my family unless we all agreed to meet in Paris). Then I returned to the city, where I had rented a room in one of the dorms that the university kept open for summer housing. ("Dear Ann, You won't believe how hot it is here! I'm working at Bonwit Teller.") The collection department, sole duty typing addresses on form letters, nine to five, seventy-five dollars a week.

Clack clack clack *ding!*

When you pushed through the store's revolving door, you got a whiff of perfume, and printed on a small card posted on the wall was the name of the perfume.

An hour for lunch. Strolling along Fifth Avenue and in Central

Park, visiting the bears in the zoo, discovering the Museum of Modern Art and the galleries on Fifty-seventh Street. My introduction at last to the city's heart. Midtown: beautiful, romantic, grown-up world. Inspiring me to make a dozen promises to myself, many of which I would keep. A stupid, boring, humiliatingly low-paying job. Yet I had never felt so free. My letters to Ann, who spent a month home in Connecticut before heading west, were full of hope.

The perfume in the air today is My Sin.

Dear George, I think it's positively wonderful we are both doing what we want to be doing this summer and not what our parents or anyone else wanted us to do. I believe that we must live our lives to the fullest while we're still young. We don't want to be full of regrets later on, about all the things we never got to do, the way so many old people are. "To be nostalgic for what was *is painful enough; to be nostalgic for what* never *was is torture." I don't remember who said this, but I know it must be true. Oh George, I miss you so much! We'll have so many things to talk about when we see each other in September!*

Later these memories would make me bleed. What if I *had* been home that summer? Could I have stopped Solange from running away?

Dearest Ann, If you can be nostalgic for things that never were, can you also be homesick for a home you never had?

Home? What home? is how I kept hearing Solange answer the question I imagined everyone she met must be asking.

"It sounds paradoxical," one of the police investigators said, "but a lot of these runaways are actually trying to *find* a home."

It sounded right on to me.

According to the police, there had been a great rise in the number of runaways—more American teenagers had run away from home that year than ever before. Fifteen was about the average age (Solange was fourteen and a half), and most runaways—almost three-quarters, I was surprised to hear—were girls. It seemed like a boy thing, didn't it: walking out of the house with just a few bucks and not even a change of clothes and hopping the next bus. Today it is still true that the majority of runaways are girls, and it still surprises me.

So many things we learned from the half dozen investigators, some local, some federal, who came to be involved. Most runaways didn't stay on the run very long. They were back with their families within weeks or even days. Tired, hungry, filthy, scared, they tended to be tight-lipped about where they'd been and what they'd done. Unfortunately, many of these returnees would try to run away again. One of the investigators spoke—inevitably—of "a vicious cycle." On subsequent tries, the runaway could be expected to go missing for longer and longer periods of time. But only a tiny number of runaways disappeared without a trace. Even a runaway who never actually came home again was more than likely to let someone, if not her parents, know at least that she was alive. The question was *when*. In some cases, it could be years. If Solange telephoned, we should try to find out where she was calling from ("carefully, now") and waste no time getting that information to the police. We were told that runaways often got in touch on their birthdays or around holidays. Instead of calling, she might write, and in that case we'd have a postmark—countless kids had been tracked down through postmarks. It helped that many of these kids were in fact hoping to be tracked down.

"Try not to worry too much, Mrs. George," said one of the men, kindly patting my mother's arm. "We know how much you love your daughter, and we believe she knows it, too. All of a sudden, out there in the cold, cruel world, it's going to hit her that home isn't such a bad place after all."

But I knew that down deep, under her shock, under her fear, my mother was as angry at Solange as she had ever been in her life, and I knew that Solange knew it, too, and however bad things might be out in the cold, cruel world—however much she might be secretly hoping to be tracked down—there was this to give her pause. One of my last memories of Solange was of her trying to cover her bruises, smoothing pancake makeup all over as if it were body lotion. When she was in a rage, my mother would often threaten to kill us, and we believed her. Enraged, she seemed crazed enough to kill anyone. According to Zelma, the week before Solange ran away, things had reached such a pitch that Zelma herself feared Mama would go too far. Worse than threatening to kill her, my mother had threatened to shave Solange's head, inciting Solange to make some serious threats of her own. "If Mama really did what she said, Solange said she was going to burn the house down, Georgie!" Poor Zelma had turned to Father DuMaurier. She began by talking about Solange and Mama but ended by talking about herself. "I

47

cannot live in a house of hate." Young as she was, Zelma was already meditating her own escape, not only from that house of hate but from the wider, hate-filled world.

Of course it was not little Zelma but Guy who had always been the family peacemaker—and Guy had moved in with Ina. It occurred to me that the move might even have played a part in Solange's disappearance. Like me, Solange had idolized Guy (I have often wondered whether our rivalry for our big brother's affection kept us from being as close sisters as we might have been, growing up). First, I go away to school. Then Guy moves in with his fiancée. It made sense that Solange was feeling abandoned.

Guy was taking his favorite sister's disappearance hard. I thought it was partly a question of masculine pride. He had not been there—and was not there now—to protect her. Also, Guy was possessive, and it upset him that Solange could have taken such an extraordinary step without so much as a hint to him. But to me, this said that Solange had probably acted impetuously.

None of this was shared with the police, who, to my surprise, never asked to speak with any of us alone, out of our mother's presence. They did, however, speak with Solange's friends. Talk about tight-lipped. My mother wanted to know why, being the FBI, they didn't tap Solange's friends' phones. If they did, she was certain they would learn something. The men explained that they could not do such a thing, because it was illegal. My involuntary sneer (these were Hoover's men, after all) caught one's eye.

"So you're the college girl." None too friendly, and no surprise. Clashes between cops and college students were routine by now, a part of the national crisis, and in spite of the reason why these particular cops were in our living room, it was a given we were still going to see each other as being on opposite sides. I was wearing purple jeans and a tie-dyed shirt. I was sitting on the couch next to Guy, whose hair was as long as mine. He'd gotten a lot of tattoos in the army, and the most visible one right now was the peace symbol below the knuckle of the third finger of his right hand. His eyes were bloodshot. Under the circumstances, this could have been taken as a sign of emotion or a bad night's sleep, but I knew better, and I worried that a cop might know better, too.

"Which college?"

"Barnard."

"And where is that?"

"Um, Columbia University?" As if I were guessing.

"Right." As if he'd only been testing me.

His partner interrupted. "Let me ask you something. Is your sister a hippie, too?" Guy and I exchanged a look. Was this about drugs? No. "Is she into free love and all that?"

It was not just a prurient question. As it turned out, Solange's sex life was more than relevant. Most runaways were girls, and "it's not the good little virgins who hop on the Greyhounds." It was the sexually active, sexually precocious ones. If we didn't know that, alas, far too many others did, and they were out there, "a vast network of predators," stalking bus and train stations and certain streets and parks and shelters in towns and cities all over the land. They lay in wait, ready to "befriend" these lost girls and lure them into prostitution. And in fact, some staggering number of runaways ended up turning tricks even before pimps got to them. And if a girl had already got herself into the life, especially if she'd become the property of some adult male, "well, let's just say this could complicate things." Who wouldn't hesitate to call her mother if . . . "It's a hard life to live, and an even harder life to leave."

Once the talk took this turn, my mother had to leave the room, and I began to sniffle, and I thought it was good that Guy was mellow.

One thing I did not understand: if this *vast network of predators* knew exactly where to go to find these runaway girls, why didn't the police know, too? In fact, they had to know—so why didn't they cover those places and get to the runaways before the bad guys did? I mean, even if they couldn't save them all, they should have been able to save most of them. Or lots of them. Or at least some. Or one. *Oh, please, dear God, just one, just one.* What was it with the cops, anyway? Why weren't they all out there rescuing poor girls from pimps instead of coming after us for demonstrating against war and racism and smoking a little harmless marijuana? Oh, this *society*.

But even the ones who ended up working as prostitutes, we were told, even the majority of those girls could be expected sometime to resurface and be reunited with their families.

Ruled out: that Solange had gone in search of our father. She had by this time joined the rest of us in believing that he was as good as dead and she was better off without him.

Because of the rising number of runaways, police had begun working with bus companies to try to raise awareness and help personnel identify such kids. You couldn't *stop* a nervous-looking teenage girl traveling alone without any luggage on a one-way ticket as far as her money would take her, but you might at least make a mental note. You might remember to look at her hard enough so that when someone came by later and showed you a photograph, you'd recognize her. Then you might be able to say where she had got off the bus.

I have no idea how successful in general this police effort was, but as luck would have it, Solange had disappeared just days before the Woodstock music festival, when hundreds of thousands of kids all over the country, and above all in the Northeast, were on the move. It was known that she had arrived at the bus station on a Tuesday morning and had taken the next bus out, a bus that happened to be going to Albany. She knew no one in Albany, we were pretty sure of that. From Albany she might have gone anywhere. Bethel, for example. Not ruled out: that she'd been making her way to the Woodstock festival. (Except, to me, this didn't make much sense. Why wouldn't she have waited and gone with her friends?) It was also possible she had got off the bus somewhere before Albany. Anything was possible. That was the horror of our situation. New York City being a place where so many runaways headed, or drifted, sooner or later, we could cling to the hope that one day she'd show up at my door. (Always—long, long after there was any need—I have made sure that my phone number, with my full name and address, is listed; I leave messages on my voice mail giving the number where I can be reached even if I plan to be gone just a day. "For god's sake," my first husband used to tease. "*I'm* the doctor!")

I was ashamed to think how unlikely it was that Solange would show up at my door or even call. We had shared a room the whole time we were growing up, but since leaving home I had all but ignored her existence. I had never invited her to come visit me in New York, though I knew this would have meant much to her. She had been right to feel I had abandoned her. I had abandoned them all. I had never given serious thought to Solange's future, and there had been no one like Miss Crug to look out for her. Besides, Solange was a terrible student. The way she was forever fussing with her hair and nails, I guessed she'd end up studying beauty culture, like Ina. When she was younger, her dream had been to become a figure skater, and she had much of what it took, the strength and the grace and a certain daredevilry, but no discipline. Same story as Guy and ice hockey.

I imagined her arriving at the Port Authority Bus Terminal, just as I had the year before, the same man stepping up to greet her and to offer, in his gallant way, to carry her suitcase. Only she had no suitcase. She had taken nothing with her besides a purse—itself the size of a small suitcase: a big black shiny vinyl zippered thing that had got her into trouble at school. At school there was a prohibition against skirts that were too small and handbags that were too large. Both were considered—*unladylike*, was the euphemism. A proper student carried a proper schoolbag, we were told. Feed bags were for horses. And: A lady never carried a purse larger than a book. I would, today, be grateful to anyone who could explain this baffling objection to large purses and just what it was about them that supposedly said *slut*. At any rate, she who broke the rule had better be prepared. Purses like Solange's were likely to be seized and searched.

Port Authority. Times Square. *Just a come-on from the whores on Seventh Avenue.*

Back in New York, everyone knew where the whores and the runaways were to be found, and I toyed with the idea of looking in those places myself, but it seemed such a wild, hopeless plan, needle hunting in a haystack, and it could be dangerous. (One day, a student who'd gone to the bus terminal to collect signatures for a petition against the war came back in tears. Besides the expected sexual cracks and pro-war verbal abuse, she'd been knocked down by a gang of boys, punched, groped, and robbed.)

Sophomore year—the year the feminists would succeed in getting us to stop calling ourselves *girls*—I had my own room, my first room of my own, and I had a new distinction. No one else had a sister who was a runaway. Not that I told everyone the story, but those I did tell were impressed.

Ann and I had signed up for single rooms next door to each other in another part of the same dorm complex we'd lived in as freshmen. Several girls—women—from our old floor were now our neighbors again. That summer, Ann had shared a house in Oakland with some other radicals she had met through Columbia comrades. She had worked long hours in a five-and-ten, donating most of her earnings to the Black Panther free-breakfast fund. She had been arrested for defacing the wall of a San Francisco bank (ROB THIS BANK AND SEND THE $$ TO SOLEDAD) and got off with just a warning. The avuncular judge had addressed her as "young lady" and would have been much harder on her, he said, had she used an obscenity. Released, Ann headed straight back to the bank, where the wall had not yet been cleaned, inserted a caret between THIS and BANK, and wrote FUCKING. She had returned to school even leaner—and more muscular—from doing karate, and brimming with her usual energy and purpose. She had her work cut out for her. Vietnam was raging still, with Nixon and Kissinger hell-bent on bombing the North to its knees. (*Nixon, Kissinger*: how those names can bring despair even now, after all these years.) First thing, she threw herself into helping organize the Vietnam Moratorium that would take place in November. Just before the school year began, Lieutenant William Calley, Jr., had been charged for his role in the My Lai massacre. All that semester, the facts about what had happened on March 16, 1968, in a hamlet of Quang Ngai province, South Vietnam, were brought to light. In December, *Life* published the gruesome photographs. (One of several reasons I would be glad not to be sharing a room with Ann that year was the poster she put up, the same poster decorating the walls of hundreds of other college rooms at the time, showing the bodies of about a score of the more than five hundred murdered South Vietnamese civilians and the words "Q: AND BABIES? A: AND BABIES.")

Meanwhile, on the home front, the power had not yet passed to the People, the racist system remained firmly in place, and the black leadership was being systematically framed, incarcerated, and even assassinated. The day after the photographs of the massacre at My Lai appeared, Chicago policemen murdered Black Panthers Fred Hampton and Mark Clark in their beds. Angela Davis, who had already lost her position as a professor at UCLA because of her political beliefs, would be imprisoned on false charges of murder the following year.

Oh—and school: Ann had already decided she would major in philosophy and had taken on a demanding course load. (I had been planning to major in English, but after the poetry class I was not sure.)

Though she had lost none of her political passion, Ann had grown disenchanted with the student movement. Students for a Democratic Society, with its commitment to civil rights, helping the poor, "letting the people decide," and ending the war, had seemed, at least when she joined as a freshman, the obvious happy home for her. But partly because of the escalation of the war in Southeast Asia, SDS itself was at war. In June there had been the organization's tumultuous national convention and the splitting off of groups such as the Weathermen with their ominous cry: "The violence of Amerika must be answered with violence." That fall brought the raucous trial of the Chicago Seven and the riotous Days of Rage; within months the Weathermen would have moved underground, and by the time the school year was finished, so, more or less, was SDS. If witnessing the coming apart of SDS did not surprise Ann (and it did not; the writing had been on the wall already the year before—but the year before, as I recalled, she had come back from those meetings charged and even euphoric, and now she came back depressed), it still shook her to the core.

Before she had given up trying to make a radical of me, she had dragged me to some meetings, and I did not remember anything so lively as the brouhaha she now described. All I remembered was talk. Talk interminable and impenetrable, at least to me. A crowded and invariably stale-aired room, a microphone, often malfunctioning, and each and every person queuing up to have his (and it was almost always *his*) say. Once again I had the sense of a language beyond my grasp. I had to ask Ann later to explain what things such as "the bourgeoisie dictating consciousness" meant. And though she was as fluent in that language as anyone, and knowledgeable about political theory, what Ann herself stepped up to say was that she was far less interested in sitting around discussing the differences between Leninism and Maoism with a bunch of college students than in tutoring ghetto children.

In fact, she never would come to terms with this: virtually every political activist and radical she knew came from a privileged background. "We're all 'haves,'" she said ruefully. But of course. In the words—the very first words—of the first official document of SDS: "We are people of this generation, bred in at least modest comfort, housed now in universities . . ." Ann thought the Port Huron Statement was a beautiful thing. She knew many in the movement who, bred like herself in something closer to luxury than modest comfort, were now striving to make up for that. Good, brave, serious, responsible haves, dedicated to improving the lives of havenots. And she did not wish to take that away from them. Still, she could not escape the belief that the attempt to create a new social order by any group made up almost entirely of children of the elite was doomed. Those born into the ruling class were corrupted by its stain; they had the blood of millions on their hands. How could they now expect the children of their victims to join hands with their bloodied ones? Wasn't this why black militants preached that any black man who called any white man "brother" was a Tom and a traitor to his race? Not even civil rights martyrs Goodman and Schwerner could escape this rule.

"You cant steal nothing from a white man, he's already stole it he owes you anything you want, even his life"—LeRoi Jones.

Everyone in the movement talked about the need for stronger ties with the working class. Ann, who gave regularly to strike funds, was all for strong trade unions and for any measure that resulted in increased power or protection for workers. But unlike most of her comrades, she did not romanticize the working class. Corrupted by the culture of the bourgeoisie, workers were if anything more fiercely attached to bourgeois values than the bourgeois themselves. Most were hostile to the civil rights movement and even to the peace movement that was trying to save their sons from destruction in an unjust war. About the people of Vietnam, one of the poorest people on earth, whose death toll from the war was climbing into the millions, they cared not at all. Activists who had gone in after white proletarian and slum-dwelling youth discovered that the building of a more equitable society was the furthest thing from their minds.

For Ann, American blue-collar workers could not seriously be considered have-nots; however hard, their lives must not be compared to the lives of those trapped in ghettos, say, or of Third World peasants. And so, though it mattered to her how they were treated, though she could—and did—fight on their side, she could never feel for them the same unconditional love she felt for the truly deprived. She could never *embrace* them.

Q: Why did Ann love the poor to death and bitterly hate her own kind?

Of course, she was not the first to hallucinate a nimbus around the poor, or to believe that all of us—"I'm talking about individuals and I'm talking about nations"—should be judged by how we treat those who are without power and therefore at our mercy.

She said, "I wish I had been born poor." ("I wish I'd been born an Indian"—Robert Kennedy.) The ideal would have been to be born poor and black. But the counterculture was full of people in the grip of the same fantasy, with some—from street fighters to rock stars to flower children—even starting to believe they *were* black.

It followed that she would be wary of the women's liberationists, now that they had begun to stir the waters. In general, Ann preferred men—not for romantic reasons, but because she had more respect for them. Eavesdrop on any conversation between women, she once said to me, and what you hear is mostly trivia. "Never ideas. Always this tiresome focus on the minutiae of the personal." I knew what she meant, but did she have to say it? Eavesdrop on any old conversation between men, and you won't hear a lot of ideas, either. But men outnumbered women in the movement, and Ann had more Columbia friends than Barnard friends, and she also had many dates, as I have said, though a date with Ann more often meant dinner and a meeting than dinner and a movie. She said that she herself was proof that the idea that even smart men were more attracted to big breasts than to brains was a myth. Besides being scrupulously clean (she often showered twice a day), she did nothing to make herself alluring. She was at one with the feminists in complaining that most women attached too much importance to things like makeup and clothes and spent far too much time worrying about how men saw them. She was fond of quoting the melancholy words of a certain aging beauty of the day: "I have wasted so much of my life being beautiful." And wouldn't it be better if everyone, male and female, wore the same simple set of clothes?

Women's liberation had, of course, played a role in the splintering of SDS. It seemed now everyone was quoting the line about women in SNCC, and some women in SDS were accusing the men of having the same sexist view. In fact, many people would later remember that it had been not Stokely Carmichael but this or that SDS leader who used *prone* and *position for women* in the same sentence. Though she hated male chauvinism as she hated all chauvinism, Ann watched the blossoming women's movement with growing unease. She sensed a fatal distraction from the main work at hand. For Ann, only the poor had rights; the rest had obligations. And she sided with the women in BOSS who said, Black women have to think about our men getting their rights *first*.

Over the summer, Ann had acquired a new gesture: lightly beating her right fist against her left palm when she was trying to drive home a point. Gradually this gesture was replacing another gesture, one that was more appealing and that I will always associate with her: clasping her hands at about the level of her breastbone and rocking them gently back and forth as she spoke.

It must have been obvious to Ann that she was making herself more and more disliked. This was no era for killjoys. Coming home late from the library, she would cast a cold eye over a group of us sprawled in the carpeted corridor amid scattered cookie and chip packages, red-eyed and knocking together with laughter. It wasn't that she didn't smoke pot herself, but she was one of the few who became more withdrawn rather than gregarious when she turned on, and amazingly, she never got carried away with the giggles or the hungries. She didn't disapprove of people getting high. She disapproved of a certain life style (it was two words then) that was coming into being. It alarmed her that people of her generation were beginning to see politics as increasingly irrelevant to them. Too many who had once pledged to change society would now sooner drop out. In her eyes, doing your own thing too often seemed to mean doing nothing, or at least nothing useful. She didn't see that there was really that big a difference between pot parties and frat parties, and she could never accept the hedonism at the heart of hippie culture. And, as always, there was the issue of privilege: "Show me a black flower child," she said, fist smacking palm.

Maybe I was mistaken, but I thought I remembered a freshman Ann who was in most ways the same, but lighter in spirit. Busy though she was, and rarely alone, she had an aura of loneliness, like the lonely child she said she had been, or some poor little rich girl—and why had none of the men she was dating captured her heart? She still liked to play music at night before she went to sleep, and I sometimes heard through our common wall off-key sounds in the music that I thought were the sounds of Ann— weeping? (A wonder she could sleep at all, with that picture of slaughtered babies in the same room.)

Sometime during that first semester of sophomore year, she developed the tense posture and watchful air of someone expecting a blow. And she would receive her share of them—one requiring stitches in her scalp. Somewhere in the archives of TV network news there exists a clip showing Ann being dragged by her long hair toward a paddy wagon at astonishing speed. Whenever she was arrested, she knew that she and her fellow protesters would spend little, if any, time in jail. And this brought her shame. "We all know what happens to people who don't have powerful liberal lawyers to help them."

I was surprised that she still wanted to be friends. And I was pleased. There was no one to whom I would have admitted it, but I took pride in Ann's friendship, not least because she was so smart and serious, not to mention so tough on women. She made me feel as if I had passed an important test, as if I had won something. I was the only friend she had kept from our crowd of the year before. Among all the wounded feelings, mine were flattered. Why me? "She's slumming," joked one woman, unforgivably.

"What do you mean, you're not going to march?" It was inevitable that I would disappoint her. Instead of reading the books she urged on me—Marcuse, Fanon, DuBois—I was making my slow (and secretly second) way through Tolkien. It had not taken me long to fall back into my habit of not going to class. Ann was appalled that I would let one bad experience stop me from writing poetry altogether. And she thought I could do better for a main squeeze than dope-dealing Dig, a Columbia dropout who tended bar at the West End (though he would make his mark some years later—as a powerful liberal lawyer).

Now that we were no longer sharing a room, Ann and I saw less of each other, but we still ate together almost every day in the dining hall, and if there was a knock at my door in the middle of the night, I knew it was her. I might have had more fun hanging out with my other friends (her enemies), but it was those times when it was just the two of us, talking and smoking till dawn—already nostalgic about our days as freshmen!—that I looked forward to, and that would later keep coming back to me.

Once, when we were riding the subway together, a beggar entered the car. Ann filled his paper cup with bills, blushing at his thanks. When he had moved on to the next car, I turned to say something to Ann and saw that she was crying.

There were those to whom I told this story who found it irritating. There were those who would not believe Ann's tears had been sincere. And wasn't it a bit show-offy, giving a panhandler a wad of bills? And what did such generosity mean anyway, when the giver herself was so rich?

Complicated people are easy to misunderstand, and I believe this was the case with Ann. But when she said, "I would give anything to have had your parents instead of mine," what could I say? I had stopped feeling anger when she came out with this sort of remark. But how was I supposed to respond? What could I do to help Ann?

"One thing you could do for me, you could come with me when I see my parents."

I had met the Draytons only briefly, once, the year before, when they came to take Ann home from school—not long enough for me to form much of an opinion about them. I knew they came into the city fairly often for one thing or another. They had subscriptions to various concert and theater programs. Ann never went along to these events. She had no interest in highbrow culture. "Too many people get left out." Show her a black orchestra conductor! And she didn't approve of the contributions her parents made to large cultural institutions like Lincoln Center. Though she knew it was useless, she was constantly badgering her father to donate money to her own causes, and in a constant rage over his ready excuse: "Now, Ann, you don't really know in whose hands that money ends up." Much better the arts. But the Draytons were also big givers to programs to save American wildlife and wilderness. "Because animals and trees are more important than people?" their daughter fumed. To be fair, her parents did, through their church, give to Connecticut's poor. But Ann was not appeased, not when "they could give so much more." When I learned that what the Draytons did give altogether to various charities each year amounted to many times the cost of our entire college tuition, I was speechless. So they were sharing their wealth, weren't they, in a pretty big way? So they couldn't really be called *bloodsucking parasites*?

Ann set me straight. "Most of that money is tax deductible, don't forget. Do you think they would give a penny if it weren't?" I didn't know. But from the way Ann talked, you would have thought her mother had *stolen* the money she spent on clothes and antiques from welfare mothers and the North Vietnamese.

It pained Ann unbearably that the family fortune derived from patents for medical equipment. "Anything as essential as a device that makes a medical procedure safe or feasible ought to be freely available to all." This old argument came back to me not long ago, when, at a dinner, I was seated next to a woman who lectured me about doctors (she'd just learned I'd been married to one), who, according to this woman, had a moral obligation to treat people for free.

Medical care was only one of a long list of things Ann thought the people should get for free.

It was a Sunday, and the Draytons had tickets to a matinee. Ann agreed to meet them for brunch if she could bring me along. But hadn't they always told her any friend of hers from school was welcome to come along! We met at the Café des Artistes on West Sixty-seventh Street. This was in the years before that restaurant had become such a popular place, before the flashy awning had been put up—a time when, from the street, it gave such a muted, clubby impression you would not have thought it was even open to the general public. Ann had told me we'd be going either there or to the Russian Tea Room, because those were her parents' favorite restaurants near Lincoln Center. Ann hated them equally. She, of course, would have preferred Chinatown, one of those holes-in-the-wall where only Chinese people went. But even if her parents had been willing to try such a place, Ann's reverse snobbism wouldn't have let them. "People like my parents don't deserve the real thing."

"You just missed the mayor," said the coat-check girl—woman—and Ann shot her a look that said *Die*. (That summer, at Bonwit's, a saleswoman had informed me in exactly the same tragic tone that I had just missed Lee Radziwill.)

I had asked Ann if we had to dress for this occasion, and she had rolled her eyes ("Of course not!"). Now I went all hot as we entered the dining room in our jeans and I saw all those suits and pearls.

We were late—Ann had made sure of it—and the Draytons were waiting for us. Mr. Drayton stood when he saw us.

"Oh, Turner, please, you know how I hate that," Ann scolded as she threw herself onto her chair.

"Yes, dear, I know," he said, but remained standing nevertheless until I, too, had sat down. Maybe this would not have occurred to me had it not been for the coat attendant's remark, but I was struck by how much Mr. Drayton resembled the man we had just missed. Which is to say, good-looking in a bland, middle-aged, senatorial way. He and his wife were one of those couples (and I, at least, have seen many of them) who look so much alike they might be related by blood: brother and sister. With the Draytons the resemblance was so strong they might have been twins. Ann had once complained to me that her parents looked like figures in a wax museum. And so they did, in a way. But so did most people in that room, and so to the eyes of youth did just about every middle-class white person over thirty—perhaps because to our minds they *were* figures in a museum.

They had already finished one round of martinis while waiting for us and now ordered another. I wondered what "dry" could possibly mean.

Turner and Sophie: both pale like Ann and blond like Ann and thin like Ann. But there was more of a family resemblance between husband and wife than between either parent and child.

It's always a shame when the daughter turns out plainer than the mother. Mrs. Drayton had poreless skin and a generous mouth. She wore her long hair in a twist (her kind of woman loosened her hair only in private). I liked the color. It looked as if ashes had been evenly combed through it. (In her husband's case, the ashes had been not combed but tousled in.) But her blue eyes were cold, and I didn't like the cold way they scrutinized me, though of course it was done slyly. She made me want to hide my hands, but I thought

I remembered hearing that it was bad manners not to keep both hands always in sight at table.

I had been reading *The Great Gatsby*. It was on the reading list for one of my courses. Because it was the shortest book on the list, I had picked it to write about for my midterm paper. Now I looked for signs of Daisy Buchanan in Sophie Drayton. Was it really something you could hear—when a voice was "full of money"? I cocked my ears.

She had the unnerving habit of not keeping her gaze on you during conversation but constantly letting it slide somewhat off to the side, as if someone or something were coming up behind you.

He had the unnerving habit of behaving as if he were having the time of his life, a bluffness, a kind of pumped-up geniality or jauntiness that, for me, went with his bow tie—an "act" that thwarted whatever desire you might have had to know what he was really thinking or feeling. He was—reaching back for a word no one ever uses anymore—*debonair*. "Let's all have something nice, a nice omelet, what do you say, or some very nice crab salad." I did not know then that these mannerisms were common among people of his class.

"Look at this place." Ann spoke for my ears only from behind her open menu. I supposed she meant all the murals of women depicted as cavorting wood nymphs, for which the restaurant was known. From our table we had a good view of *Girl on a Swing*. They certainly were striking. Under other circumstances it might have been a treat for me to be there. Some years later, when there were so many other places to choose from—I mean trendier restaurants with much better food—I would mystify friends by wanting always to return to the Café des Artistes. ("But it's all tourists now!" "Nobody goes there anymore!")

When Ann had asked me to come along, to help her get through this meeting with her parents, I'd thought of it as a simple favor. But this turned out not to be the case. Once it was over, I would spend the rest of the day nursing a headache. Closing her menu, Ann announced that nothing appealed to her and she would make do with just the bread and some ice water. It must not have been the first time she had done such a thing, because her parents showed no surprise. Her mother said only, "I hope you're eating enough at school, Dooley." To which Ann made no response— whether because her mother had used the offending name or for another reason, I didn't know. (But mark how her father bowed to her wish to be called Ann, and her mother did not.) I myself was thrown by Ann's announcement. Was I supposed to follow suit? I didn't feel right ordering if Ann wasn't going to order, too. As if sensing my confusion, Mr. Drayton exclaimed, "We'll be *crushed* if you turn out to be on a bread-and-water diet, too!" But his wife said nothing, and I was thrown again. Nudging me under the table, Ann said quietly, "Eat."

I ordered some nice eggs Benedict because that's what Mrs. Drayton said she was having. But I didn't like poached eggs, especially not with glop all over them, and besides, I was too nervous to eat. I had been nervous from the moment we walked in. It had to do first of all with the wrong clothes—not that Ann appeared in the least troubled by this. (The Draytons, of course, were well dressed, both in the same dark shade of gray, which enhanced their twinnish appearance.)

Given everything I'd heard about them, I expected at least some sign of snobbism or high-handedness from the Draytons, a certain tone with the waiter, for example. But in fact it was Ann who snapped at the waiter—"Didn't I just say?"—when he wanted to make absolutely sure she was not going to order any food. Watching him retreat, Ann said, "Am I the only one who finds it weird that people like waiters and servants are so often forced to wear uniforms like tacky tuxedos?"

In the end, she did not even eat the bread.

When they found that nothing they could ask Ann was going to get her to talk about herself, her parents naturally turned to me— and how were *my* classes this semester?—not guessing, of course, that this was a topic about which I had little to say.

It was now that they began—the first pangs on the right side of my head.

Ann would not eat. She would not talk. We were as tense around that table as if we were hostages. The Draytons and I acted our parts as if in a play. I asked them about their matinee, which brought the conversation, briefly, to life. They had discovered the ballet only recently, they said, and they were hooked. They could not get enough of Balanchine, whoever he was. It would never have occurred to me that I, too, would be hooked on Balanchine one day, with my own subscription to the City Ballet. (But then, that "dry, straight up, with an olive" would ever trip off my tongue was also inconceivable.)

I had not been paying attention to the music that was playing over the sound system, but now I picked up Judy Collins: "Both Sides Now." It was a song I associated with the last days of high school, a lifetime ago. My throat tightened.

When the waiter had brought us dessert menus, Mr. Drayton said to me, "You *must* have something."

"Can't you see she's not hungry?" said Mrs. Drayton.

But clearly Mr. Drayton had guessed that it was not lack of appetite that had kept me from finishing those eggs. "Ah, but dessert is different, isn't it?" he said in his exuberant way. "And the desserts here are *scrumptious*." Such a silly word. Such a nice man. What did he care whether I had dessert or not? It was just kindness, really. His eyes were soft with it. The sort of kindness I never forget.

The next instant it was as if someone had thrown open a window or a door to the outside air. All the lights in the room shivered and dimmed. The menu dropped from my hand. Ann knew at once. Ann, with her exquisite antennae, her passionate empathy— she was like an angel or some other spirit at such moments. She put her arm around my shoulders and told her parents, "You guys should know something. George's sister is missing. She ran away in August, and no one knows where she is."

Mr. Drayton was the first to speak. "I am so, *so*, terribly, *terribly* sorry." Blood had surfaced to his face in a way that made it look as if he had been pinched hard on both cheeks.

Mrs. Drayton needed to catch her breath. "Your poor *mother*." And the voice in which she said this was completely different from the voice in which she had said everything else.

No one had dessert.

My head was hurting on Both Sides Now.

Bellevue Hospital. The city morgue. The girl is naked under the sheet. There is a mirror on the wall, angled for better viewing from outside the booth. I am not allowed to stand too close. I am asked to stand outside the booth and look through the Plexiglas. The police had told me this day might come, I should be prepared. Now. Was I ready? The girl is dead and naked under the sheet. The attendant lifts the sheet at one end, exposing just the head, with the long, pale hair brushed straight out from the crown, and the bare shoulders. I stare at the shoulders and think: prom gown.

The dizzy dancing way you feel.

I stare at the hair and wonder who brushed it and arranged it so. I wonder if her being naked means that naked was how she was found. Such a buzz in the playground some years ago: MARILYN FOUND DEAD. "And did you hear? *They found her naked.*"

As Mr. Drayton was paying the check, Ann said, "We could have eaten five times in Chinatown for that."

"No thanks," said Mrs. Drayton. "I don't want all that MSG."

That girl did not even look like Solange. Only the coloring was the same. And of course, the age. Because it was not Solange, the police did not give me any information. What would they do if no one identified her? How long would they keep her? And then? A tender profile. Skin tight and smooth and ripe-looking, but with an unnatural sheen, like the skin of fake fruit. And even though it wasn't Solange, I thought of the deer.

"You are such a racist, Sophie."

"What?" Mrs. Drayton tried to laugh. "Now I'm a racist because I don't like Chinese food?"

"No, Sophie, you're a racist because you're a racist. But it's the way you shuddered when you said it."

Mrs. Drayton had shuddered; I noticed it, too.

"I was shuddering at the MSG!"

"Sorry, but we might have to ask you to come in and do this again sometime."

The inside of my skull lined with barbed wire.

"Sorry, we know it's tough. A dead kid ain't no pretty picture."

He was on his feet, he was giving his wife his hand, helping her to get up from the table. "I think we should go now, or we'll be late." He moved gracefully and he spoke cheerfully, as if the exchange between mother and daughter had never happened, as if we all didn't know they still had more than a half hour to kill before the performance and the theater was right there. But his face—I may have been the only one to see it, I may even have imagined it—his face was the face of defeat.

Outside, Ann said she wanted to walk home. Someone was digging thumbs into my eyes, it was chilly November, and the dorm was fifty blocks away, but I wanted to walk, too. When we said goodbye to her parents, Ann asked her father for whatever cash he could spare. As he took out his wallet and handed over a couple of twenties, I wondered why he didn't ask her what the money was for, and whether maybe he knew without asking. Ann and I headed up Broadway, stopping in different stores until we got the twenties broken down to singles. The farther north we went, especially after Eighty-sixth Street, the more boarded-up windows and broken glass and beggars we saw.

"Observe," said Ann, reaching into her pockets, distributing alms. "The richest nation in the world."

Drunks in doorways raised their bottles to her. A woman pushing a shopping cart with all her possessions started to bawl.

There but for fortune go you and I.

"The world's greatest city. Capital of the twentieth century. Where people pay two dollars for a martini." Or a penny less, as I recall, for a full steak dinner at Tad's Steak House.

I asked Ann why her parents hadn't had more children—families of three were uncommon then—and she said, "When I was growing up and I used to pester them with that same question, they kept saying that all they ever wanted was me. I was supposed to believe I fulfilled all their parental desires—and I guess I did. Of course, I thought it was rotten of them to deny me at least one sibling. But I'd say one pregnancy was more than enough for poor Sophie. My god, pregnancy is *uncomfortable*. It gives you *stretch marks*. Labor is *painful*. I mean, Sophie doesn't even like to sweat. And that whole generation was so alienated from their bodies they wouldn't even have natural childbirth, for god's sake. Most of them wouldn't even nurse their own kids! *That* was for *peasants*. If rich women could pay poor women to incubate their babies for them, they'd do it. If the revolution fails, that may well be the wave of the future. Frankly, I can't imagine Sophie having a baby. And besides, can you imagine the two of *them* having sex?"

They were over forty. The thing was, I had to admit, neither easy nor pleasant to imagine.

Ann and I both thought we wanted to have children someday. But Ann insisted, "Only if it's not in the conventional bourgeois way."

Now that we were alone, the tension had eased, and what with the fresh air and the walk, my head throbbed less, and I realized how hungry I was.

We were both hungry. About ten blocks from the dorm, we stopped at a Puerto Rican lunch counter that Ann had discovered and where she was greeted by the owner and his wife with warmth. We had pork stripped from a whole roasted pig that sat in the window, fried plaintains, and rice and beans. We were both starving, our plates were piled high, and we ate every bite. It was the real thing, and it was *scrumptious*.

But afterward, scourged by the thought of millions of famished Biafrans, Ann was upset with herself for pigging out. She would skip her next three meals as a penance.

A week or so later, Ann called her father. She wanted to talk about Arthur Mitchell, a former principal dancer with Balanchine's New York City Ballet. He had just founded the Dance Theatre of Harlem, fulfilling a personal commitment he had made in response to the assassination of Martin Luther King. Ann wanted to know if Turner would become a donor to the fledgling company.

She almost broke down my door. "He said yes!"

*

How many times altogether did I go out with Ann and her parents? I'm not sure. What I am sure about is that every time was the same. Though I got a little more used to the Draytons, I was never able to relax with them. Never relaxed enough, say, to eat with appetite. Yet in spite of Ann's attempts to demonize them, they both struck me as basically harmless. Dull, yes, like most everyone their age, and a little phony, with the artificial manners of their kind, but harmless.

There came a point, though, when Ann had delivered her umpteenth snide remark or accusation or taunt, and I began to share her frustration. Why did the Draytons pretend that nothing was wrong? I would think about my own parents, who, for so much less, would have knocked me off my chair. I would think about the browbeaten and battered children of my hometown. Now here I was a witness to the other extreme, and it irked me. It would always irk me. Once, at a birthday party for a friend of my young daughter's (yes, I had natural childbirth; yes, I nursed her), I watched a mother comfort a child who had purposely dropped a glass full of grape juice on the carpet—"It's okay, sweetie, I know that glass was slippery"—and I had to leave the room. I saw that it was true what Ann had told me about her parents: no crime could turn them against her. Irked I was, but also envious. Yes, even of that child with the grape juice.

Racist, fascist, parasite, pig—all these names and worse she called them. She mocked them and she jeered at them, and she even threatened them ("Sometimes I think it might be better if we never saw each other again"). Occasionally Mrs. Drayton would make a halfhearted attempt to defend herself, as she had done that first time over the MSG. Mr. Drayton would try to make a joke, once taking up his knife and offering the handle to Ann. "Why not go on and stab me, then, since I've no right to live. Why not chop me up into little pieces and feed me to the Biafrans." I had a moment's panic here and kept my eye on that knife. You didn't joke about Biafrans with Ann.

For the most part, though, the Draytons did not respond to their daughter's attacks. Often they pretended not even to hear what she'd said. It was part of their perfect blandness, and it could drive you perfectly insane. With Ann constantly baiting them and trying to incite them, that blandness could seem almost cruel. Was there *nothing* she could do to get a rise out of them?

My wax parents, she called them.

The kindest thing I ever heard her say about them was, "I know they aren't really truly evil. They're just weak."

As I say, those times when we got together were all much the same. (I had promised Ann I would accompany her anytime so she would not have to see her parents alone.) We always went to a restaurant (the Draytons offered to get us tickets to any event they were going to, but of course Ann would have none of that). We even seemed to have the same conversation. I remember a lot more talk about the New York City Ballet. Suzanne had left the company, Kay was adorable, Allegra was divine. "So you know these women?" I asked, and everyone laughed.

Sometimes, like that first time, Ann did not order any food, sometimes she ordered but hardly ate, and sometimes she ordered and cleaned her plate. And whatever she did, it was all right with Mummy and Daddy.

I used to believe I would have given half my adult life to have been spoiled as a child.

I have said how it seemed as if we were acting parts in a play, meaning the strangeness and artificiality of those occasions, so charged with tension and anxiety. But now may I revise that and say that it really seemed like some kind of *rehearsal*. Not this time but the next it would happen—the scene we were always rehearsing for, and which I had no doubt would be a disaster. Next time at the Café des Artistes or at the Russian Tea Room a terrible scene would unfold, something that would leave every one of us changed and that no one who witnessed it would ever forget.

The night after our first brunch, that cold November day, I dreamed about it. I saw Ann standing among the plates on our table, screaming and pulling at her hair. I saw her tear off her clothes, grab a chandelier (which existed only in the dream restaurant), and swing over the heads of the gaping diners. Among the diners were not only her parents but also mine, as well as many other people—perhaps everyone—I knew or had known. Jay Gatsby was at one table with other characters from his story (I'd finished the book that same night before bed). It sounds comical in the telling, I know, but the dream itself was sinister. It was a nightmare, and not the last nightmare I would have starring Ann.

A dead kid ain't no pretty picture.

In fact, I would not be called back to the morgue again. No other unidentified teenage female corpse that might have been my sister's surfaced in Manhattan. But back home, over time, my mother was being asked to look at Polaroid snapshots taken in morgues as far away as Texas and California.

I was astonished that she had kept these pictures. By the time I saw them, the mystery of Solange's disappearance had been solved, my mother was dead, and Zelma (now Sister Michael) and I were going through Mama's possessions, most of which we simply threw out. What little might have been worth saving was in too bad need of repair. The house itself had been so neglected for so many years it would have to be torn down. So—out went the Polaroids. But first I had a good look at them. There were perhaps a dozen, as I recall, all head shots, and on the back of each one was written "Jane Doe" and a number. (Through a remarkable error, one of the pictures was of a black girl.) Some of the faces were cut or swollen or bruised. What an ordeal for my mother—my *poor* mother, indeed—dutifully examining all these faces, most of which bore a resemblance to her own missing daughter's. (And how *clear* death was: no one would have mistaken it for sleep.) I surprised myself by momentarily toying with the idea of holding on to the pictures myself. And it was the woeful guilty feeling that surged as I dropped them into the trash that explained the hesitation on my part and perhaps also why my mother had not been able to bring herself to do the same. But once they were gone, I was able to put them from my mind. I threw the pictures out, and I don't believe I mentioned them to anyone. Zelma was working in a different part of the house that day, and I threw the pictures out without telling her about them. There was the woeful guilty feeling, but I didn't dwell on it, and I soon forgot the pictures altogether. I was a busy person in those days, and a lot of what I was busy doing was forgetting. And when, long after, those pictures did come back to mind, it happened in an unexpected way. This was during a period when I often went to a certain kind of art gallery, and it occurred to me that those Polaroids were the kind of thing you might find in an exhibition in that kind of gallery, part of some pastiche or installation, a piece that aimed to provoke or shock, a piece with a message, and if that message was not obvious enough from looking at the work or at the name of the work (which, in fact, probably would not have been very helpful), you could go to the description in the catalog and find such words as *loss of innocence, the erotic, exploitation*, and *violence against women*.

That March, the movie about the Woodstock festival was released, and I went to see it with a crowd of friends. It was showing at a theater near Bloomingdale's, which had already come out with a line of Woodstock-inspired clothes, on display in the windows. We stopped to mock those designer versions of the very fringed shirts, bell-bottoms, headbands, cowboy hats, and granny dresses we had on, and for which altogether we had paid probably less than fifty bucks. At the time, it was indeed possible to get used versions of these height-of-fashion articles absolutely free if you knew where to find them. All over the neighborhood, stores and street vendors were selling merchandise bearing the Woodstock name or the flower-power logo, and a diner near the theater had renamed its everyday breakfast offering of pancakes and eggs the Woodstock Breakfast Special. All this made us want to turn around and go home—not to mention that the theater had jacked up the ticket price just for this movie. On the other hand, there was no way we were going to miss it; tragic enough we had missed the real thing.

We sat in the balcony so we could smoke. The theater—the balcony especially—was all Woodstock Nation, and soon the joints were being passed back and forth and up and down the rows. The audience demanded that the projectionist turn up the sound, and we cheered each performance as if it were live.

It was about three-quarters of the way into the film when Solange appeared. The scene was a group of people taking a break from the music to go skinny-dipping. It was barely an instant; it

73

was the merest of glimpses. I could not be absolutely sure. The movie rolled on, and I kept looking and looking, my heart going like Santana's drummer up there, but of course I did not see her again.

But had I really seen her at all? It seemed to me hundreds of people watching that movie probably imagined they saw familiar faces in those crowd scenes. And I was high.

I went back the next day to see the movie again, alone, straight. I waited anxiously for the skinny-dipping scene and caught again the maddeningly brief glimpse of that girl standing on the shore. Every cell of my being wanted that girl to be Solange. I went back once more. I still was not sure.

I called my mother. I wanted to tell her, even if I was wrong. "I wouldn't be at all surprised," she said, "if that slut was there." I said, "Please don't call her that, Mama," and then, in a completely different voice, "Don't you ever call her that again." And though I could hear my mother starting to cry, I hung up.

✳

Snorting the crystal through a straw, I reflect that meth is probably overkill for what I am about to do, but it happens to be what I have at hand, and besides, I always crave it. It is only when I am speeding that I feel caught up with the rest of the world, in sync with the stepped-up pace of urban student life. In the time I have before the meth comes on, I shower (I'm going to sweat, so I want to be clean), I put on my most comfortable clothes, and I take the elevator down to the basement, to Fat Alley, where the vending machines are. I buy several cans of soda and two packs of cigarettes and some chocolate bars and chips to eat before the speed kills my appetite. By the time I return to my room, I feel a buzz. It is the middle of the night, but I am as awake as I think it is possible to be. I will have to be careful not to let myself get distracted into cleaning the room from top to bottom, washing windows, scraping waxy buildup off furniture, organizing the closet down to the belts. I'll have to watch out when leaving the room, say to go to the lavatory, not to end up in an hours-long conversation with someone I meet. I've got this paper to write, it is due in the morning; in fact it was due last week, but I got an extension. All week long I couldn't do it and I couldn't do it, but now with the speed coming on, my confidence kindles. How hard can it be? At the end of last year, our floormate Sylvia Lustman had just started writing a paper when her boyfriend, her beloved orgasm-giving Gabe, called to say he had found someone else. As Sylvia took to her bed, her roommate, Grace, sat down at Sylvia's typewriter, read what Sylvia had written, and typed a page. Then Grace went knocking on doors. It was a Friday, the paper was due Monday, and over the weekend one after the other of us trooped in and, after a consolatory word or two to the prostrate Sylvia, sat down and wrote. This was finals period, and we were all swamped with work of our own. But with everyone pitching in . . . Some had read the book and some had not but had seen the movie, and those of us who'd done neither just went on instinct. The last person to sit down at the typewriter saw a major problem and had a stroke of genius. She decided to separate what we'd written into numbered sections and to title the paper "Notes on *Great Expectations*." A radical notion for a term paper at the time; only a little earlier it would have been unacceptable. But academia was a brave new world. There was a new spirit of tolerance and leniency, a willingness to respect a student's individuality, her need to break the rules and try something different. And sure, the professor found the analysis somewhat disjointed and criticized Syl for not always thinking her arguments through. But he also found a sufficient number of "good observations and interesting points"—and how about that clever and original collage style? B plus.

I have left my paper till the last minute, I don't have much time, but at least the book is fresh in my mind. I feel the first real rush from the speed, followed by a tingling anticipation. I am going to work, but I am also going to have a good time. I do not feel merely alert—I feel *brilliant*. My brain is brimming and bubbling, a vast cauldron of ideas. All I have to do is get them down. I see now that this will take no time at all. And I am already way ahead of myself. Once I've finished the paper, I'll still be speeding—well into the next day and the next night—and I'm thinking how in fact I could clean my messy room from top to bottom and get a hundred other things done before crashing.

I sit down at the typewriter, fill my mouth with M&M's, and feed the first sheet of onionskin into the roller: chirp chirp chirp. I light a cigarette—oh, for three hands!

Cigarette clenched between teeth, I poise my hands above the Smith Corona like a pianist about to fill the hall with Bach. Another rush. I hit the keys. "Why *The Great Gatsby* Is Not a Great Book."

*D*on't go down to the park alone, don't walk in the park alone, don't wander too far from the entrance, and don't ever go in there at night.

I saw the two men, or boys—I couldn't tell from this distance—and I was not afraid. (A word about my eyesight: I am myopic and I was so then. I needed glasses, and I owned a pair—the tinted aviator kind that were cool back then—but I wore them as little as possible.) I went to the park all the time. Not at night, of course, and it wasn't night now, it wasn't dark yet, it was late in the day but not quite dusk. I had entered the park at 116th Street and was heading toward Grant's Tomb, at 122nd Street, and until I saw those two men, or boys, walking in my direction, I had not seen a soul. City parks did not draw as many visitors then as they would just a few years later. Most people did not feel safe in the parks, and that included much of Central Park, except maybe on a warm and sunny weekend afternoon when you could count on crowds. Riverside Park this far north was usually deserted. Dog walkers were not so common. There were fewer dogs in the city then, and you didn't see many, leashed or unleashed, in the park. And no joggers—a jogger would have been an unusual sight in any park at that time; the great running boom was still years away. There were rats. Even this close to school, you did not see a lot of students in the park. It was not a student hangout. If you were going to study outdoors or play Frisbee or touch football, you'd do it somewhere on campus. (But we all knew the story: back in Beat days, a Columbia student named Lucien Carr, who knew Ginsberg and Burroughs and Kerouac, had stabbed a man to death in the park and rolled the body into the river.)

You almost never saw a woman alone in the park, and you never saw policemen. The bums and the homeless you might have expected to see were also rare. I remember one man I used to see down around 110th Street, who, if he didn't actually live in the park, was always to be found there. He was not Indian, but he wore an Indian-style dhoti that appeared to have been made out of a pillowcase, and that's all he wore, even when it was cold, and he would sit on a large rock or stretch out on the grass, taking the sun, wearing nothing but his faux dhoti, even in winter. He was small, with short, thick bowlegs, and there was something not quite human about him; he was like some forest creature. A hobbit. So absorbed was he in his sun worship, he did not even see you pass by. I once passed fairly close behind his bare back and saw that his skin was like bark.

Deserted as it was, and close to the dorm, the park was perfect for my purpose. I did not go there for exercise or fresh air or to admire Olmsted's design, or for any of the usual reasons people go to parks. I went there to sing. To sing and not be heard. Like many people who can't carry a tune, I love to sing. I, with my tuneless voice, my tone deafness, have always gotten enormous pleasure from singing. I sang all the time when I was growing up, to the annoyance of my family, who sometimes banished me to the basement. I had not found anyplace in the dorm or on campus where I could go and sing and enjoy myself without worrying about how bad I sounded (and how bad I sounded I knew only because other people had told me; I myself could not hear how out of tune my singing was, or I suppose I could not have enjoyed it). Another place I liked to go to sing was up on our dormitory roof. But I preferred the park. For one thing, it was quieter.

Even if my voice had been fine, I would not have wanted to be heard singing the particular songs I sang, which were not the folk or rock songs that we all listened to all the time and that I myself loved as much as anyone, but songs from the Barbra Streisand albums I'd listened to in high school. "What Now My Love," "The Shadow of Your Smile": the kind of music—torch songs, show tunes, favorites of the Copacabana—that was not music at all to the youth of 1970. Streisand herself, though in age much closer to us than to our parents, was also closer to Bing Crosby than to the Beatles, a pop singer for the middle-aged and middle class and the hopelessly straight. But the summer before I left home, I would listen to her albums every day. I knew all the songs, and these were the songs I would sing when I was alone in the park, and at that time the song that was probably closest to my heart was "Someone to Watch Over Me." I sang "Someone to Watch Over Me" over and over, untiring, out of tune, in my pitiful soprano, to the Hudson River, to the squirrels and birds, to Grant in his tomb. I kept an eye out, and if someone appeared I'd pipe down, but as I say, I did not usually meet anyone.

I saw the two men, or boys—guys—up ahead of me on the path, walking in my direction, but they were still too far away to hear even my screechy high notes. I saw them stop, and then the guy on the right, my right, suddenly took off in the opposite direction and headed out of the park, leaving just the one now, coming toward me, and I could tell that he had his hands in his pockets and was looking not at me but out across the river to New Jersey. The disappearance of at least one helped ease whatever anxiety I may have had. But later someone told me that it should have done just the opposite; it should have been my cue to run away as fast as I could.

I didn't even change direction. I walked toward him, singing, until he was near enough to hear, and then I smiled. I think I mouthed hello, because that was the friendly hippie thing to do, say hello, nod and smile, flash the peace sign, whenever you met a stranger, even an obviously hopelessly straight one. For a better world. So these were the facts: I walked right up, singing and smiling, and said hello to my rapist.

Neither a man nor a boy, but that age in between: call him a manboy. No weapon, no weapon needed. He was as big as a man, with upper arms the size of my waist. Big like a man but chubby like a baby. He was fat, really. But it was hard fat. No words, no words needed. All clear as a bell, the bell that tolled for me. Big, fat, hard hands around my neck. I wanted to live, so I did not fight. But I would not walk: I made him drag me. Not far from where we stood was some kind of tree. I am not city bred, but I'm no country person, either. I don't know what kind of tree it was, but there were many in the park just like it. This one was planted in a spot where the lawn sloped to such a degree that on one side the leafy branches reached all the way to the ground, forming a dark, cozy green enclosure, like the entrance to a hobbit dwelling, or a perfect little rape room.

I don't mean to be flippant. I'm just trying to find a way that I can tell about this.

He didn't smell at first, when he grabbed me, dragged me—the smell came on only when he had pinned me to the ground. I don't really know how to say what that smell was. But I think it is true that fear makes your sense of smell more acute.

I am myopic, but what is up close I see perfectly. I saw his eyes roll so far back in his head that from below he looked completely white-eyed, freaky.

The faint peeping noises I made throughout were involuntary. A good thing he did not mind them.

I knew that I might die, and I thought I should pray, and I tried to pray but could not. Now I am suspicious of all those movies in which people who are about to die start praying. When you are filled with fear for your life, there is no room for anything else, though the fear itself can expand infinitely—as it did when I remembered the other guy, the one who had run off, and imagined him now running back here. With all his friends.

He never spoke, but just before he left me there, alive after all, he sighed a few times—these were deep, contemplative-sounding sighs, followed by a low, throaty noise that I would call a chuckle. He did not look at me. I never once caught him looking at me, directly at my face, into my eyes. He was in some profound way all unaware of me, and this *unawareness* was to me so bizarre it made me wonder if he was retarded, as his not speaking had made me wonder if he was a mute.

What was it like? It was like being mounted by a dog or some other animal. There was the slaver, the panting, the animal smell, but no speech, no eye contact, nothing personal.

I felt the vibrations of his footsteps through the ground as he loped away.

Nothing had changed. The same sun shone in the same sky. The river flowed darkly on, and a squirrel sat on a branch, eating an acorn.

Nineteen seventy. In the future, still, were bestselling books about rape and what would be damned as "our whole rape culture." In the future were Take Back the Night, Rape Awareness Month, Light a Candle If You've Ever Been Date-Raped, Honk If You've Ever Been Sexually Harassed. In the future, the definition of rape would turn out to be, like fear, capable of infinite expansion, with one legal scholar stating, "I call it rape whenever a woman has had sex and feels violated," and others going much further than that, until it came to be said that one out of four and then one out of three and then one out of two women were victims, and there was such a thing in this world as rape by word or glance.

In the past, the near past, was a movie I'd seen on TV about the sexy German girl gang-raped by American GIs who is so thoroughly put to shame during their trial that she has no choice but to kill herself. *Town Without Pity.* A movie that would have been hard to forget in any case, but was brought incessantly to mind by repeated playing of the theme song, a hit recorded by Gene Pitney. Based on a true story.

The first question is always the same: Will I tell anyone? Then: Who?

I suppose if I'd still been writing poetry, I might have tried to write a poem about it.

Ann's room. I had barely got out the story when someone knocked at the door. It was Ann's friend Sasha. That wasn't her real name. I never knew what Sasha's real name was, but whatever it was, like so many others back then, she had given herself a new one. She must have chosen Sasha because it was Russian. She owned a gold bracelet from which dangled a single charm: a tiny gold hammer and sickle. She wasn't a student; she was much older—she was twenty-six. (I say "much" because that is how it seemed; we were all extremely conscious of age, and I remember how those who turned twenty that year were envious of those who could still call themselves teens.) Sasha had been in grad school, but she quit in order to devote herself full-time to the revolution. She lived in a communal apartment on the north border of the campus. Now she knocked and walked right in before Ann could answer.

I didn't like Sasha—partly, I admit, because Ann was infatuated with her. Ann called Sasha her mentor. Sasha was a genius, according to Ann. She had read everything and could hold her own with any man on any topic. She was striking: masses of dark, wild, wavy hair, a face whose heart shape was exaggerated by a deep widow's peak. But a thick dark monobrow gave that face a stern, shaded look. Never without a cigarette, always in black, she liked to mix lace and leather. I didn't think she was beautiful, as Ann did. I thought she was witchy. I didn't think she was a genius, I thought she was a know-it-all. I didn't think she was a born leader, I thought she was bossy. Ann had told me Sasha was getting ready to go underground, and I was glad. Lately she had been coming around a lot, and she and Ann were often together, which meant I was seeing less of Ann myself.

She thought she could do that, Sasha: knock on Ann's door and walk right in without waiting for permission.

She did not expect to find me there, lying on Ann's bed, in tears, with Ann sitting beside me. She said, "Hey, what's up?" And when no one answered right away, "Hey, no secrets, remember? Secrets are bad." She stood in the middle of the room, arms crossed high on her chest, waiting, until we told her.

Though she said "Wow," it was without surprise. She was the type who would never let herself be caught showing surprise at anything. (Poor Ann had screamed when I told her.) Sasha said "Wow" a few more times, in the same unwowed voice, shaking her head, and she paced a little in the small, silent room. She was frowning the whole time, and with that monobrow of hers a frown was serious business.

Finally she sat down, perching on a corner of Ann's desk. She lit a cigarette. An air of command about her: Sasha was in charge.

"Did you call the police?" she asked, and was clearly relieved to hear we had not. "Good, that's good," she said, blowing a smoke ring. "The absolutely last fucking thing we need right now is the pigs." Ann had said exactly the same words to me just before Sasha arrived.

But of course we were not going to call the police. At that time it was understood: no matter what happened, you avoided the police. We were not going to tell any school authority, either. We did not trust authority, and that included college administrators. Trust in the police was, for us—no exaggeration—like trust in the government or trust in the military: it was madness. And besides, calling in the police meant calling in men. (One day when I was no longer living on campus, a neighbor of mine whose husband had beaten her took refuge in my apartment, and we called the police. By the time the officers arrived, her husband had taken off, and they said there was nothing to be done. But before they left, one of them asked my neighbor if she was "one of those wives who like to get beat"—sweeping away whatever doubts had been nagging me about not having turned to the police myself.)

I didn't have a scratch on me. I foresaw humiliation upon humiliation. *Miss George, is it not true that you yourself approached the defendant with a smile and said hello to him? And you say he had no weapon? Miss George, was this really all you were wearing?* (holding the miniskirt up to the eye level of the jurors). I had heard that rape victims were often asked if they had had an orgasm, and all that business about the aftermath being worse than the rape itself. Town without pity. And Manhattan was such a big town.

I believed that if I reported the rape, I would not be able to keep it from my mother. I knew nothing about police procedure or crime victims' rights. But I knew Mama.

Sasha said, "You got an old man?"

Tending bar at the West End at that very moment, but I did not want to see him. Much later I would think that maybe I had not been completely fair to Dig, ruling out beforehand that he could possibly understand. But by then it was too late; we did not know each other anymore. At the time, it was painful to think—to know, for I was sure about this—that he could not help me. I felt the same about my brother. I think it is fair to say that I could not bear to cause certain feelings that I thought both Dig and Guy would have if I told them. In situations like this, rightly or wrongly, a woman often ends up treating the men around her like children. I know this for a certainty today; then, I had just an inkling. I remember thinking also that my not wanting any part of Dig at this moment exposed a serious flaw in our relationship—but in fact this was nonsense. Flaw? We had the kind of relationship much desired and much vaunted then, part of our generation's big social experiment: we were sleeping together, but we were not a couple, we were not even very close, and we were not faithful. We *called* it love. We called it freedom.

A word about language: in those days people—our kind, anyway—used the word *ball* instead of *fuck*. *You wanna ball?* A lot of guys would put it to you just like that. The hard core took offense at *make love* and *sleep with* as uptight bourgeois euphemisms. The same people who'd mock you for saying "I have to go to the *bathroom*." I don't know how *ball* got started, but I would meet feminists who hated it and put it on the list of words they wanted banned.

Though he never knew about the rape, Dig and I stopped seeing each other soon afterward anyway, and I did not miss him. Had there ever been much between us, I suppose I would not have been in the habit of singing "Someone to Watch Over Me" all alone in the park, now, would I.

"Was he white or black?"

When I said black, Sasha looked at me as if I had given the wrong answer. Again, it was the same response I'd gotten from Ann. Yet another reason for not telling the police, who we believed would have been only too glad for an excuse to roar into Harlem and crack the head of any black manboy they picked up on suspicion.

Sasha hopped off the desk and crossed to the bed. I was now sitting up, and Ann was still beside me. Sasha sat down on my other side and started massaging my shoulders. She was wearing the bracelet with the Communist charm. My sense of smell must have still been sharper than normal. I could smell her hair—no one said "big hair" back then, but that's what Sasha had. I could smell the hair itself and her piney shampoo and the menthol from her cigarettes. Garlic on her hands as well as on her breath.

"Listen," she said. "I know how you feel. It happened to me, too. And I was even younger than you are." Briefly, she told the story. (High school, swim coach.) I saw from Ann's reaction that this was news to her, and given how close she and Sasha were and how anti-secrets they both were, I had to wonder if Sasha was telling the truth. But immediately I was ashamed, remembering the cliché: the first response most people have to a woman who says she was raped is doubt.

"Trust me," Sasha said. "You can deal with it. Just keep above it. You have to remember some things. First, you're still the same person who you were before. And second, forget all this bullshit about how a woman never gets over it. You just have to be strong. It could have been worse. You're not dead, for one thing. This guy could have killed you. He could have done something to maim or scar you for life. It could have been a gang rape. You could have been a little girl. You could have been a virgin." All true. I had

85

been telling myself these same things since the rape was over, and I would do so all my life. "The main thing now is, you survived. This is a sick, violent society, a society that breeds this kind of act. Remember what Malcolm said after Kennedy was killed, about chickens coming home to roost, and how everybody jumped on him as if he were saying Kennedy had it coming, when all he was trying to say was that America is full of evil, and if you don't do something to stop the violence of Birmingham or Mississippi, you can't be surprised when violence one day comes round to you.

"You have to try to understand how something like this could happen. And you have to be aware that a whole lot worse is happening all over the world right this minute." Also true. "You have to be tough. You can't just feel sorry for yourself."

From "Someone to Watch Over Me" to "Big Girls Don't Cry."

Ann said, "Think of all those poor Vietnamese women being raped by American soldiers." The teachable moment.

Sasha said, "Did you get the impression this guy was a militant?"

"No, he was just a kid. And I think maybe there was something wrong—"

"Because you know what Eldridge Cleaver said."

There was a copy of *Soul on Ice* in Ann's bookcase. There was a copy in at least half the college bookcases in America. It was radical Holy Writ and a national bestseller, named by *The New York Times* as one of the ten best books of '68.

Sasha found the book and the page she was looking for right away. She read aloud the passage containing Cleaver's justification of his rape of white women as a means of taking revenge on white men.

I was suddenly exhausted. I wanted to lie back down and sleep for the rest of my life. I said, "Well, this guy wasn't Eldridge Cleaver."

"No," Sasha said, slamming the book shut and holding it with both hands overhead, like a football she was about to pass. "Eldridge fled the country, man! He escaped! No way the fucking pigs can get their hands on him now!"

(Is there nothing time cannot bring about? Five years later Cleaver would return from exile in Cuba, France, and Algiers; he would renounce the Black Panthers and all his revolutionary ideas; he would become a born-again Christian, a fierce anticommunist, and a Republican, and would support the election to the presidency of the man who as governor of California had objected to an invitation to Cleaver to speak at Berkeley with these once famous words: "If Eldridge Cleaver is allowed to teach our children, they may come home one night and slit our throats.")

Ann had an evening class. When she said she would cut it and stay with me, I shook my head. I knew how much Ann hated to miss class. "But you shouldn't be alone, George." In fact, though I would have loved at that moment to be in my own room, I wasn't quite ready to be alone. But we had forgotten who was in charge.

"Ann, go to class. I'll take care of George."

I said, "I just want to go to bed."

Sasha shook her head. "Bad idea. Ann's right, you shouldn't be alone. It'll just make you brood. You should come with me. I have to go uptown to my parents' house. I'm taking the car—I have to pick up some stuff. You can hang out with me till I'm done; then I'll bring you back here. Ann will be back from class then, too."

It sounded simple, reasonable. I looked at Ann, who clearly thought that, like all Sasha's ideas, this one was brilliant. I went along partly because I didn't want to be alone and partly because I didn't want to keep Ann from her class, but also because I was feeling guilty about not believing Sasha had been raped.

The car was a station wagon Sasha shared with her numerous roommates. It was run-down and filthy, littered with cigarette butts and paper coffee cups and old newspapers. There was dog hair and doggy odor. I wished the dog itself were coming along. A dog would have been a real comfort to me. The back of the car was filled with empty boxes and suitcases. I remembered Ann telling me that Sasha was planning to go underground "in order to carry on her political work more effectively." I didn't pay much attention to this at the time, but in coming days, whenever I heard of a bomb going off or some other incident for which radicals claimed responsibility, I would wonder if Sasha had been involved.

She drove aggressively, even recklessly, a lot of lane changing, finger flipping, and horn. We didn't talk much, because the radio was on. Sasha thought some good, loud soul music would soothe me, and she was right; I could have driven all the way to Canada on those songs. ("I remember when Otis Redding died, I didn't think I could go on"—Bill Clinton.)

The news came on, and we heard an update about the Charles Manson case. He and members of his Family had been charged for the Tate-LaBianca murders, but the trial had not yet begun. The murders had taken place in August—the same week, as it happened, that Solange disappeared. Lately there had been constant breaking news about the case and about the Manson Family, which was mostly female and included teenagers, runaways, girls from troubled homes—girls (the thought was inescapable) like Solange.

On the radio, a lawyer who was not involved in the case said that Manson would probably go free because of lack of evidence against him. Sasha was one of those who wanted Manson to go free. "You see how it is, everyone freaking out because a couple of millionaires get killed, when people in the ghetto get killed all the time." Instead of turning the radio down, Sasha screeched over it. "Good for Manson, shaking up the Establishment, putting the fear of God in them, showing what could happen to the whole bad lot of motherfuckers tomorrow! You know, he spent most of his life behind bars. He's what the system made him. He's America's worst nightmare, and he's just what America deserves. And he's supposed to have killed—what, seven people? And everyone's acting like it's a bigger crime than My Lai? Is that not fucking amazing? And all because the victims were white and rich!"

Sasha's parents' house was in a part of the city where I had never been, and I was astonished to see that it actually *was* a house and not an apartment: a three-story gray house with black trim and its own garage.

"You grew up here?" I asked.

"I did indeed, but I've hardly set foot in this place in three years."

On the way there, she had told me that her parents were out of town. "I think they're coming back soon, though, which is why I have to get this done."

The house was smaller than it had looked from outside. It had the feel almost of a playhouse. I remember ornately patterned rugs, unmatched furniture, a jungle of potted plants, and what I mistook for African sculpture. ("Nah. It's from the Pacific Islands.")

I helped Sasha bring in the boxes and suitcases. In the kitchen, which was ultramodern and spotless, Sasha took two Cokes from the refrigerator and opened them. As she handed me one, the doorbell rang, startling me so violently the can slipped from my grasp. Sasha was calm. Though she had not mentioned it, she'd been expecting the people she now went to let in. Two men and a woman followed her into the kitchen, the men about Sasha's age, the woman closer to mine. The exceptional thing about them was the length of the men's hair: short, very short, like straight men's.

"These are my friends," Sasha said. They did not look happy to see me. "This is George," she told them, leaving their own names unsaid. They stood there looking at me uncertainly, without speaking. "George is cool," Sasha said, and when that failed to break the ice, "Give her a break, man. She's just been raped."

"No," I said quickly. "I mean—I mean yes, but I'm okay." I would have fled the room had they not been blocking the doorway. One of the men said, "Oh, wow, man," and turned and walked out.

I was holding a sponge. The can I had dropped had gushed a puddle of Coke. I had been about to clean it up when Sasha returned with her friends. Now I started to get down on the floor, but Sasha said, "Hey, don't you do that," and grabbed the sponge away. I thought she meant she would clean the mess herself. Instead, she tossed the sponge in the sink, and deliberately stepping into the puddle with both feet (she was wearing boots), she began marching in place, splashing Coke over everything under waist-high. She laughed, and the man laughed, but the woman glanced at her watch and said with a singsong warning inflection, "*Sa*-sha."

"Right," said Sasha. "Okay, why don't you three get started? George, you come upstairs with me." She led me out of the kitchen without drying her feet.

As we passed through the living room, I saw that the man who had left the kitchen was lying on a sofa, smoking a joint. I saw also that Sasha's friends had brought suitcases, too.

Sasha's parents' bedroom smelled like a greenhouse. There were plants downstairs, too, but the ones in here were particularly exotic-looking, and some were in bloom. "But these have just been watered," I said.

"Yeah, the cleaning person comes when my parents are gone." Like Ann: a gun to her head could not have got her to say *maid*. "Make yourself at home. That's a very comfortable bed." I sat uncomfortably on it. It was half smothered with pillows, all different sizes and covered with different fabrics. I knew that some people decorated their beds like this, but where I came from it was not done. In our own home, there was always just one small flat pillow for each bed. The unbidden thought of those meager pillows and their old, stained, sour-smelling cases filled me with despair.

Sasha was rooting in the purse she had brought upstairs with her. Now she simultaneously produced a small plastic bag full of whitish powder and asked me whether I'd ever done smack before. I had, and in that instant I forgave Sasha everything.

On a bedside table were some framed photographs. Sasha took one and laid it flat, carefully shaking some of the powder onto its glass surface. I supposed those were her parents, the bride and groom under the powder under the glass, but I wasn't really interested. I was too preoccupied with what was about to happen. I was also thinking about Sasha's driving, how incautious she'd been, once even running a red light. And all along she'd been carrying.

She said, "I wish I could join you, but I have to stay straight tonight. This shit may be stronger than what you've had before, but you'll like it. And you deserve it after what you've been through. This will make you forget, baby. This will make you forget."

I was glad the room had its own bath. If the stuff was really good, I might throw up. I snorted the powder and lay back against the comfy pillows. Why should I mind getting high by myself?

I had noticed a stereo set downstairs, and here was another one in the bedroom. Next to it was a stack of records, which Sasha was now looking through. "I swear," she said. "My parents have the worst fucking taste." She tossed aside albums of movie sound tracks: *Camelot, My Fair Lady*. "Who listens to this shit?" She tossed aside Sinatra. Rosemary Clooney. Barbra Streisand! But in spite of herself, as she kept looking, Sasha started to sing "If Ever I Would Leave You," from *Camelot*. She must have liked it once: she knew all the words. She had a beautiful voice, and she wasn't even trying. My eyes filled with tears.

"Hey, this'll do." She had found some Ravel.

There were headphones with a cord long enough to reach the bed. Sasha had me put them on before she started the recording of *Boléro*.

"Now," she said. "The only thing you have to do is stay right here and relax." She tweaked my nose as if I were a child, and she left, closing the door.

Not too long after, I had to get up. In the bathroom I vomited, very gently, very *naturally*, if that is not too strange to say, to the rhythm of *Boléro*. I felt better afterward, but then I had been feeling pretty good before. Back to the bed on boneless legs, back under the headphones. I was in the pleasure dome now: body heavy, head light, and that fluttering in the blood, as if butterflies were trapped there. The only thing I had to do was relax. Okay. You could have pulled me limb from limb like taffy.

For those who do not know, here is the way a friend of mine once described it: "The first time I ever did heroin, I thought God had bent down from heaven and kissed me on the lips."

I hadn't eaten any dinner, but I was not hungry. I was not thirsty. I had left my cigarettes downstairs, but I did not crave one. Had something been bothering me? I did not remember. Ann was right: Sasha was a genius.

When *Boléro* came to an end, I got up and started it over again. I did this more than once. It was a piece I had never heard before that night (and the kind of music I would never listen to today).

Downstairs, they were packing as much as they could carry into the boxes and suitcases. When, between nods, I floated down there, no one paid attention to me.

Later I was vaguely aware of sex happening somewhere in the house.

At some point I crashed for real and did not wake until morning. I was still completely dressed, down to my sneakers, and had slept on top of the covers. The headphones were beside me, but the stereo was gone. So was the one in the living room, and the television, and everything of value, including the sculpture. So were the people. In the kitchen—the Coke had dried and the floor was all sticky—I found a note: "You were so out of it we decided to let you be. You can get home by yourself." Yes, that was not a problem. I could get home by myself—so long as there was no hurry. I drank about a gallon of water, then went back upstairs, and the moment I lay down I fell asleep again.

When I woke the second time, it was because someone was waking me. A hand on my shoulder was squeezing, shaking. "Hey, come on now, we can't let you sleep anymore. Come on, wake up, wake up now." Sasha was back. She was sitting in a chair by the bed. She had changed into a tailored suit and aged about thirty years. Her widow's peak had turned white, and her face tragic. She said, "Who

92

are you?" And I, enlightened, shocked, and dry-mouthed, croaked, "Sasha's mother."

"No, my dear, that's me. Who are *you*?"

Footsteps pounded up the stairs, and a man strode into the room. Face like a storm. He jutted his chin at me and said, "So she finally woke up?"

I gathered they had not just arrived. They had found me but had not woken me right away. This gave me a chill. They had "creepy-crawled" me, like the Manson people. Except, of course, this was their house.

The way the man—Sasha's father, who else?—was looking at me told me I should hurry and get out of there. I got unsteadily to my feet and started babbling: how sorry I was, didn't know how this could have happened, must have fallen asleep, but now I'd be going, leave them in peace—

"You're not going anywhere till we call the police."

"The police!" Sasha's mother looked at her husband as if he had kicked her. "For god's sake, Louis. *We are not going to call the police.*"

"No?"

"No, Louis. We are not going to call the police on our own daughter."

"Oh, no? And what are we going to do, then?"

"Well—" She had turned back to me. I could tell she was more upset with Louis than she was with me. "We're going to send this little girl home, and then I'm going to go to bed and cry until next Tuesday."

"You realize the insurance company is going to call this an inside job. We won't be able to collect a penny."

"I realize."

"I suppose we should be grateful she didn't blow the place up."

Sasha's mother shut her eyes, and I knew exactly what she was seeing. It had happened only weeks ago, in Greenwich Village. The survivors—exactly who and how many not known—staggering out from the flames and the collapsing debris to escape before police arrived. Three had not escaped, had not survived; and the two, a man and a woman, who'd been making the bomb in the basement had been ripped apart. The woman just about Sasha's age. A town house, like this.

"Louis," Sasha's mother said in a voice that was somehow both harsh and imploring. "Take her out and get her a cab." She got up then and went into the bathroom, quietly closing the door. I remembered vomiting to *Boléro* the night before and hoped I had not left any mess.

I was afraid to be alone with Louis and his rage for even a minute. I ran ahead of him down the stairs but waited so that he could open the door. As I stepped outside, he asked me if I had money for a cab, and I shook my head. When Sasha and I left the campus the night before, I had taken nothing with me but my cigarettes, and somehow I had managed to lose even them.

"Then I guess wherever you're going you'll just have to walk."
Slam.
That's what he thought.

Within a few blocks I had collected twice the fare. (Hard to explain, but back then, for a little while at least, people *liked* to give money to hippie panhandlers. They *enjoyed* picking up hitchhikers. People who would never or could never belong to the counterculture were often sweetly benevolent toward it.)

On the way home in the cab, smoking a Kool I had bummed from the driver, I thought of the wedding photograph lying flat on the bedside table where Sasha's parents would find it, coated with white dust. I had a fleeting fantasy of being alone with Sasha's mother, throwing myself into her arms, and telling her everything, beginning with the rape.

I returned to a campus in uproar. American troops had just invaded Cambodia. There were calls for a student strike. In the following days, demonstrations took place at colleges across the nation. In Ohio, National Guard troops opened fire on students at Kent State, wounding nine, killing four. Ten days later, at Jackson State, in Mississippi, police killed two and wounded twelve. (Ann would make much of the fact that the second event got nothing like the attention of the first, surely because the Jackson State victims were black.) Before the semester was over, hundreds of schools, including Columbia, had shut down. So ended (early) our sophomore year. Ann and I saw little of each other those last days. But we both had come to the same decision. When school reopened that fall, it would be without us.

For me, even before the turmoil of that spring, college could seem like the very home of chaos and confusion, where students with absolutely no need for money risked jail by pushing drugs, and a Barnard senior, also in no financial need, worked as a prostitute at a fancy brothel near the U.N.; where rich kids lamented not being poor and made a fetish of poor blacks; where blacks claimed that no white teacher could criticize a black student's work and that criticism was just a white idea anyway; where one teacher got a letter telling her she'd better watch her Jew ass; and where a black classmate whose book I picked up by mistake threw the book at my head, shouting, "Now you've given me bad luck for a month!" Where Charles Manson was a hero, or at least "one of us." Where some people would have nothing to do with me because I had a brother who'd killed Vietnamese. One night that semester, we all flew out of our beds: someone had planted a bomb under the statue of Alma Mater. The noise might have been a shock, but the act itself surprised no one.

As for Ann, she had come to believe, like Sasha, that despite the growth of student power in recent years the universities remained entrenched Establishment institutions, in bed with corporate America, committed to preparing the young to take their places in a corrupt and undemocratic society. Unlike Sasha, Ann had no intention of going underground, but she could not live the privileged life of a student anymore. We were both disillusioned; we both wanted to move on, but for different reasons. Ann was still looking to change the world. And I (though I saw it only later) was looking for romance.

I once spoke to a group of young women about being raped. This was years after it happened, when I had already been married twice and had had my two kids. I had made friends with a Women's Studies professor, and I had told her my story, and it was she who asked me to speak to the small group of young women, all of whom were doing some sort of research on women and sexual abuse. I did not want to do it, but she was my friend.

I sat on my friend's living-room floor with a glass of white wine, and I began by saying that things had been different in 1970. I explained that women were different then, that they could not have been as afraid of getting raped, for example, because at that time you saw women hitchhiking everywhere, even pregnant women and women accompanied by children. They went on the road, and they got into cars and drove off with strange men—this at a time when rape, like all violent crime, was on the rise in America—and who in her right mind would do this today? I told them about the two hippie girls who'd hitched from Denver to Manhattan and crashed in our freshman dorm and who, when we asked them hadn't they been afraid, said no, because "if a guy wanted to ball, we'd ball 'im." I said that when I was finally reunited with my sister, who had hitched back and forth cross-country several times, she told a similar story, and we even joked about what a golden age that had been for truckers—you see, we could laugh about it then. But nobody in my friend's living room was laughing now. I told them about the lunatic fringe of the sexual revolution who thought it a crime that anyone should ever have to resort to rape at all, and how Solange once confessed that for years of her life she would sleep with anyone who asked. It was political, she said. Because for some, free love meant what it said, like air, like water, and no shame. And I told them how at that time you could find plenty of women who thought it rude or unfeeling to sleep with just one man if there were two men in the room. (Still no laugh.)

I brought up Eldridge Cleaver and how—though it was known he had raped black women for practice and then moved on to raping whites as an "insurrectionary act"—at least half the women I knew would have been honored to have sex with him. Sex with a Black Panther would have been the height of their dreams.

I explained why I would not go to the police, and why I did not want to tell my boyfriend, and how I had not told my mother for the same reason I had not told her about my stolen suitcase or about the way Miss Crug used to take me in her arms to talk about college applications—because it was only asking for trouble, that. Everything always had to have been my own fault. But that was my mother, and that was another story. I said it had been very interesting, as the years passed, to see whom I found myself telling and whom I did not: this friend but not that one, my first husband but not my second. (Later: my daughter but not my son.)

I said I thought walking alone in that deserted area of the park after being warned not to had been irresponsible and just plain dumb. No, not that I was asking for it, listen carefully, that is not what I said. I said—hoping not to be misunderstood but fearing I would be, dreadfully so—that if I was going to be raped, and if there could be such a thing as a best time for it to happen, I had been raped at such a time. I said I was sure it had helped that at that particular time, sexual intercourse had been demystified, that it could mean not just a casual but a meaningless act, something you might easily do with a person you didn't know or care about, someone you never intended to see again, someone to whom you were not even attracted, someone you might even dislike, someone you would almost certainly *not* have had sex with if you'd been less high or less lazy or tired. I cited *Woodstock*, the movie, the scene in which two very young kids are interviewed: "We ball and everything but like it's really a pretty good thing because there's plenty of freedom because we're not going together and we're not in love or anything like that, you know . . ."

I said it had probably helped also that there'd been so much craziness going on, not just that night at Sasha's parents' house, but the general madness of the day; and indeed, later on when I looked back, I saw how the rape had ended up blending in, a terrible moment in a terrible time, but—a *moment*, that was the thing. I said no, and again no (when they pressed me), I did not resent the way Ann and Sasha tried to play down what had happened and asked me to remember that worse things were happening right then in the world. God knows, it was bracing compared to what I remembered my high school friend Joey Turco saying after his sister-in-law had been raped: "That's the end of my brother's marriage, right there, the whole thing." None of the women in my friend's living room had ever seen *Town Without Pity*, but they knew the Gene Pitney song. I said that when I looked back on my life, I could point to many things that had happened that had been worse than being raped, and that all those worse things had, though the truth was strange and bitter to me, made the rape into a minor event. Then I told myself to put down my glass and not drink any more wine.

They told me I was in denial. They told me I was intellectualizing, and that I clearly still had a lot of emotional work to do. They told me I had repressed how bad the rape had actually been.

Here is another memory from that spring: A woman accidentally walking in on her roommate to find her and her boyfriend lying in bed. Later, the woman's voice all derision as she reported, "They were still wearing their underwear!" How we groaned. What sort of silly bourgeois lovemaking was that? Taking your clothes off one piece at a time was considered ridiculous then. As bad as turning out the lights.

Part Two

*I*t's *always who you know*. Stacy Rudolphson and I had been in the same modern dance class. "Call my stepmother," she said. "She's the features editor at *Visage*."

As it turned out, the features editor was not looking for help right then, but the health and beauty editor was. Nicole Bishop was looking for a new secretary (it was still a year or so away, our transformation into *editorial assistants*). Half a college education might have been better than none, but what got me hired was, of course, the typing test. There was also a spelling and vocabulary test, multiple-choice, easy, easy, and scrutiny of my penmanship. How I could have come to a job interview dressed the way I was, tsk-tsk—but never mind: so long as I understood that the office had a dress code. No jeans. Indeed, no pants, no bare legs, and an overall well-groomed appearance was expected. In this regard, Nicole Bishop herself could not have set a better example. She was an elegant dresser, an advertisement for her own department: a true beauty—makeup so expertly applied it was all but unnoticeable— and the picture of health. Though she would later struggle with her weight, she was for the time being what you'd call shapely. Her panache was enhanced by what I first took for a British accent; in fact, she was from the country once known as Rhodesia. We had this in common: Nicole had dropped out after two years at Wellesley. A newlywed. A husband who was also an editor, at a different magazine, and a man of some importance in the magazine world— so I would learn from the secretary of the fiction and poetry editor. The husband's name was Whit. Another smart dresser. A handsome pair. They had this sweet little tradition. Wednesday evenings Whit came to pick Nicole up after work, and they went out to an early dinner and a movie. At least once a week he had flowers delivered to her office. Still in their honeymoon phase, everyone said—the younger women, dreamily; the older ones in a tone that was knowing, ironic.

Soon it was plain: a child was on the way.

Nicole was the kind of woman on whom younger women instantly develop a crush. She had, I saw at once, everything I wanted for myself. I wanted her wardrobe, or at least her sense of style. I wanted her job and a husband like hers—important, a man of the world, but still boyish. Those Wednesday nights. The flowers. I wanted the brownstone apartment down on Bank Street (where I would go often, once Nicole was in her eighth month and had stopped coming into the office) and, when he arrived, the little prince of a child.

I was lucky. *Visage* had its share of monsters (Stacy's stepmother turned out to be one of them), and some of the other secretaries suffered under them. But Nicole had a relaxed way about her. Unlike other bosses, she permitted us to call her by her first name (speaking of names, at *Visage*, I was at last "Georgette"), and while I was learning the ropes and making stupid mistakes she was kindness itself. "Oh, you always keep a copy of any letter you send out. My fault. I should have told you that." I wondered why the magazine didn't hire real secretaries with professional training, until someone explained that the editor in chief didn't want any "Katharine Gibbs types." *Visage* did not place want ads; you really did have to know someone to get a job there.

Vee-ZAHGE. The editor in chief went wild if you did not use the French pronunciation. Its readership was mainly single women in their twenties and early thirties, women who were just starting out in life, who wanted a career but a family, too, in time. The editorial board was all female, and with a few exceptions (the mailroom clerks, the business manager), so was the staff. The real power, though—the power that said whether *Visage* would live or die (and it would say *die*, come the eighties)—lay with certain men, men with offices on another floor or in another building. I knew their names, but I never saw them.

I did not have my own office; I sat at a desk right outside Nicole's office door. This was the arrangement for all editors' secretaries. And there was a rule: no messy desks! It was hard to get used to. I felt so *exposed* in that corridor, and making sure my desk was always neat took some effort. Complying with the dress code took far too much effort. I spent many lunch hours in department stores near the office, looking for sales. Though I could not afford the clothes that appeared in *Visage*'s pages every month, and though I knew I would never possess her flair, I did my best to be like Nicole. I found myself imitating even her handwriting, or at least the way she formed certain letters. Like her, I began crossing my *z*'s and my sevens. (But my occasional lapse into a British accent was unconscious, I swear, and needless to say embarrassing.)

Surely no one had ever called Nicole "Nick."

Every day, there came to the office numerous samples of cosmetics and other beauty products, most of which were mine to take home. I was delighted. It was manna from a kind of heaven—the heaven of I-enjoy-being-a-girl. In college I had not paid much attention to magazines like *Visage*. Now I began reading not only "us" but our many competitors as well. And I began paying attention to my appearance in a way I never had before, either. I started wearing makeup, learning to apply it as Nicole did, so it looked natural. How to have shiny, tangle-free hair, how to make my eyes appear wider, which was the right shade of blush for my complexion or the right scent for my body chemistry—such things now took on importance for me. I began taking vitamin E (the beauty vitamin, we called it) and drinking six to eight glasses of water a day. I tried to eat well and to sleep more, and it made me feel good, this taking care of myself, breaking the bad habits of college one by one (except smoking: this was one way in which I would not do as Nicole did and quit). Of the knowledge of health and beauty there seemed no end. It was a whole other education, and I was a diligent student, even taking those silly tests that were included in some issues: What's Your Beauty IQ? Which of the Following Are Fashion Don'ts? (Ah, there it was again: the outsize handbag!) Consider the avocado, a food unknown where I came from, just then coming into its own as an ingredient in countless products, from shampoos to foot cream, and, in Nicole's copy, "a veritable powerhouse of vitamins and nutrients." How could such knowledge bring me as much pleasure and satisfaction as anything I had learned in school? "Cut it open, remove the stone, and fill one half with crab salad, for an elegant, healthful lunch." It was another secretary, Cleo King, the only black person working at *Visage* and whose desk was near mine, who showed me how I could also save the stone and cultivate a large, leafy plant. I got to know Cleo and the other secretaries, and gradually (or not so gradually, come to think of it) they replaced most of my college friends. These women were all about my own age and obsessed with the same things I was now obsessed with. We were the magazine's most devoted readers, and we were a sisterhood. And none of them ever called me George.

Much about popular magazines has changed, but text still mattered then, and Nicole labored over her copy, as I knew from typing revisions. Short stories and articles of general interest, some as long as several thousand words, appeared in every issue. People like Ann (who of course frowned at my new job—"And where did you get that ridiculous accent?") made fun of the pretentions to seriousness of women's magazines. But the editors at *Visage* prided themselves on publishing, all in one issue, The Best Spring Fashions Ever; a poem by W. H. Auden; an interview with Ted Kennedy; various reviews; Is Going Braless a Good Idea?; What Your Favorite Color Says About You; Your First Visit to the Gynecologist: What to Expect; Recipes for a Candlelight Dinner for Two; and A Letter from Vietnam.

Even today, when beauty and fashion concerns are far from my mind, when I open a women's magazine only to kill time, say, in a doctor's waiting room, it is easy for me to see why I was seduced by that world. The order, the structure, the simple responsibilities, the gentle mentor, the weekly paycheck, humble though it was. It used to be said that in a wise budget, a person's monthly rent should not exceed one week's salary. And so it was part of the sense of rightness I felt at the time: both my monthly rent and my weekly salary were precisely $125. I had found my first apartment, a studio, on West End Avenue near Ninety-sixth Street. It was in the basement, there were bars on the windows, there were roaches, the street was scary after dark, and the super was a lech and a drunk. But for me these were days of optimism. I knew my fortunes would soon rise, and I set my heart on something in Greenwich Village, near Nicole. Around the time the baby was born, when I was often at the Bishops' apartment, I would take walks around their neighborhood in a kind of trance. Was there no end to the romantic corners of this city? I still loved Midtown, where our offices were, but surely the Village was the place to live.

Except for the occasional editorial tantrum, the atmosphere at *Visage* was calm. The office suites were well designed and beautifully decorated. For some reason, the first thing to come to mind is the carpeting, which was very pale, the color of an unripe peach, and how—and this was what always amazed me—it never got dirty. The carpeting in the dorm had been a revolting shade of puce and, though dark enough, was covered with more stains with each passing week. Not that any effort was made to keep it from getting stained—quite the opposite. Though the kind of vandalism and thievery college campuses have become known for was rarer then, there was little respect for property. Unbelievable where some people chose to put out their cigarettes. But it is not just at this particular moment that I remember the carpeting at *Visage*. For years after I'd left the office, that plush pale expanse would, for no reason at all that I could tell, roll out in my head. I suppose it spelled luxury to me—like the big vases of fresh flowers arranged everywhere, even in the ladies' room. Nicole's office was truly luxurious, more like a study in a private house, with its brown leather furniture, antique desk and lamps, and pony-skin rug. Nicole and Whit were passionate about France, where they had spent their honeymoon, and they were passionate about photography, which they collected, and there were framed photographs of French subjects by famous French photographers on the walls. There was also a framed letter signed by Cocteau, which had been a wedding gift—but here I may be mistaken: that letter may actually have been somewhere in the Bishops' apartment, which was also hung with photographs.

On one of Nicole's office bookshelves, on a small tray, sat a frighteningly fragile tea set—cups so thin you would have thought the tea would seep right through. Coming soon, this instruction from feminists to pink-collar workers: Tell your boss, "I don't make coffee and I don't dust." But it was different, wasn't it, if your boss was a woman, and if she was pregnant, and beautiful and good, and if you loved her very much? Except for my great fear of breaking one of those cups, I enjoyed making Nicole her afternoon tea. I would have enjoyed doing almost anything for Nicole. Today I will cross a *z* or a seven and think of her sitting in a chair by her window, gazing out, one hand holding the pretty little cup, the other resting on her belly. Her expression is serene but a touch grave, an expression that suits her. And what I would not give, *what* I would not give, to be back there again just for a moment, just to see her— and myself—as we were; or even—nostalgia being the paradoxical emotion that it is—the editor in chief scowling down at me: "Don't you think all those papers should be filed away instead of cluttering up your desk?"

I have decided that nostalgia is itself a kind of love. From time to time it dictates that I absolutely must have avocado and crab for lunch.

I did not share tea with Nicole. I did not drink from those cups. I waited for the man with the coffee cart to come around to our floor. I heard his loud bell ("Oh, *must* he?" moaned our headache-prone managing editor) and went to buy coffee and a pastry, though the quality was not very good (Nicole would touch nothing from that cart). The coffee too weak, the pastry too sweet, and yet, somehow, together, they tasted just right.

As I say, it all seemed good and right to me, my new life at *Visage*. It was all therapeutic, I think—even the infatuation with Nicole. It was all part of the romance I was seeking, and a long time would pass before I missed being a student. However much I have changed, however immeasurable the distance between that life and the life I have now, I was partly formed by *Visage*, and I am still grateful (as I am still friends with Cleo). I see no mystery here. One must have something to believe in, and for a while, at least, I chose to believe what the women's magazines want us to believe: that we can make ourselves ever more beautiful, and that we *should* do this, and that if we did we would be happier, more successful, even better people. Massages, facials, visits to spas—I could no more afford extravagant beauty treatments than could many of our subscribers. But I could read about them, and just reading about them was a pleasure and surprisingly satisfying, as for some people reading recipes without actually cooking or eating can be satisfying. (Wherein, of course, lies the secret of such a magazine's—and perhaps many a cookbook's—success.) I made a connection between the pages of *Visage* and Nicole's life—I mean, those things that she had that I wanted for myself: in a word, her happiness. What made me so sure Nicole was happy? Only someone truly happy, I decided, could be so nice. She had no enemies as far as I could tell. And I was not the only one smitten with her. There is a sort of gentleness you find in people who have suffered much, and a different sort of gentleness in people to whom life has always been kind. And Nicole had this second sort of gentleness—or so I believed.

"The important thing is to glow," began one of her monthly Letters from the Health and Beauty Editor. And glow she did: eyes, skin, teeth, hair. But it was not just a reflection of physical beauty and health, it was the glow of happiness itself I believed I saw.

As she was right about much else, Ann was right when she said I would become bored with *Visage* and even ashamed of my new preoccupations. But she was wrong when she predicted it would happen soon. It took years.

Every January, as part of its New Year's issue, *Visage* included a special "makeover" section featuring members of the staff. In 1971 there were three of us, all new to the magazine: two secretaries—Cleo and I—and a woman in her forties named Joan who had just joined the art department. As always, there were "before" photographs, and the same hairstylists and makeup artists who readied the professional models for their fashion shoots buzzed about our giddy heads. I no longer recall how it was decided who would wear what, but there were several fittings, and we were allowed to keep the clothes and accessories we wore in the "after" photographs—in my case, a black-and-white houndstooth check woolen blazer and matching skirt, a red silk blouse, red leather pumps, and matching shoulder bag. By far the best clothes I'd ever owned (and so beloved, I wore them out, alas, in no time).

"We thought Georgette's long-haired waif look needed an update." I felt only the mildest twinge as the hair piled up on the floor, and I have worn the suggested chin-length blunt cut ever since.

One day later that year, I was running down Madison Avenue in the rain. I had on the matching blazer and skirt and the red shoes, and I was holding the red bag over my head—I had been caught without an umbrella. I was so afraid of ruining that suit, those lovely shoes, that, swerving to miss a puddle, I crashed into a man carrying an armload of lunch bags. "Jesus fuck." It was more than annoyance. "Why don't you watch where you're going?" Ponytail, hoop earring, head scarf, scar: he looked like a pirate, and there was blood in his eye. My apologies died in my throat. It was more than rage. I heard him distinctly yet could not trust my ears. *"Rich bitch."*

No one would tell Cleo, but Nicole told me. After the January issue appeared, several people, mostly in the South, canceled their subscriptions because they did not like seeing a black woman in the magazine. "I don't see any white girls in *Ebony*," wrote one woman. "And there's a reason for that."

A thing can shock the hell out of you and still not be a surprise. This was a time when, despite the huge success of black recording artists, most record companies refused to show photographs of African-Americans on their album covers. When albums with such photographs did appear, many stores would not stock them.

Q: Should Cleo have been told?

She would have wanted to know, I think.

I was her friend. Was it right that I should be told about those letters but not she?

She was three years older than I, she was from Philadelphia, she had her B.A., and after two years at *Visage* she would go to journalism school. "It's either that or law school," she said. At *Visage*, mulling over her choice, she worked for the fiction and poetry editor. After she left, she kept her connection with the magazine, doing occasional book or theater reviews. She became the author of a book herself, about the figure of the empathetic black in white society, which brought her some attention. Then she wrote a play, which brought her much more attention. She wrote more plays and made a name for herself. She married early and had a child. She divorced and raised the child herself. She wrote a book about that. She got cancer and wrote a book about surviving.

"We thought Cleo's six-inch-deep Afro overwhelmed her fine-featured face." So they mowed that thing down closer to her scalp. It was Kenneth, the king of coiffeurs, who said it was a mistake for a woman to keep changing her hair, because for every woman there were only one or two styles that suited her face. This was something sophisticated women (Jacqueline Onassis, Princess Grace) have always understood, Kenneth said. But such good sense was now being lost. Tell it to Cleo. Back in school again, she grew her hair and straightened it and held it in place with barrettes as she'd done as a girl. Next came cornrows, then dreadlocks. And in the way that a few faces look good in almost any hat, all these styles suited Cleo. Even when chemotherapy left her with no hair at all, the effect, we agreed, was a striking, extraterrestrial beauty. So much so that for a while, as the hair grew back, she kept shaving it off.

The last time we met, after many years, her hair was a skullcap, a thin pelt, a white rind. She saw how my eye went right to it and, patting it with one hand, said, mock-mournfully, "Like frost."

Meanwhile, something momentous had happened to Ann. She had fallen in love. She wept when she told me about it, and I felt the old envy, for though I was involved with my neighbor upstairs, I was in love with no one.

Ann wept at my table, having eaten almost nothing of the lasagna and salad I had made her. I was learning to cook. My neighbor, the one with whom I was involved, was a steadfast test subject because, as he put it, even when the meal was a disaster there was always dessert, meaning sex. (Indeed, it all began because I was dying to try *Visage*'s Candlelight Dinner for Two.)

Ann had stayed in New York after leaving school, moving into the same communal apartment where Sasha lived. She was working in a store called The People's Books. She never went home to Connecticut and hardly saw her parents anymore. She had her job and her causes, and now she had this man with whom she said she was in love. She blew her nose in her napkin and told me about him, a schoolteacher from Harlem she had met on a subway platform. (She had been sitting slumped on a bench, catching her breath, having just been mugged, when he stopped to ask what was wrong.) "He also writes poetry." She had been thrilled to learn he had once belonged to SNCC and to the Communist Party and had sown his share of radical wild oats. "But he's not a revolutionary—not anymore," Ann said tenderly. "Just a quiet guy who loves kids." During his revolutionary phase it would have been unthinkable for him to date a white girl. "He said if I knew some of the things he'd said and written about white people, especially about rich white people, I would never want to be with him." But of course she did know, she made it her business to know precisely such things, and she did want to be with him.

Once again, a life change had demanded a rechristening. He'd been Kwame Kwesi since 1966 but was now thinking of going back to his birth name. His mother would have been pleased, but not Ann. She would rather be with a Kwame Kwesi than with an Alfred Winston Blood. I said I liked the lordly sound of Alfred Blood, but she objected passionately. "Tell me the truth. When you hear that name, do you see a black man?"

He was not young, he was about to turn thirty, and he wanted to settle down. He had warned Ann not to get involved with him unless she was serious. He wanted children. Was she ready for that? I could not imagine her fooling herself into believing that she was. She had just turned twenty. Yet already they had taken the first step. They were looking for an apartment to move into together, and they would soon find one, above the Barnard campus, on Tiemann Place. He didn't like the living arrangement Ann had now one bit. The squalor. The musical beds. He didn't like her roommates. At his most radical, he had hated young white radicals most. Coming into the ghetto: we're gonna show you what to do. Till Stokely Carmichael, a.k.a. Kwame Ture, told them to keep out. He didn't like The People's Books, the manager in his Jewish Afro giving him the raised fist every time Kwame walked in. Just because he didn't hate white people anymore didn't mean he had to like them. And what about Ann's activism, her own revolutionary goals? "He wants me to say goodbye to all that."

No wonder she was crying. She must have been so confused.

Nothing was easy. The Draytons did not yet know about the relationship, but the Bloods did. Kwame, who had lived on his own since he was eighteen, had had some kind of dispute with his current landlord and had moved in temporarily with his parents. About Ann, the first thing his mother said was, "Now, why would you want to go and bring so much trouble into your life?" His two sisters, both older and married, said, "No black woman good enough?" "She's not even pretty, she's just white!" At least some of his other relations and friends had also expressed, to varying degrees, disapproval or doubts. On the streets of Harlem, strangers made their feelings known: "Hey, nigger, what you doin' with that pink bitch?" Only his father remained detached. Moses Blood had worked as a chauffeur, had been in a crack-up, and now spent all his time in a wheelchair and all his resources fighting pain.

I was a little hurt that I had not already met Kwame. That subway encounter had happened months ago. It was a sign of how much had changed, and how rapidly, since Ann and I had left school, though I did not like to admit this. I did not like to admit that it now seemed to be mostly up to me to keep in touch, that it was usually I who called, I who suggested we get together, or that when we did get together we seemed to have less and less to say to each other and Ann's mind often seemed to be somewhere else. The truth—and I shrank from it—was that I was afraid of losing Ann's friendship, because for me that would have entailed another, deeper loss. What to call it? Some important failure. I would remember— piercingly—those early days when I would hide out from Ann, putting off till late returning to our room, not wanting merely to avoid her but to snub, to reject, to *hurt* her. And how she would have done anything in the world not to hurt me. But now she was no longer careful about my feelings. For example, the dinner I had made for her and which she hardly touched—she said nothing about it, not even a polite word. As if it weren't a lot of work, lasagna. As if she were not my guest.

Upstairs, my neighbor—my lover—had just come home and put on some music (he was a drummer in a band). I had thought about introducing him to Ann, but it would never happen. Another sign: none of my new friends had met her.

Of course, I could not leave *Visage* out of account. As always, Ann was open in her contempt. I had entered the enemy territory of her parents ("Sophie reads all those magazines"), and the longer I stayed there, the less respect she would have for me. She was affectionate at times—indeed, much of the time. But she was also impatient and irritable, which bothered me in a way I would not have imagined. I saw that—much as I wished it were otherwise—her opinion of me would always matter. I did not yet know that, contrary to youth's sense of itself as tolerant, freethinking, and egalitarian, it is more often stubbornly critical and judgmental, priggish and snobbish. I would find these faults much later (glaring) in my son and daughter and their friends. But at that age myself, I did not see how we truly were, nor did I put together that these faults were often worst in those with the strongest political opinions.

The more critical Ann was, the more vulnerable I became. It was like having layers of skin peeled away. That I had disappointed her, that I did not meet her standards, that I had ceased to be of serious or special interest to her—all this was as painful as it was undeniable. It weighed on my mind and on my spirit, but there was no one with whom I would have talked about it. The only person I had ever been able to talk with about something so painful, so close to my heart, was—Ann.

I began to count the number of times she used the word *superficial* in response to something I'd said. "That is so superficial, George." George. ("I'm sorry. 'Georgette' makes me think of some kind of frilly petticoat." Never mind that it was my real name.)

On my new work clothes: "I think it's awful that they make you dress like that."

Probably I should have resisted telling her to be sure to check out the January issue of *Visage*. But I was too excited to keep it to myself. I told everyone. Whether or not she saw it, I don't know; she never mentioned it. It is possible she forgot about it completely. It would have been easy for something so *superficial* to slip her mind. (Those tempted to ascribe Ann's behavior to simple envy did not know Ann.) But I never forgave her. How could something be superficial if it was important to me?

Still. When we hugged goodbye that night, I did not want to let her go. I was confused, too. I was always confused about Ann.

"So when do I get to meet this guy?"

"Next time," Ann promised. But she did not say when that would be.

I had just started washing the dishes when my neighbor came down and rang the bell. He must have noticed Ann leaving. He was holding a small jar of dark honey. He was a good drummer, and good at one other thing, too. "Dessert?"

By the time I met Kwame, he and Ann had moved into their apartment on Tiemann Place. Ann invited me to come to dinner after work. But first I stopped at my apartment to change (I would rather Ann not see me in my work clothes anymore) and to pick up a bottle of wine I had bought the day before. Also, because Ann had admired my avocado plant, I had decided to give it to her as a housewarming gift. I would miss it—it was the first plant I had ever tried to grow, and it was thriving—but I figured I could grow another one. (As it turned out, though I tried again, twice, mysteriously both seedlings failed.)

On the short subway ride to 125th Street, the heavy terra-cotta pot bruising my thighs, the leaves nearly smothering me, I thought about how nervous I was. What if Kwame and I didn't like each other? I wondered what Ann had told him about me, what sort of person he'd be expecting. I thought about all the things Ann knew about me, all the intimate things I had told her since we'd met. She knew everything, really—and did that mean that Kwame, a total stranger to me, now knew all these things, too? (I have never been completely pleased or at ease when someone to whom I am introduced says, "I've heard so much about you.") Or had I come to mean so much less to Ann that she'd hardly spoken about me to her boyfriend at all, merely summing me up in a word or two, and one of those words *superficial*? And, as I was walking from the subway station to Tiemann Place: Had she told him what had happened to me just a stone's throw away, in the park?

It was Kwame who opened the door and took the plant from my arms.

"Oh, wow—sweetheart, come look at this." *Sweetheart!* How strange to hear anyone call her that. It made them both seem old. He was a small man, not much taller than Ann or I, and very lean. He had high cheekbones, and sideburns that covered much of his jaw, and he was wearing an African cloth cap. He was more pleasant-looking than good-looking, I decided, though he did have perfect teeth and almond-shaped blue eyes. Ann came running out of the kitchen. She clapped her hands when she saw the plant, and my heart swelled with pride. After some discussion about where to put it (the living room, which had the best light), I gave them the wine. It turned out that Kwame didn't drink wine, or any alcohol, but he opened the bottle and poured two glasses. Ann took hers and returned to the kitchen, where she was making a tuna curry with rice. She wasn't much of a cook and didn't pretend to be. She was following a recipe on the tuna can label. "This should take about twenty minutes," she said.

Meanwhile, Kwame showed me around. The apartment was freshly painted, uniformly white, and underfurnished—they had not lived there long—with the improvised look of grad-student rooms: the bed a mattress on the floor, the coffee table an old trunk with a batik cloth over it, bookshelves made of pine boards and cinder blocks. And yet it had the feel of a real home, I thought. In the bedroom, I was startled by a poster that was actually a blown-up black-and-white photograph of Ann and Kwame standing hand in hand and facing the camera—stark naked, like John and Yoko. "A friend of mine took that," Kwame said. Then, teasingly, "Why are you blushing?"

"It's the wine," I said, taking a peek into the spare room, which was furnished with only a small desk and a metal folding chair. There was a typewriter on the desk, and in the typewriter a partly typed page.

This could be my room: I could not prevent the absurd thought from forming. Have I said that I was terribly lonely? I had never lived by myself before. A room of one's own was splendid, of course, but a home all one's own was a prison sentence.

In fact, the wine was helping me relax. Back in the living room, I sat down with a feeling of relief. I was comfortable, Kwame was comfortable, Ann was happy with my gift. I had no reason to be nervous, no reason to fear the evening would not go well. The living room was warm and fragrant both with the curry and with pipe tobacco. Kwame did not drink, but he smoked everything—pipe, cigarettes, cigars. Right now he was rolling a joint. Ann poked her head out from the kitchen. "Put on some music, hon." *Hon!* How strange to hear her call someone that. Kwame turned the stereo on without changing the record that was already on the turntable. I recognized with a pang Ann's old Billie Holiday album. "God Bless the Child." I knew every scratch.

"I was sorry to hear about your sister." So this he had been told. "Any news?" I was surprised—not because Ann had told him or because he'd brought it up, but because, in fact, there was news. I had received a postcard. Not that the postcard was signed. It said only, in the puffy script of the kind used by comic-book artists, "Guess Who?" Big fat question mark. The card had been mailed from Ann Arbor, Michigan (where I knew not a soul), but showed a picture of the Statue of Liberty. Little joke. Once again I could not be sure it was Solange, but I couldn't think who else it could be. She had been missing for almost two years now. All that time I had believed she might be dead. Now I believed she was not only alive but, if not ready to go home (in fact, I was sure she would not go home), willing to be found. I believed also that she had figured out that, though still a minor, she could reappear at this point and nothing bad was going to happen to her.

"The Statue of Liberty?" Kwame said. "What do you suppose she's trying to tell you? That she passed through New York? That she's got to be free?" He was speaking in the strangled voice of the pot smoker trying not to exhale, at the same time offering the lit joint to me. I shook my head. Recently I had started to feel paranoid when I smoked pot. The only time I got stoned now was when I was with my drummer, who was one of those men who, though reckless, fickle, irresponsible, dissolute, and too hard-living to be in physical shape, somehow had the ability to make a woman feel safe. After a few tokes Kwame carefully extinguished the joint and laid it aside. "Ann's not big on reefer, either," he said thoughtfully. What made *me* thoughtful was this: there was not the slightest sign that Kwame was high. I doubted whether that half a joint had affected him as much as half a glass of wine was affecting me. I guessed that he was one of those people who smoked every day without ever getting wrecked, like those other people who would not have let a day pass without downing a six-pack or a couple of cocktails but somehow remained quite sober.

I said I didn't know if Solange was trying to send any message at all. "She probably just happened to have that card and decided to use it. But I think maybe at some point she was here in New York. Just a feeling."

Kwame was shaking his head. "I don't understand. If she's okay, why doesn't she come straight out and let you know? Why play guessing games? Why would anyone want to hurt their family so bad, going off and disappearing like that? I don't know that I could forgive my own sister if one of them did a thing like that." He was, indirectly, asking a question, but I ignored it. I wasn't sure I wanted to talk about Solange. I wasn't sure I could be truthful. I knew I didn't want to hear any stranger judge her, though.

He said, "Kids today." (Talk about sounding old!) "A lot of times, adolescence is already too late. You want to make a differ-ence, you got to reach them earlier. Much earlier." This, presum-ably, was why he taught sixth grade.

Dinner was ready. There was no dining table. I mean, there was a table just outside the kitchen, but it was hidden under piles of books and papers. We ate sitting around the batik-covered trunk. I had forgotten: trust Ann, with no experience, to make a great meal out of some canned tuna and rice. But mine was not the important judgment. Though she did not seem at all put out, I was indignant when Kwame refused to compliment her. "Don't worry," he told her. "We'll make a good cook out of you yet." What was that supposed to mean? He knew how to cook? So why hadn't he made dinner? If there was something I wasn't going to like about him, it was this. He was patronizing. It might have had something to do with his spending most of his time around children. And I didn't know if he talked down to everyone the way he talked down to Ann and me, but I noticed also that when he himself was not speaking, his attention often strayed. He did not listen. Of course, most men I have known have been like this.

Already he had been a big influence on Ann. He had persuaded her to follow his example and dedicate herself to teaching young children. So this was her plan: first she would finish her B.A. (she was attending City College right now); then on to Columbia's Teachers College, which Kwame himself had attended after graduating from City. His footsteps.

"All of a sudden it seemed so simple, so obvious," Ann said. "I mean, Kwame's right. If you really want to change the world—"

"And it's not just a job, you know, when you work with kids. They really are beautiful at that age—everyone is!"

"Kwame says it's a high just being around them—"

"It's like Chekhov said: In the animal world, you start with an ugly worm and you end up with a beautiful butterfly. But with people, you start with a butterfly and end up with an ugly old worm!"

I wanted to remember this.

As for having children of their own, they had agreed to put that off a few years. "I mean, I'm an old worm." Kwame grinned at Ann, and she grinned back. "But she's still a butterfly. We got time." They kissed.

Just as, earlier, I had thought their new apartment was already a real home, I was now thinking how Ann and Kwame were a real couple. I saw, with a tumult of mixed emotions, that it was all going to happen. Ann was going to be someone's wife. They were no longer just courting, but committed. They were already husbandly-wifely with each other. (I thought of Nicole and Whit: *still in their honeymoon phase.*) By husbandly-wifely I mean not only the kissing and the fondling (and there was much of this) but the way Kwame didn't need to compliment Ann on her cooking, and the way she did not take offense, and the way they interrupted each other and finished each other's sentences. This was all part of it, their intimacy a thing that could be sensed, warming the room like the steam coming off the rice, sweetening the air, like the curry and the pipe tobacco. Love was a rich, warm, sweet gold broth.

Love, marriage—children? That Ann would make an excellent teacher, I had no doubt. But having your own children was entirely different.

Motherhood: the one thing I was virtually certain Ann would not do well.

"And what about you, girl?" Kwame said when Ann had gone into the kitchen to make coffee. "Please tell me you're planning to go back and finish school yourself." His tone mock-wheedling. I said I didn't know. Right now, I had a job. I saw no reason to go back to school. At which, of course, he pounced, and began listing all the many inarguable reasons. If there was a second thing I wasn't going to like about Kwame Kwesi, it was this. There was the touch of the preacher about him. He was the kind of person who wanted to influence other people, I thought—who wanted, if not quite to have power over you, at least to guide your steps. Presumably another reason he was so crazy about teaching. Later that evening I would hear him say that ideally, a teacher should try to keep up with as many kids as possible after they'd left his own class. "That's how you keep being a force in their lives and help mold them." That was an old-fashioned idea, wasn't it? The idea of *molding* a kid. Kwame himself had had one elementary school teacher who'd always kept track of him. "Someone who made me believe that with enough hard work and self-respect, anything was possible." I thought, a little sadly, of Miss Crug, who probably knew by now that I had let her down. Could be it was my fate always to be disappointing people. I didn't even know Kwame, and I was already disappointing him. "Eventually, of course, I learned that it's not that simple, and all the hard work and self-respect in the world might not get you two cents in this land of apartheid. But still, I know now that that one teacher made all the difference to me—made me want to be a teacher, for one thing."

On and on Kwame went, Crug-like himself, on the importance of a higher education. But now it was I who was barely listening, distracted by Ann rejoining us with the coffee and by this straight-out-of-*Visage* observation: Love is good for the skin. (*The important thing is to glow.*) I remembered a story about some Hollywood director who supposedly tried to arrange to shoot scenes with his leading ladies right after they'd had sex (presumably with him). An apocryphal story, it sounds. Nevertheless, that *would* have been the way to capture those women at their most radiant. It used to be a commonplace: There are two times in a woman's life when she will look most beautiful—the moment when she becomes a wife and the moment when she has her first baby. When I was a girl, hearing this always irritated me. At last, at twenty, I knew why.

Here is a scene my mind would often replay. Ann and Kwame are seated on the couch, half facing each other, and she has brought her bare feet up and propped them in his lap. And as we talk, as we sip our coffee, Kwame holds and caresses Ann's feet. Squeezes and strokes Ann's feet. Pets and fondles Ann's feet. This, too, went on and on. More erotic by far than the full-frontal nudity in the photo on the bedroom wall. The temperature of his palms, the texture of his skin—I felt them myself as a tickling that made me want to tear off my sneakers and socks and scratch like mad.

I remembered that I'd wanted to ask Ann about her parents.

"Oh, god," she said. "I guess I didn't tell you. They finally met Kwame." The two of them exchanged a sardonic, long-suffering look.

The Draytons had come into the city to take Ann and Kwame out to dinner.

"It was right before we moved here," Ann said. "First they wanted us to come to the house, but I saw no point in dragging Kwame out to the white ghetto, so we agreed to meet somewhere in town. They picked this restaurant where they'd never been—small French place on Fifty-sixth Street, fancy as they come. I didn't think anything of it at first, but then, the night of the dinner, on the way to the restaurant, something started bothering me. I didn't quite know what it was—until we got there, and it hit me. Why this restaurant? Why a place they'd never been? My parents, who, as you may recall, *always* ate in their same few favorite places where they were known and treated like family and where everyone knew I was their kid. So what was this all about? I was supposed to believe it was innocent, that this particular time, when it wasn't just me, or me and my roommate, but me and my *black* boyfriend, that they'd gone out of their way to find a place where they were *not* known or sure to be going back?

"I knew I had to confront them. For Kwame's sake, I waited till we'd finished eating. Needless to say, they denied everything. I was wrong, I must be joking, how could I even suspect them of such a thing, et cetera. They'd just wanted to do something different, their best friends had raved about this French place, three stars, world-famous chef, what have you. Then Sophie turns to Kwame, hand on heart, and swears up and down that nothing could have been further from their minds than what I was 'imagining,' and he must, *must* believe that. And then Turner, out to prove *he's* no racist, oh no, not he, squeaks out in this desperate, high, choked voice, like he's just been drop-kicked in the crotch, 'Oh, why don't we all go to the Café des Artistes tomorrow and have a nice brunch!'"

She did a pretty good imitation. Like a struck match, Turner Drayton flared for an instant to life, and in that strange, muddled, heart-contracting instant I was bewilderingly happy to see him.

Ann was laughing angrily now. "I haven't spoken to either of them since."

I said, "How was the restaurant?"

"Oh, George. What a superficial question." She had scorn to burn, Ann.

But Kwame, winking at me, mouthed the word *fantastic*. His smile was mischievous.

"I know why Ann's upset," he said, patting her feet, as if that were where the trouble lay. "She knows her folks better than I do. Maybe she's right. But it's also possible they were innocent, in the sense that they were acting unconsciously. A lot of racism is unconscious, after all. They may not even have been aware of their real motivation in picking a different restaurant—if in fact it was their real motivation. I myself was willing to give them the benefit of the doubt. But L'il Miss Hothead here—" He kissed her brow as if she were his beloved, incorrigible little girl.

I said, "The real test would have been not to say anything and see what happened next time. I mean, if they always—"

"I refuse to play stupid games."

Not tonight but on another occasion, it had struck me that lately, often when Ann responded to something I'd said, her tone was exactly the one she would have used had her words been *Why don't you shut up*.

It came out that Kwame's family was not at all happy that he and Ann had moved in together. They were still hoping to talk him out of this marriage. But Kwame was both more philosophical and more optimistic than Ann. First, he said, unlike Ann, he wasn't interested in confrontation or even discussion. He had one and the same short answer for his critics: he was in love. When people called him a hypocrite, throwing his own old rabid rhetoric from black-power days in his face, he would not be riled. And he said, "Most of these people, if they really care about me, they'll come around. Just need some time. And the ones who don't? Fuck 'em."

Tiemann Place was a mixed block, and their neighbors in general were civil, though there was one elderly white man who deliberately looked away whenever their paths crossed. Another neighbor was extremely chatty anytime she met either of them separately, but tongue-tied whenever she had to face them together.

It was the hostility of total strangers that Ann found most unnerving. "The looks some people give us. The things they think they have a right to say." ("So, black ain't so beautiful after all, right, bro?") "One time, in the street, I had just kissed Kwame goodbye, and there were these two women watching us, and one of them said to the other—and I know she knew I could hear—'Look at that. Just because he's got a big cock.'"

One thing Kwame did admit made him want to strike was people saying, "But what about the children?" In fact, rather than writing poetry these days, he was working on an essay that he was thinking of calling either "No More Tragic Mulattoes" or "The Myth of the Tragic Mulatto."

"My god, all the crazy ideas and fears people have about miscegenation—it's about time they came to their senses. One thing I know for sure: whether I raise happy, self-respecting children or not is entirely up to me. Whatever shade of brown they are won't have anything to do with it."

And now, he said, if we would excuse him, he was hoping to get a little more work done on that essay before bed.

It was after eleven. I said I would help Ann clean up and be going. We all stood then, and I discovered I had drunk too much wine.

Saying good night to Kwame, I saw that I had been wrong about his eyes. It was the navy shirt he was wearing that brought out the blue, but in the light of a tall lamp standing between us, they were just as much green. "What beautiful eyes you have," I said. The compliment caught him off guard. Rather than thank me, he merely smiled and looked down at his feet, as people do when they feel embarrassed, before heading toward the back of the apartment.

Ann had slipped into the kitchen. I heard her turn on the water, and then, from the spare room, a burst of rapid-fire typing. I gathered up the coffee cups, and as I carried them into the kitchen, I said, "Kwame types faster than I do."

"You know what? I don't really need any help here, George. Why don't you just go home?" Ann had attacked the dishes so furiously she had slopped water all over.

I put the cups down on the counter. Carefully, for my hands were shaking. I said, "What's wrong?"

She did not speak or turn to look at me. She stood at the sink, giving me her profile (that hatchet sharp-looking as ever), and I saw the veins standing out in her long, thin neck.

"Ann, why are you angry?"

She shook her head, but it was a gesture of frustration, of impatience, not denial. There was no mistaking that she was angry.

"Is it because of what I just said, about Kwame's typing?"

"Of course not!"

"Is it because of what I said about his eyes?"

"His *beautiful* eyes, don't you mean? Those eyes that happen to be the *beautiful* color they are because once upon a time some son-of-a-bitch master of some fucking plantation *raped* one of Kwame's slave ancestors? Is that what you're talking about?"

When sarcasm drips, as we say, it drips from fangs.

"I didn't mean—"

"Whatever you *meant*, it was unforgivably insensitive."

"I was just saying something nice about what I thought was an attractive feature—"

"And you just *happened* to pick, as his most attractive feature, the one that's obviously *white*."

"I didn't say it was his *most* attractive feature. And I didn't think—"

"No, of course you didn't think. Now the damage is done. So why don't you just leave."

"What damage? I don't want to leave. What damage?" I wished my head were clear of the wine. I didn't think I had done anything unforgivable, but I didn't know how to defend myself. And I did not feel free to do what I wanted to do: go fetch Kwame and the

Benefit of the Doubt. I had that all over squeamish pins-and-needles sensation you get when you know you are about to witness some violence. I could not help observing that Ann had several knives within easy reach.

"Ann, please, please try to understand." (My god, I thought, I was begging her.) "Ann, you're going to break those dishes." She turned off the faucets (they shrieked from the force), and though she had a dish towel draped over one shoulder she dried her soapy hands distractedly on her shirtfront. I saw that she was shaking, too. How much wine had *she* drunk? She looked sick. But her face said it was me: it was me Ann could not stomach anymore, her expression said. I was what made her sick.

"You're the one who doesn't understand. And how could you? You know nothing about history. You know nothing about politics—you don't *have* any politics. You're completely, hopelessly apathetic. You always have been. And you don't try to change, George. You don't even try to educate yourself. You're perfectly happy getting all your ideas from places like *Vogue* and *Visage*."

"Which is probably a whole lot better than getting your ideas from people like *Sasha*." (*There!*) "And besides, what are you talking about? You don't know how Kwame got those eyes. You don't know that it happened back in the days of slavery. You don't know when or how it happened. *How do you know it was rape?*"

The typing in the back room had stopped. Our voices were far too loud not to have carried. Ann was gripping the edge of the sink as if to hold herself upright. I had the sure sense we were just seconds from calamity, and I saw myself like some cartoon character: trying to stop an oncoming train with my two little hands.

"Look," I said, "why don't we go ask Kwame—"
"Don't you dare speak to him."
"I'm sorry?"
"No, *I'm* the one who's sorry!"
She had found the dish towel. She tore it from her shoulder and flapped it like a gauntlet in my face. "For all the time I wasted on you! You unteachable—hopeless—you stupid, stupid—"

Once upon a time, when I was being bullied by some girls at school, I went crying to my brother. "What can I do?" he said. "I'm a boy. I can't fight with girls." The bullying grew worse, and Guy said he would teach me how to fight myself. "Use your fists," he said. "And make sure your thumb is outside. Never go to hit someone with your thumb inside your fist. You hit them hard enough, and you'll break it."

He was right.

It was worth it.

There is another story I want to tell now, a story that, though it did not happen next, seems to belong here. In this story, I am still working at *Visage*, where for some time Nicole has been having me write some of the copy. For example, I am the one who writes the answers to readers' beauty questions. ("In winter, when my lips are chapped, how can I get lipstick to go on smoothly?" "Try brushing your lips lightly with a dry toothbrush first.") I have a list of cosmeticians and dermatologists and other experts to call when I don't know the answer, though by this time I have become something of an expert myself. As for Nicole, she is looking for another job; she has been wanting to move on since the arrival of a new editor in chief, who, for reasons no one understands and which she is at no pains to explain, is hostile to Nicole. The first person I have ever known to dislike Nicole, and I see how it takes Nicole herself by surprise and how ill-prepared she is to cope with it.

Nicole's son is now a robust toddler, as cuddly as his name: Teddy. The kind of pretty, smiling child that fills you with yearning for a child of your own. Though he does not see me often, he is especially affectionate toward me, which pleases Nicole and makes me want to cry. Nicole and Whit no longer keep their tradition of Wednesday nights out, but there are more flower deliveries than ever. There are also rumors. One says they are on the verge of divorce because Whit has had an affair—"and that's just the one Nicole found out about." Poor Nicole. I do not want her to be unhappy, but I do not want her to divorce Whit, I have always liked

Whit, I am stuck on the notion of their lifelong romance, and besides: Teddy.

They do not break up. Instead, they buy a second home, a weekend house on Long Island, and decide to have a second child. Around the same time, Nicole receives an ·offer from another magazine—as it happens, the same magazine where our new editor in chief worked before coming to *Visage*. Not a bad arrangement all around. I am promoted to beauty editor. Things could have worked out worse.

There is a big farewell party for Nicole, who has worked at *Visage* almost a decade. The party is in a loft on Greene Street, one of the first living spaces to be created out of an old shop floor, in a SoHo that is still largely industrial. Nicole is pregnant again, and this time she is having difficulties. She is exhausted from headaches and lack of sleep. I have never seen her look bad, let alone this bad. The doctor has assured her she will feel better after her first trimester (in fact, she will miscarry). She spends most of the party reclining on a giant leather horseshoe of a couch while Whit and I fetch her food and drink and this or that guest whom she wishes to see. Smokers must stay clear of the couch—cigarette smoke is one of several smells that can make Nicole gag.

I take my cigarettes and head for the far end of the loft, making my way slowly (the crowd is deep) and keeping an eye out for Cleo, who, though no longer working at *Visage*, has been invited to the party. I pass Whit standing near a window, smoking and talking with a few people, most of whom I know from work. I pause here to light up, and Whit calls, "Georgette! I want you to meet a friend of mine. This is Dickie Smythe." A big, bearded man, as tall as one of the models in the room, and dressed in what must be an acre of forest green velvet suit. Grains of face powder in the goatee, eyebrows professionally waxed. "You must know his work," says Whit. "He wrote *Nuclear Waltz*?" I have never heard of *Nuclear Waltz* or of Dickie Smythe. But something is up: Whit is looking inexplicably sly, and everyone is observing me too closely. I say, "Oh, really?" and they all crack up.

"You see? I told you!" Whit is triumphant.

"Don't be embarrassed. You're not the first victim," says the jolly green giant in exactly the flat, nasal voice I was expecting. As it turns out, he is not a writer. He did not write *Nuclear Waltz*. I am not sure any such work even exists.

"But every single person gave that exact response—*oh, really?*—and pretended they knew what it was," says Whit.

I am annoyed, but I play the good sport. Whit is now telling me what Dickie Smythe really does, but I have lost interest. I am distracted by the way Whit has put his arm around me and drawn me chummily to his side, his hand resting high on my rib cage so that it is touching part of my breast—that old maneuver that can be very daring and very seductive when executed by the right man at the right time. Now Whit is telling Dickie Smythe about me, flattering words ("Nicole says Georgette will be *running Visage* one of these days") that confuse me because they do not sound like Nicole at all. I remember the rumors (*"and that's just the one Nicole found out about"*), but Whit has never touched me before, and I wonder if he is drunk. I don't think I have ever seen Whit drunk or high. There is a heat coming off his body that is like an alcoholic heat, and his breath is hot on my cheek: "That's some sexy skirt you're wearing." He is drunk. Gently, I pull away from him ("Oh, look, there's Cleo") and remind myself that I have always liked Whit and that he has never touched me before. Cleo is indeed here, but moving in the opposite direction. I see her being led by our retired editor in chief toward the bar. Before making my way to her through that crowd that is now even denser, I slip behind a Japanese rice-paper screen and find the bathroom.

When I am finished using the bathroom, I open the door and find Whit. He pushes me back inside and shuts the door on us.

All men are rapists, radical feminists say without shame. But I don't believe there are many men who would dare to do what Whit does next. Even drunk. One hand on the back of my neck, he presses his mouth against mine. He fills my mouth with his whiskey-soaked tongue, stifling any protest, his other hand nimbly working to undress me under the skirt. This takes practice. So the rumors are true. I am practiced, too, meaning I know what is going to happen, what he thinks is going to happen. All men are not rapists, but there is a kind of man for whom a show of force has been so often rewarded it is always worth a try. He is rich-boy handsome and full of nerve, he is drunk and strong, and he is bad. He knows himself, and he knows what a winning combination it is: looks, money, balls.

All the rotten rumors are true.

His cry reverberates off the tiles. Running through the loft, I keep my head down. I think I hear my name called, but I do not stop or turn. I keep my head down, my chin is wet, I cover my mouth, my hand is wet, I run.

"Yeah, that was me calling you, all right. You should have seen yourself, you crazy thing." Cleo. "It took us all about two seconds to figure out what had happened. Someone said he probably needed stitches. Someone else said he would definitely need a tetanus shot. I think he threw up. Nicole wanted a doctor to take a look at him, but he refused. Someone brought ice. He went home muffled in a big bloody towel."

Days passed. Weeks. I waited for Nicole to call me, and when she didn't I called her. "I can't talk to you now," she said. I discovered that this meant *I won't talk to you—ever.*

"Well, what did you expect?" said Cleo. "You exposed the woman's husband in front of everyone they know—you think she's going to thank you for that? You totally humiliated both of them, don't you see? Not to mention ruining her party."

"You think that's fair?"

"I think you could have stopped the man without"—here she started to laugh—"without drawing blood!" She laughed and laughed. "I hear his tongue's all black now—like one of those chow dogs! He *is* a dog! But seriously, you can't blame Nicole. He's her husband, the father of her child. There are rules, you know. You break them, you pay the price. Believe me, Nicole is never going to forgive you for this."

"You're saying it would have been better if I had just let him fuck me over the sink and kept my mouth shut."

"No! But from her point of view, Nicole would be a lot better off now if you'd done that instead of what you did. Well, wouldn't she?"

"I guess."

"You overreacted."

This, I would learn, was the majority view.

It was the kind of story people like to repeat. Over the years, it has come back to me—sometimes distorted, embellished versions gossiped by people unaware that I myself had been involved. Years later, at a millennium New Year's Eve party, I struck up a conversation with a young woman who happened to bring up Whit Bishop's name. She had once worked for him. "And do I have a story," she told me. "It happened long ago when he was still young." At a club, she thought it was. Whit Bishop was locked in the restroom getting a blow job from some girl who was so coked up she nearly bit off his dick. He almost bled to death, this woman told me. Ambulance, ER, stitches—she shared all the details.

At the time, I remember thinking that now for sure Whit and Nicole would get a divorce, but they did not. They never had that second child, but they stayed together until Nicole died. That was in 1998. I had forgiven him long before. Her, only then.

*I*t began soon after the debacle on Tiemann Place. Several times a week, the phone would ring and when I answered, the caller hung up. Once, when the caller hesitated an extra beat, I said, "Ann?" Click. These hang-ups infuriated me. I did not want to hear from Ann—I did not want to have anything more to do with her—but I did want to know whether it was she making these calls. It was a relief when, after a few weeks, they stopped. By then also my thumb had healed.

June 1972. I feel a pang. This was when I would have graduated.

That summer, a store opened in my neighborhood, selling new and used books. A cramped, overflowing space that was never cleaned. I don't believe the owner even swept out the store (formerly a check-cashing place) before moving in. He certainly did not paint it. "Who's going to see the walls with all these books up, anyway?" That was Ruben, the owner, whom I got to know quickly, stopping by the store almost every day on my way home from work, even minding it once or twice in an emergency. And when I had bought so many books I had nowhere to put them, it was Ruben who spent all one Saturday hanging shelves in my apartment. And who stayed for dinner and who stayed the night, and that is how *that* romance was born. (I know that I have failed to give the name of the drummer. I am ashamed to say it is because I do not remember it. Nor do I remember what ever happened to him. It isn't always easy to tell the truth. Women's liberation changed a lot, but it did not change this. At the very least, a woman is expected to remember the names. And say one day you open a book and read, "That summer alone, I had more than a dozen lovers." Think how much the meaning changes, depending on whether "I" is a he or a she.)

Ruben, avid reader, bookseller, book collector, and builder of bookshelves, was forever recommending books to me. He sold me many volumes, but more and more were gifts. At that time, beginning somewhat before the summer, I was regaining something I had lost: the pleasure of voracious reading. I did not have a television then—few of my friends did. We—the first generation to become addicted to TV as kids—had got out of the habit when we went away to college. Movies were a different story. I saw several movies a week. I saw almost all of them in the same theater, not far from Ruben's bookstore. It was another shabby, unswept place (they smelled just like two rooms in the same house), where, for a dollar or so, you could take in double features of Hollywood classics and old foreign films. There were quite a few art houses like this one in the city, and there were many more bookstores like Ruben's, and I never doubted they would be part of New York— and of my life—forever. And to think how little money mattered. By this I mean how much less someone starting out in life had to worry about money compared with today. I had not had to worry about paying for school or, when I left school, about staying in Manhattan and finding a job and an apartment whose rent I could cover myself. I had no savings account and of course no credit card, and there were countless desirable things that remained out of reach. But those books and the movie tickets and eating out a couple of times a week at one of the Chinese or Cuban-Chinese restaurants on Broadway—all this could be had on $125 a week. I recall no sense of deprivation. And when I think of that time and of the life I led then, around the summer of '72, a life I would have described as full of pain and difficulty and doubt (and not untruthfully, since all these things were part of my life then), it seems to me to have been as nearly perfect as any life could be. (At various times in later years I would try to re-create that life, and fail, for the most important element—youth—was missing.) I had wanted romance, and in many ways I had found it, though still elusive was what I'd begun to think of as Big Love. This, too, would come, and given how much I listened to a certain kind of song in those days, I should have known it was not going to come from the direction I was looking. In those days I was convinced that nothing could possibly be random, that everything I did, every book I read, for example, was part of some elaborate preparation, and I did not see what else this preparation could be for if not Big Love. My affection for Ruben was not Big Love, and I knew it. It was perhaps more than I'd felt for other men (he was devoted, Ruben, he was my best friend), but it was not love at all. Never having experienced Big Love did not stop me from having Big Ideas about it. Between me and the world hung a veil. I did not always know what was real and what wasn't, and it was this that love would change. When I fell in love, the veil would lift. I would see the world as it really was and know the difference between a thing and the shadow of a thing—yes, I had been reading the Greeks.

I had saved the reading lists from those courses I had registered for but had scarcely attended, and though far from eager to sit in a lecture hall again, I was now ready to read the books. How Ann's final, harsh accusation rang in my ears. But of course it was false; *of course I wanted to be educated!* Most of my time in college I had found it hard to read, impossible to study without the help of drugs, but now that trouble was gone, and I wanted to read everything. Arriving at Barnard, I remember feeling, among other shames, the shame of not being as well-read as someone like Ann. Except for the ones we brought home from school, there had been no books in our house. In high school, when I grew hungry for more than what had been assigned, the books I brought home from the library were mostly popular books written for girls: stories about cheerleaders and candy stripers and young equestriennes—stories that were almost always really about first love. There was one book, about a beauty contestant, that I read so many times it remains today the book I have read more times than any other.

I like the details that have stayed with me from books I read as a child and of which I can recall little else. A bag of pretzels, a horse wearing a straw hat, an orphan's cardboard suitcase, patent-leather bows on a dress, a dollop of cold gravy, a red wagon, red shoes, a lost cap (red plaid). A boy ashamed of a mother who sliced and buttered her bread too thickly, a young woman's surprise that a boy's lips could be so soft. I have the feeling if I let myself go on like this, the list would be many pages. And then I think there was nothing wrong with the way I read as a child, nothing at all.

Heroines. The name Jacqueline Cochran was familiar to me from the label on a cold cream jar on our bathroom shelf. And lo, that name again, on a book, on a library shelf. *The Stars at Noon.* Autobiography. A spectacular rise against spectacular odds, among them a brute of a foster mother. Up from dirt. Shoeless till she was eight years old. "My story went from sawdust to stardust." Besides building a cosmetics empire, Cochran was one of those rare birds: an aviatrix. An air racer, a breaker of records. Yet nothing she achieved in adulthood compared with one amazing thing she had done as a child. " 'Mama' decided to whip me. I took things into my own hands in the shape of a good chunk of firewood and we talked things out with my eyes flashing fire. She knew I meant what I said and she retreated, never to touch me again. She was a coward to let a six-year-old girl get the best of her."

Moving house is an ordeal, not least because of the unpacking of the past that is usually involved. How much we forget—even things that once touched us deeply, events that changed who and what we are. But every house has them, those boxes and trunks filled with old clothes and papers and pictures and souvenirs of all kinds. Along with everything else, we forget what we have saved— until one day some move brings all these things into the light again. Out they come ("Oh my god, I can't believe I kept this!"), and in and in dig the needles and pins, and occasionally something more serious: a real knife, shucking the heart like a clam. And so one day I would open again that notebook in which I made a list of books read in the summer of 1972. Greek philosophy, Greek plays. Novels: Henry James, George Eliot, Thomas Hardy. Poetry (thank god, it was only the love of *writing* it that had been killed in me): Yeats, Auden, Eliot, Wallace Stevens, Anne Sexton, Sylvia Plath. I did not make a list of movies seen, but I'm pretty sure that was the summer I saw, for the first time, *Grand Illusion, Citizen Kane*, and *Tokyo Story*. What a life! Wordsworth may not have been on the reading list, but it's his lines, about bliss and being young and heaven, that leap to mind when I look back on that time—when Time itself must have been a different element, or how did I manage to do all that reading and get anything else done? But Ruben, as I recall, read even more—at work, between customers (some of whom complained about his inattention, which on the other hand was a great boon to shoplifters), and in bed, staying up long after I had fallen asleep.

In the same box where I found the notebook with its list of books, I found another notebook with another list, this one of new beauty products that I tried (an important part of my job) and my comments about them. A night cream: "too rich: woke up with a blemish and bags under my eyes." Flavored lip gloss: "yummy and refreshing." A new kind of mascara had left my lashes "spiky and full of dry flakes." And strawberry vaginal deodorant spray "made R want to barf."

What else. An old typewriter eraser, the wheel-and-bristle kind, hard as a fossil. (What was I saving it for?) An old journal, most of the pages still blank. Old term papers. My first passport, which I got that same year, 1972.

My daughter, Zoe, and I have been working all day. She has come home from school for the weekend to help me. Now that she and her brother, Jude, are grown and I'm on my own, I am moving to a smaller place. I am finally moving to the West Village. All day, Zoe has been hugely enjoying herself. "I can't believe you ever fit into this skirt!" "You saved my *Barbie?*" "*Daddy* wore this hat?" "Hey! We're reading *The Great Gatsby*, too. Is it any good?" I've had enough. I feel drained and lightheaded and lightly bruised, as if after a hard swim through rough waters. I get up stiffly from the floor. "Let's take a break."

"You got an A on this paper!" My only one.

In the kitchen, where most of the dishes have been wrapped in newspaper and boxed, I put on the kettle and take from the refrigerator the remains of a spice cake. We drink hot lemon tea and eat cold, stale spice cake, and I listen to Zoe read aloud from "Why *The Great Gatsby* Is Not a Great Book."

Ruben: darkly handsome, smart, devoted, doting, true. At the end of the summer I broke his heart. I had been seeing someone else, a teacher I met at the French Institute, where I was taking a course. I took my two weeks' vacation and went with him to Paris. More romantic, I suppose, it could not have begun. But it would be brief. I believed something I had heard, that when you went off the Pill, you'd still be protected for at least a couple of months. When I broke the news, Romeo hit me. "You never told me you were not on zee Peel!" "You never asked!" And so it ended, in a tumult of rage and recriminations and thick blood and cramps.

I could have gone back to Ruben, but I would not allow myself that solace. All my life, though, among my daydreams about careers that might have made me happy, has been this one: a small shop somewhere, some partner and I buying and selling used books.

When the hang-ups began again, I no longer thought of Ann. I knew now the caller had never been Ann. It had been unreasonable even to think it was she: it was not the sort of thing Ann would do. No, not Ann. But no stranger, either.

Sister Sister, as our family called Zelma after she *took the veil* (an expression that made her wince: "Please, we don't really use it anymore"), liked to say, "When Solange got on the bus that day, her guardian angel got on with her."

Actually, it was a couple, and they did not board the bus until the next stop.

It had been as I'd thought: Solange did not have a plan that day in August 1969. Later she said she had obeyed a voice in her head—she wasn't even sure at first that she was running away. ("I just wanted to go somewhere.") She hitched a ride to the bus station, and after she bought her ticket (to Albany: destination of the first bus to depart), all she had was a dollar and change and the light clothes she was wearing and her giant but mostly empty pocketbook. On the bus, she headed for the rear, where you could smoke. Scared now as the bus pulled out, she lit up and began puffing in a hyperventilating way. But once they hit the highway and were rolling merrily along, Solange almost burst her seams. She was joyful, excited, and proud all at once. Everything had changed. "I was already different." In her mind, anyway, she was *someone else*.

Grover and Pam, in their early twenties, dropouts from the state university in Buffalo, were on their way to the Jersey Shore.

They had a friend who was working there and living with other employees in a beach bungalow provided by their boss, who ran some boardwalk concession booths. Grover and Pam were traveling with sleeping bags. They were planning to crash at their friend's place for a while, but that was only the first stop on what was going to be a cross-country journey. When they boarded the bus, they went to the last row, where Solange was sitting alone, smoking. They broke out their own cigarettes and immediately started a conversation. Solange gave the mélange of truths, half-truths, and lies that would soon be habitual to her. If Grover and Pam had any doubts (about her age, for example, which she gave as eighteen), they did not challenge her. The main thing was that they liked her. And Solange liked them, too. By the time they got to Albany, they were friends.

In Albany, Grover and Pam had to change to a bus to New York City, where they would have to change again to get to the Shore. In the station restroom, Solange showed Pam the bruises on her arms and legs, and Pam made a decision. She and Grover agreed to pay for a ticket for their new friend. In New York, they put their half-hour layover to good use by panhandling. Solange was amazed at how readily people dropped money into her hand, including one man (looking so much like Father DuMaurier back home that her heart nearly stopped) who glared and shook his head and growled, "Take it, girl." Ten bucks!

Solange was absorbing an important lesson, one that would be crucial to her survival. In Albany she had caught a glimpse of herself in the grimy restroom mirror as she was showing her bruises to Pam. She saw herself as she must look to others: helpless and in need of protection. She saw a pretty, pretty girl. A face that could not lie. And the fact that she *was* lying? A few days earlier, carrying laundry to the basement, she had taken a tumble on the stairs. But where was the sin in letting those bruises stand in for all the past ones she had received from Mama? If it was a lie, it was a white one. If it was a sin, it wasn't mortal.

She was the best-looking of the girls in our family, and though this did not make her a beauty, she did have that look some girls have—alarming to many adults, irresistible to some—of a sexy child. Long after they lose their innocence, these girls keep an innocent guise. With Solange it had to do with a particular flatness of face, doll-like cherry lips, and an air of solemn wonderment, a way she had of fixing and blinking her eyes. She seemed always to be staring hard at something she was too young to fathom. And maybe it really was so, and we can call the unfathomable thing Life. Even when she was much older, high heels looked too big on her feet, a cigarette in her hand looked extra long, and almost any makeup she wore made her look painted. Once, when she came to visit us, my son happened to have a friend over to play, and after Solange left, this five-year-old looked around and said, "What happened to that little girl?"

Glancing in the restroom mirror, Solange thought of a word, and the word was *waif*. A type that has probably always had some appeal but perhaps never more so than then. This was a time when those wildly popular reproductions of Keane paintings—mostly thin, starved-looking girls with eyes like ink-filled saucers—were ubiquitous. (What ever happened to them?)

Grover and Pam: not angels, but hippies, of course. They might as well have been angels. I don't know about Solange's soul, but I believe they saved her life. And had that been a different time, had it been nowadays, say, I doubt whether Solange would have been so lucky. I doubt whether she would have found, at almost every turn, people like Grover and Pam, eager to befriend her or take her under their wing. She would not have found, almost everywhere the wind blew her in the next three years, a helping hand, a place at the table, a bed for the night or for as long as she liked if need be, a "family" happy to adopt her. She might have been forced to grow up fast instead of blossoming into a flower child and remaining, as she did, forever young. Everything had changed, all right, and she was about to join the part of the youth movement that was constantly moving—all those rootless, restless kids who began taking to the road, sometimes alone but more often not, never working but never wanting, constantly breaking the law (drugs, trespassing, hitchhiking, shoplifting) but somehow avoiding arrest. During the Great Depression, hoboes used to draw pictures of cats on sidewalks and fence posts outside certain houses to let other hoboes know: *Kind lady lives here.* The new drifters had their own ways of letting one another know where to find help: the earth mothers cropping up all over now as if in response to the very need, the crash pads and youth hostels and communes—a network not unlike the one that brought underground radicals like Sasha to safe houses (in fact, there were places that functioned as both). After Woodstock, there would be such a swell of destitute vagabond youth that it created a kind of national emergency, and official and unofficial charities organized to cope with it. In many places, there was not only such a thing as a free lunch, but free breakfast and dinner and takeout, too. There was free clothing, free shelter, free soap and hot water, free health care and counseling and rehab. There was even free job training and placement for those for whom the work ethic had not got completely confused with materialism and selling out. And for getting around, of course, there was always a free ride. (Because I so rarely left Manhattan, to me it seemed to happen overnight: One day hitchhikers could be seen almost every mile. The next, they were few and far between. One day you could count on a ride within minutes. The next, the only car that would stop for you would be a police cruiser. Some people put the blame for this on the Tate-LaBianca murders. Drivers no longer saw a romantic budding writer out On the Road but a long-haired psychopath on a killing spree.)

By the time they got to the Shore, it was the middle of the night. The house was full. Besides the four boardwalk workers legitimately living there, a dozen or so friends were camped out on the floor. Grover and Pam's friend was called Moose, and the first thing he said was, "What are you doing down here?" Upstate New York was where it was all happening that weekend. Didn't they know?

In fact, Grover and Pam had tried but had not been able to get tickets to the Woodstock festival. Moose said that shouldn't stop anyone from going. There would never be another concert like this one, three days long, the biggest bands in the world, and it was outdoors, in this big field—it would be easy to gate-crash. And they wouldn't have to hitch or take another bus: Moose had just bought a used van from some surfers. He was going to put a mattress in the back, and— But what about his job? (He worked a french-fry stand.) Moose said he didn't care, he was sick of the boardwalk, he'd been going to quit anyway. His boss was a pig, he said. In fact, he was afraid of his boss, afraid to cross him by leaving him shorthanded at the height of the season, and afraid to lose a week's pay. His boss paid him in cash every Friday after Moose's shift. They could not leave till then. They would miss a few acts, but that was okay. Just as long as they didn't miss The Who or Janis.

That settled, they all went to bed, which for Grover and Pam and Solange meant a place on the floor of the screened-in porch.

Not that anyone had asked her, but Solange was a little uncertain about heading right back in the direction of home. And she was anxious about being paired up with this Moose, who had nice muscles and a gorgeous tan but the greasiest skin she had ever seen, probably from eating too many french fries. She didn't even have a change of clothes, let alone her own sleeping bag, and he had glanced sidelong at her when he mentioned the mattress. But she was also excited about going to the concert, which everyone had been talking about back home, and she was already attached to the idea of being swept along by other people, of following wherever they might lead. By an odd logic, this made her feel safe. And if she and Grover and Pam were friends after just a couple of hours on the bus, by morning they'd be brother and sisters.

They joined the litter curled up on the sandy porch floor. Solange lay with Pam beside her and Grover on the other side of Pam, and though they were quiet about it, Solange knew perfectly well what those two were up to. And she ached in her belly and in her breasts—she wanted Grover herself (and in due time she would have him, and it would be with Pam's blessing). In fact, soft moans and heavy breathing could be heard from one or another corner of that house all night long. There was a dog—Moose's dog, Deuce—a small mutt with mismatched ears (one black, one white, one folded, one open) and a black patch over one eye that gave him a raffish appearance. He lay down next to Solange, and she put her arms around him and held him close and felt tired and happy, like a child that has played hard in the sun all day long. She could hear the surf and smell the salt water, and she thought how tomorrow she would play on the beach with the dog, who in her mind was becoming *her* dog, just as Grover and Pam were becoming her family.

How easy it was for Solange to replace us should not cause surprise. I met a man at a party once who confessed at the end of the evening that he felt closer to me than to any of his three sisters, and I never doubted he was sincere. Often, the last people a person expects to know him are those who conceived him and with whom he was raised. Isn't this the reason for those disappointing birthday and Christmas gifts families come up with year after sad year? How could I be surprised? I knew how normal it could seem, embarked on a whole new life, having fallen in love with your peers, to forget all about where you came from and what kind of mess might be stewing *back there*. I knew how it was possible to avoid thoughts of family for weeks and months at a time. How could I hold Solange's behavior against her? When she said to me, "I've always thought of myself as an orphan," how could I find it strange? I had had the same thought (the same *fantasy*, I should say) myself.

It came, of course—horror at what she had done, guilt for not contacting us. But Solange had her excuse: fear that if she wrote or telephoned, she would be found. Among the people she met who would hear her story were many who urged her to send us word, some of them even offering to do it for her, and there was one good woman, a church volunteer in Madison, Wisconsin, who went so far as to write our mother herself, a letter Mama never received. Two things Solange was careful never to reveal: her real age and her real hometown.

But her bad conscience kept coming back, and again and again Solange resolved to find a way to let us know she was all right. Yet somehow she never got around to it, and somehow the more she put it off, the harder it became. And the more time passed, the more certain she was that she could never go home again. Not that she had her heart set on going home. (I have never found the absolute fixation of that famous runaway, Dorothy, on hurrying back from over the rainbow entirely convincing. It does not fit with the imagination of any child I have known.) Not only was Solange not unhappy being far away; she did not think anyone back home—not even Guy—could possibly still love her. In her mind, we were all so angry at what she had done, we would never forgive her.

But once, passing through New York, she screwed up her courage to call Barnard—only to learn I had left. She found my name in the telephone book, but by now her courage had failed. Instead of calling, she took down my address. Later she bought a postcard at a newsstand in Times Square, and much later, when she was on the road again, she scribbled a line and mailed it to me. So: I had left school, but I had not gone home, either. For the first time in a long while, Solange was curious about me. She knew how to reach me now—but who could say how long I'd be at that address? She herself was rarely more than a couple of months in the same place. Later she would tell me she had been to every major city in America, and it's certain she covered a lot of ground in three years. But sorting out the truth from the tall tales, I gathered she was mostly out West. Usually she ended up in a particular place for no other reason than that others she'd hooked up with happened to be going there. Someone knew someone in Madison or Denver; someone had a gig in San Francisco; there was a Grateful Dead concert in L.A., some work in Portland or Seattle, a friend in Vancouver with some land where they could camp for the month of July. Long after she had lost track of Grover and Pam, another couple she met took her along for the ride, picking up a load of dope in El Paso and driving it back to New York. From time to time, curiosity (and other feelings, more difficult for her to name) got the better of

Solange, and she picked up the phone and dialed. Always the sound of my voice unnerved her, a current turning the receiver into a hot potato in her hand. Until, finally, she paused long enough for me to rush in: "Please don't hang up this time Solange I know it's you." But she did! She did hang up on me once again. And she burst into tears. Later she said it had been my tone. Anger was what she claimed to have heard, anger and exasperation. But I remember very different feelings. After she hung up on me that last time, I, too, burst into tears. But Solange was in town now, she was in New York, and instead of calling next time, she would arrive in person. Came a night of wind and heavy rain—like the beginning of a mystery, not the end of one—a night where someone is lost rather than found again.

I opened the door and saw a pretty, pretty girl.

By the time we got to Woodstock—but in fact they never got there. Though Solange would often tell people she had been at Woodstock, she never actually saw any of it. They had set out too late and made it only as far as the outskirts of the town of Bethel.

Moose turned out to be right: no tickets were needed. Early on, when it was clear that the gate-crashers would number in the tens of thousands, the organizers of the festival had declared it free. But by this time such a multitude of fans had converged on the site, many had to be turned away. Warnings were broadcast over all the airwaves that no one who had not already arrived would make it within miles of the stage. Police and the National Guard were deployed to control the hordes (many of whom refused to turn back), and the governor declared a state of emergency. The state thruway and other main highways had to be closed.

Bummer! No one took it worse than Moose, who had turned the wheel of the van over to Grover and dropped a tab of mescaline in hopes of peaking around the time they arrived and found the concert in full swing. Now, stuck in traffic, surrounded by disgruntled, disoriented hippies, many in the same condition as he was, and by an unexpected army of pigs, Moose began freaking out.

Solange had by certain signs already let Grover know her desires, which included not being paired off with his friend. But there seemed little danger of that now. Moose had forgotten her existence. He had got it into his head that his boss back at the Shore, who he insisted belonged to the Mob or at least had gangster connections, was going to come after him for running out on the job and for stealing the mattress from the house.

All around them, people were abandoning vehicles and attempting to walk off the highway, hoping somehow to make it to the concert on foot. A rumor that the Beatles (or the Rolling Stones) were going to make a surprise appearance was rapidly spreading. No one wanted to accept that you could be this close and still not get in. Others were ready to give up for the moment but wanted to stick around and see what would happen tomorrow. After all, there were still two days of peace and music to go. They were setting up camp anywhere they could (anywhere they wanted, really). With darkness had come chaos: car horns and radios, loud arguments, singing and guitar strumming, laughter and crying, police bullhorns, choppers. Not a whole lot of peace. Moose had brought the dog along, and he, too, was freaking out, though Moose paid him no attention. Setting out hours before, no one had thought about food or water. All they had brought was dope. Like all of them, Deuce was frantic to get out of the van. He pawed at the door and whined, looking with that eye patch less raffish now than demented.

Grover was deeply displeased with his friend Moose. It was beginning to dawn on him that the van they were in had not been sold to Moose by some surfers but in fact belonged, like the mattress, to Moose's boss. But it was Moose's paranoid raving about the Mafia that set Grover off.

"You're scaring the chicks, man," he said. "So cool it!"

Thinking this rebuke was directed at him, Deuce promptly wet the mattress.

They had not budged in two hours. Slumped together in the front seat, Grover and Pam dozed off. Solange huddled with Deuce on the dry side of the mattress. Moose was still raving, albeit in a whisper. "What's happening out there? *What the fuck is happening?* I still say they can't keep us from getting near the stage." Finally he opened the door and bolted into the night. Watching him disappear, Solange thought of a story she had overheard Guy telling Ina soon after he'd come back from the war, about a GI who dropped acid when they were out on patrol, had a bad trip, and fled into the jungle, never to be seen again.

Moose had not returned by the time traffic finally started to move again.

They had to eat. They had to find a bathroom. They no longer gave a damn about the music. They just wanted to get off the road. Following the parade, they found themselves rolling into a small Catskills village where they were met by a vision. It was the middle of the night, but all the lights were ablaze. It was like a movie set, with a cast of thousands milling about, waiting to be directed. Everyone in the town was awake, even the children. Many had come out just to gawk, but others had heeded the call for help. The church and the high school were open, as were the pancake house and the gas station. There were stacks and stacks of bologna and white bread sandwiches in the school cafeteria and rows of cots in the gym. The school nurse was on hand. Volunteer firemen were directing traffic, telling people where to park and where to pee. Tents had been pitched and bedrolls laid down in the village green and on the lawns of private houses. There was a sense of overwhelming confusion and fatigue but also of reckless merriment. Certainly the mood was more festive than what might be expected in any state of emergency. Campfires had been built in places they had no business burning. There was singing and dancing and shedding of clothing with no thought to how much this added to the general bedlam. Reefers and hash pipes were being passed around openly, and no one was being arrested. When a girl wearing only a Navajo blanket tried to pass a pipe to a state trooper, he covered his eyes with his hands good-humoredly—see no evil—winning cheers and a round of applause.

Pam said, "You know, when we tell people back home about this, who's going to believe us?" And if this was what was happening on the perimeter, what must it be like at the center?

They had given up on Moose. "You're *my* dog now," Solange whispered into Deuce's open ear. It turned out he fit perfectly into her giant purse.

Pam said, "You know, Grove, if that van really is hot, I say we ditch it. Wherever we go from here, we can hitch." So they went back to where they had parked and got their packs, leaving the keys in the van.

There was an inn on the green. The manager of the inn did not want any dirty hippies inside, but he agreed to let some sleep on the wrap-around porch. From the windows of their rooms, guests took in the astonishing sight of girls and boys sleeping together out in the open.

This time, Grover slept in the middle.

With the light of day, the truth could no longer be denied. Police and rescue workers were going from group to group, trying to appeal to reason. The last thing they needed was more bodies massing on the concert site. It was still a big question, how they were going to get enough food and water to the ones who were already there. They were concerned about exposure, both to the sun and to the storms that were predicted for the weekend. The day before, serious thought had been given to canceling the performances. But now that they had all those acres of kids out there, many in an overexcited state, many on potent psychedelics, it was agreed that entertaining them, fixing everyone's attention on one mesmerizing thing, was probably the safer measure. In any case, no one liked to think of the riot that calling off the concert at this point might cause.

So the show would go on, but not for everyone.

In the course of the morning, scouting for something to eat, Grover and Pam and Solange attached themselves to a group of people who had come all the way from Iowa. They had come in several vehicles, like a Gypsy caravan—except every one of them was blond. One of the vehicles was an old school bus that had most of its seats ripped out and was painted Day-Glo yellow. They called it The Yellow Submarine (written in block letters on both sides), and they called themselves the Mellow Yellow Heads. Some of them were related by blood, some by marriage, and some not at all, but they all lived together on the same farm back in Iowa. When Grover and Pam and Solange first saw them, they were holding hands and dancing in a ring in the parking lot of the pancake house. The whole tribe refused to be bummed out about how things had turned out. They'd had the time of their lives just getting there, declared their patriarch, a man so tall and leggy he looked almost as if he were on stilts. And now they'd have twice as much fun going back. "It's always the journey that matters," he said. He wore bib overalls without any shirt, and a stovepipe hat that made him even taller; he had a jutting jaw, and the way he trimmed his beard turned him into a Swedish Abe Lincoln. He was called Big John and also Papa John, or Big Papa. His wife was as beautiful as her own name: Fleur. All the women were beautiful.

There were about twenty-five men and women altogether, including one very beautiful pregnant woman. There were two little babies, and several other children of various ages who took an instant liking to Solange and Deuce. (Children in general, my own included, tended to bond with Solange, perhaps for an obvious reason. *What happened to that little girl?*) For Solange it was the beginning of what would become one of her sweetest memories. Traveling west with Grover and Pam and this big, sunny family whom she came to love, especially the children, who were always naked and happier than any children she had ever known, and whose fair hair when she brushed or braided it gave off the smell of both kinds of grass. Riding that crazy bus into the heartland, under spacious summer skies, past ripening fields and farms and factories: so this was America.

No hour worth living, went Mellow Yellow creed, without a song. They sang when they rode, and they sang when they stopped. Among them they had a couple of guitars, a flute, bongos, tambourines, harmonicas. By the time they reached the Midwest, Solange was sure she had learned every folk song ever written.

They liked to stop often on the way, and wherever they stopped, people would gather and stare. Sometimes it would be more than stares: bad vibes, hostile words, even rocks. Once, at a truck stop outside Cleveland, someone slashed the bus tires.

But somehow the tribe never lost their sweet temper. They were genuinely sorry for those poor folks who could want to hurt other folks whom they did not know and who had done them no harm. "It's not us they hate," Big Papa reminded everyone, "it's themselves." And, added Fleur, "they're our brothers and sisters, too."

Often, when they pulled out of someplace where they had drawn a crowd, they would stick their hands out the windows and wave and waggle the peace sign, crying, "Goodbye, we love you, we love you, goodbye!" And even, "Why not come with us? Come!" And of course, they did pick up countless hitchhikers all along the way.

They had little money, and what they had they needed for gas. They would descend on a town and go with their shopping lists separately into different stores and lift everything they needed, from milk to batteries. (Yet another excellent use for Solange's capacious purse.)

Once they had reached the Come Together Farm, Grover and Pam and Solange did not stay long. Living with the Mellow Yellow Heads turned out to be less fun than being on the road with them. For one thing, there were rules: everyone had chores to do, and meals were strictly vegetarian. (Whenever anyone got a craving for meat, he or she was expected to go discuss it with one of the cows.)

Grover and Pam were not big fans of cows, vegetables, or folk music. And they considered themselves on vacation; they didn't want to do chores, especially not crack-of-dawn ones. And they were still a long way from California. They were itching to get to the Haight.

Solange could just as happily have stayed on the farm, where not much more was expected of her than of the children, with whom she spent most of her time. She would have liked to stay at least until the pregnant woman, who was called Moon, gave birth, an event that was supposed to take place in an open field, all invited. But Solange had persuaded herself that where Grover went, she must follow. He was no longer her brother; he was her old man. Meanwhile, Pam was moving in the opposite direction. She still loved Grover, but even before Solange had entered the scene, something had cooled, and Pam's feelings for Grover were now more like what she might have for a dear friend or a brother.

Though it broke her heart, Solange agreed that Deuce would be better off staying behind with these good vegetarians than on the road again. In exchange, Fleur and John gave Solange some clothes and a sleeping bag.

The three had not gone far when they discovered they had brought along a bad case of crabs. An old geezer, a World War I veteran who gave them a ride in his pickup, was surprised they did not know the cure. ("Ya shave off half yer pubic hair, set the other half on fire, and when the crabs run out to escape the flames, ya stab 'em with an ice pick.")

They ended up having to throw all three sleeping bags and most of their clothing away.

But all of this has been written. All of this has been told by Solange herself, in different form, in the memoir she published in 1990.

I heard bits and pieces of her story for the first time that wet night when she showed up at my door. No umbrella, soaked to the skin, teeth chattering. *You look like something the cat dragged in!* was one of Mama's favorite sayings. But that night Solange looked like the cat itself, dragging her thin, wet, sunken flanks into my living room, leaving a trail of water on the floor. She looked bedraggled and pitiable now, but once her fur had dried and she had warmed up at the radiator, she'd be herself again, ready to preen and to lap her saucer of cream.

That night when she came to find me, Solange had been in town for a couple of months. There she was, living right down in the East Village with a man called Roach, a friend of the couple who had made the drug run from El Paso to New York. Solange did not let me meet this Roach for some time. By then I had imagined a character so like his name, the actual person could not but look good. He worked as a stagehand at the Fillmore East. He had a way about him, as if all he wanted was to steer clear of hassles, keep his head down and his nose clean: the way of certain ex-cons. Roach looked like what he was, a survivor of an era that had tipped over into madness, a type that was just emerging around this time, guys whose histories could be read in their tattoos and prematurely lined faces, like a map of every wrong road they'd been down, and in their pupils, like spent match heads. As for their futures: though they might shorten their hair and give up heavy drugs and start using their real names again, they would never be able to return wholeheartedly to the straight mentality; they would never put on a suit or work in an office or take seriously the things their fathers or sons (or most women) took seriously. Hang a sandwich board on them with DON'T MEAN NOTHIN' on one side and IT DON'T MEAN SHIT on the other. Many would smoke pot every day for the rest of their lives. Sixties casualties, some people called them. But were they the most unhappy of their generation? I would say no. Anyway, no need to dwell on Roach; he and Solange were not for long. They lived in one of those old East Village tenements with the bathtub in the kitchen. Covered with a piece of plywood, the tub also served as the dining table. A lot of their neighbors seemed to be musicians; it was the loudest building you ever heard, a miracle all those good vibrations didn't shake down the walls.

Music was Solange's thing now, too. She had her own guitar, and she was writing songs. On her travels she had met many musicians, she had followed certain bands, and for a time she had lived the sad, low life of a groupie. Now she dreamed of being a star. But though she had learned to play the guitar well enough, and I thought some of her lyrics were at least as good as Joni Mitchell's, her voice was not much better than mine. Not that Solange was going to let a small thing like that distract her. Once she learned what I did for a living, she kept pestering me to get her into the modeling business. She wouldn't listen when I told her that I had no power to do this, and in any case, she was not tall enough to be a model. All she knew was that most people found her attractive. (And to be fair, a few years later she did end up doing some catalog modeling.) It would be an ongoing struggle trying to get Solange to be realistic about her prospects in life. I considered it a major victory when I finally persuaded her to get a high school diploma. If I had accomplished nothing else that particular year, I would still have patted myself on the back.

After she ran away, Solange told everyone she met how terrible her life at home had been. Don't let the pack know you're wounded? My sister wanted the whole world to know. It was the subtext of her memoir and at the root of almost every song she wrote.

She told everyone how her father had abandoned her and her mother had mistreated her, and how she might as well be an orphan. But in Solange's version Mama was beautiful. Solange made this part of Mama's power—her great, cold, stern beauty. Mama was wicked, but she was beautiful and vain. Solange left out the bald patches, the bad veins and rough skin. Avaunt, slatternly employee of school cafeteria and nursing home! Solange transformed Mama into royalty. She was the fair, homicidal Queen in *Snow White and the Seven Dwarfs*.

Everywhere she went, people seemed to have trouble with her name. A lot of people had never heard it before, and too many mispronounced it. She needed something different, something pure and simple and evocative. *Rain*. Now, that suited her. Like, rain was a beautiful thing, a natural thing, but sad, too, you know, like tears.

I told her I would rather not call her that.

Roach and Rain, of East Sixth Street.

To my children, she would be Aunt Crash. *Is Aunt Crash coming? Is Aunt Crash coming? Is Aunt Crash here yet? Is Aunt Crash going to stay with us? When is Aunt Crash coming? When is Aunt Crash coming back? Why can't Aunt Crash stay longer? Why can't Aunt Crash come live with us?*

Et cetera.

Say she had come of age in a different era. Would it have been so easy to mistake or ignore certain signs? That *voice* she heard, for example, telling her to get on the bus. Say it had not been a time when you saw the weird every day: people letting it all hang out, freaking, goofing, dressing funny, being crazy, acting out. If there hadn't been so many runaways, especially in places like the Haight, where she ended up, maybe she would have stood out? The wish to be high all the time. The flight from reality. The mythomania. Where was the line between sexual liberation and promiscuity? Between promiscuity and nymphomania?

I had a theory about Solange, which I shared with Zelma: if the way to be popular had been to take the veil, Solange would have taken the veil. (Zelma: "Do you see a veil on my head?" No. "So quit saying that.") She'd been a pretty tough kid, once, prone to fights, prone to pick them. Now she was all turn-the-other-cheek and what-would-Gandhi-do. No wonder people found her attractive: she was not just pretty; she was open, spontaneous, full of love. A free spirit, a wild (but gentle) thing, a natural woman, instinctive, unschooled. A female type that was as romanticized as the revolutionary or outlaw male. Two types, in fact, that often found each other and, unsurprisingly, romanticized and romanced each other (like Roach and Rain).

She never wore underwear. She did not shave her body hair. She did not use deodorant, perfume, makeup. Said she was eighteen but looked twelve. *Good mornin', little schoolgirl.* Urchin. Waif. *Got an old man? Who's your daddy? Somebody's mama must be crying.* She loved to party, and she loved to share. Don't get her started on those days. Never again would she be so popular or receive so much attention. And so, in spite of her regrets, she would talk about them as if they had been the best days of her life.

Don't get her started—

But my children could never resist.

Oh yes, everything was different then. People were so generous, so warm and openhearted. You could just travel anywhere at all, you could knock on someone's door, tell them I'm a friend of so-and-so, and they would take you right in. Kids set out and roamed all over the world without having any plan! And there was a kind of puppy love kids felt for one another, even if they were strangers. If you were young, you were one of us, and the young would take care of the young. Money? What was that? Who needed it? Who wanted it? And this idea we had, that if we just passed around enough love and shared whatever we had, everything would be all right. We really believed we could create a new world. No more war. No possessions. No more hunger or envy or greed.

Imagine.

One of the songs she wrote back then was called "All I Had to Do Was Hold Out My Hand." Another was "I Am a Wound."

"Why does it bother you so much, Mom? What's the big secret? What is it you don't want us to know?"

Years after the fact, Jude told me how Solange had turned him and his sister on to pot. "Am I a cool aunt or what?" At the time, they were both still in grade school.

And when they were in college, I listened to some of their friends talk about their parents. One said that at first she'd been proud to know her parents were hippies, but now she was just embarrassed. "I *hate* hippies," said another.

This was what their parents told them: "Don't think you can shock *us*, no matter what you do. We did every crazy thing you can imagine, and we did it first. You call Desert Storm a war? Hah! *We* had Vietnam. The LSD *we* took was much stronger than what's out there today." (I have no idea whether this is true, but I have often heard it.) "You kids have it easy. *We* were involved, we *cared* about politics, we had *ideals*, we *fought* for great causes. You wouldn't have the *rights* and *privileges* you have today if *we* hadn't done all the work."

Et cetera.

What were some of her regrets?

1. Her tattoos. Modest though they were (a circlet of stars, the head of a unicorn)—especially compared with, say, Zoe's and Jude's—Solange came to hate them.

2. In spite of all those people who were supposedly taking care of her, there were times when she suffered from malnutrition, and this, along with a bout of hepatitis (all those shared needles none of us worried about back then), would affect her health all her life. She was always sick, it seemed to me. She had no resistance; she caught every cold or flu going around. She smoked, of course, and always too much. She hacked her way through every winter. Like Zelma, she had inherited Mama's migraines and, in time, even without having children, those "very coarse" veins. Early on, she began losing teeth.

3. Rote sex with too many partners had robbed sex forever of any deep magic or charge. She had learned to use sex both to get basic needs and to barter her way out of trouble ("Okay, but then you have to leave me alone"). Another runaway had given her this tip about cops: If you blow them, they don't have much choice afterward. They either have to kill you or let you go. ("All I Had to Do Was . . .")

4. Somewhere along the way she contracted a disease that remained asymptomatic, undiagnosed, and untreated until it had done enough damage to her fallopian tubes to prevent her from ever having children.

She had no intention of going home. And her drifting days (she said) were done. Even after she and Roach split up, she was determined to stay in the city. She was not eager to go home even for a visit, and in fact she and Mama would see each other only once before Mama got sick and died. No reconciliation, not even then. That was us. We were just not the kind of family who forgave one another or who asked forgiveness or tried burying the hatchet or hashing things out. "In our house," Solange wrote in her memoir, "it was either silence or violence." (When the book came out, a reviewer bemoaned the appearance of "yet another memoir about growing up grim, in a world marked by poverty, dysfunction, abuse, and bad blood.")

After our mother died, I was haunted by the thought of her working in the nursing home. I'm not sure why it was that particular chapter of her life my mind kept turning to, but I kept thinking of her, in middle age (but in a life such as hers, did it even matter what age you were?), working in that sinister place. I knew it was sinister, because that was why, after a multitude of complaints, the authorities had finally shut it down. Now I was haunted by the thought of my mother at her job—some kind of attendant. To be honest, I never knew exactly what her duties were, I never wanted to know, and she certainly never talked about it.

Who can say how much her daily proximity to decrepitude, sickness, and death contributed to her own decline? My last visits home—I am talking about a time before she became sick—I had to brace myself not to flee her presence. She no longer went to bed at night. Instead, she fell asleep around eight or nine fully clothed on the couch and stayed there till dawn. And so it went, sleeping and waking, same clothes, day in day out. This alone made it hard for me to be in the same house with her. Once, I discovered her sitting all by herself in the kitchen in the dark. The sun had gone down hours before. For a few minutes after I turned on the light, she had not seemed to know where she was. No one could persuade her to see a doctor. But that was the way of most people where I came from. The most alarming and even painful symptoms could not budge them. They just drank more. People wanted little truck with modern medicine. *Never let them cut you.* This rule was passed down through generations. The worst alcoholics would knowingly warn, "Never take none of their poisons."

As a mother, she had abdicated. She said, "I wash my hands of you!" Why should she give a damn about any of us? We were *all* monsters of ingratitude. (Just what it was she thought she had given us for which we were so monstrously ungrateful was a question we children would always be asking ourselves.) We were all our father's children—*bad seeds*, she called us, as if she had been only some kind of incubator or surrogate mother.

Even at her calmest, all she could do was blame. In the end, it was against Solange that she rested her case. When Solange ran away, Mama said, she destroyed this family.

When I talked about all this with Solange, about the thoughts that were haunting me and how guilty I felt now that our mother was dead, she told me she herself was not haunted; she did not feel guilty about Mama at all. She said, "Remember that time Noel wouldn't let her put on his snowsuit, and she got so angry she knocked him down and broke his arm?" Oh my god. I remembered. And I remembered how remorseful Mama had been. I remembered how afraid she had been that someone at the hospital would call the police on her. But at the hospital no one questioned the story she told them, no one called the police, and that scare had done nothing to reform her. Mama never changed her ways.

I want to repeat something I have said before: where I came from, my parents did not stand out. There was nothing exceptional about the behavior of either of them. I bring this up partly to help answer the bedeviling question, why didn't someone try to do something? This was childhood. We accepted it. We were just another six kids growing up grim, in a world marked by poverty, dysfunction, abuse, and bad blood.

Mama was hopeless, Solange said. Mama was *a criminal*. No way Solange was going to waste time feeling sorry or guilty. "You know I've always thought of myself as an orphan." Nevertheless, she had one of her worst breakdowns after Mama's funeral. And years later, when she sat down to write, it was Mama who dominated Solange's memoir.

And now here she is again, like a figure in a children's pop-up book. And though I would like this to be Mama's last appearance in these pages, I cannot say for sure.

*

What were my feelings when my long-lost sister turned up at my door?

I cannot resist a purplish phrase I once read somewhere: "I felt my blood leap at the sight of her." Of course, for some time, I had been expecting her. From the time of that first postcard, I think, I had been preparing myself for what was nonetheless a great shock.

First there was the distraction of getting her out of those wet clothes. I gave her my bathrobe and some thick socks, and I hung her things to dry in the bathroom. She curled up immediately on the rug near the radiator, but it was some time before I could bring myself to sit down. She was smiling at me, but it was a nervous smile. She had taken a huge step coming here, and she was nervous, uncertain, anyone could see it. She had something of the meek, penitential air of the returning prodigal. But she was not humiliated. She was not crushed. There was an element of pride or perhaps defiance that flashed through—I saw it more and more often as the night wore on and she grew more relaxed. It was there, I saw, in certain gestures, a way she had of twitching her long hair back from her face, and the way she smoked, or more precisely the way she flicked her ashes from too far away into the shellacked clamshell I used for an ashtray, missing it. (We both smoked Newports—how about that?) And don't think she was here to ask anyone's forgiveness (she was a George, remember). I had the impression that were I even to hint to Solange that she had been guilty of the slightest sin, she would have drawn herself up and flounced from the room. Her sauciness, which I well remembered, and which had driven my mother and not a few teachers mad, had become something else, less playful, harder-boiled, a kind of knowingness—oh, she'd seen a few things these past three years, she knew all about life, so don't go thinking she was a kid anymore, she was all grown up, far older than her years, older than you, Big Sister, make no mistake. She would lock eyes with you and then let her glance slide sideways right off your face: insolent. The dry, throaty chuckle she sometimes emitted now, and which I certainly did not remember, had a mocking, crowlike tone. (When Zoe was a teenager, she would develop some of these same mannerisms, a glance, a laugh, that got under my skin.) I knew it was mostly a pose, but it was Solange's favorite pose for quite some time, and she struck it so often I was tempted to say, as some parents do when a child keeps making a face, *Keep it up, missy, and you'll stay that way.*

But that early glimpse of her vulnerability (she had taken the big step, now how would she be received? Welcomed with open arms? Door slammed in her face?) brought out the tenderness in me: as if her heart were in my hands.

Right off, there was something reassuring to me about the way she looked: poorly groomed and underfed, perhaps, but in general like almost any other girl her age. And she behaved, too, like any girl her age: giggly and vivacious, fast-talking and *very* talkative— she could talk all night. And *yes*, I wanted to hear every word of her adventures, even the upsetting and scary parts, but first I wanted to feed her. I picked up the phone and ordered a large pizza, and when it came we wolfed it down straight from the box, sitting on the floor. A festive spirit had taken hold of us, and a sense of complicity in something vaguely naughty, like kids staying up past bedtime because their parents are away, that was the mood, and it brought back certain nights in the dorm. It brought back *Ann*, oh my heart, who'd had the same habit of leaving the crusts piled in the pizza box like small bones. Softly the radiator hissed, the room filled with heat. I watched the color come into Solange's cheeks and felt the color in my own. As they dried, two locks of hair framing her face corkscrewed fetchingly. Tomato sauce stained her lips, making the tales that poured from them seem even more lurid. I had put on some music. "Oh, wait!" she interrupted herself. "I love this song!" We had to be quiet and listen all the way through, and then I had to pick up the needle and play it again. *Who knows where the time goes?*

"That's what I want," Solange said excitedly. "That's the kind of song I try to write."

She was full of dreams.

After we finished the pizza, she produced an expertly rolled joint from her pack of Newports. It had become an increasingly rare event for me, getting high, but Solange could not remember the last time she had gone a day without getting high at least once. She smoked far more of the joint than I did. The effect of the pot was to make me quieter and her livelier; her talk became more and more dramatic. It was not unlike watching a piece of alternative theater of the kind that was beginning to be popular: lone performer onstage, rapping. Even the bathrobe was the right touch.

I was entranced. A dizzying thought struck me: I had a sister. A real sister, not a fake one like Ann. I had Solange and Solange had me—no room in my head for the thought that we would ever again be separated. And in fact, between then and now, with very few lapses, Solange and I have spoken with each other nearly every single day.

Watching her, I felt surges of love that threatened to choke me. I told myself she was my responsibility now, and the thought filled me with pride. I remembered a time when, as a child, I had found an abandoned cat and bundled it home, throbbing with tenderness and with this same pride. Kitty was now mine to love, mine to care for (little did I know she would run away the very next morning), and this feeling of being someone's savior and protector was so elating I wanted it to go on forever.

Listening to Solange—her talk increasingly birdlike, sharp and twittering, the effect of the dope on her speech or on my hearing, I was not sure which—I was grateful, too, for the chance I saw being given to me, a chance to atone for not having been a better big sister before, a chance I had secretly prayed for.

It may be significant, and so I put it down here, that around this time I had begun to fantasize almost constantly about having a baby. I had no husband, I was not even serious about anyone, but the conviction was growing in me that the kind of love I was craving could only be satisfied by having a child. And I was not wrong. Shortly, indeed, there would be no doubt in my mind whatsoever: having children was the one thing in life I knew for certain I wanted. And when I was feeling despondent, I would even comfort myself with fantasies of the children who would one day love and be loved by me. Just the sight of a pregnant woman or a woman with a baby or toddler could make my heart beat faster.

These feelings set me apart from most women my age I knew. Most of these women were torn about motherhood. If there was one thing they knew for certain, it was that they did not want to end up like their own mothers, women whose lives had been given over to the demands of marriage and family and who seemed, in the eyes of their daughters at least, to have missed out on just about everything. In fact, in one generation, the lives of women had changed drastically enough so that countless girls grew up to discover they had almost nothing to say to the women who'd raised them. By this time, one was used to hearing girls and young women vow never to be saddled with a family—it was the feeling of many of my co-workers at *Visage*, for example. Others were open to the possibility of marriage, and perhaps one child, someday (provided they could pursue careers as well), but they had a lot of living to do before settling down, and they were certainly in no hurry.

I was the only one in a hurry, the only one who could not wait, the one who had got it into her head that her real life would not truly begin until that first child was born.

I knew these feelings might not be understood or might be frowned upon, so I kept them mostly to myself. But why curb my dreams? At times I'd be seriously carried away and imagine myself with a whole slew of kids—why not five, why not ten? At the very least I must have two, for I must have both a boy and a girl.

Listening to Solange and, later, thinking about all she had experienced since I'd last seen her, I committed the sin of envy. It was like the envy I had so often felt with Ann—or even, strange as it might be to recall now, when Guy announced he was going off to war. When did I fully see and accept it—that my life would be short on adventure? Solange was right when she said—and she said it often—"You're a lot more like Sister Sister than you'll ever be like me." (Except it was not the Trinity but the tutelary spirits of house and home that would win *my* devotion.) In my whole life I would never see half the places Solange had already seen by the age of eighteen. She had lived out one of the big dreams of the day. *See the U-S-A in your Chev-ro-let!* (In those first days of television, when Dinah Shore belted out the *Chevy Show* jingle, whole families would sing along.) *America is asking you to call!* I had made my way to the Big City, but she had vroomed from coast to coast, zig-zagged all over the patchwork quilt of states. (*America's the greatest land of all!*) No skills, no money, a girl, a mere child, she had managed somehow not only to keep herself alive but to have an extraordinary time. Eighteen, and fixed for stories till her dying day. When did I figure out that life had nothing like that in store for me? I have gone through bad spells, times when, thinking about others' lives, the challenges faced and the risks taken, I have felt shame and loathing for myself. I have accused myself of cowardice, lack of imagination, of ambition, of will. (And if truth be told, it has not always been I myself making such accusations. I have been blamed by others for my timidity; I have heard my passionate love of reading denounced as an addiction, a vice, a cowardly avoidance of the challenges, dangers, excitements, and even duties of real life.)

That night, because it was much too late for Solange to go back downtown, we slept in the same bed. We slept head to foot, as we had done when we were little girls.

In the morning Solange was up first. I was driving a car over a waterfall when I awoke to the noise of the shower and the muffled strains of "Amazing Grace."

———

At work, people remarked on something different about me, which I was hard put to explain. Except for Cleo, no one had been told that I had a sister who had run away.

I once was lost but now am found. Around that time, it seemed you could not go anywhere without hearing that song.

Solange was delighted when I told her I had hallucinated her in the movie *Woodstock*. She wanted to see some mystical meaning in this. Another movie had come out, another documentary, about the Rolling Stones concert that had taken place a few months after Woodstock, and though I did not glimpse Solange anywhere in *Gimme Shelter*, this time she was truly there.

She had been living in Berkeley then. She had stayed on in California after Grover and Pam returned east, thoroughly burned out from the struggle for survival in the jungle that the Haight had by then become, and having decided they wanted to be with each other after all. She had been taken in by some students, was being passed from dorm room to dorm room like some kind of clandestine pet or mascot. Again—and in spite of warnings from astrologers—everyone wanted to be there. The concert was being billed as a second Woodstock, the West Coast Woodstock, Rock 'n' Roll History—free: a gift from the Stones to American fans. But according to Solange, you could tell it was not going to be a love-in long before the first punch was thrown. Much would be made of the fact that the first thing many people saw when they began arriving at the Altamont Speedway the day before the concert was a large butcher's cleaver lying in the dirt road leading to the concert site. People hiking past it slowed down to stare, but no one wanted to touch the mean-looking thing. All gave it a wide berth, as if it were indeed the ill omen hindsight would make it.

The flying fists, the flying beer cans, the Hell's Angels with their whirling chains and thrashing pool cues, the stretchers bearing the wounded away, the killing. I had heard about all this—everyone had—right after it happened. But it was one thing to hear about a murder and another to watch it on-screen, knowing it was not just the new, real-*seeming* violence of, say, *The Wild Bunch* or *Bonnie and Clyde*.

It had been reported that a fight had broken out between two men—something about a girl, something about race—and one of the men, who was black and who had a gun, was killed by the other man, who was white and who had a knife. But in the movie the gunman *appears* to be aiming at the stage, and the knifeman, a Hell's Angel, *appears* to be doing the job for which he'd been hired, and possibly saving Mick Jagger's life.

> *Mick Jagger, Mick Jagger—*
> *You make my heart stagger—*
> *I'll be the sheath, baby—*
> *You be the dagger—*

For years his name would be a kind of measuring device. I would count the number of times Solange mentioned Mick, and when that number began to climb I'd begin to worry. I could even see a direct relation between the number of times Solange mentioned Mick and the number of pills she had skipped. I got good—expert, even—at this sort of thing over time, but in the beginning I was helpless. I was naïve. So my sister swooned for Mick Jagger; millions of other girls did, too. Everyone knew how susceptible girls were—Beatlemania was still a fresh memory. And popular music was now a force in people's lives as it had never been before. I had never questioned Solange's devotion to the Stones, which began long before Altamont and before she ran away; I was a big Stones fan myself. And I'll bet we weren't the only ones who played our forty-five of "Satisfaction" so many times we destroyed it. I remembered that back in school, digging the Stones more than the Beatles made you cooler—though the coolest of all scorned the whole lot of British Invaders as faggots stealing off their black betters, and to someone like Guy, if it was not black (sole exception: Elvis), it was not rock and roll. As for the posters covering every inch of Solange's bedroom walls; the bubble gum cards and T-shirts, the pendants, belt buckles, key chains, and other fan paraphernalia she collected; her bottomless hunger for every detail about her idol to be gleaned from teen magazines and other sources, from the dullest news item to the wildest gossip; the way she had whole chunks of his biography by heart; and her threats of suicide over the affair with Marianne Faithfull (who would attempt suicide at the end of that affair herself)—well, all this just meant Solange was hard-core. And once she started writing and singing songs herself, I supposed it made sense that her idol, at his peak then, one of the biggest pop icons of all time, should have become an even greater obsession, so that when Solange told me she had written over a hundred songs to or about Mick, I saw this as extreme, but I did not see the harm. It would take a long time for me to accept that Mick Jagger was to Solange what Jesus Christ, Napoleon, Hitler, and JFK were to others in whose company I remained stubbornly reluctant to put her. She had a drug problem, no kidding, and she had always been an excitable, reckless, unmanageable girl—no surprise this combination could lead to trouble, that the drugs could exacerbate whatever emotional or personality problems might lie underneath. This I could believe. But I also believed that *underneath* underneath, my sister was normal. And who could have known, watching *The Ed Sullivan Show* that Sunday evening in 1964 ("And here they are, ladies and gentlemen, please—welcome—the Rolling Stones!"), how could Solange and I, still grade-schoolers then—how could we ever have guessed what role the band's front man, with his delightful resemblance to the girl star Hayley Mills, whom we adored, would come to have in our lives?

※

"All women are groupies"—Mick Jagger.

Dear Mick,
I know it was only yesterday I last wrote you and you have not even received that letter yet but I just had to write you again. I have not been

able to sleep nor can I eat for I cannot stop thinking about you. I am writing a new song for you but it is not finished, when it is finished I will send it as always and I hope you will like it as I hope you have liked all the others. I know I have said this before, but as it has once again begun to prey relentlessly on my mind so that I can think of little else and leaving me no peace I need to say it again. I WANT YOU TO KNOW I DO NOT AGREE WITH WHAT SOME PEOPLE ARE SAYING ABOUT ALTAMONT. I DO NOT BELIEVE YOU ARE IN ANY WAY TO BLAME.

I think most people if they are fair will understand that you could not have prevented that Tragic Death. As you know, I myself was in the audience, and anyone who was actually there knows how valiant you were, how you tried to reason with the unruly crowd and calm people down. It was, as is now widely known, a fruitless battle. What is more, I have seen Gimme Shelter *a total of twenty-two times, I have studied and studied it, and I say no one can know for sure what the man with the gun in his hand had on his mind. And when I think what MIGHT have happened! My god, it could have been another ASSASSINATION! When I think of what a close call that was—well, this is what has robbed me of sleep and appetite for many days and nights running. But when I think how scared you must have been up there and how valiant and heroic you were, when I hear you say "If we are all one, let's show we're all one," I feel such love for you as cannot be fully measured. For at that moment you showed the world who you really are, which is a GOOD PERSON as well as a ROCK STAR and not the BAD BOY so many people out there want to make of you. (Hint: this is what the new song I am writing is all about.) I know a sensitive soul like yourself might well be hurt by the hateful things that have been and continue to be said about you in this regard. Words like ARROGANT and SELFISH PRICK and CRIMINALLY IRRESPONSIBLE have been thrown around ad nauseam. Certain loudmouths are still saying what could you have been thinking, hiring the Hell's Angels as security, like hiring the Weathermen to guard the Pentagon, and if you hadn't done such a stupid thing that poor kid might still be alive.*

I know how painful it must be for you to hear such harsh accusa-

tions and how sad you must feel about the whole mess, when all you were trying to do was give us a good time. In the movie, it is so clear that you are suffering. Last time I saw it, I could barely stop myself from jumping up and screaming MICK, DON'T BE SO HARD ON YOURSELF, THERE IS NO BLOOD ON YOUR HANDS. And maybe I did scream something, or maybe it was just that I was sobbing so loud, but some people sitting near me got up and moved. Oh, if they only knew! Someone went and got the manager, but when he saw it was me he just sighed and reminded me how I'd promised not to disturb the other patrons. To which I replied, well, how many other patrons have bought as many tickets to this movie as I have? To which he just sighed again and said he would give me one last chance, and left, like he was sorry for me. As if anyone who has embraced a demigod needs pity from a mere mortal, especially a fat, zit-pocked, wimpy mortal like this guy, who doesn't even have the balls to throw a ninety-eight-pound girl out of his theater. But to repeat: you are not responsible for any of the sick things that happened at Altamont, most especially not the murder, which was fate. Ask Santana, ask Jefferson Airplane, ask Crosby, Stills, Nash or Young. That scene was out of control long before the main act came on. Ask the astrologers. The sun was in Sagittarius, the moon was in Scorpio. It was in the stars, man! Who could pin the blame on you?

Needless to say, I do not believe for one minute the story going around about how that kid was out to get you for having made yourself rich and famous by ripping off the music of his people, stealing their rhythms, their blues, their dance moves, their soul, their gestures and even their accent—as if you were no more than a common thief and good mimic with no soul or original musical ideas of your own and for this deserved to be shot. I put this story in the same category as those rumors that you have had surgery to make your lips look more African, or that in fact you really do have an African ancestor somewhere, or that you and Keith Richards are lovers.

I understand that you have received a lot of hate mail and even THREATS AGAINST YOUR LIFE. This has really freaked me out and has made me decide to write you LOVE MAIL every day. I don't want you ever to forget that your true fans cherish and adore you and will always stand by you. Oh Mick, I do hope Keith and the other Stones have been a support to you during this trying time. I hope Bianca is a comfort to you, as is of course her duty as your wife. And now that I have brought up Bianca, which I had no intention of doing when I began this letter, I want to take a moment to ask your forgiveness for those letters I sent a while ago in which I said all those terrible things about her.

Jealousy is an evil emotion, and I don't have to tell you how totally crazy out of my mind I can be when the subject comes to your love life. The thought of you with another woman—what it does—well—think of dropping someone's heart in a blender and hitting Chop. I don't recall my exact words but I remember how I was feeling when I wrote them, so I know the gist. But since that time I have changed. I have grabbed myself by the shoulders and given a good shake, I have sat myself down and given myself a good talking to, and I swear to you, Michael Philip Jagger, I have left those ugly feelings behind. Now that I see how serious you and Bianca are about each other and that she has given you a precious baby girl, I can finally be happy for you and send BOTH of you my much belated congratulations. (My wedding gift to you, as you probably guessed, was "Bianca, Ma Belle," which was included in the last batch of songs I sent you.)

I will not lie. I will not say my jealousy is completely cured— perhaps that is asking too much. But I have come to accept that MICK and RAIN were not meant to be, that you will never belong to me, and that I must content myself with the memory of the one brief shining moment that we shared. I do not know if you have told Bianca about me or are planning to tell her, but of course I understand if the answer is no. I myself have come to see Bianca through your eyes, and what I see is a very beautiful, sexy woman who could be your very own twin sister. And this is good, for how would it be, after all, for The Sexiest Man Alive to be with some Plain Jane or Homely Hannah? I want to say also that I am sure you must be a wonderful wonderful father, though I *can imagine lots of people will disagree, given your much publicized and much criticized way of life. But again, they do not know you as I do . . .*

Et cetera.

There were hundreds of such letters, many of them a staggering number of pages long, all written in what I called Solange's spider writing: a thin, squeezed, spiky scrawl, unlike her usual hand. This, too, was something I learned to watch out for—a change in her handwriting. Graphomania: Solange scribbling away furiously on a yellow legal pad or in one of the many expensive leather-bound Italian notebooks she bought on her many shopping sprees. (She was—she became—a bulimic shopper, buying all sorts of things she didn't need or even really want and later literally throwing them away.) Words, words, words. If she stopped writing at all, it was only to start talking. Endless monologues, endless switching of topics, the queen of non sequiturs, tireless, exhausting.

Not every letter she wrote actually ended up being sent, but of those that were sent, many received replies. Not from the demigod himself, of course, but from an agency hired to handle fan mail. Eight-by-ten glossies, publicity about upcoming gigs, thank-you notes with printed signatures: *Love, Mick XXX.*

When John Lennon was shot, Solange had a breakdown. She had gone the moment she heard the news to join the growing crowd gathered behind police barriers near his apartment building, where she alarmed people by carrying on about assassinations and how Mick Jagger was next. I suppose to some it could have sounded like a threat. The police brought her to the emergency room at Bellevue Hospital, where the staff recognized her, admitted her, called her doctor, called me. It was December 9, 1980 (Lennon had died in another hospital the night before), and by then I was no longer helpless. I was no longer naïve about Solange's illness, and I knew all about Mick. This time, however, there had been none of the usual warning signs. She had gone from zero to five hundred mph in a heartbeat.

In the Bellevue ER, as soon as they heard about the shooting, they had braced themselves for an influx of patients, and that is what they got. Later I was stunned to learn that although Solange could not possibly have known this, Mick Jagger was indeed on the assassin Mark Chapman's hit list.

*

I had heard the story about Altamont so many times, this particular day—a couple of months after Solange came to find me in New York—I wasn't really listening, at least not at first. Besides, we were tripping. It was a weekend. Roach had left town to go to some relative's funeral. I had gone to help Solange, who had got it into her head she wanted to paint her apartment, each room a different color. But when I arrived, there were no paint cans or brushes or rollers to be found. I was only a little surprised, though, since I had seen this before: the big plan or project that somehow never got off the ground, usually because Solange had got distracted by some new one.

She had gone to the paint store, she said, but the wide choice of colors, the dizzying variety of shades of each color, had given her what she would later know as an anxiety attack. Anxiety attack, panic attack, hypomania—these terms were not yet part of our vocabulary. "I don't know what happened, man. I was scared—all that *paint*—I couldn't breathe—I just *freaked*." And fled. Back home, she decided that rather than snort crystal and paint the apartment as planned, she would drop acid instead.

Now that she had got me downtown, I was more than happy to blow the day with her. I just wished it weren't so hot. There was no air conditioner in the apartment. There were two fans, both broken. I sat in a chair near the open window. There was another chair—we were in the kitchen—but Solange sat on the floor. In

173

those days, she always preferred to sit on the floor, even when there was no rug or when the floor was rough or dirty. There must have been a reason for this preference for the floor so many shared back then, but what could it have been? It was like the preference for going barefoot even in places such as hot city sidewalks, where shoes would have been far more comfortable. From where I sat, it was hardly more than two arms' lengths to the window across the air shaft, which was also open. As Solange rattled on, I found myself listening more and more to the sounds coming from that kitchen, where a woman was feeding her baby from a jar, coo-coo-congratulating him on every mouthful he ate. With the acid, I became that woman.

Mick was wearing a red-and-black satin shirt with a ruffled bib and scarves hanging from the sleeves. Solange was so close to the stage she could see his face. She could follow the exaggerated movements of his lips and tongue, as if he were not just singing the song but making a meal of it, licking up the crumbs. Tears dripped from her chin. The night before, a few hours before dawn, as she and her friends were camped around a bonfire trying to stay warm, a figure in a large red hat and a long red scarf had appeared to them.

"Allo, people. Y'all ready to rock tomorrow?"

He had come by helicopter to check out the stage for the show. He had lingered to walk among these most devoted of fans who had arrived so many hours early to get the best seats and were now braving the winter cold.

"Hey, little girl, how 'bout you? What song do you wanna hear me sing tomorrow?"

She said "Honky Tonk Woman," and he laughed.

"Now, how did I know you were gonna say that, luv? How did ole Mick know dat? All right. Give us a kiss. When you hear it tomorrow, you'll know it's for you."

And right in front of everyone, he put his arms around her, pulling her close. "Oh, look at you now, shaking all over, and I haven't even done anything yet." Under cover of his big hat, he tongued her ear. Under cover of his scarf, he took her hand and plunged it down his pants. "Lookee here." Showing her he was hard. Probably he was always hard. "What do you say you come find me tomorrow, after the show? You come to my trailer, baby, you promise? I'll give you something to shake about."

Since then, she had not slept. She had kept her hand pressed to her face, inhaling deeply, until his smell had faded away.

The baby had finished eating. I lifted him from his high chair and cuddled him against my shoulder, gently patting his back. I carried him out of the kitchen to the nursery, where I changed his diaper, discovered that he was a girl, and laid her in her crib.

"People," pleaded Mick. "Brothers and sisters. Come on, now, just cool out."

Somewhere in the middle of "Sympathy for the Devil," she managed to catch his eye. Fans—some partly naked, some totally naked—kept trying to climb onstage, were attacked by Hell's Angels and tossed back into the crowd.

"*People.*"

Tears dripped from her chin. During the hour and a half between the end of the last act and the moment the Rolling Stones finally walked onstage, she had gone up to one of the Angels and asked him how to get to the Stones' trailer. She had told him what Mick had told her the night before. Without a word the Angel grabbed one of her breasts and twisted, hard, one way and then the other, like a knob on a locked door.

My hearing muffled as if by cotton or water, catching only an occasional word, I realized that woven into Solange's otherwise wholly familiar tale were some things I had not heard before, possibly important. (To sort it all out—what had actually happened from what Solange remembered from what she imagined from what I remembered she had told me from what she or I had seen in the film— would prove a hopeless task.)

I wanted to listen more closely to what she was saying, but just as her attention had been riveted on the stage, so was mine now riveted on the crib. At the very least, I wanted to wait until Baby had dozed off. And then I might have to stop in the bathroom.

Out of the crowd rose a desperate wail. "Pablo! Pablo! Help! I can't see you! I can't *see*!" Too much LSD, or she'd got separated from her old man. Scores of people would end up freaking out or OD'ing that night, and many would get separated or lost.

"SHUT THE FUCK UP EVERYBODY, CUT OUT THE SHIT." Hell's Angels strode the stage, all pumped up like gladiators. One of them hoisted his pool cue to his shoulder like a javelin. He shook his big, shaggy blond head and roared, "YOU MOTH-ERFUCKERS WANNA HEAR MUSIC OR YOU WANNA FIGHT?"

Blam! Pow! Whup! Thump! Whack! Smack! Stomp! Crunch!

"This is so weird, man. I always heard the Angels didn't even dig the Stones."

"This concert's a fucking *bummer*, man."

"It's not a concert, it's a fucking riot!"

"People," said Mick, interrupting the song. "Who's fighting and what for? Why are we fighting?"

"Fuck you, Jagger, it's all your fucking fault."

"*Why* are we *fighting*?"

"Stop the concert!"

"We need an ambulance and a doctor," Mick said wearily. "By that scaffold."

Those who had seen it earlier now remembered the butcher's cleaver. Or had it been an axe?

A German shepherd had got onto the stage and was churning in frantic circles.

"Gun! Gun!"

"This could be the most beautiful evening," said Mick. People in the back, far from the stage and the mayhem, clapped and cheered, eager to get on with the show. "I beg you to get it together. Hell's Angels. Everybody. Let's relax, get into a groove."

The friends with whom Solange had come wanted to leave. A lot of people had already left or were trying to leave. Solange was still weeping. Her breast still ached. The bruises—blue fingerprints—would last for weeks. Someone doused her head with beer, but she stood firm. "Not before 'Honky Tonk Woman.'" She was determined to find Mick after the show. She had caught his eye. *I'm scared*, his look told her.

"Come on, guys, this is insane. The Angels just knifed some cat two feet away. Let's get out of here."

"Not before 'Honky Tonk Woman.'"

I'll give you something to shake about.

The tang of urine on her palm.

Her friends left right after "Brown Sugar."

"Honky Tonk Woman" was the next-to-last song.

It was just like morning sickness. To keep from vomiting, I concentrated on Baby's eyelashes resting like tiny gold half-moons on her plump pink cheeks. The palest pink suffused with the palest blue—just like my own plump, milk-filled breasts before she was weaned. The nursery was painted pink and blue and white—and so had Baby come into the world, all pink and blue and *trailing clouds of glory*. Oh, sick. What had I eaten? A pill to make me small enough to climb into Baby's crib.

"George! What the fuck are you doing? Get away from that window! You okay? Here, sit on the floor. It's safer down here. You scared the shit out of me. You okay? You gonna be sick? You need air? Oh, man, oh, man, you really scared me. Where'd you think you were going?"

Everyone always said the same things. Oh, the colors, the colors, and it was like you were seeing everything for the first time, and if you didn't fight it, you would lose your ego and find bliss. You would meet God. Everyone said you would never forget those trips. But everyone I know has forgotten them, even the part about meeting God. We all swore we'd take acid as long as we lived, so we'd keep growing spiritually, but for most people I know, it happened more or less the same: one day you dropped, filled with all the usual jittery anticipation, and when you got off, you found yourself thinking, Here I am again, watching the world come apart again, and after that, no matter how many other drugs you might take or how often you might take them, you were never in the mood for LSD.

As it turned out, this would be my own last trip, though I did not know it then, as I did not know that even though Solange and I had each swallowed half a tab, we were not traveling through the cosmos at the same velocity. Solange was one of those people who had taken so much acid so many times they couldn't always count on getting off. She was stoned, all right, but she wasn't flying, like me. She was tempted to take more. But that was Roach's stash she'd got those purple tabs from, and bad enough she had helped herself to a whole one without asking. Roach, who had supported himself for years as a dealer in the past, still had a few special customers he supplied now and then, and for all she knew this acid had been meant for one of them.

That Solange was nowhere near as fucked up as I was was just one of many realities right then eluding me. Had I known, I might have been less scared. I kept my eyes narrowed to slits. When I opened them wide, too much world rushed in—think of two tunnels and a pair of highspeed trains—and the nausea intensified. Some time passed—a minute, a day—while I hugged the floor, which was crawling with something. (Later on this trip I would turn my head and encounter at eye level a cockroach that appeared to be walking on stilts.) I threw up. (Oh, the colors, the colors.) I looked helplessly for my sister and found her standing in front of the refrigerator. Flat as a pancake—no, flatter. She was one of those plastic stick-on peel-off figures kids play with—she was a Colorform! And then to my—I don't believe there is a word for what struck me—she was not even that. I saw a child's finger painting on the white door, brown and pink and green, which I had still enough mind to know were my sister's hair, her face, our brother's army T-shirt. I shut my eyes against the unbearable sight of a living person being erased.

I had never reached this stage before, but I had heard about it, as I had heard about the next stage, said to bring about the total dissolution of the visible world, the disappearance even of abstractions and colors, in which you experienced a kind of blindness, as it was described, except rather than seeing darkness, you saw light. Enough mikes, I had heard, could cause this blindness, which I imagined to be like snow blindness, and more mikes could take you to the next stage, where, out of this blindness, this nothingness, this light, it was said you would hallucinate, you would behold your own self, you would see your body outside your body, like an identical twin or a clone. All in your mind but real enough to touch. And it was said, in order not to go mad, because at this stage you were that fucking vulnerable, you had to be very steady, very strong. Strong enough to do absolutely nothing.

Once, it had filled me with awe, this kind of talk. It had thrilled me and tempted me. Would *I* ever trip like that? Would I ever be ready to go *there*? But now that I saw that I might be going there willy-nilly, ready or not, I wanted none of it. It was already too much for me, my god, Solange running like a cracked egg down the refrigerator door. All I could do was mumble those three awful words that everyone hopes no one tripping around them will say: *Make it stop*.

"You didn't actually say it," Solange told me later. "You didn't say anything at all. You couldn't speak. And you couldn't hear, either. I would say something to you, I was trying to get a sense of where your head was at, but you didn't hear me. I asked you if you wanted a soda or something from the fridge, and you stared right through me."

Solange, experienced in these matters, able to guess without my telling her exactly where my head was at, took charge with the efficiency of a psych nurse. She weighed the option of giving me a hit of Placidyl. Had I actually said the three awful words, she probably would have given me the Placidyl. Instead, seeing that she herself was well in control (which is not to say she was very happy about it), Solange decided it was safe to let my trip run its course. (Understand her reluctance to see *both* halves of a tab of Purple Haze go to waste.)

She laid some newspaper over the vomit (deal with that mess when she was straight) and gently coaxed me to my feet and into the living room, a journey that took several minutes. In spite of the heat (in fact I no longer felt the heat; I was sweating but I was cold), Solange closed all the windows in the apartment and locked them. She pulled down the shades but kept the lights off (later, she would light candles). She sat on the floor in front of the stereo, and for the next couple of hours she did nothing but play disc jockey.

Solange and Roach took their music seriously. Hundreds of albums filled an entire wall of nailed-together milk crates, and though most of their other possessions had been salvaged from junk shops or off the street, their sound system was one of the best money could buy. (Not that they actually had bought it, but that is a whole other story.) Solange chose what to play now with care—not her beloved Stones, or Led Zeppelin, her second-favorite band at the time, but the gentler sounds of the Beatles, Donovan, Neil Young, Jackson Browne. She even played a little Mozart. Though she was always watching me out of the corner of her eye, she avoided looking directly into my face. She avoided talking, and she avoided moving about. If she had to move, she moved slowly. She didn't blast the music but kept it turned up loud enough to block out other sounds. Had someone knocked, for example, we would not have heard it. When I screamed, though, Solange, who had her back to me, heard. Turning, she saw me eye to eye with that cockroach (it was on the back of my chair), and this time she did not move slowly. With astonishing, graceful, warriorlike moves, Solange chased and slew the invader.

Wow.

A lifetime later, having survived the perilous peaks (without, thank god, ever losing my sight), I entered the miraculous stage when the threat of freaking out has receded but reality has not yet retaken hold. I was not ready to talk, but I was able at last to stir from that chair, to move about gingerly on legs that felt as if I had borrowed them from someone taller. I was able to smoke my first cigarette since the acid had come on, and the most deeply satisfying cigarette of my life it was.

Everything I laid eyes on now had a pattern, and I surprised myself by remembering what that pattern was called: *herringbone*. ("Surprised" because I seemed to have lost half my vocabulary, and many simpler words, such as *thirsty* and *match*, would not come.)

Solange had been smoking hash while I was coming down, and because it was very good, opium-laced hash, she and I soon arrived at about the same plateau. She lit a few candles around the room and she lit some joss sticks and she got out her guitar. I listened to her sing and wondered when she had become so good. Her voice was assured and pure and vibrant with feeling. The songs she sang were mostly songs she had written herself, and they were about love and pain and what was right with the world and what was wrong with it, and for all she had suffered she praised the wounded world and sang of her tender feelings for man, she sang angelically of hope and forgiveness, and I was blown away by this kid's wisdom and goodness, and I was proud. Maybe my little sister didn't have to go back to school. Maybe she knew everything already.

By the time Solange put away her guitar, it was evening. She went through the apartment opening all the windows, and the cool, ash-smelling city air blew in. From the street came the enchanting music of children at play. From the air shaft, a medley of kitchen sounds as neighbors prepared and sat down to their supper.

Someone on an upper floor was watching a game show. Someone on the show was winning big.

That morning, when we dropped the acid, Solange had turned off the phone. Now she turned it back on, and when almost immediately it rang, we both jumped. While the phone rang and rang, Solange told me a story about Roach, how once when he was tripping, the phone rang and it was his mother, and she became so suspicious from the way he was talking that, in spite of his assurances to the contrary, she knew something was wrong. To her it sounded exactly as if someone was holding a gun to her son's head, like a bad guy in the movies ("Just make like everything's fine, mister, or else . . ."), and after they hung up, she called the police. "So there's Roach, tripping his brains out, when two pigs bang at the door."

The phone had stopped, and the room rang instead with our laughter. For the next hour or so, just about everything would strike us as hilarious, and tomorrow our stomachs would hurt as if we had done hundreds of sit-ups.

I heard a story once about a kid who dropped acid and went to the zoo. It was one of those cautionary tales acidheads liked to tell. The kid had some kind of food on him, say an orange, which he tossed through the bars to an ape, say an orangutan (because of "orange"), and the orangutan peeled the orange and ate half and then tried to hand the other half back through the bars to the kid. And the poor kid—well, it was a cautionary tale: Don't take acid and go to the zoo.

Or: You never knew in what Oz the twister might drop you.

We were in the kitchen. Solange opened the refrigerator and brought forth nectar and ambrosia. Iced licorice tea. Lemon custard. A sweetness to flood the mouth with saliva and the eyes with tears. It might have been childhood we were eating.

I looked out the window, and there she was, the woman of many moons ago. There they were, mother and child—and father, too. They were sitting around the kitchen table, the baby in a high chair, and there were plates of spaghetti on the table and bottles of beer. There was a loaf of Italian bread, and the familiar bright green shaker of grated cheese. The Holy Family.

The man was wearing a white undershirt with the sleeves rolled up over his shoulders. He had a laborer's arms and dark curly hair spilling out of his V-neck, and though I have never liked hairy men that chest did something similar to what the custard had done to me.

Now I wanted to go out. I really wanted to go for a walk, to strut around the block on my new long legs, but Solange, little sister, Big Nurse, said no. Instead, we went up to the roof, where a breeze blew the faint scent of fire our way and we heard faint sirens and saw the evening star. Solange, goofing, started to sing "When You Wish Upon a Star," but a catch in her throat made her stop. *Yesterdayland.* Bittersweet. Jiminy Cricket! *Makes no difference who you are?* But that song could make you weep, even then. Walt Disney the fascist had declared a ban: No longhairs permitted in Disneyland! But think how they must have broken his heart: *after all he had done for them, and this is how the kids turn out!* It was thanks to the hippies, though, that *Fantasia* was given a long second life. It was one of their favorite films and, along with *2001*, highly recommended for viewing on psychedelics.

Mercifully, Disney did not live to see it: the hippie mob storming Sleeping Beauty's castle, invading Fantasyland, liberating Tom Sawyer's Island, battling police, and causing the whole place to shut down (Anaheim, 1970).

I once heard that there exists a secret trove of cartoons, made many years ago by some of the original Disney animators, in which such characters as Snow White and the Dwarfs, Mickey, Donald, Pluto, and Pinocchio engage in graphic sexual antics. It is hard not to hope this story is true.

Somehow up on the roof we got to talking about love, and how we loved each other and how we loved the world, and how love really was the grooviest thing there is. We told each other that we would always love each other and always be there for each other, and never, whatever might happen, be separated again.

Back downstairs, Solange put on the Stones' *Beggars Banquet* album.

The last song of the concert was "Street Fighting Man." Mick blew kisses and thanked everyone, saying, "We leave you to kiss each other goodbye." But the Stones did not dare return to their trailer. They ran straight to where a hovering chopper with lowered rope ladders was waiting to lift them out, as from enemy country.

Solange knew where the band was staying in San Francisco, and later that night she made her way to Nob Hill. In his crowded hotel suite, Mick was beating his breast, blaming himself for what had happened. He was threatening never to do another concert again. He would quit this rock-and-roll life! As soon as possible he was flying home to London. He didn't know if he would ever see America again. The last thing he said to Solange was, "Promise you'll come to London, little girl. I'll introduce you to the Queen."

It must have been around ten or eleven that Roach came home. By then Solange and I had lapsed into a kind of stupor. But when Roach appeared, Solange snapped to, like someone who'd been under hypnosis. One look at him, and she began to wail. She stood there with clenched fists raised, jaws wide, and tears spurting from her eyes, like a child—like the child I once knew: prone to flailing, crying fits nearly grand mal in force that used to terrify us all and that only Guy seemed able to quiet. *Wah!* she cried. *Wah! Wah!*

She hurled herself at Roach, wrapping her arms around his neck and her legs around his waist. Loud though she was, I could barely understand what she was telling him, her voice was so thick with mucus and emotion. She confessed to having raided his stash. "Don't be mad at me, Roachski!" Then: "I was so scared! I was so fucking scared!" Scared, I gathered, first of all out of concern for me, but also because she had not gotten off. What did that mean? Was it brain damage? Was she never going to be able to trip again? "I'm no good!" she wailed. "I'm no good. I've never been any good. I'll never be any good. I hate myself. I wish I were dead!"

What was happening? At no point during that astonishing day had it occurred to me that *Solange* might be in danger of freaking out. It was almost as if the strain of keeping herself together for my sake all this time had been too much, and now that Roach was here, she could let go at last.

Awkwardly clasping Solange in his arms, Roach lowered himself onto the couch (really a single mattress and some throw pillows on top of some crates), and he rocked her gently back and forth, one hand on the back of her head. After a minute or so, he peeled her away and got her to lie down on the couch. She was still sobbing, but she wasn't talking anymore. She lay facing the wall, kicking it and weakly pounding it with her fists. Roach disappeared. I heard him in the kitchen, turning on one of the stove burners, and figured he was making tea. I knelt on the floor beside Solange and stroked her heavily perspiring back, helpless for something to say. I heard Roach turn on the bathwater. A minute later he returned with a syringe in one hand and a dog's leather collar (though they had no dog) in the other. Somehow, while holding the syringe, he managed to tighten the collar around Solange's left arm, and he injected the needle. The whole time, Solange never flinched or turned her head, and the whole time, no one spoke. When he removed the needle, a trickle of blood ran down Solange's arm, and before it could drip to the floor, he leaned forward and licked it up.

Roach gathered Solange into his arms and carried her to the tub in the kitchen. When he had finished bathing her, he wrapped her in a towel and carried her past me into the bedroom. He closed the door, and I went into the kitchen where the tub water was lazily draining. On the sink counter was the blackened spoon in which Roach had cooked the heroin. I saw the stained newspaper on the floor and remembered what had happened earlier, though it did not seem possible that this could have happened on the same day. It did not seem like the same place, either. That apartment felt now like a place where I had no business being. I was sure Roach and Solange were having sex back there, and I did not want to think about it. Solange had looked pretty unconscious to me as she was being carried, all floppy limbs like a giant rag doll—and not that Roach was hurting her, but you couldn't really call it consensual, either.

Roach came into the kitchen and finally noticed me. He said, "What do you want to do?" This I'd had plenty of time to think about. I wanted to go home.

"You sure? You can handle being alone tonight?"

I said I was sure, and Roach said he would walk out with me and get me a cab. When I told him I didn't have money for a cab, he said, "No problem."

When I asked him how Solange was, he shook his head. "She gets like that," he said, clipping his words. "She's got problems. Real problems. It's not about the acid. She needs help." Then he caught himself and said, "Hey, shit, man. I didn't mean to lay all this on you. Everything's cool now. Let's go."

Up close, if I had to guess, this had not been a drug-free day for Roach, either.

Just before we stepped outside, he said, "You'd better prepare yourself. It's R. Crumb–land out there." East Village, Saturday night, summer. Leading the parade was a guy with a head like a jack-o'-lantern. At least half the people we passed seemed to be in some sort of disguise. I could not help staring into faces. One block brought you every kind of expression: smiling, angry, lost, frightened, zonked, secretive, ashamed, paranoid, smug, heartbroken, bored, stupid, hopeful, hopeless, guilty, calculating. And with my special vision, of course—my special herringbone filter—I could tell: not every one of them was alive, and not everyone was human.

After I had accidentally bumped into some person for a second time, Roach put his arm around my waist and kept me close to him. As for *his* facial expression, it was a touch fierce. Roach was no biker, but that was *his* disguise: caveman hair, gladiator arms, nothing over his big barrel chest but a black leather vest. Wait a minute. For a funeral? "Who died?" Roach looked surprised at the question. "Whose funeral did you go to?"

"None of your business, girl," he said, patting my shoulder at the same time to show he wasn't being mean.

Roachski. I had never heard Solange call him that before. By now I had met Roach often, but I would never know him. I didn't think Solange really knew him, either. He was the kind of man who preferred not to be known too well. *None of your business*. His real name was Joseph and he was from Rhode Island and he had never been to college; under torture I could not tell you more. A few months later he and I would sit together drinking bad coffee in a hospital cafeteria, and I would listen to him explain why I wasn't going to see him again.

"Now, I know what you're going to think, but I got to tell the truth here. Staying with your sister, I know what that means. A life sentence, that's what it means. And I'm sorry, but I know I can't do it. I love her, my heart bleeds for her, but I'm just not the man to take care of her, and better that everybody knows it right here and now, up front."

A life sentence. Cruel, but honest, and I forgave him. I would hear versions of this speech other times, from other Roaches, and usually I forgave them.

One of the last conversations I'd had with Solange before she was hospitalized, she told me all about the trip to London, the rollicking time she'd had with Mick, and what it was like to meet the Queen. The only thing she left out was how she'd managed to do it without a passport.

And soon after that conversation, Solange swallowed everything in her medicine cabinet, bottle of this, bottle of that, aspirin, cough syrup, rubbing alcohol, and one used razor blade.

In those days there were a million hippie cabdrivers in Manhattan, and right now about half of them seemed to be converging on St. Mark's Place. Roach hailed one by eyeball. Have I said that I'm a Catholic? This cabbie was the image of the image of Our Savior that used to hang in the front hall of the house where Solange and I grew up. He had his window rolled down, and Roach reached in with an opened pack of Camels and shook a joint halfway out. "Will this get the chick up to Ninety-sixth Street, safe and sound?"

"Sure, man," replied the Redeemer with a beatific expression, and the two men did a soul shake.

He did not light the joint until we had passed through Midtown. He drove like the wind and delivered me, safe and sound, to my door. Before he drove off again, he brought his palms together and nodded, in the Hindu gesture of *namaste*.

I wanted you—
I did not count the cost—
I was just a runaway—
In love with what I'd lost—

According to an ex-roadie I once knew, there were basically three kinds of groupies. First, there were the national groupies, the girls who were the real pros, who charted every move their favorite bands made and would arrive in the cities where the bands had gigs even before the bands got there themselves and make whatever deals they could with hotel people and production people and others, in order to gain access. They usually had no money, these girls, but they had something that was just as good and that they were perfectly willing to use. Some of these groupies became famous in their own right. Some could boast of having been with more than one rock star; some had serious romances with stars and lived with them and had babies by them. Some would eventually sell their stories or write books about their experiences. And one became a rock superstar herself. Then there were the local groupies, different from the first tier mainly in that they did not travel, they did not devote their entire lives to the bands or become close friends with them. And finally, there were the "beginners," girls who hung around the fringes, groupies of groupies in some cases, trying to learn all they could from the big girls. These teenyboppers might have had what it took to get themselves into a sold-out concert, but they lacked the aggression and skills needed to get closer to their idols than the edge of the stage. Among all three groups, but especially among the last, you found a lot of runaways. You also found some boys.

"Most groupies were just trying to do their thing," the roadie told me. "They could be a nuisance at times, but they were basically harmless, and pretty much no one was against the idea of having a lot of loose young girls around. But some of them were crazy. I mean, really wild, fucked-up, crazy girls who would do *anything*. They'd get themselves set up in one of the trailers, say, and let not just the musicians but every roadie and bodyguard and passing stranger have their way with them. You felt sorry for these girls, but it was hard not to get disgusted. You just wanted to round them all up and bring them to the ASPCA."

Some of them kept score and got into a spirit of competition. They set outrageous goals for themselves that went well beyond I-want-to-do-the-whole-band. There was Velvet Mouth, for example, who made her name on a Rod Stewart tour. Staggering around a hotel lobby one night, boasting, "Three hundred and fifty, man!" before passing out.

True or false: Many Stones groupies had the famous tongue-lapping logo from the *Sticky Fingers* album cover tattooed on one of their butt cheeks, close to the cleft.

✳

In the last days of disco, the following conversation took place between me and a friend in a Thai restaurant around the corner from the old Studio 54.

"Guess who just sat down behind you."

"Who?"

"Mick Jagger."

"Oh, my god. Are you sure it's him?"

"Of course I'm sure."

"Is he alone?"

"No. He's with two other guys. Not Stones. I don't recognize them. I'll bet they're going to Studio 54."

"Probably. How does he look?"

"Fantastic. After all, he's not that young anymore. You know, everyone says he's really homosexual. If so, he does the best impersonation of a heterosexual I've ever seen."

"I have to get his autograph."

"You have to be kidding."

"No. I have to do something."

"What are you talking about?"

"It's hard to explain. It's about my sister."

"The crazy one?"

"She's not crazy when she takes her medication."

"So you want the autograph for her?"

"No. It's for me." For me.

"Aren't you a little old to be a groupie?"

" 'All women are groupies.' "

"What?"

"Look, the truth is, I don't really want the autograph. I just want some—exchange. I want some sort of contact. How else can I get that without asking for his autograph?"

"But you can't! The kind of people who do that— It's too embarrassing. It's also rude. Do you think he wants people bothering him like that?"

"He can say no. That's okay, too."

"Well, *I'm* saying no. I say it's *not* okay. I must insist that you not humiliate us."

"I'll never have this chance again."

"What? A chance to make a fool of yourself?"

"You don't understand."

"I understand you're about to do something horribly tacky."

"Yes. But I know that if I don't do it, I will always regret it."

"Oh, this is absurd! I won't ever be able to show my face in this place again!"

"What's he doing now?"

"Looking at the menu."

"I'd better hurry before the waitress comes. It will be less awkward."

"Oh, Georgette, this is too ghastly for words! I had no idea you were this kind of person. If you do this, I'll be furious. I'll never forgive you! And what if he tells you off? I hope he does. It would serve you right!"

He was kind. He took the pen and the piece of paper I slid across his table without looking up. The other two men looked patiently on. He handed the piece of paper back. Of course, I recognized it.
Love, Mick XXX.

Part Three

olange, who suffered agonies of guilt over being "such a terrible burden," liked to remind me that had it not been for her, I would never have met my first husband, who was working at one of the hospitals where she was a patient. In fact, we all used to say that I had married Jeremy because, given Solange's situation, we needed a psychiatrist in the family. We were joking, of course. But when Jeremy and I were getting divorced, he took to saying it often, unjoking, until it became "the *only* reason you married me." And in that extreme moment, when I was having such a hard time remembering why on earth I *had* married a man with whom I had nothing in common, who was not really my type, and who was so obviously incapable of making me (or, as I sometimes insisted, *any* woman) happy, I quit arguing and accepted the possibility that this ridiculous reason had been there all along. After all, I certainly was desperate when I became engaged to Jeremy. Solange was at her worst then, and I had never felt more overburdened and in need of help. And, as will become clear, I had other reasons for feeling wretched.

Look at me: married and divorced in the same paragraph—dispensed with Husband One in a few lines! And yet we were together for five years. He is the father of my daughter. In the way of many exes, he has come to hold but a small place in my thoughts. I almost never remember Jeremy, and were it not for Zoe I might know nothing about him today. For the sake of nostalgia, I bring to the surface one magical week in Rome, my shameless pride in his medical degree, and the sweetness of shared joy as we fussed together over our newborn.

I will add that in fact Jeremy never was much help with Solange. She is not my patient, he would say. I cannot make decisions as if I were her doctor just because I happen to be a relative. Not that he was much help as a relative, either. Over the years Solange has had many doctors, some good, some bad, but the only relative she has had throughout this ordeal has been me. She has had many kinds of therapy, from analysis to electroconvulsive treatments (the latter at least temporarily effective, the former not at all), and though we cannot know for sure, it seems the worst may be behind us. As I write this, Solange has gone almost ten years without needing to be hospitalized (before that, it was at least once every two years), and for this we give thanks to a certain Dr. Well (nice name for a doctor) and increasingly effective drugs.

The first time Solange was hospitalized, when I was asked by her attending about family history, I thought of our mother—her rages, her depressions, her inability to love—all of which I now saw in a different light. Later, I would watch my own children closely—too closely—panicking again and again at any sign of moodiness or low spirits. It was Dr. Well who suggested that if Solange tried putting her troubles into words, it might help her to order and understand them. These words would eventually pile up into her memoir. And once she had accepted that her dream of being a pop star was never going to happen, she went from writing songs to writing poetry.

Solange had come back into my life immediately after Ann had gone out of it. There followed a number of years when I wasted little time thinking about Ann; I was sure we'd never have anything more to do with each other. (I believe you have to reach a certain age before you understand how much life really is like a novel, with patterns and leitmotifs and turning points, and guns that must go off and people who must return before the ending.) For one thing, I had my hands full with Solange. (This was before I met Jeremy.) For another, Ann belonged to a time from which I felt very distant (more distant than I do today, in keeping with one of the many paradoxes of memory). I was not nostalgic at all then for school days; I was merely relieved they were over. I was lackadaisical about staying in touch with old classmates. I did not even like to be reminded of college, where I had been so miserable, where I had felt like such a failure in every way. And of course I had good reason not to want to think about Ann. In certain weather there'd be the throb in my thumb that would bring back our last meeting, and my entire being would throb with shame. If I never told anyone that disgraceful story, perhaps somehow it would be as if it had never happened. For a while I lived in fear of running into Ann or Kwame. I never did, but recently I had heard something about them. They were no longer living on Tiemann Place. A fire had destroyed their apartment, and they had had to move. I had no idea where they'd gone. Once, when I had drunk too much at a party and returned home alone and awash in sentiment, I looked for their names in the phone book. I looked under Drayton and under Kwesi and under Blood, but I did not find them. After that, as if a line had been cut, Ann all but disappeared from my thoughts. This changed abruptly in the spring of 1976. And from that time to this, it is no exaggeration to say I have never stopped thinking about her. There was a period—endless in memory though probably actually just a few months—when she would be the first thing on my mind when I woke up in the morning, after nights through which thoughts of her had disrupted my sleep.

At that time, I used to buy the newspaper on my way to work every day. And so that is where I was, standing on the platform at the Seventy-second Street subway station (I had by then moved from Ninety-sixth Street to Seventy-third Street and Riverside Drive), when I read the news—news I knew instantly to be false—throwing me into confusion. Had the train just then hissing into the station turned out to be Puff the Magic Dragon, the shock could not have been worse. Dooley Drayton (*Dooley!* I had all but forgotten) had killed a cop.

I did not board the train. Instead, I climbed the stairs back up to the street and walked into a coffee shop. I sat down at the counter and ordered a cup of coffee, which I would leave untouched. I laid the newspaper flat on the counter, and I read the article and read it again, unable to fathom how a story that could not be true could be printed there, in black and white—as if this particular copy of *The New York Times* had been one of those joke editions found in novelty shops, no more factual than the *National Lampoon* or *Mad* magazine.

Ann had killed a cop. She had shot a cop twice, in the head and in the neck, and he—an Officer Sargente, thirty-one, of Bay Ridge, Brooklyn, husband and father of two—was dead. She had shot his partner as well, wounding him in the leg. This extraordinary event had allegedly taken place in the meatpacking district, in broad daylight, just after noon, in fact, but on a Sunday, when the area was completely shuttered and deserted. According to police, Sargente and his partner, an older officer named Heffernan, had been pursuing a motorcyclist later identified as Alfred Blood, a.k.a. Kwame Kwesi, from a few blocks away. Kwame had not been wearing a helmet (in later reports, he was wearing a helmet, but the chin strap was not secured). He had been driving erratically (later: he had run a red light). Once the police officers had got him to stop, Kwame was said to have become disorderly. He had shouted threats and obscenities and refused to obey the officers' commands. They had been attempting to calm him down when, without warning, from a second-story window of a two-story building on Gansevoort Street, came shots. As Officer Sargente went down, Kwame turned and ran. Almost at the same instant, Heffernan was hit in the leg, and he fired at Kwame, hitting him in the back. Heffernan managed to crawl behind the police cruiser and call for help. Officers who arrived on the scene entered the building and found Ann, who surrendered peacefully. She had just called an ambulance. As she was being taken away, Ann asked the police if she could see Kwame. Later: "I didn't know if he was alive or dead." The police would not let Ann see Kwame, and he was dead.

The article in the *Times* began on the front page, and on the inside page where the story continued was the photograph I have mentioned once before, showing Ann outside the police station where she would be booked, her hands cuffed behind her and her long hair hiding her face. "The petite, attractive blonde is the only child of Turner and Sophie Drayton." I had completely forgotten her father's first name. Sophie's and Turner's photographs, too, would soon be appearing in various papers, and they would be glimpsed on television, and I would remember how, when I first met them, they had looked to me blood related. They looked that way still, and they looked harrowed.

The article did not mention that Kwame had been an elementary school teacher or that Ann was enrolled at Columbia's Teachers College. But these facts, along with much else about them, especially about Ann, made their way into later reports, as did the photograph from our freshman year, the one in *Newsweek*—Ann glowering between the faces of Malcolm X and Ho Chi Minh, with the quote that would now be quoted again and again: "What we want is for America finally to face up to its crimes."

I went on to my office—what else could I do?—but I did little work that day. I spent the morning making phone calls. I was trying to reach someone who might be able to tell me more than what I'd read in the paper. But no one could. Everyone I spoke to was dumbfounded, and I was reminded of the mood on campus the day we learned about the town house blowing up on West Eleventh Street. I thought of Sasha, and for the one and only time in my life I wished I knew where she was or how to get in touch with her. Many times in coming days I would think of calling Ann's parents, but this never seemed right to me. I was a stranger to them. I was not even a friend of their daughter's anymore. Besides, I knew they were probably the last two people on earth who'd be able to enlighten me.

That day, I went out to lunch with Cleo. I told her how certain I was that the report was all wrong. "It makes no sense whatsoever."

"But didn't you tell me she was with the Weathermen or something?" Cleo would not be the only one to make this mistake. It would even find its way into print here and there, along with the untruth that Kwame had once belonged to the Black Panther Party.

"She joined SDS when she was a freshman, but she was never with the Weathermen, no. She knew them—I mean, she was friends with some of them, yes. But in fact, she was completely disillusioned with SDS and the whole student movement even way back then. Anyway, she would never do anything like this—never. I don't know what really happened, but the only witness is the other cop, and why believe him? He killed Kwame. He could be lying."

"But that doesn't make any sense, either," Cleo said. "The cops didn't shoot themselves. And why did she have a gun? And what was she doing way over there by the river in the first place? No one lives over there. It's just meat storage and packing places and leather bars. What was she doing in that building standing by a window with a gun, like some kind of sniper? Where did she learn to shoot like that?"

"A lot of radicals learned how to use guns. It was part of their training. They learned street fighting and karate, too. The revolution was coming, and you had to be prepared. And you had to be ready to defend yourself, especially from the police." Had there really been a time (and not all that long ago) when this would not have sounded completely idiotic? I remembered the summer of 1969, when Ann had spent time at some kind of radical boot camp in California. I remembered, too, with a drowning feeling, that she had been a superb marksman, at least with a bow and arrow. Typical Ann: good at anything she put her mind to.

Cleo said, "All I can say is it's a good thing she's rich. She's going to need the best lawyer money can buy. I mean, we're talking about a cop killing. Not too long ago that could get you the death penalty. Your old roommate could end up in jail for the rest of her life."

"That would be completely insane," I said—so loud, people at neighboring tables stared.

Back at the office, I got hold of a radio and listened to the news at the top of each hour, but the story remained frustratingly unchanged. The mystery as to what Ann had been doing on a Sunday in an empty building in that nonresidential area would not be answered until I got home. According to the evening news, the room from where the shots had been fired (and there was no doubt about who had fired them: Ann had been all alone inside, and the police had taken the "murder" weapon from her) was an illegal loft space above a meat-storage center. There the police had also found, besides the Smith & Wesson taken from Ann, a cache of weapons, including various handguns and knives, grenades, shotguns, and assault rifles; illegal drugs (sleeping pills, marijuana, and amphetamines); and literature calling for the overthrow of the government, death to the police, and death to the rich. (In court, the defense would point out that you could find the very same "inflammatory" literature on many campus bookshelves and bulletin boards and in many ordinary bookstores as well.)

By the late news, the storage space had become "a possible safe house used by the Weather Underground or other political extremists." Evidently the name on the lease was a false one, thought to be an alias of a suspect long sought by the FBI in connection with several bombings.

The phone rang, and it was Cleo, who had just watched the same program. "See? There definitely seems to be a political connection here." Though I was still convinced otherwise, I had to admit things were beginning to look very, very bad. Then I remembered the fire.

"It was an emergency. They came home one day and their building was gutted. I think they were crashing in that loft because they knew someone there. Just because radicals might have stayed there too doesn't mean Ann and Kwame were involved with them."

"Uh-huh. Like, the jury is really going to believe that."

But in fact I had guessed right. Ann, who would plead not guilty, gave exactly this explanation for what she had been doing in the loft space, where she and Kwame had been staying for about two months. She did not deny knowing the loft was illegal or that it had been used by political radicals, including fugitives. But she refused to give any names or information, as she also refused to give any information about the training camp she had been to in Oakland. She said, "I realize how grave my own situation is, but that is no reason for me to betray friends and comrades."

Why did no one believe her? Ann's explanation did not seem to me so incredible. It was not nearly as preposterous as some other explanations people would turn out to have no trouble swallowing. "We believe that the crime may have been planned. The officers may have been lured to the site precisely so as to be murdered there. At this point, we also believe there may have been more than two suspects involved." (A spokesman for the police.) When questioned as to where Kwame was coming from the day of the shooting, Ann replied—with the haughtiness that would be the despair of her defense counsel and of anyone else concerned with her fate— that she didn't know. "We did not have that kind of bourgeois relationship, in which one always has to know exactly where the other one is and what he or she is doing."

At an early press conference, the district attorney had answered journalists' questions about motive with a wild guess. "Possibly this attack was intended as some kind of loony left action in response to the nation's bicentennial. Possibly there is some connection to the case of Patricia Hearst" (whose conviction had come just a little earlier that year). "We're still in the first stages of our investigation, but we do know for certain what kind of element we are dealing with. We are dealing with an element that has made hostility to the American government and to law enforcement abundantly clear. We are talking about an element with known associations to radical terrorists and close ties to fugitives from justice. We are talking about murder and attempted murder, and about a cold-blooded killer who has yet to show the least sign of remorse. We will prosecute this case to the fullest extent of the law, and our goal will be to ensure that the executioner of Officer

Thomas Sargente, who leaves behind a young wife and two small children, will never spend another day of freedom in her life." (Starting immediately. Because of her close ties to radical fugitives who, with the help of an organized underground network, had been eluding capture for years now, and because of her access to considerable family wealth, Ann was deemed a high flight risk and denied bail.)

Tommy Sargente had a beautiful face, a pretty-boy face, younger-looking than his thirty-one years. For a time, that face seemed to be everywhere. His poor widow seemed to be everywhere as well. Always with one or the other of her children in her arms, often flanked by her stone-faced in-laws. And even though there was no death penalty in New York State at the time, Mrs. Sargente kept bringing it up. "For me, that would be the only true justice." It seemed capital punishment was on other minds as well. The prosecutor himself was a strong advocate of reinstating the death penalty and of making it once again mandatory for anyone convicted of killing a police officer. (He just had to wait another nineteen years.)

"She's going to need someone like Kunstler," said Cleo. And she could have had him. William Kunstler would have been willing to take Ann's case, but Ann refused. Her parents would have been willing to pay anything for her defense, but Ann would not have this, either. She had no intention of taking advantage of the special privileges the Draytons' fortune and social position gave her. She would not follow the heiress Patricia Hearst and hire a formidable hotshot lawyer like F. Lee Bailey. She would make her way through the criminal justice system in exactly the same way as any poor, unknown person, with a court-appointed public defender. I thought she must have been pleased that the appointed attorney turned out to be black.

But this decision won her no points with most people. "What the hell is she trying to prove?" "Now she can plead insanity and no one will doubt it." "Oh, I get it: the martyr syndrome." "If you're rich, you can't play poor." These are some of the things I remember hearing around the office. "She's just putting her principles into practice," I said. But why did this sound so lame? It was the same now as it had been back in school: Why was I always so bad at defending her? I remember also how, among some of those covering her story, Ann was called stupid, wildly inappropriate names. The Ice Princess, for example. And, after Patricia Hearst's famous guerrilla alias, Tania Two. Someone writing in the *Daily News* referred to Ann's "Joan of Arc complex." (*Joan of Arc?*)

Soon after Ann's indictment I wrote her a letter in which I tried, albeit clumsily, to express my feelings, including my regret over how we had parted—was ever any letter harder to write?—and how sorry I was about Kwame, and was there anything at all I could do for her? No reply. (I confess, with shame, to the childish hurt this gave me.) So I watched the whole spectacle as just another outsider. But during the whole time, beginning with Ann's arrest and all through her trial, I felt often physically ill, as if instead of a daily vitamin pill I were ingesting something mildly toxic every morning. I had the feeling you get from riding a long time in the back of a bus. My appetite decreased, and I lost weight—though nothing compared to Ann, who would appear on the first day of her trial looking, as someone described her, like a walking skeleton. "Was it the jail food, Dooley?" shouted one reporter, in that familiar, ribbing tone so many would take with her. Ann looked at the man with a stunned expression, as if she thought she could not have heard right. "No," she said. "It was grief."

COP SLAYER DENIED REQUEST TO ATTEND LOVER'S FUNERAL.

Ann was neither a blood relative of the deceased, her jailers explained, nor his legal spouse. But this cruelty may have turned out to be for the best. There had been a big demonstration outside the Harlem public school where Kwame was teaching at the time of his death, with sobbing children and thundering spokesmen. "The black community is outraged that the police officer who shot Kwame Kwesi in the back has yet to be charged with a crime." (That death would be ruled a "justifiable homicide.") But it was as if Kwame's death and Ann's case were two entirely separate incidents. Whatever feelings about Kwame were seething among African-Americans appeared not to extend to his girlfriend. The only one who had a word for her was Kwame's elder sister, Dee Dee: "If it weren't for that crazy fool, my brother would still be alive." No member of Kwame's family would attend Ann's trial. And even before the trial got under way, news coverage tended to focus almost exclusively on Ann. With time, Kwame came to be mentioned hardly at all.

"Are you a political prisoner, Dooley?"

Her blue eyes, immense now in her gaunt face, turned a pitying gaze on the reporter who'd asked her this. "Yes," she said. "And so are you."

From her downtown jail cell, Ann, who had refused all interviews, issued a statement:

> *I killed Officer Thomas Sargente. I did not conspire to kill him. Allegations that Kwame Kwesi and I, possibly acting with other persons, had devised a scheme to lure police to a place where they might then be executed in keeping with some extremist political position are totally false. I am not now (though I was at one time) a member of any radical political organization. I do not advocate the violent overthrow of the government of the United States. I shot Thomas Sargente and his partner, Theodore Heffernan, for one reason only, and that was to protect my beloved friend and comrade, Kwame Kwesi, from a danger in which I perceived him to be at that time, meaning a danger to his life.*

According to Ann, it was shouting in the street that had brought her to the window.

I knew right away what must have happened. Kwame, who had been out riding his new motorcycle—it was his first bike, and he was still getting used to it—had been followed and stopped by the police. It was clear that he was very angry. He was shouting at the officers, demanding to know why he had been stopped. I want to say that as a rule, Kwame was not a hot-tempered or belligerent person. As anyone who knew him will attest, he tended to be calm even under pressure, and he had exceptional patience, the kind of patience you must learn if you are going to dedicate your life to young children, as he had done. But at this particular moment Kwame did not appear to be himself. I do not know how else to describe it. He was shouting at the police. He was cursing them. He was so worked up I hardly recognized him.

Watching this scene from behind the window curtain, Ann said, she was deeply afraid.

It was an angry confrontation between an Afro-American male and two white officers, the kind of confrontation that might easily turn violent. I had in mind the countless instances of brutality against Afro-Americans at the hands of police. I had in mind men like Fred Hampton and George Jackson, to name only the two most famous black men murdered by members of law enforcement in recent years. And here were the police shouting at Kwame to get on his knees, and here was Kwame shouting back, challenging their authority, their right to have stopped him when, as he kept shouting, he had done nothing wrong.

In fact, Ann said she could not explain Kwame's behavior to herself. "He had to have known he was in danger." And after all, as a former member of SNCC, he had undergone training in how to behave so as to minimize antagonism in confrontations with police. Recently, though, he had been having difficulties. There had been the fire, just two months earlier, in which they lost their apartment and all their possessions. There had been ongoing tension between Kwame and members of his family, who did not approve of his relationship with Ann. Add to this the daily pressures of working as a schoolteacher in the ghetto, and a recently diagnosed incurable illness: diabetes. Finally, Kwame's father, whom he loved very much, had died that past fall.

Perhaps as a result of this cluster of stresses and strains, he was in such a vulnerable state that at this moment of confrontation something in Kwame snapped. I must add that it was not the first time Kwame had been stopped by police for no legitimate reason. He did not even have to be driving. Once, walking near the Metropolitan Museum of Art, he was stopped by a patrolman who wanted to know what Kwame was doing in that neighborhood at that hour. It was the middle of the day. He was on his way to the museum.

Longer ago, in his Communist and SNCC days, Kwame had been involved in several clashes with police, and during those years when the FBI was engaged in its full-out assault against the Black Panther Party, African-Americans like Kwame who also happened to be political activists were routinely subjected to police surveillance and harassment.

It was when she saw Officer Sargente pull his gun ("He was standing about three yards away from Kwame, with Heffernan a yard or so behind Sargente and to his right; Heffernan had not pulled his gun, but his hand was on his holster") that Ann ("as if by blind instinct") went to the closet, where she knew the weapons were kept, and returned to her post with the Smith & Wesson.

The scene had changed. Kwame was now completely silent.

Sargente (shouting): Get down on your knees, nigger, and get your hands up over your head.

Kwame (still calm): Oh. So now you want to *shoot* me for driving a motorcycle while black?

Sargente: Nigger, I am going to blow your fucking nigger head off if you don't do as I say.

Kwame: Nigger this, nigger that. How about I teach you a new word, motherfucker?

Heffernan: Don't be a fool, now, boy.

Sargente: Nigger, do you want to die? Because I will blow your fucking nigger head off.

How could I not believe Officer Sargente? Anyone hearing his voice would have believed him. Those who say he was only trying to intimidate Kwame may be right. But that is not how it seemed to me at the time. I believed— indeed, I have never been so sure of anything in my life—that the worst was about to happen. I saw it as clearly as if it were happening already: Kwame was not going to obey the officers. He was not going to put up his hands and get down on his knees. He was going to be shot by Officer Sargente. He was going to be killed before my eyes. And so I shot first.

According to Ann, it was not true that Kwame then turned and ran.

He had no time to run. He spun around and looked up at the window. I am sure he knew exactly what had happened. He turned, and he was looking for me. And I made the mistake of looking back at him. And in that split second that I took my eyes off Heffernan, he pulled his gun. I fired at Heffernan, but it was too late. He had already shot Kwame in the back.

These are the facts. When I shot at the officers Sargente and Heffernan, I was acting in the belief that I would save the man I loved. Had Officer Sargente merely been threatening Kwame with his gun, it would have been terrifying enough. But it was the way he was pointing the gun and at the same time screaming nigger, nigger, nigger*—the word itself was like a bullet.*

And then some demon prompted Ann to add the line that would make her briefly world famous and help seal her fate.

If Thomas Sargente had said nigger *one less time, he might not be dead.*

It was said you could hear the champagne corks popping all over the D.A.'s office. Ann had made it possible to argue that she not only shot Sargente but shot to kill, and even that she *regretted* not having blown Heffernan away as well. And in all her lengthy statement, she had included not one word of remorse.

"She's a killer *and* a liar," said Heffernan, whose leg was still far from healing (indeed, he would never walk properly again). "Officer Sargente never said no such word." (Under oath he would amend this somewhat. "It is possible, I admit. We were under a lot of stress. We did not know if this wild man was armed or what his next crazy move might be. But if that word was used? I don't know. Maybe once. I would remember if it was over and over, like she says.")

As it turned out, nobody had ever heard Officer Sargente say such a word (nobody in those days called it the N-word, either). His wife told reporters he would have smacked his kids silly if he ever heard them say it, and his parents insisted "he just wasn't raised like that."

The defense attorney's motion to prevent Ann's statement from being brought up during the trial was denied on the grounds that Ann herself had chosen to make it part of the public record.

Why would anyone go and do something so blatantly against her own interests? was the question everyone kept asking.

Well, she had this thing about always telling the whole truth, I explained. But every time I gave this answer, I would think, How lame. How utterly lame it sounded. (As lame-sounding as the explanations some radicals give today for their past behavior: we saw what America was doing in Vietnam, and it drove us crazy.)

"Because it's bullshit," said Cleo. "Her whole story. All she had to do was stick her head out the window and let the police know she was there, she was watching, so whatever they had in mind, there'd be a witness. Isn't that what any sane person would have done? Or was she scared they'd shoot her blond head off? I don't think so."

"Well, I think she must have been worried about drawing attention to that place."

"Well, *I* think she just wanted to shoot someone. And I think she's nuts."

"You don't know her."

"No, but I know her kind. These spoiled rich kids who want to play revolution, and all they end up doing is making a big fucking mess and destroying other people's lives. These rich white girls who have the hots for black men, so *proud* of themselves for being with poor black men, these girls who want to be black themselves, never realizing that if they *were* black, these men wouldn't even be with them. *Ghetto groupies.* Make me sick."

Cleo's harsh judgment of Ann, her contempt and utter lack of sympathy, were hard for me. Our friendship cooled during this time, we had quite a few words over Ann, and the trial would long be over before Cleo and I could be comfortable enough to enjoy each other's company again.

Not that Cleo was alone in her feelings. Riding the subway to work, I eavesdropped on three young black women huddled over a copy of the *Daily News*.

"Oh, what is *wrong* with that woman? Who does she think she is?"

"This rich white lady trying to be the black man's big friend."

"Now she wants everyone to believe this was a righteous thing she did."

"Like she was just trying to defend her man."

"All she did was get him blown away!"

"I don't believe a word that woman says."

"She's a crazy woman. They should lock her up."

"What was he doing with her, anyway?"

Should I have jumped in and said something? What should I have said?

———

Remember what the Panthers had to say about the Weathermen: We do not support them or share their agenda. They might think they are helping black people, they might see themselves as engaged in a revolution to liberate blacks from white oppression, but we do not see ourselves in alliance with them, and we do not authorize them to speak in our name.

A sympathetic columnist in the *Amsterdam News* suggested that Ann was being used as an antimiscegenation object lesson: See what disastrous things can happen when you don't stick to your own kind? (The Supreme Court decision to strike down interracial marriage bans was then not quite ten years old.)

I learned later that Ann had begun receiving hate mail, sacks of it, and would go on receiving such mail for years. *"Dear Nigger Lover."*

*

Nineteen seventy-six—and by the time the trial was over almost 1977—that is, much closer to the eighties than to the sixties. By the year of the bicentennial, the movement had lost most of its steam. This had everything to do with the end of the draft, followed by the end of the Vietnam War. The underground was said to be rapidly dissipating. The last bombing for which the Weather Underground had claimed responsibility had been in June 1975. (Still ahead, though, lay the huge surprise of the 1981 Brinks robbery, which would bring things full circle with the capture of radical Kathy Boudin, last seen fleeing the bombed Greenwich Village town house, eleven years before.) A number of radical fugitives were making plans now to come up and surrender to the law, which may partly explain why there was silence from the underground about Ann's case. During the trial itself, outside the courthouse on some but not all days, a sad few held signs reading FREE DOOLEY DRAYTON and JUSTICE FOR KWAME KWESI—and to see those people and those slogans was to understand just how bygone the protest era really was. It was like hearing one voice singing "We Shall Overcome."

And from the beginning it was impossible for Ann to escape the shadow of Patricia Hearst. For one thing, the Hearst case, in all its bizarre details, had been publicized as no case before, beginning with her kidnapping by the Symbionese Liberation Army in 1974 and their demand that her family donate millions of dollars' worth of food to the poor. Next came the startling communiqué from the victim herself—she had joined the SLA and was henceforth to be known as Tania (after Che Guevara's mistress)—followed by her participation in an armed bank robbery, her capture by the FBI, and her trial (hyped as the Trial of the Century), at which the jury refused to believe she had been brainwashed. At the time of Ann's arrest, Hearst had just begun serving a seven-year sentence in a federal prison. (About two years later, President Carter would commute this sentence to time served, and President Clinton would grant Hearst a full pardon in 2001.)

Between Patricia Hearst and Ann there were indeed some slight similarities. They were both young women from wealthy families who had renounced the privileges to which they'd been born and condemned their own class, their own families. They both had taken up guns; they both had had sexual relations with black men, though Hearst would say that her relations with SLA leader Donald DeFreeze (killed along with several other SLA members in a shoot-out with Los Angeles police) were part of the "Stockholm syndrome" that had been her unsuccessful defense. Photographs of Hearst had been widely published, including one in which she was wearing a revolutionary-style beret and holding a submachine gun, with the SLA's seven-headed-snake symbol in the background. As it turned out, in some photos, and in that one in particular, she bore a resemblance to Ann. They could have been sisters. And that was exactly how a lot of people saw them, as sisters.

In at least half the articles I read about Ann's case, the name of Patricia Hearst was also mentioned.

During the time that Hearst and the SLA were making head-lines, an article about political radicals appeared in *Rolling Stone*. "Once upon a time, radicals were cool. Radicals were sexy. You looked up to them, even if you didn't always completely agree with them. Secretly, you wished you could be like them. But now, let's face it, all that has changed. *Death to the fascist insect that preys on the life of the people!*" (The SLA slogan.) "Remember when you could hear somebody say something like that without giggling? Remember when everyone who had a bank account *ran with capitalist dogs?* It's not just that radicals no longer seem cool. They have come to seem downright ridiculous. Looking back at the violent excesses of such groups as the Weathermen (to say nothing of wackos like the SLA), you find yourself asking, What was *that* all about?"

Remember when *Soul on Ice* made the *New York Times* list of the ten best books of '68?

Like Patricia Hearst, Ann was warned by counsel how important her demeanor with her parents could be to the outcome of the trial. But in Ann's case the warning went unheeded. The Draytons were in the courtroom every day, and later, more than one juror would remark on Ann's obvious detachment from them, as opposed to the genuine warmth she quite clearly felt for her lawyer. Also noted was Ann's seeming indifference to the hostility from the police officers who packed the courtroom and who glared murderously at her and sometimes even made comments.

"She did not seem to be at all intimidated," a juror said. "It was like nothing could intimidate her." In fact, that was the general impression: the defendant was fearless, she was strong, she was consistent, and as the jury foreman would put it, "She just did not seem to like white folks."

efense attorney Lester Prysock would have to persuade the jury that whatever Ann was, she was no cold-blooded killer: "This woman never *intended* to kill anyone at all." The jurors must begin by remembering exactly who this young woman was *before* the tragedy that had brought her to this courtroom—a fate no one who had known her at any point in her life so far would ever have predicted. Several witnesses (including former teachers of Ann's, among them Barnard professor Otis Keeble, with whom she had studied Afro-American literature) gave testimony about Ann's character, giving proof, according to the defense, that all her life she had been admired as much for her ethics and idealism as for her academic performance. According to one witness, Ann had "the strongest conscience of any young person I have ever known." Another called her "the most truthful person I have ever known." A third remembered how, in high school, she was sometimes referred to as "our future first woman president."

"Ladies and gentlemen, could this same youngster also have been *our future heartless murderer?*"

Yes, it was true that Ann had participated in antiwar demonstrations, and no, those demonstrations had not always remained peaceful, and yes, she had been among those unlucky enough to be hauled off by police. But now that the war was over, now that the American government itself had seen fit to end the conflict in Southeast Asia and bring the troops home, who could say that those protesters had not behaved with just cause? The prosecution's attempt to paint Ann as much more than an antiwar activist, as some kind of loony left extremist allied with those seeking the violent overthrow of the U.S. government and the capitalist system, was simply wrong. There was no evidence whatsoever that she had ever been a violent person. No. But she was a *passionate* person. And she was, make no mistake about it, a person of strong beliefs. She was a person who believed first of all in caring passionately about the poor and the oppressed—about anyone less fortunate than herself.

At the time of her arrest, what kind of life had the defendant been living? A life of crime? Of course not. The life of a disaffected social dropout—or a revolutionary urban guerrilla? No. Ann Drayton had been preparing to take her place in society as a member of that most noble and selfless of professions: teaching. Her intention once she had earned her degree was to serve where the need was most urgent—our troubled inner-city schools. Her goals were what they appeared always to have been. To help other people. To do good.

In fact, it was clear that from a very early age Ann had been unusually sensitive to the suffering of others. Her mother described for the court an incident that occurred when Ann was a little girl and was taken by her parents to the city of New Haven. And there in a park they encountered a man all filthy and in tatters and lying on the ground. And little Ann, all of six years old, seeing such a sight for the first time in her young life, had forced her parents to stop. She had demanded they take the poor fellow home with them. And when her parents refused, she wept. And Mrs. Drayton, with a gentle smile on her mournful face, told the court how, the next day, little six-year-old Ann had set out from their house, alone, with food she had taken from the kitchen and a blanket she had taken from her own bed, determined to find her way back to New Haven and that park and that man—only to be stopped by a neighbor who led the poor little thing back home.

But a week later Ann was still trying to talk her parents into adopting the stranger.

"And to this day," said Mrs. Drayton, wiping a tear, "I honestly don't believe she ever forgave us."

And the jury heard about other incidents from Ann's youth: her hysterical response to photographs of thalidomide victims and of people in different parts of the world suffering from famine or disease, to news coverage of police dogs attacking civil rights protesters down South and of carnage in Vietnam. During a classroom discussion of the crimes of Adolf Eichmann, Ann had begun vomiting and had to be sent home. Her reaction to the murder of four girls of about her own age in the bombing of a black church in Alabama had left her unable to eat for days.

The psychologist from whom the Draytons had sought help for their young daughter also testified at the trial. In another patient, he said, he might have read such behavior as self-dramatizing and a bid for attention, which would hardly have surprised him in a girl her age. But Ann's case was different. For one thing, she was already receiving more than her share of attention; she was not clinically depressed, and in most ways appeared to be not only normal and well-adjusted but thriving. What she lacked was the necessary coping mechanism when faced with evidence of life's cruelties or man's inhumanity to man. No, he would most certainly not describe young Ann as mentally ill.

But could such supersensitivity cause distortions of perception and leave a person vulnerable to emotional scars?

Of course.

The prosecution would not have the jury forget for one moment that, unlike the sad majority of those indicted for felony crimes, this defendant had not come from a bad home, she had not been abandoned or deprived as a child, she had never herself been a victim of violence or of any sort of abuse or neglect. A fairy-tale childhood, the prosecution called it.

A fairy-tale childhood? Ladies and gentlemen, there was a fairy tale going on here, all right, and it was the fairy tale that *any* child in our day could be protected from the harsh realities of our planet. For a time, at the advice of the psychologist, the Draytons had tried to limit their daughter's exposure to newspapers and television, but of course this had not worked. Birmingham, Vietnam, Auschwitz, war, racism, riots, needless death, disease, torture, starvation, violence, and misery of every kind—there was no hiding any of this from Ann or from any other child of her generation. But without a doubt these things had cut deeper with Ann than with other children. If her parents had only known, perhaps they could have locked their little girl away somewhere, in a little hut at the heart of some fairy-tale forest. Or if only that doctor had been able to prescribe something, some *pill*, let us imagine, to make her grow a second skin.

The prosecution wanted the jury to bear in mind the defendant's coddled upbringing, her immunity from hard knocks. But in fact, upon examination, the truth turned out to be quite different. The truth was that at the same time young Ann was learning about all the evil that existed in the world, she was also learning that *she herself was the cause of it*. She was learning that all the wonderful advantages and good things she enjoyed in life were hers *only through the exploitation of others less fortunate*. For such was the teaching of the sixties, the era in which she had come of age. Those victims whose suffering tore at her insides—by whom were they being victimized if not by her own? *Her* race, *her* class. *They* were the guilty ones, the evil ones, the scourge of society, the cancer of history. Rich, white, and American: morally, spiritually, you did not get any lower than this—wasn't that what people were saying? The history of her kind was a history of hideous brutality, to be a have was to be a mass murderer—this was the terrible truth from which Ann could not hide.

So appalled had she been to learn that her given name, Dooley, was the surname of a southern branch of the family whose ancestors had probably owned slaves that she rejected it. Her very own name, the name her parents had chosen for her, had become hateful to her, tainted by association with the worst abomination she could imagine. But she was no fool; she knew that salvation was not so easy as changing your name.

But what did it mean to be a young person of such precocious sensitivity and to have it carved into your heart and brain that the worst sins committed all over the globe, the worst sins committed down through the ages, sins that had caused the most horrendous suffering to countless millions of innocents, sins for which no proper amends or adequate reparations could ever be made, were your *true* inheritance, the legacy of your kind?

The rich are pigs, the rich are dogs, the rich deserve to die. Nothing the rich man owns has not been paid for with the blood of the poor man—weren't we all familiar with the rhetoric by now? What happens to a vulnerable girl who, in her teens—those years when she is perhaps most susceptible to criticism—undergoes this kind of barrage, constantly being told she is an enemy of the People?

Yet another psychological expert was called to the stand to suggest what conflicts might arise, what agonies of self-hatred and abysses of despair. (Overheard: "I can't believe the state pays for this crap.")

And this unhealthy situation only worsens once Ann is in college. She throws herself into the movement, and to many it seems she is in her element. She is even something of a campus star. But by her second year, disillusioned both with the ways of the elitist university system and with student politics, she drops out.

It is just over a year later that she meets Kwame Kwesi, a soul mate who has struggled with many of the same issues as Ann but who appears to have found peace. At least, he is living the kind of quiet but meaningful life she herself has come to crave. He is older than she by almost a decade, and he takes the role of mentor. They fall in love. They move in together. There is talk of marriage and of starting a family.

But alas, this rosy picture is not the whole picture—not by any means. Ann soon feels the weight of that heavy cross our society lays upon the interracial couple. A list of some of the insults she and Kwame were subjected to is read (against the prosecution's objection) to the courtroom. Evidence in the form of journal entries proves the defendant often feared that she and/or Kwame might be physically harmed.

And so, during the period leading up to the day of the shootings, how should we understand the defendant's state of mind? Upset, to some extent, surely, at having just lost everything in a fire and being temporarily homeless. Unhappy, naturally, at the ongoing tension caused by the difference in her and Kwame's skin color. And yet, for the most part, optimistic. For Ann had much to look forward to in life and was in many ways happier than she had ever been. Thanks to Kwame's influence, and doubtless also to growing older, she had shed much of her anger and discontent. Like so many of the protest generation, she was now ready to say goodbye to youthful rebelliousness and to assume a more mature role in society. Not that she had ceased to care about the world's have-nots; nor had she abandoned her own high standards for right living. For one thing, she would not be rich. She had cut herself off from family money, and as someone who abhorred Western consumerism and materialism, she had adopted a modest, disciplined life style. Whatever little money she could spare, she gave to those who had less, and whatever little spare time she had was put to community service. Of course, she still cared about politics—why wouldn't she? But here was no extremist or firebrand. In fact, except for certain ties and loyalties she had kept for friendship's sake, there had been absolutely nothing linking Ann to any radical activism in years.

The defense asked that the jury give particular weight to the fact that Ann had no siblings and, at the time of the shootings, was estranged from her parents. Because what this meant, ladies and gentlemen, was that at the time, Kwame Kwesi was all the family Ann Drayton had. And given this, was it so hard to understand how it must have affected her when she saw that this beloved person—remember, all she had in the world—might the next instant be blown to kingdom come?

"Ladies and gentlemen, the question you must ask yourselves is this: Was it really so incredible for Ann to draw the conclusion that an irate police officer pointing a gun at a black man and shouting 'nigger' at the top of his lungs might represent a real threat? Did Ann read the newspapers? Was she knowledgeable about Afro-American history and about the long, vexed relationship between this city's minorities and police? Did she not know the statistics? Did anyone seriously think her fears were—"

(Here, the members of the police force who were in the court-room that day began to jeer, and the judge, after making free use of his gavel, ordered a ten-minute recess.)

There were moments during the trial, Ann's father would later tell me, when he was convinced that the defense was going to sway the jury. "I didn't even mind that the whole world was hearing what Ann thought of her mother and me."

"Ladies and gentlemen, before coming to a verdict, you must do this: you must place yourselves with the defendant at that window. You must try to see through her eyes and enter her thoughts. For then, surely, you will understand that her fear was beyond a doubt a reasonable one."

Nigger, nigger, nigger. The slur of slurs. An epithet so violent and abusive it had already provoked god knew how many incidents of violence in retaliation, a word that had pulled how many triggers and led to tragedy how many times before.

The prosecution wished the court to decide that the use of the word, even if it had been uttered repeatedly as stated by the defendant, was irrelevant. For the law is clear: No matter how vile or vicious or hateful they might be, *mere words* could never be used to justify the taking of a life. But in this case it must be remembered that it was not just the use of the word, it was the use of the word *backed by a gun*.

"To the window, ladies and gentlemen, if you please. The defendant can hear the word and she can see the gun and she can see Officer Sargente himself, who is not only angry but youthful-looking, possibly inexperienced, certainly jumpy. And his gun is in his hand, and his hand is aiming, and his finger is on the trigger. What person would not see in this a situation ripe for explosion? A white man pointing a gun, a white man screaming, *'Nigger, get down on your knees or I will blow you away.'* "

A plan, a plot, a purpose, a design, an intent to kill? For this the prosecution has produced not one shred of evidence. No, something else was at work here, and that was the defendant's *reasonable* belief of *imminent* danger to Kwame Kwesi at the hands of Officer Sargente.

In the defendant's own words, written soon after the event, "I have never been so certain in my life . . . he was going to be shot . . . he was going to be killed before my eyes." Not in an hour, not tomorrow or next week, but *right then and there*. And it was this belief—this *reasonable* fear—that caused Ann Drayton to do what she would never *under any other circumstances* have allowed herself to do.

For consider, after the shooting had taken place, what had the defendant done? Had she tried to escape, as she certainly had opportunity to do, and to slip away into the underground, her connections to which the prosecution had sought to make so much of? She had not. Why? *Because, never having had any plan to kill, she had not made any plan to escape.* The defendant's actions had been entirely of the moment. Of course she had not tried to escape. And what had she done instead? She had phoned for an ambulance. She had not been trying to save herself, she had no thought for herself just then, but at that moment she was still trying to save her friend. And what had she said, exactly, what were her exact words, according to the police emergency tape? "We need an ambulance. Three men have been shot." *We. Three.* Clearly, the defendant's instinct had been to get help for the officers as well. And what did Ann do once the police arrived? Remember, she still had that gun. And as we know, there were other, more powerful firearms in that house. Well then, did she try to shoot it out? Did she try to take out as many "enemy" as possible, in true urban guerrilla style? No. She surrendered. Now, this was a woman who knew the law. She knew what it would mean to be indicted for the murder of a police officer. But although she had time, and although at that point she had yet to be identified, she made no attempt whatsoever to escape her fate.

Murder in the first degree? Every last thing the jury had learned about Ann Drayton's past and about her character proved that she was in fact incapable of committing the crime for which she was on trial. A person who had been known her entire life for caring more about other people than she cared about herself did not suddenly turn ruthless killer. An unfortunate set of circumstances had placed her in the terrible position of having had, to her mind, *no choice* but to act as she had done if the life of Kwame Kwesi was to be saved.

"'Nigger' pulled the trigger!" her enemies dubbed Ann's defense with glee.

As in the trial of Patricia Hearst, the jury reached a verdict much sooner than expected, catching everyone by surprise. Later, some of the jurors made themselves available for comment. "We did not believe there had been any conspiracy, but we also did not believe it was any 'tragic mistake.'" "We came round to believing the defendant was telling the truth and that everything happened more or less like she said." But the victim was still a police officer. And the crime was still murder one.

At Ann's sentencing, Mrs. Thomas Sargente read from a statement, and though it was very short it took her a long, tearful time to read. She said the hardest part for her was going to be explaining to her children as they grew up why they did not have a father.

The only person in the courtroom who was as emotional as Mrs. Sargente was Mrs. Drayton, who had missed the last three days of the trial on doctor's orders, out of concern for her heart.

Ann was reported, as defendants so often (strangely) are, as showing *no* emotion.

The judge asked Ann whether, before hearing her sentence, she had anything she wished to say, and when she said she did not, he gave her a look that was severe. He said that he was profoundly shocked and disappointed that the court had never heard the defendant express any shame or remorse for having taken the life of an innocent human being. He paused.

"Your Honor," said Ann in a voice that would be reported by some as "hostile and sneering" and by others as "weak," "trembly," and "full of fatigue"—"Your Honor, I am not a monster. Remember, I too have lost the man I loved. But I confess, it is still very difficult for me to accept that anyone who would point a loaded gun at another person while calling him a nigger is an innocent human being."

The judge looked as though she had slapped him. He paused again.

"People like you," he said at last, "who think you are the true arbiters of right and wrong, and that however you choose to act is justified—you want the world to believe that you are good, that your heart bleeds for the little man and you are the champion of the poor and oppressed. But in fact you are nothing but a spoiled, ignorant, arrogant girl, and you have nothing but contempt for other people—or at least for all those you cannot fit into your own childish fantasy of how the world ought to be. But people like you could never create a better world. How could you, when what you do best is to hate? You hated Thomas Sargente because he was a police officer, and therefore beyond love and forgiveness. That's right, to you he *wasn't* a human being. He was just a pig, and that's why you were able to pull the trigger that day.

"In prison, you will have plenty of time to reflect on this and perhaps with God's help will come to understand what you have done. There can be no possibility of atonement, for you can never restore Officer Sargente's life to him, but you may perhaps yet save your own soul.

"It is also my hope that your knowledge and talents as an educator might be used to serve and benefit your fellow inmates, the vast majority of whom have never had anything like your opportunities to better themselves.

"I do not know who or what is responsible for the behavior of young people like yourself, who start out in life with every promise, cherished by fine, decent parents, given every means to pursue good, productive, happy lives, and who end up throwing it all away, but God knows we've seen enough of you. It would be a blessing to think this sorry chapter in our country's political history is coming to an end. Your crime was reprehensible, but your lack of feeling is diabolical."

The sentence, twenty-five years to life, could be taken as good news. There had been speculation that Ann might receive the worst: life without parole.

"I will lose no sleep over this," said the judge. "May you serve as an example to others, and may you be the last of your kind."

Officer Heffernan, now walking with a cane, said a life behind bars was too good for her.

⁎

A month or so after the sentencing, Lester Prysock gave an interview to *The Village Voice*.

A fair trial? No. That's what I was afraid of from the beginning, even though the jury was mixed—there was an equal number of men and women, and five of the jurors were nonwhite. There was just too much confusion and too many wrong assumptions about who this defendant really was.

For one thing, I think a lot of people have trouble seeing Ann Drayton and Kwame Kwesi as a couple—as being in love. People just will not give her that. I was close to Ann, I saw how devastated she was by Kwame's death. She still is. But that didn't get to be part of the story. You get a feel for this sort of thing in a courtroom. When I was describ-

ing them as a loving, devoted couple planning a family, I felt some-thing, a stiffening or coldness, like people didn't want to hear too much about that. But it was important that their relationship be taken seri-ously and treated with respect.

No, it was not.

Sure. In fact, uncomfortable isn't the word. The interracial thing brought out something—I mean, the letters Ann got! And you know, I got letters, too, and just about all of them contained messages of racial hatred. I'm telling you, if I hadn't known it before, this would have been all the proof I needed about the kind of society we live in. Then I discovered there was a rumor going around—this was in some of those letters, too—that there was something sexual between Ann and me. So what was going on here? Would this have anything to do with my be-ing the same color as Kwame, and her being white?

Well, they can call it paranoid if they want. Just like they can accuse me of "playing the race card."

People just didn't know what to make of her. When she came out with that first statement, before the trial even began, about how if Sargente had said "nigger" one less time he might still be alive—those words were just too shocking. They were unacceptable. It was not just that they could be taken as a justification for what she'd done. Those words em-barrassed people everywhere, black and white. America was just not ready for this. It wasn't that this kind of talk was new to people. It was typical Black-Panther-Party-for-Self-Defense talk. But coming out of this young white woman's mouth? After shooting a cop? It was unac-ceptable. It turned Ann into a total scary monster to some people, and to others into a laughingstock, a clown. And then, consistent to the end, she goes and says basically the same thing at her sentencing. And this time it was even more shocking. It was like the whole courtroom gasped with a single breath. Reporters' pencils froze above their notepads. Even the cops were silent. The judge turned puce. But it's less shocking to anyone who knows how Ann felt about Kwame.

Of course. I had made it perfectly clear to her what the consequences would be of not expressing remorse.

That is between her and her conscience. I will not speak for her on that matter.

Ah, yes, the Patty Hearst connection! Can't leave that out. Talk about a laughingstock! Mind you, those two women are nothing like each other, and their cases were completely different. But try telling that to the American public. Well, in this way they were alike: Hearst didn't get a fair trial, either, in my opinion.

Yes, I do believe both women were victims of their times. The judge was speaking for a lot of people, I think—or at least that large part of the population that has become totally fed up with anyone radical and outspoken. But everyone can find a reason to hate Ann. To rich, conservative people she's an ingrate, a traitor to her class, a horrific warning about what could happen to their own kids. And those at the other end, leftists and poor people and minorities, they're all free to despise Ann for being nothing but a spoiled, rich white brat. It didn't matter that she walked away from the life she was born to. You know, the days of idealism are over, and we live in cynical times. Most people aren't willing to believe anyone isn't just as selfish and self-serving as everyone else. She's one of the last of her kind, all right, but not in the way the judge had in mind. People aren't willing to believe there really is more decency in Ann than self-righteousness, that her sensitivity and compassion aren't all just a pose. There's always something about the do-gooder that gets under other people's skin, whatever color it is, and if that person comes from money, it just makes matters worse. What it boils down to is something like this: if what you're doing comes out of your own personal guilt complex, then your motives can't be pure.

You know, I seem to recall a reference in some article about Ann and Joan of Arc. But the person she really brings to mind is Simone Weil.

Yes. I spoke to her just last week. She's okay. She's doing okay.

I think race had absolutely everything to do with everything in this case.

You'll have to ask her.

Who was this Simone Weil? At the time, just a name to me, someone I knew Ann idolized and one of several writers she was forever trying to get me to read.

I decided to find out about her.

A short life: 1909–1943. A terrible death. Suicide, her doctors called it, by starvation. In an English sanatorium, refusing to obey the orders of those treating her for tuberculosis; refusing (as she had been doing for some time even before her diagnosis) to eat more than the rations allotted to French citizens then under Nazi occupation (though most likely she was eating even less than that). The same person who, at age five, had refused to eat sugar because she knew French soldiers fighting the Germans had to do without it. And who, as a university student, broke down and wept at the news of famine in China. Her class: privileged, cultivated. Though her books would not be published until after her death, her intellectual gifts drew notice long before. She earned top honors at school and grew to be "a woman of genius," according to T. S. Eliot, "of a kind of genius akin to that of the saints." But this same great mind struck not a few people, including General Charles de Gaulle, as *deranged*.

Other descriptions: arrogant, difficult, violent, egotistical, obtuse, blind, melodramatic, noble; mystic, visionary, radical, ridiculous, passionate, humorless, selfless, selfless to the point of selfishness. Her great concerns were human suffering, the soul, and the degradation of the life of the spirit in the materialistic modern world. The fate of the poor and the oppressed obsessed her. What would it be like to be one of them? This she had to know firsthand, and so for a time she worked in a factory and later as a field hand. But she was first of all a teacher. She taught Greek and philosophy to girls.

All her life she strove—never to her satisfaction, to say the least—to live up to her ideals. She had no use for money or for the comforts it could buy. Most of her salary she gave away. She loathed bourgeois comforts—or any comfort, it seemed, at times rejecting a bed for the hard, cold floor. Never enough sleep, never enough nourishment, never enough rest. Never *any* sex: she had no use for pleasure, and besides, she disliked being touched. Killing migraines, chronic bad health. Never a complaint. She inspired many people and doubtless repelled many more. There was much hatred in her. Self-hatred, accused some. Hatred most definitely of the class she had been born into, of all bourgeois habits and values. And though Jewish, repudiating Judaism. "If there is a religious tradition which I regard as my patrimony, it is the Catholic tradition . . . The Hebraic tradition is alien to me." Because she wrote this in 1940, as anti-Jewish laws were being passed by the Vichy government, many have condemned her.

Though she did not treat her parents unkindly, she wasted little time or emotion on them. "If I had more than one life," she told them near the end, "I would have devoted one of them to you. But I had only one life." And she seemed to have known that it would not be long.

I felt the hairs on my skin rise at times, reading her.

"In this world only human beings reduced to the lowest degree of humiliation, much lower than mendicancy, not only without any social position but considered by everybody as deprived of elementary human dignity, of reason—only such beings have the possibility of telling the truth. All others lie."

"I wish my parents had been born poor!"

And: "I always believed and hoped that one day Fate would force upon me the condition of a vagabond and a beggar . . . I felt the same way about prison."

Prison?

She did not dream of love or fame or of being a great writer. She did not want happiness or success. About what she wanted she was consistently clear: to be poor, deprived, trampled, mortified, tortured, caged, starved, spat upon. Anyone forced to suffer profoundly, including Christ—*especially* Christ—provoked her envy.

If no one was willing to martyr her, she could martyr herself.

She never changed.

I was not surprised to learn that she judged women unequal to men, that she believed there was something about women's nature, some weakness or failing, that prevented them from developing first-rate minds. Femininity: like Ann, Weil despised it. But no doubt she would also have shared Ann's contempt for women's lib. Now I discovered that Weil, too, believed the world would be a better place if everyone wore the same simple clothes. And I had to smile when I read about her brief visit to New York, in 1942: the one and only thing in the capital of bourgeois corruption and materialism to find favor with Weil was—Harlem.

I could never bring myself to agree with those who, like Cleo, believed that Ann had a deep wish to kill someone. But that somewhere in her tangled depths lay the wish to be incarcerated had occurred to me more than once. I remembered how tormented she was over those times when she'd been arrested for acts of political protest and had got off with a slap on the wrist. How different things would have been, she said, if she had been black. (In 2003, when Kathy Boudin, having served twenty-two years for her part in the 1981 Brinks robbery, is granted parole, some of her former comrades will not be able to refrain from commenting that she'd still be behind bars if she were black.)

Simone Weil started out as a pacifist but ended up itching to fight. The outbreak of civil war drew her to Spain, but she had to be evacuated almost immediately after burning herself in a clumsy accident. Later she begged de Gaulle to allow her to be parachuted into occupied France so she could take on the Nazis—or at the very least help nurse wounded French troops. She had no fear for her own life. Certainly she saw herself as capable of taking a life, and when I tried putting her in Ann's place, I could even imagine her behaving as Ann had done.

✳

The Maryville Correctional Facility was about halfway between Manhattan and the town where I was born. One night not long after Ann had been transported there, I got drunk with Solange. "My god," I said, "she doesn't even *like* women. Now she has to spend the rest of her life locked up with them?" "At least most of them will be black," said Solange. True. And they would all be wearing the same simple clothes.

I was one of those for whom a life behind bars seemed a worse punishment than death. (After her sentencing, the Draytons had expressed concern that it might be necessary to put their daughter on suicide watch, to which Ann responded with her usual disdain, "You see how little they know me. What reason have I to want to kill myself, please?")

My own fear of imprisonment went way back. It began, I suppose, like so many other fears, with Mama (*Mama again!*), who was forever predicting this fate for her incorrigible brood (and to such a degree, you would even have said she *wished* this fate on us). In our town, there were always a couple of kids temporarily missing, doing time in juvenile hall, and among the grown-ups who had done or were doing time was our own Uncle Claude, who'd been caught stealing cars. But what swelled my fear to irrational size had nothing to do with any of these people or their real-life experiences, and everything to do with a movie Solange and I caught one night on *The Late Show*.

We were too young to be up for *The Late Show*; we were much too young to be watching a women's prison movie, but there we were, lying on our stomachs on the floor, just inches from the screen, the sound turned low so as not to wake Mama, who'd been snoring on the couch since prime time. Though more than forty years later I can recall almost every scene, the names of the characters have vanished. There is the girl: a pretty nineteen-year-old who is sent to the prison for helping her husband commit a robbery, and who arrives pregnant. She gives birth there, the doctor who has been called in for the delivery deploring the primitive conditions. The girl is told she has no choice: she must give up her baby. It is only the beginning of her sorrows.

There is the evil matron who inflicts as much pain and humiliation as she can. She has an opposite: a decent, caring woman who, though head of the prison, is no match for the matron and the corrupt male officials who support her.

The prison is an institution that can achieve only one thing: turning a tender, sensitive, reformable girl into a tough, irredeemable con.

The sufferings of the girl and her fellow inmates broke our hearts. We buried our faces in our arms to stifle our sobs. Mama slept. *We* would not sleep that night or for many nights after. For years, just knowing the movie was being shown on TV again could depress me. You could not have paid me to watch it a second time—but how to stop it from playing in my head?

One of the prison inmates, a friend of the girl's, hangs herself. In the yard one snowy day, the girl finds a kitten. The matron tries to take it away, and she and the girl fight, slapping and clawing at each other. This sparks a riot. The matron's revenge is to tie the girl to a chair and shave her head. This is the movie's climax and most horrific scene. There is an unforgettable close-up of the girl's screaming eyes (her mouth is gagged) as the hair is sheared with an electric razor. (I made my husband Jeremy throw *his* electric razor away.) It was a punishment not unheard of where we came from. Usually inflicted by mothers on daughters. In some cases, it was done with scissors, the hair hacked off close to the head, the scalp sometimes cut into the bargain. The day you showed up at school in this condition, you lost every friend you had. That moment of stunned silence followed by an explosion of noise. Children—boys, especially—were merciless, and such girls would be shunned completely, at least until the hair grew back. I never heard of any mother getting into trouble for doing this thing. Our mother only threatened to do it, but that threat had played a large part in Solange's running away.

To win parole, the girl prostitutes herself. (This part of the story I understood only years later; at the time I had no idea what those men wanted from her.) To the head of the prison, the decent woman, believer in rehabilitation and reform, is given the last word. As she watches the girl walk away, she says, "She'll be back."

It has been a long time. I may be mistaken about some details, but I still cannot bring myself to watch that movie again (it doesn't come around on TV anymore, but it must be available on video). The story may even be different from the way I remember it. But it is the way I have remembered it all my life that concerns me. Because my mother always harped on how we kids were going to end up in jail, I could have been watching my future on that screen. By the time I was nineteen myself, I knew better, of course, but I still had every reason to worry about Solange, especially after she ran away. "If he hadn't gone into the army, he'd have ended up in jail." About how many boys of my youth—including Guy—did I hear this said? "The army straightened him out" was another line you heard all the time. People said it about Elvis Presley, for one.

That bleak story with its pessimistic message rang true to what I knew about life, not just about the existence of brutality but about how suffering could destroy you. There was another view, of course, and it could be found in other movies and in many books, a view to which you were exposed in school from an early age and to a much greater extent in church: suffering as the path to sainthood and heroism, and even to ordinary goodness. But where was the evidence for this? Who in real life, among people I knew, had been strengthened and ennobled by suffering? How could being "reduced to the lowest degree of humiliation" bring out anything but the worst in a person? How could being deprived of reason lead to the truth? This idea of Weil's, an idea shared by Ann and others whom I met at the same time I met her, the idea that the have-not was closer to God, that he alone possessed the truth about life, and that his spirit was greater than that of all those who had never known his wretched condition, a condition that was to be envied and imitated—this idea was completely alien to me. I never got it: the glorification of the dispossessed, of the slave and the prostitute, of the lunatic and the con—what good was it supposed to do?

Among Solange's admirers could always be found the kind of guy who is attracted to female madness—on the condition, needless to say, that the female is pretty. Of course, it was not madness at all, but some romantic idea of madness, that these men were attracted to. And I have learned that when a man says he has a weakness for crazy women, he means it as a compliment to himself. I have often had to be tough with this type; the last thing Solange needed was guys who are turned on by her illness. I saw them as predators, and I saw the creature of fantasy that danced in their heads: the mad girl, all pale and thin and quivering, with great big eyes and floating hair, barefoot and naked under a white nightgown (even if Solange *did* appear exactly thus one winter night in Washington Square Park, drawing much attention, until a concerned NYU student gently led her to Saint Vincent's Hospital). Anyway, few of those swains lasted much past the first sign of real trouble: her unromantic habit of refusing to wash, for example, or, in a restaurant, helping herself to food from a stranger's plate.

It was inevitable that I'd be the kind of mother who lived in terror of what her children might catch on TV. Indeed, I would drive them to distraction with my constant monitoring. (*Smother*, the little brats called me.) How I enraged them, and how they attacked me—especially when it was a question of censoring some program all their friends were watching. Once, Zoe got so angry she threw the *TV Guide* at me. *"You Victorian witch."* Another time, I had an argument with one of their teachers, who had assigned a war documentary that I, admittedly without having seen it myself, refused to believe should be seen by seventh graders. (I didn't believe they should be reading *The Diary of Anne Frank*, either.) Just once, I tried explaining what it was I was so afraid of, what had happened to Aunt Crash and me, the insomnia, the haunting, but my kids didn't get it. Thank god, they had no idea what I was talking about. (But you can't rule their lives forever. A very bad day for me, the day Zoe came home from college with her head shaved.)

And now, it was impossible for me not to be haunted all over again—now that Ann was behind bars. I was no idiot. I knew that life in prison was not a fifties Hollywood B movie. I knew it was worse.

As it happened, Ann's incarceration would coincide with a huge shift in attitudes toward crime and punishment—though who knew then that what was taking shape was the greatest moral debacle in American history since slavery? We—Ann and I—had come of age in the era of human rights movements, which had included the prisoners' rights movement, with people both inside and outside the walls protesting prison conditions and demanding, and winning, reform. The great hero of the movement had been George Jackson, who came to be seen all over the world not as any ordinary transgressor paying his debt to society in San Quentin, but as a political prisoner and, after his death at the hands of guards, a black revolutionary martyr. Ann had read the letters and the autobiography Jackson wrote in his prison cell, and she had been deeply affected by them, but imagine how it would have been had she known as she read that she, too, would one day be facing a life sentence. Between Jackson's death and Ann's conviction, prisons across the United States had instituted reforms protecting inmates' constitutional rights and making prison life more bearable. The rehabilitative value of counseling and of literacy and other educational programs came to be taken for granted. But around the time Ann began serving her sentence, the idea of reform was already falling out of fashion. The conditions in American prisons were "like little concentration camps," in the words of the Reverend Maurice McCracken, political activist, pacifist, and another hero of Ann's. "I would never do anything that would contribute to sending someone there." Reverend McCracken himself had been sent "there" for acts of civil disobedience, and, in 1978, at the age of seventy-three, he was jailed again for refusing to participate in a case against two convicts who had kidnapped him during a prison escape. "I think if conditions in prison ever come to the surface, people will say, 'I had no idea these things existed'—just like they did after Hitler's war."

Nineteen eighty-six. I open *Barnard* magazine to a photograph of Ann and the words of Sharon Woodward, Class of '87.

How many people on campus today would recognize the name Dooley Ann Drayton? It was ten years ago that the former Barnard student (she dropped out after her sophomore year) was convicted of killing one police officer and wounding another in a dramatic shoot-out in Lower Manhattan. The incident began with a traffic violation, according to police, and escalated when Drayton's boyfriend, an Afro-American schoolteacher named Kwame Kwesi, became belligerent. Drayton's defense was that she had acted out of fear for Kwesi's life. At the time of the shootings, Kwesi was being held at gunpoint by the two officers and, according to Drayton, verbally attacked with racial epithets. The jury didn't buy Drayton's defense, however, and she received a penalty of twenty-five years to life. For the past ten years she has been an inmate at the Maryville Correctional Facility, a maximum-security prison for women in upstate New York.

On a bright, crisp October day, I drove to the prison to visit Drayton, who had agreed to an interview. The ominous gray-brick structure sits atop a hill on the site of what was once a popular resort hotel. (The hotel's former icehouse, the only part of the original establishment that still stands, is used today, chillingly enough, to hold prisoners in solitary.) The electric fence and the ubiquitous razor wire struck an incongruously somber note in the midst of the gay autumn foliage. The town of Maryville itself has a certain storybook charm, with a row of hand-

some historic houses and several bed-and-breakfasts boasting NO VA-
CANCY *signs at this, the height of leaf-peeping season.*

*From an exchange of letters, I knew that Drayton had left the
prison grounds only once in the past decade, to attend the funeral of her
mother, who died within months of her daughter's conviction. (Drayton,
an only child, bristles at suggestions that her mother died of a broken
heart.)*

*Approaching the prison, I noticed that my palms were sweating. It
was not just that I had never been inside such a forbidding place before,
or that this would be the first interview I had ever conducted. I found
the prospect of meeting Drayton face-to-face intimidating. And yet, before last semester, I had never even heard of Dooley Ann Drayton.
(Though we both happen to hail from the state of Connecticut.) I first
learned about her case from Professor Leon of the Barnard history department. He described her as one of the best students he'd ever had and
"quite possibly the most misguided one." Professor Leon suggested I contact Drayton for a project I was doing on women and radical politics.
Drayton was a special case in that, not counting a brief undergraduate
flirtation with SDS, she eschewed all political affiliations and was especially wary of leftist groups made up of young men and women who
come from privileged, wealthy backgrounds (as does Drayton herself).*

*I was most definitely nervous about meeting the woman I had come to
know from the trial transcripts and related articles. At the time of her
conviction, much was made of Drayton's lack of remorse, and her refusal
to issue an apology to the family of the police officer she had killed was
seen as particularly heinous, even by her few supporters.*

*Our interview took place in a small visitors' room to which Drayton
was escorted by a young, beefy male guard who left us alone but remained sitting just outside the door. A petite blonde with delicate features and a strikingly long neck, Drayton exudes an air of steely
self-possession. When she speaks, she looks directly and unblinking into
your eyes. Her hands remain still, she does not fidget or even gesture
much, and she speaks always at the same level, no matter what she is
saying, rarely raising or dropping her voice—a monotone that I, for
one, found unsettling.*

I had arrived at Maryville with a long list of prepared questions, but it turned out that Drayton refused to answer anything I asked about her crime or her trial, nor would she discuss anything of a personal nature. It didn't take me long to see that Drayton had her own agenda and that she'd agreed to this interview for only one reason: she had a message she wanted to get out.

Although there was a radiator in the room (its clanking and hissing were indeed quite distracting), I was mysteriously cold. I could not help remembering having read somewhere that Drayton was sometimes referred to as the Ice Princess. Though she never once laughed or even smiled, I did not get an impression of someone deeply depressed or unhappy. Tragic, yes, but not unhappy, was how I would describe her, paradoxical as that might sound. And terrible as her fate might seem to an outsider like myself, Drayton appeared resigned to it.

Though she was perfectly polite, I could not escape the feeling that Drayton had formed a knee-jerk negative opinion of me. I also had the sense that my nervousness made her feel contempt, which only succeeded in making me more nervous. I almost dropped the camera when I was taking her photograph.

By the end of the interview, I was so cold my teeth were chattering! Bidding me goodbye, Drayton made me promise to report what she'd said accurately, and softly though they were spoken, her words had the force of a command.

I had not been at all prepared for the emotional impact this meeting would have on me. Walking through the numerous gates to exit the building, I found I was hyperventilating, and as I drove away down the hill I began to cry.

*Q*uite a good photograph, I thought. Also shocking, at least to me: I would have expected a person to look very different after ten years behind bars. But Ann did not even look that much older. In fact, if I had to judge, I'd have said that of the two of us, I was the one who had aged more. But this is something that has shocked me in other instances as well—how ordinary, how perfectly normal a man or woman can appear in spite of having been through hell. One would never know, looking at certain former prisoners of war, that they had suffered prolonged torture, and it was not written in the face of the Sudanese man I saw interviewed on television the other night that he had passed his youth as a slave. (Another mystery: the tendency of mental patients to look years younger than they are, something I'd never have known had Solange not made me a regular visitor to psych wards, where the fact was both evident and often remarked on.) It did not prove anything that Ann looked fine in her photograph, or that she had seemed fine to her self-absorbed young interviewer. (Though I knew, somehow, that "tragic but not unhappy" was probably right on the mark.)

The interview itself was hardly a scoop. Ann had been getting her message out for some time—practically from her first days of incarceration. This was not her first interview, and she had written many articles as well, her words appearing regularly not only in prison publications but also in law reviews and other journals. She wrote all the time, including dozens of letters to various officials and to newspapers. She wrote open letters; she initiated petitions.

In fact, Ann's life could not have been more different from that of the girl in the haunting movie I saw on TV. She had not been corrupted, she had not despaired, she had not become a hardened con. She had remained exactly who she always was. To me, it was nothing less than a miracle.

It seems every day I read about some person out there—some actor or writer or even some politician or other elected official—confessing to having used drugs at some point in his or her life or even to having been an addict. These people are all free to tell the world about how much dope they've done, safe in the knowledge that no one is going to come after them. They've broken the law, but they don't have to hide it: no one is going to punish them. That such people do not feel the need to hide what they've done and that their confessions provoke no outrage suggests that, in fact, society does not consider what they've done to be so terrible. How, then, are we to understand our increasingly harsh anti-drug laws?

In America, among people who use drugs, the number of whites and the number of nonwhites is just about equal. But among those arrested and imprisoned—under the Rockefeller drug laws, for example—the numbers are nowhere near equal. It's okay to be rich and snort powder cocaine all you want, but if you live in a housing project and do crack—that's who the police go looking for, that's who gets busted, and that's who the courts lock up. How long can a society calling itself a democracy accept such a state of affairs?

And, echoing the Reverend McCracken: "Between the destruction being wreaked by the drug culture on the poor and black today and America's way of dealing with the problem, what we have is nothing less than a holocaust in the making." (The editors had taken the last five words, added a question mark, and thus had their title.)

As a challenge to the shame and silence surrounding abortion, a feminist magazine had got a long list of well-known women who'd had abortions to agree to publish their names. Now Ann was calling for a similar action. Would all people out there who had ever been in possession of four ounces of narcotics, the same amount for which other people were now serving mandatory sentences of fifteen years to life, please step forward and identify themselves? And would those same people, now enjoying all the pleasures and privileges of freedom, make an effort to find some inmate in their community convicted of the same drug crime, and reach out and do whatever they could for that person?

I call on all of you to do what is right. People of conscience cannot allow the present situation to continue. And for those who have committed no crime, I call on you to join the fight as well. Make contact with the jails and prisons in your community now. Find out who is incarcerated, and why, and what their conditions are like. Do not turn your backs on your brothers and sisters behind bars.

I had known about Sophie Drayton's death and about the funeral, Ann's presence in chains, armed guard at her side. Ann had had to remain separate and at a specified distance from the other mourners. She did not weep, and she did not speak—in fact, she was forbidden to speak, even to her father. But as Turner Drayton himself said, "Would she have had anything to say to us, anyway?"

Stiff and silent and tearless she stood, as if in a trance. Most likely she was thinking of that other funeral, the one she had missed. About that other, more meaningful loss.

I *must change my life.*

Something about Ann's trial and imprisonment, something about reading Simone Weil—it was then, right after Ann disappeared into the dungeon of Maryville, that I was overwhelmed by the wish to be back in school. Partly nostalgia, no doubt. For as I already knew, it is not just for places and times in which one has been happy that a person may find herself yearning.

At *Visage*, we agreed to think of it as a leave of absence. I would find part-time work of some kind. I took out a student loan, and I was back, a junior at Barnard College.

Nostalgia? Give me a better word than this for what weakened my knees whenever I happened to pass our old dorm and glance up at the windows of what had been our room.

I remembered how, back in freshman year, Ann had tried to talk me into taking the same course in Afro-American literature that she was taking, and surely it was partly nostalgia, again, that made me take it now. And—as if such a thing could possibly have mattered to her—I could not help wishing that she knew I was taking it.

The course was still taught by Professor Keeble, who had been one of the character witnesses at Ann's trial. Professor Keeble was something over fifty now. He had lost most of his hair and, as if to make up for the lack, had grown a beard as full as Santa Claus's. He was barrel-bodied like Santa Claus, too. The cigars he smoked could be smelled as soon as the elevator door opened on the floor where he had his office; no one complained. His class had become very popular with both Barnard and Columbia students, partly because he had published a popular book on Afro-American culture. Famously short-tempered and hard to please, said to be tougher on black students than on white ones.

One day in his office I did what I'd been wanting to do all semester: I brought up Ann's name, and when he said he'd been in touch with her, I felt a stab of envy.

They had exchanged letters, he said.

And how was she?

"Oh—working hard. Doing a lot of tutoring. She's helping some of the other women in there get their diplomas, mostly high school equivalency, I gather. She spends a lot of time reading, she says. Doesn't complain. Doesn't feel sorry for herself—not her style. She doesn't want our sympathy. Only complaint I've ever heard from her was about not sleeping well. She also said something about getting a magazine started. She has lots of projects. I believe she's turning herself into something of a jailhouse lawyer up there. She always did have a way of getting things done, didn't she." He smiled, or so I thought. At any rate, the beard rippled.

The next time he was in touch with Ann, I asked timidly, would he say hello from me?

"Why don't you do that yourself?" he said rather sharply. And when I simply cleared my throat and cleared it again, he added, more gently, "A person in prison can't have too many friends." Again the beard rippled.

I said yes, yes, I would write to my old friend. And I meant it. I meant it for sure. But somehow I did not—I could not do it.

It would have been easier if I'd believed she would have been pleased to hear from me, but I had no reason to believe this. After all, she had not answered the letter I sent her while she was in jail awaiting trial, though I supposed she might never have received it. And it was quite possible, I thought, given all that had happened, that she had forgotten me, that she had forgotten all of us from the old Barnard days. Just look how much I had forgotten myself. People I used to see and speak to every day—who'd have dreamed their features could ever be so vague, that even some of their names would be a struggle to conjure. (I wonder: if we knew how much was going to be lost, would we pay *more* or *less* attention to our lives?) It would have been much easier, too, if we had not parted as enemies. (When I thought of that evening now, I saw the avocado plant and the Billie Holiday album and Kwame's typewriter and the photo of Kwame and Ann naked on the bedroom wall—I saw each thing separately, twisting and blackening in the flames.) And when I tried to think about what I would actually *say* in a letter—I could not presume to talk about *her* life but was afraid that whatever I'd have to say about my own must seem trivial. And I was not like Ann, for whom writing had always come naturally. I had never regained the confidence I'd lost my freshman year, and putting down my thoughts even in a simple letter would have been an effort for me.

The more I thought about writing her, the more daunting the task became, and truthfully, it wasn't that I wanted to write to Ann so much as that I wanted to hear from her. I was still having a lot of trouble imagining her behind bars. I was still haunted by my own lurid visions of penitentiary life, and I could not accept the way Professor Keeble had made it sound, with his talk of teaching and reading and starting a magazine—as if Maryville were just some other women's college. I thought of my brother, and I would have said that in the same way Guy would not talk about Vietnam, either in letters home or after he'd returned, Ann was probably not talking about what being in prison was really like to Professor Keeble.

But she was an inescapable presence at Barnard. In Keeble's class, we read George Jackson's *Soledad Brother*, his letters from prison, where I found these lines:

"Understand that fascism is already here, that people are dying who could be saved, that generations more will die or live poor butchered half-lives if you fail to act . . . Join us, give up your life for the people."

And: "Jon is a young brother . . . Tell the brothers never to mention his green eyes and skin tone . . . Do you understand?"

And: "I have heard the term nigger 350 times today. Just a word—but I *don't* understand."

In another course, we read *De Profundis*, the prison memoirs of Oscar Wilde. "The poor are wiser, more charitable, more kind, more sensitive than we are. In their eyes prison is a tragedy, a misfortune . . . something that calls for sympathy in others . . . With people of our own rank, it is different."

That semester, I was also taking a course on the English novel, and among the books assigned was *Middlemarch*. I bought a copy on my way home from school one day before catching the bus. As we headed down Broadway, I opened the book and began reading the Prelude. Saint Teresa as a child; she and her little brother running away from their aristocratic home in Ávila, hearts set on a pilgrimage to Morocco, where, if all went well, they would die as martyrs; turned back by some uncles met on the way. I was already thinking of little Ann, setting out to save the homeless man in New Haven, already possessing, as George Eliot writes of little Teresa, "the rapturous consciousness of life beyond self."

But here is the sentence that made me want to cry out loud: "That Spanish woman who lived three hundred years ago, was certainly not the last of her kind."

Part Four

March 12, 1990

Dear George,

I hope you don't mind my writing to you out of the blue like this. I remember the kind note you sent me during my trial. What I don't remember is whether I answered it. If not, I hope you understood and forgave me then and will accept my apologies now.

I know a little about what you've been up to since those days. I know that you went back to school and finished your B.A. I know that you got married and had a child and got divorced. I know these things from Otis Keeble. A few weeks ago, he sent me a copy of the first issue of Caracara *with a note saying that you and Val Strom are not only co-editors but also husband and wife. I enjoyed reading it, especially Otis's piece on Toni Morrison and your husband's scathing attack on Broadway musicals. (But what does "caracara" mean? I want to say it's a bird, but I'm not sure.) At any rate, as you may know, many publications offer free subscriptions to prison libraries. Is there any chance* Caracara *might do this for us?*

But that is not the main reason I am writing. I have a much bigger request. I want to know whether you'd consider publishing work by some of the inmates here at Maryville. It seems to me that, though of course very different from what appears in your first issue, such work would not be out of place in a journal like Caracara. *So, if you don't mind, I'd like to send you a selection—poems, stories, personal essays. In general, the essays tend to be the strongest pieces and probably of most interest to your readers. (Though perhaps to someone who used to write poetry, the poems will appeal more?)*

As you must know, prison literature has a long and distinguished history, and I'm sure you'll agree that the voices of the incarcerated are voices that deserve to be heard. I cannot say how deep is the prisoner's wish to share her experiences with those outside the walls. It is no exaggeration to say that in some cases writing has saved an inmate's sanity or even her life, and needless to say, the development of literary skills can be invaluable when the time comes to leave the strange planet of prison and rejoin the world.

For many years at Maryville it was possible for certain inmates to participate in writing workshops that were taught by various teachers from local schools. It was an excellent program, but we lost the funding for it a couple of years ago, along with support for our magazine, Sister Says. Alas, getting funded again won't be easy. Educational programs are being cut back in most prisons these days—the emphasis being increasingly on punishment rather than rehabilitation—and ever since the Jack Abbott affair there's been a kind of backlash against prison writing. It would be immensely encouraging if we could persuade literary journals all over America to publish prisoners' work as a matter of course. Not just for our sake but for the sake of all society, a true picture of life behind bars ought to be common knowledge.

Please do write me soon and let me know if you are willing to help. I would also be very happy to hear more about how you are. I do not have much contact with anyone outside Maryville. There's Otis, and there's Lester Prysock, who was my defense lawyer and who has since become a friend. Do you remember my parents? Sophie died in 1977. Turner has a new wife, someone he's known most of his life, the widow of an old Princeton classmate of his. She was also a good friend of Sophie's.

Oh—I almost forgot: I know it must have been you who arranged to have Visage donate all those samples of cosmetics and other beauty products to Maryville years ago. I can't tell you how much this meant to the women, and everyone was very sad when the magazine folded and we no longer had those packages to look forward to.

Well, George, how does it feel to be middle-aged? In my mind, at *least, you are forever that seventeen-year-old whose suitcase was stolen your first day in the big city. And how does it feel to be a mother? I confess, it's hard for me to imagine you in that role. Do you have a boy or a girl?*

Ann

Actually, by the time of this letter, both children had been born. When Val and I got married, Jude was already on the way.

Jack Abbott. Like Kathy Boudin, a name I had not thought about in years. (And both names back in the news again recently, both for leaving prison, she by winning parole, he by hanging himself.) When, in the late seventies, a young convict whose crimes included bank robbery and homicide wished to share his experiences of prison life, he picked a large, famous ear. Abbott's letters to Norman Mailer became a book in 1981 (the same year as the crime that would bring down Boudin). The book's success helped win Abbott's release, but it was only weeks before he'd committed homicide again. At the time, the Jack Abbott affair seemed to be all anyone was talking about. Now I have to explain to my children who he is. Ditto Kathy Boudin.

Q: Just how do you hang yourself with a bedsheet and a shoelace?

Is it for the children that I am writing this? I have sometimes thought so, and then, what a vain and silly idea. And if true, if it *is* for Zoe and Jude, why include so much they do not need and doubtless would prefer not to know?

Take Orwell's notion that what drives people to write is demons they can neither resist nor understand. Ask me and I'll tell you: it was the demon loneliness that got me started. It was boredom. Orwell speaks also of a mysterious instinct that might just be the same one that makes a baby squall for attention. Sometimes I feel as if that were exactly what I was doing.

But I have not yet told the story.

I had some friends who used to rent a summerhouse on Long Island for one month every year. But this particular year, things went wrong. Husband and wife were not getting along. The idea of spending a month's vacation together was now unbearable, the idea of one of them going while the other stayed home more unbearable still. They dithered till the last minute, then told me, "It's yours if you want it." I tried not to act too excited. I knew the house, I'd been a guest there, and I saw myself happy and at peace among the strawberry and potato fields, catching up on my reading on the beach. The cure for loneliness, according to Marianne Moore, is solitude. But solitude is harder to find than you might think and certainly requires more than merely being alone.

The day after I arrived, in the evening, a storm blew up. A serious storm, a storm with claws: I thought they'd pry that little cottage apart. Just as it was turning dark, the electricity went off. Supper by candlelight. How romantic, I thought, but not bitterly.

I sat at the kitchen table, which was made of oak, the surface deeply scored and scarred, curiously satisfying to the touch. I ate the grilled cheese sandwich and tomato salad I had just finished preparing. Normally, I would have read a magazine while eating, but the light from the candle was too dim. I stared into its flame instead—flicker, flicker, beat, beat—and soon began to feel sleepy, my head so heavy heavy, and by the time I'd finished eating, I had no desire to get up. Flicker, flicker, beat, beat: a pretty sight, soothing, with the storm still tearing at the house, and pitch-darkness pooling in all the corners, and my mind like a cup or a bowl that was being slowly, slowly drained. But before I could nod out completely, I got up and took the flashlight I'd found in a cupboard earlier, and I scrounged up paper—a steno notebook that, though not new, had never been used—and a well-gnawed ballpoint pen. Back in my chair, following an urge I felt no need to examine, I began to write what seemed to be a letter but was addressed to no one in particular. I was still writing when the lights came back on. It was after twelve, it was past my bedtime, but now I was not in the least bit tired or sleepy. I didn't remember noticing when the storm had stopped. I made myself some coffee, put Mozart on the CD player, and wrote on.

Later, I thought how exactly like being hypnotized the whole experience had been.

I keep certain papers, letters and other documents, in an old cedar chest, and that is where these pages, when they are finished, presuming they ever will be finished, doubtless will end up, too. (Anything having to do with the children, though—baby albums, old report cards, handmade Mother's Day cards, school photos, and the like— these I keep together in a different place.) Once, long ago, there was a lock. Once, there was need for a lock, but no more. Anyway the lock is broken. The key lies rusted at the bottom of the chest.

The sight of faded ink has always made me sad. Some ink, like hair, turns gray. This letter from Ann must have been written in black ink; it has turned brown. I remember writing back, and the memory shames me. Yes, please do send us those pieces, I said— knowing full well there was no chance of any of them ever appearing in *Caracara*. Val would never have allowed it. Yes, our names appeared together on the masthead, but we were anything but equals. *Caracara* was Val's baby. I had the real thing to look after. (Don't misunderstand: This is not a gripe. Though I always wanted to work, I never wanted the kind of job that would have made full-time care of the children impossible. I thought I was lucky to be spared the pain of being torn that most working mothers I knew endured—women who, nevertheless, looked at me and my life with less envy than scorn. I gave up trying to explain why I did not feel trapped, why, so long as the children were there, so long as there were plenty of books, I had no great desire to get out of the house. Besides, I was much too anxious a parent to leave Zoe and Jude with anyone else except for short periods of time. Forced to be apart from them all day, I would have resented missing so much of their lives—as many working mothers do resent this. And possessive though I was, I believe that, in the end, spending all that time with them actually made it easier when I had to let them go. Not that this was ever easy. The day Jude followed Zoe into school was a day of panic and mourning. I thought of the time our neighbor's cat had her five kittens taken away, and how she went back and forth between her basket and the laundry basket until she'd assembled a litter of five socks.)

Everything was clear from the start. Val would be the real editor in chief; he would do the major work and make all the important decisions (of which naming me co-editor was one). This was only reasonable, given that the idea of publishing a literary magazine had been his and his alone, as was all the effort required to get it going, including finding the money. And he was the one who had the connections, and who was able to get work from good writers for less than good pay, and whose own name among contributors could be expected to be a draw, for already by then he had his reputation. Listing me as co-editor would help when he needed to be diplomatic, he said, allowing him always to fall back on "we," and I was aware that without consulting me, he occasionally told an author whom he didn't want to offend that he'd have been only too happy to run that author's piece but that I, alas, was against it. (*Alas* was a favorite Val word.) With this lie, he could remain on good terms with the rejected author, and as for me, well, there was not really much at stake; unlike Val, I was not making my way in that world. Of course, no one who knew anything about Val Strom would ever have believed for a second that I could overrule him; it was just a game we all played. And there had been another thing in the back of Val's mind when he made me co-editor. Giving at least the appearance of power shared equally between husband and wife might temper criticism when it was observed that nine out of ten *Caracara* authors were men.

In reality, Val was not someone who could have shared power

with anyone. I think we can probably all be grateful that he was willing to leave domestic matters to me, including most things having to do with raising his son; otherwise, our family would not have lasted a day. Val was a born tyrant. We had trouble keeping staff, which made me and my still-sharp secretarial skills often indispensable. Our office was in a run-down loft building on lower West Broadway, above a Chinese restaurant. But much of the work I did could be done at home (in those days, a very comfortable apartment on Central Park West that Val had inherited from his grandparents). Besides fact-checking and editing copy, I typed correspondence, kept records, and took care of the slush pile. I insisted on writing personal rejection letters, even though Val thought we should be like most other journals and use a form. Eventually we would start using a form, but I held out against this as long as possible, who knows why. It was all such a sham, anyway. We never published unsolicited manuscripts, and I didn't see why we couldn't just announce this and save everyone a lot of bother. But to Val it was out of the question. He said it would hurt us in the eyes of readers and subscribers; it would make us look bad. The rest of our staff agreed. I said, Worse than anonymous rejection forms? The mysteries of literary publishing. Was it any wonder I preferred the company of children? (Remember the great Chekhov quote about worms and butterflies? Watching my own children grow, I thought of it all the time.)

I knew exactly what Val's response to Ann's letter would be. How about something written by *her*? Now, *that* we would have published in a heartbeat.

"Yes," I wrote Ann, "you are right. A caracara is a large South American bird of prey, something between a hawk and a vulture." Like everything else about the magazine, the name had been Val's idea. Something about how we were going to be hawkeyed in our pursuit of the best writing—like vultures pouncing on the most significant, stimulating, provocative news and ideas about culture and the arts—and ruthless in attacking the bogus, the meretricious, the overpraised. How silly all this sounds today. But the magazine, like Val himself, was nothing if not serious, and from the beginning it was a grand success. Which was only what everyone expected of Val Strom.

He died suddenly one day in a highway accident. Needless to say, *Caracara* did not survive him.

He was a friend of Cleo's, an old college friend. He had been living abroad; mostly in London, and when he returned to New York (unlike Cleo, he was from there originally), she threw a party for him. That was how we met. At the time, my marriage to Jeremy was over—all but the paperwork. Little Zoe and I were on our own.

I should say here that after my graduation from Barnard, I did not end up back at *Visage*, which in any case was not the same *Visage* I had left. Since I'd first started working there, many changes had come to the world of women's magazines, to the magazine industry in general. Though it was still more or less the same editorial board, there was a new vision at *Visage,* a whole new way of thinking and a new set of rules. Less text, more pictures. More famous faces, more celebrity profiles and features about personal relationships and lifestyles (it was one word now), fewer articles about current events. Some saw the future of women's magazines as no articles whatsoever, just page after page of images and shopping details (I see the first such magalogs are already here). There had been a time when I'd thought that perhaps once I had my degree in English, I might try moving over to the fiction and poetry department, but that department had been completely dropped, and for good. And for all the changes that were made in order to keep up with the eighties, *Visage* was struggling. It had more competition than ever, with a new women's magazine being born every few months, it seemed, though now there was less and less to distinguish one of them from another, or one issue from the next.

But in fact I was not really affected by any of this. I had outgrown *Visage* and all its sister publications, old and new. In school, I had stopped reading them, and by this time I was scarcely more interested in beauty secrets (why are they *secrets?*) than was my sister Zelma, the bride of Christ, now living in a convent in Syracuse.

When I met Jeremy, I had just started working at a small press that published only poetry. I stayed on after we got married, but once Zoe was born I gave notice, with Jeremy's blessing. It was only when the marriage began to founder (which, admittedly, did not take very long) that I began working again, this time at home. I did freelance work, mostly editing, of which there seemed to be no end in those days. I was offered far more work than I could possibly have accepted. I worked long hours, though, finding this particular kind of work undemanding and even soothing. Stopping run-ons, mending sentence fragments and split infinitives (but not in every instance!), tidying clutter, clarifying sense—all this was good to do. (Bless old Crug for teaching me English well.) The only bad thing was being constantly reminded of how American English was deteriorating. In the years I did such work, I saw a steady decline in proper usage and well-turned prose, and mind you, I was dealing mostly with professional writers. I used to have some hope that this trend would somehow be reversed, but by the time my kids were in high school and I was running an appalled eye over their homework, I feared the battle was lost. (Among other problems, Miss Crug appears to have been the last of *her* kind.)

I was lucky. Not only had I found plenty of work for which I did not have to leave the house (messengers delivered, messengers picked up), but I also had Jeremy, who, if less than generous with time (he was a doctor, after all), was more than generous with child support, even after he'd remarried and had two sons. He would always do his best by Zoe, I could count on that. So it was not, in the end, a rancorous divorce. I was not heartbroken. I did not feel abandoned. Fair's fair: the divorce had been no more Jem's fault than mine. And besides, I had a secret that kept me from ever being too hard on him.

Husband Two was a different story. Although she was his friend, Cleo had cautioned me from the beginning against becoming too serious about Val. He, too, had been married before. Now, *there* was a rancorous divorce. Thankfully, there were no children to be caught in the cross fire, and an ocean now separated the enemies. Aurora was British and lived in London. I was grateful never to have met her, though it chilled me when one day, out of curiosity, I asked to see a photograph and Val said he had none. ("What would I want with that madwoman's photograph?") Cleo, although Val's friend, had taken Aurora's side. (" 'Madwoman'! He cheated on her so badly she went round the bend.")

A woman in love lies to herself. *He will be different with me.* I didn't have much choice but to cling to blind faith. Six months after Val and I had begun seeing each other, I was pregnant again. A pregnant unmarried woman is a desperate woman, willing to believe almost anything.

Cleo, who would regret having brought us together, admitted to having once been smitten with Val herself. No mystery there. He was charming, intelligent, handsome. He had the kind of smart, masculine look most other men achieve only by putting on a uniform: he had it in his shorts. A high head, a regal profile, military posture, long legs, and long back. ("At Penn we used to call him the Prince.") Sharp as a whip, the Prince. Was he really always the brightest person in the room, or did he just give that impression because he was always the best informed and the most articulate? (I remember how people would call and say, "Is Val there? I just wanted to pick his brain." Disgusting phrase. Or: "We're going to the movies and wanted to know what Val recommends.") But never pedantic. Not boring. On the contrary. He told a good story; he told a good joke. He made you listen, and he made you laugh.

"You'll see," said Cleo when she called to invite me to the party. "He's quite a package. You'll like him. He's got that thing, you know—the ability to make people like him instantly, especially women. But watch out you don't get swept away."

Easy to be smitten, to be swept away. At parties (and we would go to so many parties, that kind of socializing being not only one of

Val's main pleasures but also, he insisted, essential to his work), I enjoyed watching his effect on people, especially those meeting him for the first time. I enjoyed—how much I cannot say— watching others be charmed by him. I enjoyed—I cannot believe I am writing this—watching him set women's hearts aflutter. Now I see it as a clear and early warning sign: I was happier with Val in company than I was alone with him. Alone, I often felt as if I were somehow not enough. As if he needed more than me—than us, the children and me—to expand to his fullest self. He was at his best in the company of people just like him—bright and up to the minute, passionate in their own opinions but clamoring to know what *his* opinion was. I knew it was a failing that I could not keep up in such company. I'd be alert and engaged at first, but soon my mind would weary of so much discourse and my thoughts would start to wander. But I'd be lying if I didn't say I was proud of Val, very proud indeed of how other people hung on his every word. I can remember dinner parties where, when he really got going, the others would simply give Val his head, interrupting only with a question here and there, and I was reminded of the one or two professors I'd had whose lectures could hold a class in thrall.

All this was a lot, at least for a while. And for a while longer, it was even enough.

Solange: the only one who always remained invulnerable to Val's charms. "What kind of creepy little kid says, 'When I grow up I want to be a critic'?" A fair question. But at the time, one that only exasperated me.

It was one of his stories. He came from a well-educated family: both parents and both grandfathers had taught college. Like his two older sisters, he had learned to read almost as soon as he could talk. According to the story, when he was taken to see his first play—it was *Death of a Salesman,* he was about eight or nine—he jotted notes on his program during intermission, and that night after everyone else had gone to bed, he stayed up writing a summary of his impressions, which he read out loud the next morning at breakfast. He was enchanted when his father opened the newspaper and showed him a review of the very performance they had been to see. It was Val's first understanding that such a profession existed, that it could be one person's job to go to the theater, just as the Stroms had done, and to write about what he'd seen, as Val had done—only what the critic wrote was printed for everyone to read, and sometimes the critic liked what he saw and sometimes he didn't, and when he didn't like what he saw, he didn't have to pretend and say that he liked it anyway, as Val had been taught to do in just about every situation. ("Never tell someone you don't like what he or she is wearing. You will only hurt that person's feelings. It may be honest, but it is not nice.") The critic did not have to worry about hurting anyone's feelings or about not being nice; he could say what he honestly thought. And then people would read what he thought and decide whether or not to go to the play. And sometimes, if enough critics said enough bad things, a play could be closed after just one or two performances, even if tickets for future performances had already been sold, and even if a lot of people still wanted to see it. So, said Val's father, a critic had a large responsibility. A critic was a man of power! his mother said. And according to the story, Val had made them both laugh by announcing that this was what he wanted to be when he grew up.

"He must have been one creepy little boy."

Today these words can make me smile. But back then, Solange's dislike of Val was no laughing matter. They never got along; at best they might be content to ignore each other, but often they clashed. I kept them apart as much as possible. First of all, I didn't want Zoe and Jude witnessing that kind of behavior. Here I was trying to teach them compassion and understanding in the face of mental illness, and there was Val repelled by Solange and not even trying to hide it. (Calling someone mad was, indeed, one of his favorite insults, and he was not above using it, albeit watered down to insinuation, in a review.) For her part, Solange believed that Val was evil. You watch, she said. You can't trust a man who talks about his first wife like that.

True enough.

A woman in love lies to herself. *He will be different with me.* He was not different, but when I look back, do I see a woman in love? Or maybe it's just that I don't want to believe I was ever in love with a man like Val Strom. It is all so confusing. There are times when it seems to me that none of what I am describing could have happened. I have to be making up every word of it.

Once, in one of her irrational states, Solange attempted to seduce Val, supposedly in order to save me.

When friends of John F. Kennedy asked, "Why do you do it? Why, with so much at stake, do you risk everything by cheating on your wife and flagrantly carrying on with all these other women? You are the most important leader on earth. How can you be so reckless?" "I cannot stop myself," he said.

Cleo said, "I could have forgiven Val maybe if he had just left *certain* women alone." Married women. Women with families. "But he was a home wrecker."

I didn't think young girls were fair game, either. Like the ones just out of school who came to work at the magazine. Starry-eyed little cunts who believed Val could help make their careers. Wouldn't you know, one of them happened to be with him when he died.

Couldn't stop himself.

Where did he find the time? (Well, think of JFK, think of Bill Clinton.) Val was a man of wondrous energy (in this way he reminded me a lot of Ann). He needed less sleep than most people, and he liked his waking hours *full.* He was the kind of person who could write all morning, see a movie in the afternoon, then go to the theater and still be up for a late dinner or a party. It was in the blood, apparently: all the Stroms were like this, and they all shared the same passion for culture.

Long before he'd published a word, he was poring over reviews (his desire one day to edit his own journal supposedly also went as far back as high school) and, with few exceptions, not liking what he saw. Most reviews were badly written, often by people who didn't seem to know or care much about their subject. A lot of critics were lazy; they wrote the same damn review over and over. They made stupid mistakes. They took far too many of their ideas from one another. They were overawed by Names. They opened wide for pablum and pap, but whatever was truly original and brave and strange set their teeth on edge. They swallowed the false and choked on the real. All this he told me the first time we met. He was on the rise then, a cultural critic at large, writing for a number of different publications. He wrote about books and movies and the theater, but also about painting or photography, and occasionally about restaurants or about some cultural trend or fad. The best of his essays would be collected and published, and then it was his turn to be reviewed, and though largely praised he was also faulted—for being too harsh.

"Because I care. These are matters of life and death to me": his justification when he was accused of brutality. (But then, when has it not been the justification? No one ever says, *Because I was feeling mean, because my wife had just dumped me, because my own book had just flopped, because I'm a misogynist, because I know the author he is a fucking prick I have always hated his arrogant guts. I couldn't stop myself.*)

But—here we go again—I do not trust myself, writing about husbands. I fear I am making Val out to be too flat and cartoonish. Why did I not begin by saying that he was very good, since that is the truth? He *did* care, he *was* serious, and he wrote very, very well. He wrote about things that mattered, and he wrote about them deeply, intelligently, and bravely. He always said exactly what he thought, regardless of what people would think of him—and wasn't that his job? And yet, and yet. Why were the majority of the reviews he wrote pans? I lived with the man. I knew how much was out there that he loved and admired—why didn't he write more about those things? He thought this was very cute of me, but as he explained: to take some mediocrity that had been wildly promoted and praised as a masterpiece, and to show not only how much it had been overrated but also what dupes and philistines most critics were—didn't I see? Sometimes I thought I saw. And yet. I was never comfortable with how much he relished his role. Publicly humiliating people, catching them with their pants down, tearing the guts out of their work: I supposed the job could not have been done at all if it did not give pleasure. But one day I was reading C. S. Lewis aloud to Zoe—about a boy who eats from a box of enchanted Turkish Delight (a witch gave it to him), and the more Turkish Delight he eats, the more he craves, though it sickens him; it also turns him mean and nasty—and I was horrified to find myself thinking of Val. Wasn't he, too, like someone feasting on some "sweet corrupting food" and, as some people accused, turning ever more mean and nasty? It could not be good for the soul, I thought, to be constantly attacking other people, to be making fresh enemies daily—no matter that Val's reputation was growing and his work had begun to receive awards. The more successful he became, the more loudly certain people would protest. He was patronizing and destructive, they said. He was "the most feared and hated critic of his day." But Val was never shaken by such attacks. Don't expect *him* to be cowed into hypocrisy, he said. There was much to admire in this, I supposed, as there was in the fact that he never let the importance of the person whose work he was judging influence what he said. It took courage, what he did—more than I, for one, would ever have had. Val was fearless. And he was not afraid to slaughter sacred cows. On *Death of a Salesman*: "I saw the play for the first time when I was a child, and surely only a child could be moved by such bathos."

Further samples:

"At times, ——'s novel seems as long as life itself."

"If you wish to learn how to take two beautiful, talented, popular stars and get an audience never to want to set eyes on them again, study this film."

"We learn from the press release that, alas, there is to be a second volume."

"Reading this slight, flowery book is like spending an hour with an incompetent hooker: her perfume is distracting, and you could have done the job better yourself."

"I finished ——'s new book of poems while in a café, sitting at a very wobbly table. Before I left, I slipped the book under one of the table legs, delighted to have found some use for it."

"This morning I woke up with a pain in my arm: the result of my wife's repeated jabs in her effort to keep me from snoring through last night's performance."

"Someone ought to tell —— that the camera is not the director, and there is nothing to be gained from making love to it."

"Perhaps it was ——'s family themselves who persuaded her they would make a fascinating subject for a memoir?"

It has often been said—and I don't think Val would have disagreed—that it is easier to write a bad review than a good one, to bury than to praise. Why this should be I wouldn't know, but it reminds me of what has been said about writing fiction: that wickedness makes a more compelling story than goodness and that the most memorable and true-to-life literary characters are not saints but sinners. But when I read somewhere what W. H. Auden said—that it is impossible to write a bad review without showing off—I thought how true this was of Val. His knowledge, his wit, his intellectual acuteness and moral authority were always on display, and it did appear to be practically a rule: the worse he made the work under attack sound, the stupider and coarser and more bungling its creator, the cleverer and more dazzling Val himself came across. Again, why this should have been so was a mystery to me. An even bigger mystery was Val's confidence. How could any person be so sure of his own taste? After all, as Solange loved to remind us all, Val himself had never created anything.

I am a coward. I died a thousand deaths when we crossed paths—at some party, say—with one of Val's victims. (It happened all the time.) Val thought this was cute of me, too. "Don't exaggerate, darling. A bad review is hardly the end of the world." And, he assured me, "people aren't as sensitive as you may think." (*Now* who was mad?)

You might have thought someone like Val must have been hypercritical in general, in every respect, but in fact—big surprise—

he turned out to be much less critical of people than Jeremy, who, as a result of all those hours listening to patients talk about themselves, had grown deeply pessimistic about human nature and, like most psychiatrists, was quite fed up with the race. But Val was no misanthrope and, away from reviewing, was fairly tolerant of human weakness—except, unfortunately, in the case of Solange. He was also gregarious, much more so than I, and popular, with more invitations than he could accept, and he had many good friends, of whom he was not particularly critical, as he was not particularly critical of me—though I accept the hypothesis that this was partly because, with me, he always had a guilty conscience. It never bothered him that we did not share comparable powers or ambitions, or that so much of my life would be absorbed by motherhood. He understood me in a way others did not. A woman I met once at a party, learning I had no career, said—not unkindly, she was simply taken by surprise—"Why would you want a life that was just like your mother's?" (I have noticed this about middle-class people: they always assume everyone they meet must be middle class, too. Same evening, different guest: "And where did *your* parents go to college?") At worst, Val was a tease. He often teased me about my naïveté, my lack of sophistication, my incuriosity about the world. He made jokes about my "barbarian roots" and referred to where I came from (and where, of course, he had never been) as "the tundra."

It came as a shock to learn he did not always finish a book he was reviewing. He claimed to be shocked in turn. Surely I did not believe other reviewers read every book all the way through? In his case, yes, some books—just a few—he did not bother to finish. That was because it wasn't always necessary for him to finish a book in order to write about it. Besides, a reviewer wasn't supposed to reveal how a book ended (though in fact Val did this all the time— it was one of the complaints against him); nor did he have to read every single page of a book in order to form an intelligent opinion about it. But then one time he got caught. A certain novelist had saved a twist for the final pages. Written in the dark, Val's critique of the plot made no sense. The angry author managed to kick up a bit of a storm, but when the dust settled, Val emerged more or less unscathed. It was not a famous author; it was not an important book. Then came a more serious incident. Another author killed himself. Nobody could justifiably point a finger at Val. Almost every other review of this particular young man's book had also been bad. But Val's had been most prominent and especially cruel, and it was his response to the suicide that troubled me: "Why should I feel one iota of guilt? Obviously, the man was unbalanced." I no longer recall whether this was before or after I had stopped reading Val's reviews. I stopped at a point when they had become predictable, at least to me; when I'd gotten to know his taste, his special peeves and no-nos and unbreakable aesthetic commandments so well that the reviews seemed all more or less the same. Sometimes I'd start to read one but would not finish it. Not irrelevantly, our marriage was a flop, and the high moral tone of much of my husband's writing had begun to grate on me.

※

Portrait of a (second) marriage.

"Well, what do you think?"

"We think not."

"You could at least take a look. You never know what might—"

"If you want to waste your time, go right ahead. But we're not publishing anything just to be politically correct. How many literary geniuses do you think you'll find behind bars?"

"Well, Jack Abbott—"

"—wrote a sensational, vastly overrated book that would never have been published at all if Mailer hadn't been involved. Anyway, if this weren't your old friend, we wouldn't even be having this discussion. Sure, if you can persuade her to write something for us herself—that would be of interest. But we don't publish anything for any other reason except its literary value. We're not going to publish some trash just because you have a guilty conscience."

"Gee, I don't know. We published Celia's poem about the windshield wipers."

"What's that supposed to mean?"

"You were screwing her. That was the only reason we ran that dumb poem."

"Oh, we're not going to go down *that* dreary path again, are we, dear?"

"That poem sucked."

"Now you're a poetry critic, are you, my dear?"

"And that wasn't the only time we published something because you were screwing—or hoping to screw—someone, and you know it. Literary value, my ass."

"Have you taken complete leave of your senses, Georgette?"

✳

I have digressed too far. I do not know why. Certainly I had no intention of dwelling so long on my second marriage. But I see there remains some lingering fascination . . .

Now I want to turn back to that cedar chest, to the fading brown script of Ann's letter. *Sophie died in 1977. Turner has a new wife.* Ann does not say exactly when her father remarried.

Another letter. Not here, not in this chest among all the other documents and mementos. "My darling girl, though it breaks my heart, I have decided not to see you again." Not saved. Destroyed. Read often enough to be learned by heart, then destroyed.

Now comes the part where I tell about Love. Here is some advice I once read, from one writer to another: "The trick is to be cold about the hottest thing there is: love." But that writer was talking about fiction.

Trial and error has shown that I cannot accomplish this difficult thing unless "I" becomes "she."

Part Five

Each time she saw him, it was like a ritual. The getting ready, for which she always left plenty of time. As if it was not to be hurried, this part, no more than the lovemaking for which it was a preparation. The slow bathing and the careful dressing, and the dreaming, the imagining ahead. He will touch me here, he will kiss me there. Her awareness that never before, not for anyone else, had she taken such pains—a sign of the importance of this love: not the least part to be taken for granted. Sometimes her hand would tremble as she combed her hair, or she had to struggle with a button or a zipper. Sometimes she cried. Why did she cry? For happiness and for fear. In two more hours, in one hour, in less, I will see him. Between ecstasies, it was all waiting. Not once was one of them ever late for the other; neither ever forgot or canceled or postponed a date. Always there remained, despite their intimacy, a kind of formality between them. They would never reach a point—would never be permitted to reach that point—where they could become forgetful of each other, where one might take the other for granted. The bittersweetness of a love broken off before its time. So that decades later, looking into a mirror, combing her hair, she would recall, Never an unkind word.

A strange love to measure future loves against. She would not exaggerate to the handful of people whom she would ever tell about him. She was proud always to have seen him clearly: an ordinary, decent man transfigured by grief. What was not ordinary was the depth of her feelings. What was miraculous was that those feelings should have been returned. How it had happened—no one could have predicted it—was a mystery, the everyday mystery of love. The knowledge from the beginning that their love was doomed—there was a fatal flaw in it, the angels were against it, the gods would make sport of it—gave unnatural poignancy to their time. Every hour together had the feel of being stolen. It was, one or the other of them said, like being caressed one moment and lashed the next. Always an air of the illicit and even of danger about their meetings—as if at least one had been committing adultery, as if the price to pay might be blood. Without a word of explanation, from the beginning, it was understood: it would be a secret love.

Looking back, she sees first of all her own lost youth: hardly more than a girl then, without much experience of life and none at all of love. Big Love, wasn't that what she used to call it? First love was what it had turned out to be. Two husbands and two children lay ahead. Sometimes he would say just this to her: "You will marry and have children, and you'll forget all about me." It was supposed to be a comfort to them both when he said that. And so he tried to smile. His melancholy smile. But he no more wished to be forgotten than she wished to forget him. Whenever they were together, she would stare and stare. He understood. He had just the same fear that one day her face would be just a blur to him.

He said, "I feel as if I were doing something terrible to you—to both of us—but mostly to you. After all, I've been through so much, but you—" But she protested. It seemed to her that already she had suffered more than most people her age. At which he grimaced and shut his eyes. It was one of the ways by which she knew she was loved. He could not think of her in pain. He said, "I am afraid"—*I am afraid*: they said it to each other as often as *I love you*—"I am afraid one day you'll look back and see how young you were, and you'll be hard and bitter toward me, and you won't be able to forgive." Now, *this* was pain. This vision of herself through his eyes, bitter, no longer young, and without him. This was pain. And he had placed a hand on either side of her face, gently tilted back her head, and wiped the tears away with his thumbs. For the rest of her life, in moments of grief, the memory of this gesture would come back. In worst despair, just the memory could calm and comfort her. No other man's touch, ever, would mean more to her.

My dear girl, he called her. My darling girl. And the first time he saw her naked: "You do understand, I hope, I mean, you won't mind if I, that I"—touching her breasts—"I cannot call you *George*."

*

"*George!* Why, it's you, isn't it?"

If she did not recognize him in that first instant, it was not so much because he had changed (though he had changed quite a bit) as that she would not have expected to see him here, outside a secondhand bookshop on Eighth Street. They had found themselves side by side, looking in the window at the books on display, which included, as she would always recall, the old two-volume Modern Library edition of *Remembrance of Things Past*, with a photograph of Proust propped next to it, and the price: $15.

"What a lovely surprise! It's been ages, hasn't it?"

It had nearly broken her heart then and there: the old bluffness, which she remembered so well, the forced joviality ("*Let's all have something nice*"). That he could summon that tone even now . . . Perhaps it was the pity in her own expression that undid him. While the false smile remained frozen on his lips, his eyes spurted tears. The effect was grotesque, but instead of being repelled, she had felt her heart swell with tenderness. It had come to her automatically what to do. She took his arm and led him around the corner, to a café. He had let himself be led meekly, waving a handkerchief that he had taken out, surrendering to her care. That handkerchief. The only man she would ever know to carry one: so old-fashioned, the large, snowy man's handkerchief.

Mercifully, the café was empty, and dimly lit.

"Anywhere you'd like," said the young waitress, her voice imparting not welcome but indifference.

They chose a table toward the rear.

"I am so sorry," he said, sitting down, words muffled by cloth. And it came back to her like an echo: *"So, so terribly, terribly sorry."* "It was—seeing you—you know—" He did not have to explain. For him, she had only one association. He had never seen her before without Ann, and no doubt Ann, too, had appeared to him on the sidewalk a moment ago: the lost and wayward daughter, the ghost of her pre-murderess, pre-convict self.

The waitress came, a girl in loose peasant blouse and tight miniskirt, and took their order for tea.

The handkerchief was gone, discreetly folded back into a pocket. The smile was back. The gracious manner was back. "You are extremely kind," he said, looking straight into her eyes. And now that the crisis was past and he was all right again, enough about him! How was *she*?

She was in love. It had begun already outside the bookshop, with his tears and her pity, and Proust looking on.

It had been a bold thing she had done, taking charge of him, but now she felt hopelessly shy. Earlier, she had been to the movies. She and her sister had seen Max Ophuls's *The Earrings of Madame de . . .* The film was from 1953, and it had affected her in a way few contemporary movies about love ever did. Later she would recite the entire story, and he would say, "Maybe none of this would have happened if you'd seen a different movie that day." Maybe.

She had walked her sister home and was on her way home herself when she passed the bookshop.

"I live uptown," she said, "and Solange lives down here, but we see each other a lot. She works in a record store." She did not add that Solange was probably not long for that job, or how difficult it was for her to hold any job, or how she had just been released from the p-ward.

"How wonderful that she found you," he said almost rapturously. "I remember how terribly upset you were when she ran off." And another echo came pealing: *"Your poor mother."*

He asked her about *Visage*—it pleased her that he had remembered this about her—and she explained that she was now back in school. "I have one more semester."

The waitress arrived with the tea.

The table was only the size of a chessboard. They were forced to sit close. Knee bumped knee. Hand reaching for sugar brushed hand.

How different he looked. He had aged, of course. It had been ten years. But the real difference she was seeing was not about age.

He was still handsome. He was one of those lucky men whose hair thinned slowly, and mostly at the sides. He still bore his resemblance to former mayor of New York John V. Lindsay, whose exact age—fifty-nine—he was. His face had lost some of its sculpted shape; there were lines, there was a pallor, a look of less than perfect health. She remembered how she had always admired his immaculate appearance. But today she noticed a stain on his shirt collar, a patch of gray stubble on his neck, fingernails that needed trimming. (This would change. Each time she saw him after this, she would find him, as in the old days, flawlessly groomed and dressed. "Because of you," he would say. "*You* made me care again. You gave me back my pride.")

He said, "I suppose you know all about Ann. From the papers." She nodded, but she did not speak. Then he told her something she did not know: his wife was dead.

"Her heart," he said, briefly closing his eyes. "She had already begun to have trouble in her thirties—not the usual thing with women, but it ran in her family. It was something we always worried about. It was why we didn't have more children. The doctor advised against it." (Why had Ann never spoken of this?) "And Sophie always said it was a mistake, because it was bad for Ann, being an only child. When things started to go wrong, Sophie insisted it was because Ann had been so lonely growing up, though I myself have never believed this. And then came all the stress of the trial and so on. Of course, it isn't right to blame Ann for Sophie's death. I would never do that. As I say, there was a family history. Sophie's brother died before he was even forty. Though I can tell you, the whole terrible business was very hard on poor Sophie. You cannot imagine what she went through." His eyes watered, but he did not reach for the handkerchief.

She thought, If it is true he does not blame Ann for Sophie's death, it is a miracle.

Suffering builds character. No, she did not believe that. But one thing she did believe suffering could do was to lend character to a person's face. It was ironic, she thought, how suffering could make a person more attractive. Like melancholy, which, for whatever odd reason, often beautifies and dignifies. He had always been hand-some, but there was now this important change. The old blandness was gone. The old wax-figure look. Tragedy had etched him, and there was a new intensity and intelligence about Turner Drayton's face.

He had retired early, he was telling her. It had been years since he could concentrate on work. A nephew was running the family business. After Sophie's death he had not wanted to go on living in their house in Connecticut ("I was sure I'd go mad"). He had not sold the house, but he had closed it up and signed a lease on a fur-nished apartment in a new high-rise on Manhattan's Upper East Side. It was a gamble. He did not have many friends in the city, but the move had brought the distractions he'd been hoping for: new neighborhoods to explore (which was what he happened to be do-ing in the Village that day), concerts and exhibitions, and, above all, the ballet, to which he might go several times a week during the season. Some days he set out early ("like a tourist") and took in various sights, getting around as much as possible on foot, stop-ping in various restaurants for meals, not returning to his apart-ment till late. He wanted to be as tired as possible—exhausted, ideally—when he went to bed. There was a pool in his building where he swam every day. Weekends, he drove to Westchester, where his brother lived, and the two of them played golf.

His brother and his brother's wife were now his most frequent companions. Their names were Clifford and Edie, and they would come into the city a few times a month, and the three of them would go out together. Clifford and Edie had just talked him into signing up with them for a group tour to the People's Republic of China.

Listening, she formed her own idea of this brother and sister-in-law, imagining them not only trying to keep their bereft relative busy but also to find him a new wife. The trip to China was almost a year away, and they would be gone for about a month. She could tell by the way he spoke of it that he had agreed to go along more to be a good sport than because he was truly excited by the prospect. In the same spirit, he had allowed his brother to talk him into seeing a therapist, but this had not worked out well. "The doctor kept wanting me to go back and tell him about my childhood, as if that had anything to do with what happened to Ann or Sophie. He kept saying there were deeper roots to my sense of loss, for heaven's sake, as if the obvious weren't reason enough. He gave me pills to help me sleep, but beyond that he was worse than useless. I once burst into tears of frustration, and he was triumphant. 'Aha! Now at last we are making progress!' I never went back."

He was not used to talking so much. He was not used to talking about himself at all. She was careful not to interrupt. The café began to fill with people. The waitress turned up the music. It was noisy but not unpleasant. They were perfectly content to linger as the room kindled into life, and even the waitress warmed up. "Hi, guys. You getting hungry?" And so they ordered sandwiches.

The last time he had seen Ann, he said, had been at Sophie's funeral. Though he had never accused her, Ann was convinced that he blamed her for her mother's death. She said it would be better if he did not visit her after that, because it would be too hard for her. "That was her excuse, her reason for not wanting to see me anymore." Some demon drove him to keep up the habit of writing to her, sending whatever there was in the way of family news, though he knew this was of no interest to her, and she rarely wrote back. About her life in Maryville he knew almost nothing. "Except that I'm sure she prefers her fellow inmates to any of her relations, especially me." He did not think he would live to see her released. He knew it was possible he might never see her again. After her trial, with Sophie's blessing, he had set up a trust fund for Officer Sargente's two children. At first he had hesitated to tell Ann, but Sophie said of course they must tell her, and Ann might have ended up hearing about it anyway.

"She wasn't angry. She wasn't against it, but she thought I should have done something to help Kwame's family, too. As always, it came down to the same bitter quarrel. She said I was incapable of feeling the same generosity toward the Bloods because they weren't white."

To her surprise, he took her hand. "You're so good to let me go on and on like this, George. But it's such a comfort to be able to tell you—there aren't many people who would understand the way you do. You knew Ann. You knew how—how *tangled* everything was with her. Oh, just listen to me: talking about her in the past tense as if she were dead. But don't think she's dead to me, please don't think that. I may be dead to her, but she is not dead to me." His eyes watered again. He let go of her hand. "Not a day goes by that I don't relive the whole nightmare. People tell me I have to stop obsessing like this and move on. But I'm still a long way from being able to do that. If she would only agree to see me again, needless to say I'd be there as soon as they let me. She's the only child I have. Just imagine, if you had never found your sister again."

Which of them knew it first, that they would go home together?

Before, she would not have believed she could feel desire for a man almost sixty years old. Before, he would have been ashamed to think of himself seducing or being seduced by a woman half his age. But both at some point that evening knew that they would go home together, and both wanted it desperately to happen.

Forty-eight hours later, when they finally left each other (though not for long), she was more his than she would ever be anyone's. And he, for the first time in years, felt hope, permitting himself to believe that perhaps his life had not come to an end after all, that there existed still the possibility for some kind of happiness, and that he had every right to seize it.

Names. To him she was now Georgette; and, "I have to get used to calling you Turner, Mr. Drayton."

She went back to the bookshop on Eighth Street. She wanted to buy the copy of Proust that had been in the window. She wanted to buy it as a gift for Turner. But it had been sold.

The next time she saw him, he was carrying it. "I bought it for you!"

It was a time of small wonders. A few nights later he took her to the ballet. An all-Balanchine program, ending with *Vienna Waltzes*, which Balanchine had choreographed not long before. Turner had seen it several times. ("I could see it many more times and never tire of it.") But for her, it was not only her first *Vienna Waltzes* (she, too, would see it many times); it was her first night ever at the New York City Ballet.

She had heard so much about the company, she thought she was prepared. But she was not. She watched each performance with mounting excitement, squeezing Turner's hand. By the end of the last waltz, she was shaking. She did not understand how the dancers—of a beauty and ethereality that seemed scarcely human—could return to ordinary life when the curtain came down; could go home, like any mortal member of the audience, and brush their teeth and go to bed. As for the man who had created what they'd just seen—

"Well, in one way he is most definitely mortal."

They were in a restaurant. Not the Café des Artistes, not the Russian Tea Room, but a much smaller Midtown restaurant that, though completely full, remained almost as hushed as a study hall, and where the menu the waiter handed her—with such an air of gravity it might have been a declaration of war she was about to sign—did not show any prices.

"Yes," Turner explained apologetically. "They're very old-fashioned here. The ladies aren't supposed to worry their pretty little heads about prices."

It was a French restaurant, and she could not help wondering whether it was the same French restaurant he and Sophie had chosen for that first (and last) luckless dinner with Ann and Kwame. Ann! She knew exactly what Ann would have made of such a place—"a bourgeois horror show"—and what she would have made of *Vienna Waltzes. It's everything in the world I hate. All that beau monde frippery, the clothes and the jewels, all that luxury and waste . . . The glorification of a society from which ninety-nine percent of humanity would have been barred . . . The diamonds would have come from South African mines . . . the fruits of slave labor . . .*

She glanced around the room, surprised that no one else appeared to have heard that loud, angry voice.

The waiter arrived with their first courses. The thought of Ann in her cell at that moment while the two of them sat here threatened to—

"Do you remember the last waltz?"

Who could forget? The woman in white satin and bejeweled hair who seemed to awaken alone in a ballroom and proceeded to dance her ravishing, heartbreaking solo.

That woman, the dancer who had performed the role, Turner was explaining, was the love of the choreographer's life. "He created that dance specifically for her."

Were they married?

No. It was not as simple as that. In fact, it was quite complicated. Suzanne Farrell had joined Balanchine's company in 1961, when she was sixteen years old. "But he was more than forty years older than she, and he was married to someone else." Now all his passionate love went into making ballets for this unattainable girl and molding her into his ideal ballerina. The result was some of the greatest dance of all time. When at last Balanchine was able to get a divorce, he wanted his beloved to marry him, but she would not. When she married someone else, Balanchine was devastated. And vengeful. Suzanne Farrell, now the City Ballet's beloved star, was forced to leave the company.

"But then he repented and asked her to come back?"

No. It was she who, after performing in Europe for several years, wrote to him and asked to come back. He was past seventy then, and she was thirty. Whatever suffering they had caused each other was forgiven, and with his favorite's return he threw himself once again into making new dances for her, including the last waltz in *Vienna Waltzes*, one of the greatest roles he would ever make for her—and what was this ballet about if not love, the enchantment of love, the hope and the hopelessness of love, its beauty and strangeness and the suffering it brings?

Call it a happy ending. The setting for *The Earrings of Madame de* . . . also happened to be Vienna, and in it, too, the lovers danced and danced—in fact, that was their courtship, one endless waltz—perhaps to the very same music she had heard at the ballet that night. (All waltzes sounded the same to her.) As in the ballet, the same beau monde trappings: ball gowns, tailcoats, dress uniforms, decorations, ostrich plumes, jewels—the diamond earrings that mean so little to the Countess when they are a gift from her husband the General that she sells them without a pang, only to have them become her most cherished possession when, by a twist of fate, she receives them back, a gift from her lover the Baron.

"You know," Turner said, "after all the trouble started with Ann, Sophie lost interest in just about everything she used to care about, her antiques and her gardening, her charity work, even her friends. Going out. She did not see the point in going to something like the ballet anymore. But for me it was the one thing that I found took me completely out of myself for an evening and gave me real consolation. The sheer beauty of it. In fact, it had never meant more to me."

The music stayed and stayed with her. The vision of couples spinning endlessly in each other's arms. The swooning music, man and woman looking burningly into each other's faces, into each other's eyes, as they dipped and turned and flew, fabulous birds in a courtship ritual, lost in the delirium of love.

Years later, she would be there, alone, at the theater the night Suzanne Farrell gave her final performance before retiring from the stage; would see her dance the last waltz in *Vienna Waltzes* for the last time—no less ethereal at forty-four than she had ever been—and take her last bow under a blizzard of roses from which every thorn had been removed by volunteer fans.

It was November 1989, and George Balanchine had been dead for six years.

W hat would you say," Solange asked me, "if I were to move out of the city?"

"You mean . . . with Drew," I said carefully.

"Yes."

Enter Drew Michaelman. Solange had met him in the hospital. I had met him there, too. He was a regular visitor, like me, and his patient, the one he came to see, was a young woman named Trish who was called Slinky on the ward because of her eccentric locomotion. Her case was more serious than my sister's; it was as serious as could be. She was harmless, yet she terrified me. A human being who never made eye contact with anyone—I had no idea how terrifying this could be. She looked right through Drew, who had known her since kindergarten, had been her close friend for more than two decades during which, he explained sadly, she had been normal. Her inability to recognize people, or even to acknowledge their presence in the same room, had been all the excuse her family and the rest of her acquaintances appeared to have needed. No one else ever came to see Slinky but Drew. At the time, she was the only schizophrenic on the ward, and she had her own private nurse, a woman in a cheap platinum wig who passed most of her shift crocheting. The nurse snapped her gum while she worked and was glum and unfriendly and not big on eye contact, either. Stealthily, now and then she used her hooked needle to scratch under the wig.

Drew lived in a suburb across the George Washington Bridge, where he sold real estate, and he drove down to the hospital two or three times a week. I thought he was a nice person, a good person, even a heroic person, to do what he did. I thought he deserved a medal and was probably a wonderful real estate agent, but I also thought he was strange.

Something about him—his long, white, beautiful but cold-looking hands in particular—made me think of a priest. I would look at him, and the word *surplice* would come into my head, though I wasn't even sure I knew what a surplice was.

I don't think it occurred to me until later that perhaps, after a certain point, Drew had started coming to the p-ward as much to see my sister as to see his friend. I could understand how Solange must have seemed to him the picture of mental health by comparison. They spent visiting hours talking and playing Ping-Pong together, while the oblivious Trish slunk about the ward, muttering to herself and twirling her hands on either side of her head—so exactly like someone overacting the part of a nutcase she might have been faking (and there *were* fakes on the ward, there always are, people just that desperate for attention, expert malingerers)—and the wigged nurse sat on a straight-backed chair, chewing her gum and crocheting and largely ignoring her charge.

When I was at the hospital visiting Solange, I, too, chatted and played Ping-Pong with Drew, and sometimes the three of us ordered Chinese food and ate together in the dayroom. And though his business was not so good these days, Drew always insisted on paying, obviously because he felt this was what a gentleman ought to do, and he tipped the delivery boy generously, and he served the ladies first. I was grateful for his kindness and his attention to Solange, and I thought that when she was discharged, she would miss him. But she would miss the other patients, too, as well as some of the staff members: this was to be expected. That's what happened on any p-ward: you spent weeks, months, living with strangers almost like family, and then you left and never saw them again. So I was startled—a little squeamish, I confess—when, even before she'd been discharged, Drew and Solange began dating. Once Solange was deemed stable enough to be granted the privilege of passes, she and Drew went out to the Chinese restaurant;

they went to the movies. To my alarm, they went to Solange's apartment.

Was he taking advantage of her? Was that what he'd been doing on the p-ward, visiting someone who didn't even know he was there—*cruising*?

I hated such thoughts, but I could not stop them. Nor could I stop Solange from seeing Drew—night and day, once she'd left the hospital.

But why should I stop her? I argued with my cynical side. Wasn't it as good for Solange as it was for any other woman to be romanced by a man? What, after all, was wrong with Drew Michaelman?

He was a loner. That was one concern to me, right there. Besides Slinky, he did not seem to have any friends.

I understood how vulnerable Solange was at this moment. She did not have many friends herself, and she had never liked being alone. She'd had several relationships since Roach, and though none had worked out she was always wildly eager to throw herself into the next one. It was part of her illness, the ease with which she gave her heart and body. (When she was at her worst, she would offer herself to any passing male stranger, and, among other complications, she had once been arrested for soliciting a police officer.) I understood what it was about Drew that made her cling to him. He was the part of the p-ward she did not want to let go. His loyalty to his childhood friend had made a deep impression on Solange (never mind that he now appeared to be losing interest in poor Slinky). I had observed how well the two of them got along in the hospital, but I had trouble imagining them together on the outside. For one thing, he was much too straight for her. Though he drank (more than was good for him, in my view), he had never taken drugs and had a low opinion of those who did. He had never worn a beard or long hair. He did not like rock and roll; he liked pop. He voted Republican. He was about as far from Roach (not to mention Mick Jagger) as could be. (He knew all about Mick. "Good thing I'm not the jealous type," he said, laughing, and I was more than happy to add this to the plus side of the ledger: a sense of humor.)

I thought Solange's feelings for Drew would soon pass, but until they did, it was not right for me to interfere. Meanwhile, he appeared to be making her happy. And who was to say straight wasn't the best thing for her, anyway?

So when Solange told me over and over how mad she was about Drew, I just listened. I listened with a smile, tapping my foot to the beat of a waltz and to lyrics that went something like *I've got a love of my own*. I was glad that she was happy, glad that she was too distracted by her happiness to notice anything different about me, to suspect that as she talked on and on, my mind was elsewhere, usually on either my last or my next encounter with Turner. But when she started talking about moving in with Drew, I snapped to attention.

"Drew thinks city life is bad for me. He thinks I'd be a lot better off in a less stressful environment. He says I could find work at least as good as the record store anywhere. He says he wants to take care of me."

It's true that I myself had often wondered whether someone as fragile and labile as Solange would have been better off in a less chaotic place than New York City. But further than that I would not go, since I could not bear the thought of leaving.

Now I said—carefully—"I don't know, Ange. I mean, you two practically just met. Maybe it's too soon to take such a big step. What's the harm in getting to know each other?"

"But we're totally in love!" she sang. "If it works out, we'll get married. And if it doesn't, I can move back into the city." This, too, was part of her illness: reducing complex issues to simple formulas. She used to freeze my blood regularly with this: "And if I don't get better, I'll just kill myself."

At the time, Solange was in the care of a shrink named Rowe, a man I had mixed feelings about. Dr. Rowe was a great believer in medication; in his opinion, for anyone with Solange's condition, talk therapy was largely irrelevant. Well, he was the doctor. But it seemed that whenever Solange (or I, for that matter) wanted to talk with him about anything at all, Dr. Rowe grew impatient. The most important thing was to stay on her medication, was all he ever said: his answer to everything. Her medication, I agreed, was a gift from God, which was not to say I didn't have my concerns about that bridge mix of antipsychotic, antidepression, antianxiety, and anti-insomnia pills (if I'm not forgetting one) that Rowe prescribed to replace the lithium she would *not* stay on, because she hated how it made her feel: dull, fat, logy, unsexy, and "as if I didn't have a creative bone in my body." For what ailed Solange there was no cure. This point Dr. Rowe had driven home to me. "You have to understand she'll be dealing with this her whole life. The possibility of future suicide attempts cannot be ruled out. And she'll never survive without medication." I like a doctor who is straightforward with me. But I didn't know what to make of the fact that doctor and patient had no rapport. Dr. Rowe appeared to have no curiosity about Solange, no interest in her aside from her chemical imbalances. He wanted to help her, but he made no effort to get to know her. In fact, with the exception of Dr. Well, who would not be in the picture for some years yet, none of Solange's shrinks seemed to believe that in order to treat her they needed to find out first who she was.

Still, it was important for me to know what Dr. Rowe thought of this new situation. We spoke briefly on the phone. Solange was a grown woman, he reminded me. When not delusional, she was perfectly capable of making her own decisions, and it would do no good to treat her like an incompetent or a child. And after all, she was not going to the other side of the world. She would still be living reasonably close to me, and she would still be under Dr. Rowe's care. The most important thing was (I could not refrain from saying the words aloud with him) *"to stay on her medication."* He had met Drew once or twice, in the hospital. "He seems like a nice enough fellow." And then Dr. Rowe gave a chuckle and said, "I mean, he's no Mick Jagger, but . . ." He, too, had a sense of humor.

We agreed it was a good thing Drew was aware from the outset of the serious nature of Solange's problems. He had met her soon after her admission to the hospital, when she was still raving about assassinations; in other words, he knew what he was getting into. Also, having spent so much time visiting p-wards, he was more knowledgeable than most people about mental illness in general, and as alert to certain danger signs as I'd had to become myself. He promised to see that Solange took her pills every day.

Let me be honest. I knew this thing with Drew probably was not going to last. Dr. Rowe I was sure knew it, too. But after our phone conversation I felt as if I had been granted a kind of reprieve. Drew was a nice person; even Dr. Rowe thought so. He was generous, responsible, kind. His house when I visited it was tidy, decently decorated, not at all the squalid bachelor pad I had feared, with (aha!) a small crucifix mounted in the front hall. His widowed mother when I met her was a dear old thing who made sure to tell me how lucky she was to have such a good son. (In fact, to her he was not Drew, but "Sonny.") Every week he escorted her to Mass. He had a tank full of striped and polka-dotted fish and an exuberant sheepdog named Boz. All this added up to a reassuring picture. It is true that by this time I had begun to suspect that Drew Michaelman was hiding something. But I was hiding something myself, and I knew that not everything hidden is evil. Whatever happened, I told myself, Solange had made her own decision, and for the moment, at least, she was more Drew's responsibility than mine. Already he had adopted a possessive, even uxorious, way with her. A woman observing the two of them in public nudged her husband. "See how nice he treats her," she said instructively. The man shrugged. "I'd be nice to you, too, if you looked like that."

But wasn't it amazing that this should have happened at precisely the moment when I'd been guiltily wishing my intrusive, high-maintenance sister off my hands? Because of Turner, of course. First of all, because I wanted to spend all my free time with him, but also because I did not want her to know, not yet. An incredible coincidence, wasn't it? Neat as a novelist's twist.

*L*ove is superstitious. Tell the world, expose yourselves too soon to other people, and the spell might break.

Turner's brother was concerned. Turner hardly came out on weekends anymore to play golf. "He keeps making excuses. I hope he's all right." But Edie had guessed the truth—partly from observing how much sprucer her brother-in-law's appearance was these days. And there was something else that a sharp woman will always sense: he had as much the aura of a man with an active sex life as Clifford, for example, did not.

Well, said Clifford, if Turner had started seeing someone, why couldn't they meet her? Patience, said Edie. "Don't say anything. He'll introduce us when he's good and ready."

But Turner did not want to introduce them. He did not even want to tell them about Georgette, and she did not want to meet them or anyone else from his world, not yet. She and Turner were of the same mind: keep their secret as long as possible. They had already had a taste of how unpleasant exposure could be. It was one of their nights at the ballet. During the intermission, they ran into some people Turner knew—quite well, in fact, though he had not been in touch with them recently. These were the Holts, from Connecticut, part of the Draytons' circle for years. Though no one alluded to it, the last time they had all seen each other was at Sophie's funeral. Had Turner been alone, the Holts would have embraced him. Instead, greetings were exchanged with an air of confusion. It was not just awkward, but painful. "And this is my friend Georgette George." A stage name, anyone might have guessed. In those days, she still enjoyed dressing up. And in those days vintage clothing was not only all the rage but made it possible for a person to dress up and look chic even if she had no money. It was a little like wearing a costume, with small imperfections acceptable as they would never have been in clothing that was new. That night she was wearing a cocktail dress that had been made in the fifties: a full black taffeta skirt gathered at the waist and a red velvet bodice with a sweetheart neckline. "That may be the sexiest dress I've ever seen," Turner had said, arriving to pick her up. Now, a related but distinctly different impression seemed to have occurred to the Holts, and though no doubt they tried to hide it, disapproval came off them like a mist. His "friend"? Imagine if they had known she was his daughter's college roommate. Their children had grown up with Ann.

The incident had been enough to taint, if not spoil, the evening. The Holts had a subscription to the City Ballet—as did others of Turner's acquaintance. This problem would arise again, would always be there to haunt them.

But why should they have been *haunted*? Why was it a *problem*? What were they doing that was *wrong*?

When they were alone together (as they were most of the time when she was not at school), there was rarely a moment of discomfort between them. Everything seemed to fall naturally into place; they were content and at peace with each other. Some things they were reluctant to discuss: the future in general was a formidable subject. They never spoke of his upcoming trip to China, for example. But later the same night that they had run into the Holts, they were both pensive. If only they could be somewhere else, somewhere far away, where nobody knew them. A place where they could begin a new life together. It was the sweetest of fantasies, one they would often indulge in, but though it eased their torment and deepened their lovemaking that night, they knew it was no solution.

What were they like as lovers? Different generations. Half his age, she had already had many more partners than he. But he was the one who had known this kind of love before. Compared with any other generation, hers had been the most laid-back—often, paradoxically, aggressively so—about nudity. Nineteen sixty-nine: visitors to the Museum of Modern Art encounter a group of naked men and women in the fountain of the sculpture garden. Today such an incident—far from the only one of its kind then—seems to belong not to the historical past, but to myth. *All bodies are beautiful* was a counterculture moral. But he did not believe his body could be beautiful to her. Oh, he knew he was not bad for his age. He weighed the same as he'd weighed at twenty-five; he was naturally lean, and he swam laps daily. *For his age* he knew he looked great. But he was also all too sadly aware of the looseness of the flesh at his waist, his skinny shanks with their patches of flaky skin, and the coarse hair on his chest, half gray, half white. Now she, whose many partners had all been close to her own age, would learn what time did to a man's erection. And he was indignant for her: she deserved better than this. But he never doubted that she loved him. And how could he tear himself away, he asked himself. She was saving his life with every kiss.

There was the difference in their ages, which was problem enough. There was the difference in their backgrounds. And there was Ann.

Q: Did they have an obligation to tell Ann?

He said, "It will be difficult to tell her."

She said, "I am not in touch with her . . ."

"I don't want to tell her," he said. "What good will it do to tell her?"

"Wouldn't she want to know?"

"She would want to know, I think, yes."

"Yes. And she would be appalled."

"Yes, and no doubt angry."

Pause.

"And she would laugh."

"Yes!"

It was not hard to imagine Ann's corrosive response.

He said, "Not now. I cannot bring myself to tell her now." It was rare for him to speak bitterly of Ann, and the words were terrible to hear: "She has already poisoned so much."

Love is superstitious. Tell Ann, expose themselves to her attack, to her corrosive laughter, and the spell would break for sure.

*

By chance, outside a bookstore. That was how Turner had told his brother and sister-in-law he had met Georgette, leaving Ann out altogether. "We were both interested in the same book."

The four of them were gathered at Turner's apartment for dinner. He had hired a cook, as he sometimes did when it was just the two of them. Introductions were hardly less awkward than they had been with the Holts. Edie in particular could not hide her feelings, though she'd already been told much about the person she was going to meet. On the way to Turner's apartment, Edie had been lightly fuming. It was her great wish—a wish shared by her husband and many of their friends—to see Turner—poor Turner, who had suffered so much and so unjustly—find a second wife as good as his first one. But even before meeting her, Edie was sure this position could never be filled by a woman half his age, without money or family (he had been grilled and had been forthcoming about everything except how he'd met Georgette), with a name like a cancan dancer, who had appeared at the ballet looking, according to Bev Holt, "like a valentine."

Edie said, "It's so unlike him." Which only made it more worrying. Were Turner the kind of man to chase after young things . . . But he had never been that kind of man. He had never chased any woman except Sophie. And since her death, though any number of eligible, attractive women had sought his attention, he had shown no serious interest in any of them. Partly loyalty, partly depression.

"From what I can tell," Clifford said, "he really likes this woman. I think he's finally—"

"But he shouldn't be wasting his time in a relationship that has no future, should he? I mean, it's not fair to her, either. Unless, of course, you think they'll get married!" In fact, Clifford did think this. Turner himself had led him to think it. But the note of outrage in Edie's voice told Clifford not to say it. "He's so vulnerable right now," Edie went on. "My god, given all he's been through, wouldn't it be terrible if he were to end up with his heart broken." And, after a beat, "Or his pocket picked."

"Oh, come now, Edie. My brother's nobody's fool, you know that. And there's no reason to think this woman's like that."

"Isn't there? So you honestly think she'd be with him if he were a pauper?"

Clifford shrugged. Fairly or not, the lovers of rich people, unless rich themselves, were always automatically suspect. "I guess it's a bit odd she wouldn't rather be with someone her own age. But maybe she's one of those girls looking for a daddy."

"A *sugar* daddy."

All this meant was that they loved him. He was family. They felt protective of him, they did not want to see him hurt, they wanted him to be happy.

Arriving at the apartment, handing Turner her coat, Edie reminded herself to do a bit of snooping before she left. She wanted to get a sense of how ensconced Georgette was. (On the way home, she reported, "I found some of her clothes in the bedroom closet and not much else. But as I understand it, she doesn't have much in the way of possessions.")

Over dinner, Edie kept bringing the conversation around to the trip to China. Could this have been to make Georgette feel left out?

"We'll have an interpreter, of course, but shouldn't we try to learn a few phrases, just to be polite? We don't want to come across as typical ugly Americans. What do you think, Turner?" Turner hesitated before saying quietly that he didn't think an American tour group would have much chance of contact with any Chinese people besides their official guides. He caught Georgette's eye and smiled and looked away again, and she thought, Wait till they find out he's not going.

"How can you eat that?" Clifford asked, playfully puckering his lips. He was talking about the preserved lemon that the cook had served with the Moroccan chicken. In fact, Georgette found the stinging, bittersweet briny taste of it just what she craved at the moment.

"It's really supposed to be just for garnish," Edie said, forcing Georgette to take another bite. "Speaking of food, I don't know about you boys, but I'm a little concerned about eating on our trip. All that salt and lard and MSG."

What was it Ann had said that time, about Chinese food, about not telling Sophie and Turner about a certain great restaurant she knew in Chinatown? *"People like my parents don't deserve the real thing."* Georgette wished she hadn't remembered.

Mercifully, the evening was short. "We've got the long drive back and the dogs waiting to be walked." The door shut behind them, and Georgette began to cry. Turner held her, saying, "You know, sometimes all you need to do is give people a little time." She remembered Kwame saying something similar about people's response to his being with Ann.

On her next vacation from school he took her to Mexico. They had not traveled together before, and the trip had the feel of a honeymoon. They had planned to start out in Mexico City and move on to Acapulco. But three days after they arrived, she fell violently ill. The hotel doctor prescribed antibiotics even as he warned they might not do anything. The doctor was an American and had the cloaked and slightly disreputable air often associated with expatriate doctors. The first time he came, he'd been interrupted at lunch and arrived reeking of tequila. Something about their situation appeared to amuse him. He behaved deliberately as if they were father and daughter, though it was plain they were sharing the same bed. For several days she was as weak as an infant; she had intermittent fever. The hotel doctor came every morning, Turner's anxiety drawing patronizing smiles along with assurances that Georgette was not in mortal danger. Turner, who did not entirely trust the doctor, wanted to take her to a hospital. But the idea of ending up in a foreign hospital and having to stay there alone, especially at night, terrified her. As it was, Turner was always at her side. He might easily have hired help, a nurse, and gone out by himself, but instead he took complete charge of her, bathing her and feeding her the tiny amounts of food she was able to swallow. Even when she was asleep, which was a good deal of the time, he kept watch. He carried her from the bed to the armchair, where he wrapped her in a blanket (she was always cold) and sat with her on his lap while the maid changed the sheets.

If not in mortal danger, she had never been so sick in her life. And as physical sickness can often make a person homesick as well, she found herself missing Solange. "Call her," urged Turner. "Talk as long and as often as you like." Solange knew about Turner by now and had even met him, but she remained too absorbed in her new life with Drew to pay much mind to anything outside it. Careful what you pray for. In her vulnerable state, Georgette could not help feeling her sister's inattention as a wound. So far, she had avoided talking at length with Turner about her family, but now, in her illness, and in the intimacy of the sickroom, she opened up.

"Solange and I, we're like our own separate branch of the Georges, the only connection to family either of us has. Even before our mother died, we were both estranged from her, and we haven't known anything about our father since we were little girls. When we were growing up, we were both very attached to Guy. Now we never see him. We haven't even met all his kids. Zelma got herself a whole new set of sisters when she joined her convent. And the twins, who've always been close to each other, spent so much time living with relatives they're more like cousins than siblings to the rest of us. They both went into the army straight out of high school, and they both decided to stay in. They move around a lot. We might get a card from one of them around Christmas, and once in a blue moon someone calls. These calls never last more than a couple of minutes, though, because it's like strangers talking: no common ground. And I always feel horribly guilty afterward. I feel guilty whenever I remember the twins, as if their being sent away from home was something I could have prevented. At least they weren't separated, and the truth is, they were probably better off than they would have been with Mama, but that doesn't mean it was right. I feel horrible and guilty about Guy, too. I hear about him mostly from Zelma. He was in drug rehab for a while, but now Zelma says he drinks all day and can't hold a job. He cheats on his wife, and sometimes he beats her. In rehab they said a lot of his behavior had to do with his having been in Vietnam. But I see something else. I see our father all over again. I feel guilty when I listen to Zelma talk about Guy, but I also don't want to hear it. I try not to think about him or his wife and kids. His wife used to be my best friend in school, but now she hates us all.

"The last time we were all in the same place was at our mother's funeral, and since then, there hasn't been any reason for us to get together. Some of us may never see each other again. Sometimes I think, Well, this is what happens to families. I know plenty of people who are alienated from their parents. But other times I feel tormented. I want to say no, no, this was all a mistake, something that should never happen to any family, and why did it happen to mine?

"Now, Solange—she's always seen things differently. I guess that's because of her time on the road and the people she hooked up with then. Hippies were always bigger on friendship than on blood. You know what Robert Frost said, about home being the place where, when you go there, they have to take you in? Well, during her Rain period Solange met kids who'd been kicked out of their homes by their own parents. Because of drugs, often, or because a girl got pregnant. And some of these kids were even younger than she was. Solange herself still thinks running away from home was the best thing she could have done."

When Georgette was somewhat stronger, they began taking meals in the hotel restaurant, and later, when she was stronger still, in a much better restaurant in the same square as the hotel. They would sit a long time over their meal (what little she could eat had to be consumed very slowly), talking. She remained fatigued enough so that she often needed to sleep during the day, and then she might have trouble going to sleep at night. And so they stayed awake, in bed, in the dark, long after the noises of the street had died away, talking. And the effect of all this talk was such that, if as a vacation the trip could only be called a disaster, it brought them closer than any perfect honeymoon might have done. Before they left Mexico, she would find herself telling Turner things she had always hesitated to tell him before. She told him the story of her last meeting with Ann, filling in an earlier, elliptical version. She had told him about the fight, the accusations and brutal words. Now she told him about the punch, the broken thumb. Confessions. A desire to come clean. She told him what had happened with Whit Bishop. And she told him about the rape.

When they talked about Ann, Georgette was more than ever moved by Turner's loyalty. Nothing Ann had done (and could she have possibly done more?) could turn him against her. This had always been so, and had been true of Sophie as well. (*"I could murder one of them and the other would stand by me"*—how astonishing that Ann had actually once said those words, some of the first words Georgette had ever heard from her.) Something that occurred to Georgette often these days, whenever Turner was being especially tender and paternal: Ann had this, this was hers by right, she had only to reach out her arms, and she had rejected it. She had spat on it. Ann hated this man. She rejected her father, and she spat on him. How could that be? *I hate every bourgeois capitalist*, Ann would have said—had, in fact, more than once said. But this answer only maddened Georgette, only deepened the mystery of Dooley Ann Drayton.

Shame.

"Her lawyer understood," said Turner, "and we began to understand better, too, as the trial moved along and he tried to explain how deep it went, Ann's shame at having been born wealthy and white, and what this meant for someone coming of age in those politicized times. The term he used was 'white skin privilege.' He talked about Ann and the curse of white skin privilege all the time. He interviewed Sophie and me for hours. Then he asked for a short biography of Ann—he wanted us to put it in writing. Of course we did whatever he asked. And it was such a relief the way he treated us, not as if we were monsters, but with sympathy and respect. He was especially gentle with Sophie. He'd lost his own mother when he was a boy, and he seemed to understand that Sophie's health was in danger. I don't know. Maybe he was just a good actor. Maybe, underneath, he despised us every bit as much as Ann did. If so, the mask never slipped. As for us, we liked and trusted him, and we had great faith in him—not that he'd be able to save Ann from prison, but that he'd fight for her as hard as he could.

"I never doubted he was on the right track. If you knew Ann at all, you knew exactly what happened that day, you knew what was going through her head when she shot at the police and that no word of her testimony was a lie." (Georgette was in complete agreement with this. She, too, believed every word Ann had said, and she thought if this had not been the case, her affair with Turner would probably not have been possible.) "And it was so like her to refuse to compromise, to refuse to make things any easier for herself. I know there are a whole lot of people, including most of my friends, who believe that even though we always supported Ann in public, we must be deeply ashamed of her. But in fact, no matter how wrong I think she was or how terrible I feel about what she did, I never saw it in that light, that she had disgraced herself and her family. I'm afraid Sophie did see it this way at certain moments, but not I, and this might have made the whole ordeal somewhat easier for me, I don't know.

"I never doubted that Ann thought she was saving Kwame's life. In her mind, she had no choice. This I have always understood. What's been so much harder to understand is her stubbornness, her refusal to express remorse, because I cannot believe Ann did not feel remorse. You know that after the trial she made it clear that she did not want any appeals or petitions filed, no pleas or campaigns of any sort on her behalf, as if she was absolutely determined to see the whole experience through to the bitter end. When you look at everything, it's hard to believe Ann didn't want to go to prison. I think no matter how right she thought she was, she wanted to take responsibility for what had happened and, even though she didn't believe in the system, would bow to its punishment. And it seems to me there must have been some element of remorse in this."

According to Lester Prysock, with whom Turner kept in touch, Ann had not approved of President Carter commuting Patricia Hearst's sentence to time served. "It infuriated her, the way some reporters insisted on throwing them together in the same pot. Patty Hearst is everything in the world Ann hates." Hearst had betrayed people who'd helped her and had proved herself willing to do anything, regardless of the truth or of the consequences to anyone else, to save her own skin. Ann thought it absurd for radicals to speak out for Hearst as one of their own. When Andrew Young was asked to give an example of an American political prisoner and named Patty Hearst, Ann gnashed her teeth. "She predicted the commutation, by the way. She said no one with parents that rich and that powerfully connected to the Establishment was going to have to serve out a sentence, no matter what the judge and jury said. It was just further proof, as if Ann needed any, of how corrupt the justice system was."

As far back as the trial, Georgette had begun to see that Ann had not been as open as she always pretended or believed herself to be. The incident with the homeless man in New Haven—it seemed incredible to Georgette that this had never come up between them, not once in all those nights of endless talk. Much that she learned from Turner was also new, beginning with Sophie's bad heart and the reason for Ann's being an only child. So Ann had her secrets like anyone else. Perhaps some of the details about Ann's past that were now being revealed for the first time had been too painful for Ann to mention? Of only one thing was Georgette certain: it was not because Ann had forgotten them.

"Hard as she might have been on me," Turner recalled, "she was always harder on Sophie." Ann had contempt for the way Turner made money, but in her eyes Sophie was the worst kind of parasite: no occupation, lolling in all the bourgeois comforts, with all the housework done by servants. To Ann it seemed that Sophie cared about nothing but material things, because her house was precious to her, and the way it was decorated. And she loved furniture, and she loved clothes. Scarves. "Oh, such a fight about scarves." Sophie adored pretty scarves; she collected them and almost always wore one. But to Ann it was both absurd and obscene. In a world where millions went hungry, this idiotic passion for an *accessory*. The whole house, every room, every drawer and closet full of useless, decorative *things*. Ann had a horror of bric-a-brac, of which Sophie was also overfond. Didn't Sophie see how it made the work of the maid who did the dusting that much harder? Sophie's love of silver was even more objectionable. Ann said that cleaning it exposed the servants to toxic substances.

But even Sophie's charity work was suspect, because it never brought her into actual contact with the beneficiaries, the poor themselves. Sophie never even laid eyes on them, the Invisibles, the Untouchables, and this was so typical of women of her caste, and to Ann it represented such a moral failing that it ended up being more significant than anything Sophie might have accomplished, canceled her good deed right out. But Sophie had been raised to believe that the fortunate had a responsibility to help the less fortunate; it was a social duty she would not have dreamed of ignoring. In fact, this was where Ann first learned the rule—*he who has is obligated to help he who has not*—it was at home that she learned this, at her mother's knee.

Understand: Sophie never questioned her own upbringing, never doubted that the values instilled in her by her parents were sound, never suspected that raising her daughter exactly as she herself had been raised might turn out to have been in any way wrong, let alone disastrous. Here, she was at odds with most women of her circle and many women of her generation. She said, "Why does everyone believe this man Spock knows more about raising our children than we do?"—so confident was she in her natural ability to be a good mother, which no doubt came of having deeply loved and always believed in her own mother. When Ann accused Sophie of thinking there was nothing on earth wrong with her or the way she lived, it was true.

Turner said, "Neither of us ever experienced the kind of class guilt that would end up tearing Ann to pieces. I, too, was raised to believe that a portion of my income must go to others. But no one ever suggested to me, nor did I ever imagine, that the people to whom I gave were in fact my own victims. Ann wanted us to believe that our people were thieves, and that everything we possessed belonged legally to the generations of workers who'd labored to make and keep us wealthy, and she was forever trying to get us to confess to that crime. She wanted Sophie to give everything she had to the civil rights movement, as reparations, because a branch of her family once owned slaves."

Until Lester Prysock entered their lives, the Draytons had all but forgotten the incident of the homeless man in New Haven. But as they obediently worked together on their assignment to write about their daughter's life, this and many other memories came flooding back to them.

His biggest regret, said Turner, was that he had not had a closer relationship with his only child. "I'm not saying that Officer Sargente would be alive today or that Ann would never have gone to jail, because of course I can't know that, but I do wish I'd been more involved in her life when she was growing up." For one thing, if he hadn't left so much of Ann's upbringing to his wife, perhaps Sophie would not have placed such a heavy load of blame on herself.

"When Ann was born, Sophie tended to be rather fussy and overprotective, surely partly because she knew Ann was going to be her only baby."

And in those early years, life between mother and child is blessed, no hint of the sorrow and struggle to come. Dooley-Ooley is a goo-good baby, a quick-learning toddler with a big-girl laugh and immense blue eyes that seem to take everything in. Patty-cake, patty-cake, have you ever seen such an alert, sensitive child? That sensitivity could cause concern now and then, but real trouble does not begin until Dooley is old enough to observe certain facts—for example, that toys and ponies and party dresses are not given to everyone equally. When she asks Sophie *why* things are the way they are and Sophie replies, "Because that is how God arranged it," Dooley says, "Then God must be a very bad man." She learns to read and for a time devours stories about orphans and changelings. She reads and rereads stories in which, say, a child born to peasants somehow or other ends up in a rich or royal family. The first story she herself ever writes will be in this vein. At its happy ending, the prince—who, of course, is not really a prince—is reunited with his true parents, "a humple farmer and his humple wife whose hands were dark with soil but whose hearts were all of gold." Her parents save the neatly handwritten pages in a special folder, proud, even though, according to Turner, "the rich parents, the king and queen, the ones who are obviously us, are all of shit."

School. Year after year, so much to learn, including many things to make a sensitive child question her parents and shudder at their ways. Lost illusions, paradise lost. Dooley is not alone. Other students and many of her friends are passing through the same stages of disenchantment. The schools she goes to are progressive, and quite a few of the teachers, not so privileged themselves, are determined to open the eyes of their overprivileged students.

"Oh, I'm not blaming the teachers," Turner said. "It was the times, after all, and needless to say, we wouldn't have sent our children to those schools if we hadn't approved of what went on there. Nobody was seriously worried then about creating a Kathy Boudin or a Patty Hearst. We still could not imagine such a thing. But I think Lester Prysock was right: this was where at least some of the more impressionable kids began to feel marked. They took the ills of American society personally, and they began to feel very guilty and to wonder if anything they ever did could remove the curse of white skin privilege."

In Sophie's mother's day, a woman would put on a dress and a hat and gloves to go into town, even if it was just to visit the post office. But now it is the fashion to be casual, and an outfit popular with Sophie's set is a pair of dungarees with the cuffs rolled, penny loafers, and a sweatshirt or a man-tailored shirt with a bandana tied at the neck. Dooley protests. What does her mother mean by dressing herself up in this takeoff of workingmen's clothes? (She will be equally bothered, a few years later, by college students in patched jeans and clogs and peasant blouses.) In school, they have been studying the French Revolution. Dooley thinks of Marie Antoinette and her friends dressing up as milkmaids and shepherdesses at the little play farm the queen had built on the grounds of the palace at Versailles. French quiz. *Q: Croyez-vous que Marie Antoinette et les autres membres de l'aristocratie française aient mérité leur destin? Expliquez votre réponse.*

Going into town, Sophie sometimes carries a pocketbook, but she does not carry a wallet. Sophie rarely carries money. She takes little Dooley into town, they go from store to store, they shop, they stop for lunch or tea, they smile and greet each person who waits on them, they say hello, they say goodbye, but no one ever says a word about money, and no bill or check ever appears. When Dooley comes to understand what this means, and how well-off a person has to be to enjoy this particular privilege, she is mortified. She discovers that it is the sign of a certain type of person from a certain class, this never carrying money, and she sees it as the height of bourgeois pretension and hypocrisy. Money? *Qu'est-ce que c'est?* She sees herself in the eyes of those store clerks and waiters as something detestable, the wormy little apple that does not fall far from the tree. They smile at her, but she believes those smiles to be forced, fake, and what those people secretly want is for something bad to happen to her. Off with her head! Her mother scolds, "What has gotten into you? Why are you so rude? Why do you look away when people say hello to you?" The truth is, Dooley can no longer look them in the face. "Sweetheart, why are you crying?" To Sophie, her daughter's shame is inexplicable. "We pay those people, sweetheart, don't you understand? We pay them later, that's all. It's just a matter of convenience." Dooley's request that her mother start carrying a wallet like any normal person strikes Sophie as ludicrous. If she did not know that other people's children were exhibiting the same kind of irrational behavior these days, she might fear her daughter was mad. But if not mad, why so mean? "Mummy, don't you realize how much those people must hate the very sight of you?" Sophie's turn to cry.

Turner said, "Ann hated that we didn't know any people who weren't just like ourselves, how everyone we socialized with was the same color, the same religion, same class—which was true. But the constant socializing itself was something she objected to. Sophie always liked to entertain; she liked giving dinners and parties and hosting charity events. Sometimes her name or her picture would be in the newspapers, and Ann would get upset. How could any reasonable, decent person want to appear in the society pages? It was like flaunting your privilege. Ann said it was like taking out an ad to announce you were rich."

But the most serious battles of all in the unhappy Drayton household will be fought over servants. Over the years, many different people will work for the Draytons, tending to the house and grounds. There are the regular domestic servants, and there are the extras hired to do heavy cleaning or seasonal jobs, or to help with parties. Almost without exception these people are black, and several of them are related, or at least acquainted with one another. They are paid by the hour, most of them above the minimum wage, though not by much. They are paid the going rate for such work in this particular part of the country. Sophie has grown up with servants, and she deals with them as she has been taught to deal with them, in a manner she considers above criticism. She does not know what Dooley means when she says that the tone her mother uses with the servants is subtly different from the tone she uses with the people who work in town, or with the white workers or repairmen who are sometimes called to the house (and, needless to say, vastly different from the tone she uses with social equals). Sophie crosses her arms high on her chest and taps her foot. Well . . . ? But Dooley cannot describe what she means, exactly. "I just know what I hear." Not that she hears it very often, since the only time Sophie addresses a servant is to tell him or her what she wants done. She never engages in conversation, not even with those who have worked for her for years. She knows little about her employees' pasts or about their daily lives apart from what they do on the job. "They're *hands* to you," Dooley says. "Hands and backs, not whole human beings." There are many days when the only words Sophie might exchange with a servant are *hello* and *goodbye*.

In school, they have been studying slavery, and Dooley is appalled that her parents can bear to have black servants at all.

"Oh, would you like me to fire them?" Sophie says. "Maybe that would solve all their problems."

"Well, how about for the moment you double their salaries."

"Really, Dooley, you are becoming impossible."

Turner said, "Things that seemed perfectly nice to Sophie, such as offering old clothes to the maid before giving them to Goodwill, or letting her take home the leftovers from a party—to Ann, these were patronizing, demeaning gestures. She believed these things were accepted not with genuine gratitude, but out of the need to avoid looking ungrateful. I don't know. I suppose this might be so, though I confess it never occurred to me."

When she is small, Ann does not understand why she cannot visit the servants' homes the same way they are "visiting" hers.

There is a woman named Doretta Weems. Everyone calls her Retta. She will work for the Draytons for several years, starting when Dooley is in kindergarten. Sophie is forever reminding Dooley that Retta has work to do, and Dooley mustn't pester her. But Dooley is as curious about the servants as Sophie is incurious. She follows Retta from room to room, repeatedly offering to help with the chores, and when she sits in the kitchen eating the lunch or snack Retta has prepared for her, she pelts Retta with questions. And so, though Retta has never been the talkative kind, Dooley manages to learn much about her. Dooley has picked up something different about Retta's speech, and Retta says it is because she is from South Carolina. Dooley goes to get her schoolbook with its map of the United States and asks Retta to show her where South Carolina is. Later, this memory will break her heart: Retta anxiously scanning the map, frowning, until finally Dooley cries, *"I found it!"* and Retta says, "Oh yeah, that's it." Retta has two children, a boy and a girl. The girl is big, almost a grown-up, but the boy is around Dooley's age. Why can't Dooley meet him? "Oh, one day, maybe one day," Retta says. She has a habit of chuckling after she finishes saying something, as if everything, on second thought, were amusing.

Dooley especially likes hearing about Retta's people down South. The brother home from the Korean War who sat down and ate ten pieces of fried chicken and two whole peach pies with peach ice cream all by himself. The father who could catch fish from a stream with his bare hands, until he went blind from glaucoma. In Retta's town lived a boy whose tongue was scorched when he was struck by lightning, and a preacher with a peg leg whose real leg had been chewed off by a gator. A woman who died giving birth sat up in her coffin at the sound of her infant crying.

Ann remembers these tales and repeats them at dinner, banging the table with one elbow to show how the preacher stumped to his pulpit.

In school, they are assigned a theme: "My Favorite Person." Dooley is too bashful to read what she has written to Retta, so Sophie does it for her while Retta dabs at her eyes with a corner of her apron. But later, when mother and daughter are saying good night, Sophie says, "You know, sweetheart, Retta is too nice to say so, but you only make her life harder by hanging around her so much."

"Is it true?" Dooley asks Retta, and receives a cryptic response:

"That's for your mama to decide, don't you think?" As Retta so often says about one thing or another: That is for the Lord to decide.

Sophie reckons it is not too soon to begin teaching her daughter the Proper Way to Behave with Servants, using the same method her own mother used to teach her. Make it a game. You be Retta, and I'll be you. Now I'll be Retta, and you be you. Now, let's say you want to tell Retta you are having friends over after school and you'd like her to bake some brownies. Or say you want Ora (another maid, and Retta's sister-in-law) to hem a dress for you.

Dooley has fun with the role-playing. But the first time she tries out what she has learned, she catches such a look of surprise and recognition and disappointment on Retta's face that Dooley feels as if her tongue has been scorched, like the tongue of that boy struck by lightning. In fact, she *has* been struck by lightning of a sort; she has experienced a bolt of recognition herself, one that will haunt and shame her the rest of her life. She will never forget Retta's look. She will never forgive herself for playing her mother, for not seeing through the game.

The teachers at the school Retta's son, Israel, attends hold a one-day strike, and Retta gets Sophie's permission to bring him to work with her. Israel spends most of that rainy day in the kitchen, reading *Sinbad the Sailor* and listening to a transistor radio. By now Dooley has met Israel once or twice before. When she comes home from school, it is still raining, and Dooley takes him upstairs to her room to listen to records. Israel has a rash on his chin, an archipelago of small scabs.

Turner told the story in a pained voice, pausing often and occasionally stuttering. "Sophie was terribly upset. She insisted Retta ought to have known how contagious impetigo was." Not that Sophie knew it herself; in fact, she'd never even heard of impetigo until she took Dooley to the doctor, who explained that it was a staph infection, adding—unfortunately, in the light of things—that it was caused by unsanitary conditions and was rampant among the poor. "Sophie was not one to lose her temper. But she spoke to Retta in a way she probably had never spoken to her before." Sophie could not contain her horror that Israel's infection had spread to her daughter's face—and what if it left a scar? But what Retta heard was an attack on her son and on the way she took care of him. "My boy is clean, Mrs. Drayton. He is as clean as you or anyone." That was all she would say, she just kept repeating it, louder each time, and nothing more.

"Eventually they both calmed down, they even apologized to each other, but too much damage had been done. Retta became depressed. For weeks afterward she would look down at the floor when she was spoken to, sometimes she would slam things around in the kitchen, and she broke a fine old bowl, a wedding gift, dear to Sophie. Worse, Sophie could not stop thinking about what the doctor had said, about those 'unsanitary conditions.' How had Israel caught impetigo? How sanitary was the Weems home? How careful about germs was Retta? It was absurd, really, when you think how Retta had been working for us all those years. Sophie wanted to be sure Israel was being treated with penicillin, as Ann was, but whenever she brought up the subject, Retta would say only, 'We are taking care of it ourselves, thank you. Don't you worry about that.' Which did not put Sophie's mind to rest at all. Sophie was beginning to think she was going to have to let Retta go. And then one day Retta called in sick, and the day after that, she gave notice. And thank god it happened that way, because I don't like to think how much worse things would have been if Retta had been fired. As it was, Ann called Sophie—and me— terrible names. In her eyes Sophie had done the unforgivable: she had humiliated Retta, she had made Retta feel 'like dirt.' My sin was to stand by and do nothing. 'You're so weak, Daddy. You let Mummy do whatever she wants.'

"Part of it was that she missed Retta so much. She went to pieces when they said goodbye. I remember she called Retta at home a few times, but then Retta asked her not to call anymore, because she did not feel comfortable about it.

"It was a couple of years later. Edie was visiting us, and somehow the subject of Retta came up. Edie was entirely on Sophie's side in the matter, and she started talking about her own ordeal once with a maid who turned out to have lice. Ann was there, too, and she went absolutely wild. 'You two sit here talking about these people as if they were chattel. You should be ashamed of yourselves.' And she started weeping hysterically. I remember being frightened. The force of her emotion—she was crying like someone whose heart was completely broken. Sophie was shaken, too. She could not calm or comfort Ann. She could only try to defend herself. 'I was protecting *you*!' she said.

"When I think back to that scene, it seems to me Ann was already lost to us. She had already made up her mind that anyone who would ever have black people waiting on them as we did had to be racist. In a couple of years she'd be arguing that every black prisoner, no matter the crime, was a political prisoner. It was a question of historical oppression, and her mother and I were accused of doing our part to keep black people oppressed."

By this time she is in high school, and her attacks have become relentless. Long preaching fails to get Mummy and Daddy to acknowledge their sins, let alone reform. She begins calling them by their first names. And, "If you want me to answer, you'll have to start calling me Ann." She takes pleasure in the pain this causes. And she will take perverse pleasure in her mother's disappointment, which (added pleasure) Sophie has to struggle to hide, as it becomes increasingly clear that, though a beautiful baby and a pretty girl, Dooley Ann, unlike Sophie, will never be anything but a plain-looking woman.

It is as if the daughter's flesh, in collusion with her spirit, had revolted against being made in the mother's image.

Turner said, "Ann was always a good student, but as she got older, she got more and more serious about school, and she complained that Sophie and I were not intellectual enough. She said Sophie was more like someone who'd gone to finishing school than to college. Sophie had majored in French but had forgotten most of it, she was not a big reader, and neither was I. We might enjoy certain cultural events, but we did not seek out what was intellectually challenging. Ann called us superficial. She pointed out bitterly that as members of the overclass, we'd been given the opportunity to get the best possible education, and what had we done with it? Meanwhile, the brightest black people in the country could only dream of such a thing. And then there were people like Retta, who'd had so little schooling she could barely read and write.

"Ann thought her mother was a beautiful, empty-headed ninny, and she accused me of marrying her for her looks and her social standing. She did not want to believe that I loved Sophie."

Georgette said, "Why did you choose that restaurant? I mean, the restaurant you went to the first time you met Kwame?"

Turner sighed. "The truth is, I stopped pleading not guilty to Ann's charges of racism a long time ago. I'd be lying if I didn't say we were not happy about her being with Kwame Kwesi. We didn't know if she was really in love with him or merely infatuated because he was black. Given her complicated feelings, her enormous guilt, and her tendency to romanticize poor people, we honestly did not believe it was ideal for her to be involved with someone from the ghetto. We worried she might have some idea that by being with Kwame, she could somehow escape her own privileged white identity. We worried about her being with someone who was political, someone who might encourage her extreme side. We thought Kwame was too old for her, and we worried about the fact that at his age he was still a bachelor. It crossed our minds that he might in some way be using her. Of course, we never said any of this to Ann. All we said was that we wanted to meet him. But hadn't she already decided we were incorrigible racists? Wasn't that how she must have described us to him? So what would this meeting be like? We did not know what to expect, but we were certainly nervous. Finally meeting him put at least some of our fears to rest. He was very friendly at dinner, gracious, kept the conversation going, praised the food—he treated us better than Ann did. But we didn't like the way Ann seemed to take a subservient position to him, and we thought if she married him, she'd be marrying beneath her. She was our precious, brilliant daughter, destined for extraordinary things, and so far as we could tell, this man, if nothing bad, was nothing special.

"Why did we pick that restaurant? Was it, as Ann accused, because it was a place where we weren't regulars? Well, I know we didn't discuss it and plan it that way. I do remember Sophie and I agreeing that we should go someplace new. But it's not as if we chose some dive to hide in. It is still one of the best restaurants in New York."

"And *did* you ever go back?"

"No, as a matter of fact."

On the way home from Mexico, Georgette had a relapse and needed a wheelchair to get from the plane to a taxi.

Lying on Turner's bed, she listened to him talking on the phone, describing her symptoms to his doctor. "May I bring her in right away?" he asked. And, after a pause, "More than a friend, actually. We're going to be married."

Turner's doctor ordered various tests and prescribed different drugs from those prescribed by the hotel doctor, along with a special diet. He said it might be some time before she was entirely herself again. And he wished them both much happiness together.

While Georgette and Turner were away, Edie happened to speak with her son Theo. This was not the son who was now running Turner's business, but his younger brother, an attorney who specialized in entertainment law and who lived in Los Angeles.

Theo said, "What did you say her name was again?"

"Georgette George."

"Oh. You mean Dooley's old roommate."

"What? You know her?"

"Not at all. But I remember the name. I remember Aunt Sophie making some joke about people thinking Dooley was rooming with a boy because this girl was called George. You were there, too, don't you remember?"

"I do not."

"You must be getting old, Mums."

Indeed.

"Does that really make such a difference?" Clifford wanted to know.

"If it didn't," said Edie, "why did he lie to us?"

Clifford shook his head. "It's sad."

"Yes, and if he marries her, it will be more than sad. It will be tragic."

"You women," Clifford said tiredly, "understand these things."

You men, she thought irritably, would understand, too, if your minds weren't so lazy.

————

After Turner had been back for about a week, Edie phoned him. She was coming into town to do some shopping, she said. Could they meet for lunch? She needed to talk about something.

Excellent, said Turner, who had a few things he wanted to talk about himself.

No matter how hard she thought about it—and she still thought about it all the time—Edie was sure she was never going to understand how two perfectly sane and civilized people had managed to bring forth such a child. The blow had struck much too close to home. She must thank the stars she'd never had serious trouble with any of her own three children—all, if not exactly always obedient or mother-and-father-honoring, sensible enough to resist the extremes to which so many of their generation had been fatally drawn—though Theo had gone perhaps too far in the opposite direction and become a conservative Republican, a little too narrow and much too smug in his views for her taste. He disappointed at times, he infuriated, but at least he had never disgraced his family; he had not driven his own poor beautiful mother to her grave.

Ann. From now on everyone must call me Ann.

Edie remembered the Thanksgiving gathering at which her niece had made this announcement, followed by a diatribe about dead Indians and black slaves and the cancerous imperialist white race, and how no one had dared to stop her. They had all just sat there in mute misery while the food cooled on their plates, and one of the smaller children, too young to understand the words but sensing something murderous let loose, began to cry.

Okay, then: *Ann.* Abominable Ann was right where she belonged at this moment and deserved to stay, was how Edie saw it—though now and then she would recall a luminous little girl thrilling her parents by teaching herself how to skate backwards, and her heart would soften.

These were her thoughts as she arrived at the restaurant, where

Turner was already waiting at a table, looking, it struck her at once, better than he had in years. (She had married the more handsome brother, all agreed at the time, but as the men grew older, this had gradually changed, and despite all he'd been through Turner was much the better-and-younger-looking one now. For this, Edie was inclined to blame her husband's lifelong spurning of exercise, an opinion she did not keep to herself.) It was rare for Edie to see Turner alone, and whenever she did, she experienced a certain nostalgia; for some reason, being alone with her brother-in-law brought back the happier days of her youth.

"I have something to tell you," Turner said as soon as they had looked at their menus.

So he was going to make a clean breast of it, Edie thought. Should she play dumb, pretend Theo hadn't already exposed him?

"Two things, actually."

"Two?"

"I've decided not to go with you and Cliff to China."

"That's an awful lot of money to throw away." (Most of the expenses for the tour had had to be paid in advance.)

"I don't care about that. I'm going to marry Georgette."

"You can't."

"Edie!"

"I'm sorry, Turner. I know how that must have sounded. It was partly shock. I thought you were going to say something else. I thought you were going to tell me the truth about Georgette and how you two met. Turns out Theo remembers Sophie talking about her."

"Ah, yes," he said. "My little sin of omission. I figured it would eventually come to light. I don't know why I didn't simply tell you and Cliff the whole truth right away, Edith. It was foolish."

"Think hard, Turner. Think hard why you didn't tell us."

The waiter who arrived to take their order noticed this as he collected their menus: the hands of both were trembling.

"You were ashamed to tell us, Turner," Edie said. "I think if you weren't so smitten, you'd see it. You'd see how completely wrong this relationship is." Turner brushed the air with one hand, as if to erase what had been said, but Edie ignored this and pressed on. "Nothing would make me happier than if you were to marry again, Turner, but how can you possibly think this is the right person for you? An affair is one thing, a good thing, probably something you needed—"

"Edie!"

"Oh, I know. I *know* what you must be thinking. But I couldn't live with myself—I promised. I promised." Her voice cracked. To help compose herself, she lit a cigarette. (Normally, she would not have smoked until the end of the meal.) Turner gazed at her sadly, waiting, but in his mind her voice went on: *I promised Sophie I would take care of you.* He could hear those words, and he could hear Sophie, half mad with grief over Ann and the pain of dying, extracting this promise. In Turner's mind it was a scene out of opera: the two women in a circle of light, hair loosed, clutching hands. Duet for mezzo and soprano.

They had been the best of friends—more like sisters than sisters-in-law, everyone said—and Sophie had trusted Edie in the same whole-hearted way she had trusted her mother.

"Edie's so sharp," Sophie used to say, "especially about people— she understands what makes them tick. She knows me better than I know myself! She would have been a good psychiatrist."

And Sophie had often used Edie as a kind of therapist, confiding in her about everything, relying on her advice—even more than on Turner's—in matters of importance, and generally admiring Edie's way of always speaking her mind. Turner admired Edie, too, but with reservations. In his view, she was often tactless, she was manipulative, at times she bullied Cliff, and she did what Turner and Sophie would never have done: she spied on her children when they were growing up, going through their pockets and schoolbags, reaching under their mattresses, listening in on their phone conversations. She had called it a necessity, an extreme measure demanded by extreme times. There was alcoholism in Edie's family, and to her the new drug culture presented the gravest threat. (The children joked that Edie had flushed more marijuana down the toilet than the three of them put together had ever inhaled.) Of all the people Sophie and Turner knew, Edie had been the most critical of Ann. She had kept after Sophie to take a harder line with her rebellious daughter, constantly warning about things coming to a bad end. But once her prediction had come true, Edie never spoke another word against Ann, at least not that Turner knew (though Cliff did tell him: "Edie has this crazy idea that when Ann shot that policeman, she was really shooting at you"). From the moment of Ann's arrest, Edie had offered nothing but support. Always mother-hennish about her sister-in-law's health, Edie had been shattered by Sophie's last illness.

"Look," Turner said gently. "I know you're only thinking about what's best for me. But I do love Georgette, even if you can't see it. I love her very much."

"Tell me something. Does Ann know? Are they in touch with each other?"

"No. They had a bad falling-out years ago. And no, Ann doesn't even know that I've been seeing Georgette."

The waiter approached, and they fell silent as he set down their plates and fresh-peppered their omelets. When he had gone, Edie said, "Here's what I think. If you'll just hear me out, I want to say a few things, and then we can finish our lunch and say goodbye and you'll do as you wish, and so be it. But I would not be able to live with myself if I didn't tell you why I think you're making a mistake.

"Let's begin with Georgette. You love her, she loves you. But do you really believe you'll be doing the right thing by her if you marry her? What about children? She wants to have children, doesn't she? Well, are you ready for that, to be a father again? If the child were born tomorrow, you'd be seventy when the child was ten. I know it's been done, it can be done, other men your age have done it, but is this what you really want? And is it fair to Georgette, not to mention to the child? And do you think she's ready to have a baby right now, when you two have just met?"

"Needless to say, Georgette and I have talked about all this. We've done the math. We know it's complicated, but we want to find a way to work things out."

"But what about Ann? You haven't told her yet, because you've been afraid to tell her. You knew how she'd respond. You say she and Georgette parted on bad terms. How will she feel about your making Georgette her stepmother? I know you and Ann are barely in touch these days, and she says she doesn't want to see you. But life is long, Turner. Life behind bars is longer still. Anything can happen. Even Ann can change. My understanding is, people serving life sentences usually do change. She may finally grow up. She may finally come to her senses, and then you'll have to be there for her. You'll want to be there, I know. But if you're married to Georgette? Look, the last thing you need is another obstacle, one more grudge for Ann to hold against you, one more reason to keep you two estranged. And how do you know what effect your starting a new family with Georgette might have on Ann's morale? Remember, she has to be strong to survive in there, and though she may be angry with you, you're still the only family she's got.

"One day, God willing, she'll be released. And, God willing, you'll still be alive. You'd be a very old man then, but not too old to be there for her. And what if she gets out sooner? Don't shake your head, Turner. I know you've said it's impossible, but things do change. I don't pretend to know all the legal ins and outs, but I don't believe her sentence is carved in stone. There's always a way. I've heard Cliff and other people say all you need is her cooperation, a ton of money, and the right legal team."

She paused, and when Turner did not speak, she said, "You know, Turner, just because you've—taken her on a honeymoon doesn't mean you have to marry her. Things are different from the way they were in our day. I'd hate to think part of all this is about your being a gentleman. You don't want to hurt her, of course. But she's a whole other generation, and her generation understands these things differently—better than we did, I'd say. She's not going to be destroyed if you don't marry her, trust me. Not if you explain it carefully to her."

"I'm afraid my feelings are much more selfish than you seem to think, Edie. I can't keep her without marrying her. Neither of us wants it to be like that. I would have to give her up completely. And I don't know if I can do it."

Edie allowed an even longer pause this time before she spoke. "Let's not talk about it anymore for now. You've hardly eaten a bite of your lunch. Just promise me you'll think about what I've said."

She changed the subject then, and they talked about other things, and they ordered coffee, and Edie smoked another cigarette.

But as they were waiting for the check, she gripped his arm lightly and said, "Go to China, Turner. It's so far away. You'll be separated from Georgette all that time. It will make it easier for both of you. There's a lot at stake here, for you and for her, and for Ann, too. Everyone needs you to be strong now."

They had paid the check and were about to leave. The waiter was hovering. Edie decided to pretend he was deaf. "I have one last thing I want to say, Turner, and it's something I want you to think very, very hard about. Marrying each other won't do what I believe you two may be subconsciously wishing. She can't replace your daughter, and you can't replace the father who abandoned her."

The waiter, who in his free time wrote screenplays, tried to remember these lines until he had a chance to write them down.

"My conscience is clear," Edie told her husband. "You know as well as I do Sophie would never have approved of this marriage."

"And you told Turner that?"

"No." It was the one thing she had held in reserve, the one arrow she had not pulled from her quiver. The one dipped in poison.

"And what do you suppose will happen now?"

"We'll see."

"What a sad story," Clifford said. "What a sad life my poor brother has had. How did he seem when you left him?"

"He seemed all right."

In fact, Turner had seemed utterly downcast when they said goodbye.

Which Edie took as a good sign.

Part Six

I did not try to kill myself, but they pumped my stomach anyway.

It was Solange's fault. She had just moved back into the city. Little surprise: after years of forcing himself to lead a straight life, Drew had finally decided to come out.

"There's no reason we can't always be friends," Solange said bravely.

"You're certainly taking it well."

A few years earlier she would have written a song about it.

"I'm just sorry he's had to suffer so much. Being Catholic made things even harder. He was afraid it might hurt his business. And he still can't bring himself to tell his mom."

So we were back to seeing a lot of each other, Solange and I. "What a pair!" we kept saying, and we laughed and we cried. But secretly, I was not happy with the timing. Misery doesn't always love company.

Among other complaints, I had insomnia. I asked Solange to give me some of her sleeping pills. That night, she tried to call me, but I had taken the phone off the hook. I had taken the phone off the hook because I had gone to bed early. She kept calling and getting a busy signal, and she started to worry. She was having second thoughts about those pills she had given me, and about how much I'd had to drink at the bar where we'd met. Around midnight she took a taxi to my building. A neighbor coming back from walking his dog recognized Solange and let her in with him. Rather than wait for the elevator, she ran up five flights of stairs and rang my bell. She rang the bell and she banged with her fist on the door and she shouted my name, but I did not hear her. I did not hear her because I had taken four of the sleeping pills. Later I would be indignant with those who could believe I was stupid enough to think you could kill yourself with four little sleeping pills. "So tell me," said the counselor who came to interview me. "Say you *were* going to try to kill yourself—how would you go about it?" Tired and irritable though I was, I counted the ways: the gas, the rope, the bridge, and so on—for who has not at some time or other thought about it? But the counselor looked at me as if he'd never heard of such things.

Damn Solange. She panicked. Neighbors, most of whom had already gone to bed, came shuffling out to the hall, where she blubbered her fears to them. The super was roused from his basement apartment, and he opened my door with his key. I lay in bed—naked, unfortunately—and through all the shouting and slapping and splashings of cold water only fluttered my eyes and groaned without fully waking. The police came, and the ambulance came, their sirens drawing more people to the scene. At the hospital, Solange told them she had no idea how many sleeping pills or what other drugs I might have taken, but I'd definitely been drinking, and though it was unnecessary the fools pumped my stomach anyway.

When I was conscious again, but hardly what I'd call myself, I had to answer questions. Why, if all I'd wanted was to get to sleep, did I take a *quadruple* dose of medication? "Because I wanted to sleep *a very long time*," I said. Wasn't the answer obvious? But what turned out to be obvious was that it was the *wrong* answer.

The bright side of being held on the p-ward for three days was getting to put off facing the super and all those neighbors whom Solange had arranged to see me drugged and naked. Every night I was there, I'd be given a sleeping pill, which I thought ironic, but in fact everyone on the p-ward always gets a sleeping pill, even if the problem that put him there is the exact opposite of insomnia: it makes the staff's life easier.

Flowers? They were waiting for me in my room, a fat, smelly bouquet. They had been sent by one of the policemen who'd been part of my rescue team, whom in my oblivion I had never seen. How old was he? What did he look like? A cheery little card. Mama and Papa and Baby Bear wanted me to Get Well Soon. I started to cry and could not stop. Could not stop and could not stop. One of those jags that knock you out like a beating. But when I woke an hour or so later, I had the feeling you have when a long, high fever finally breaks.

Though I was still seriously pissed at Solange, she and I had a giggle over our reversed roles. (*Oh, what a pair!*) But this was not the same ward where Solange was known as a Frequent Flier; it was not the same hospital.

My last morning, I was asked to attend a group session with one of the recreational therapists. The therapist was a fanatically jovial, painted woman who carried a book called *In Writing Is Healing*. At their last session, a week before, patients had been given an assignment—write an imaginary letter to someone who you believe has done you wrong—and almost everyone, even the elderly (always a high number of elderly on any p-ward), wrote to Mom or Dad. Now people were invited to read their letters aloud. There was a lot of gulping and sniffling, a few voices failed, one person fled the room, and more than once I felt my blood run cold.

Edie, if you are still alive, read this and know that I don't blame you.

I can do it now, look back and say the marriage would have been a mistake. The seed you hoped to plant—that a marriage between Turner and me could have ruined his chances for a reconciliation with Ann, or might have stopped him, say, from doing his all for her—that seed was already there, a torment from the beginning. Looking back, I think how we might not have had children after all (he did not really want to start another family, and I knew this). I might be childless today, and blame him. (For, of course, the existence of Zoe and Jude has made it impossible to imagine true happiness without them.)

We saw each other up until the day before he went away—I, begging him to stay—and then he was gone, and I had his first letter. I told myself he would come back; I would get him back again. We did not have to marry, then; this did not matter anymore. Only not to be without him, this was all that mattered. The love I remembered, his love, which I had never doubted, gave me strength, even made me cocky. Of course he was not gone for good, of course I had not lost him. Mexico. He needed only to return. He needed only to see me.

But when you and Clifford came home from China, he did not come with you. Instead, he went to Egypt, dropping in on an old boarding school pal, now an archaeologist supervising a dig outside Cairo. From Egypt he went to Greece, and from there he traveled on—visiting every friend and friend of a friend who happened to be abroad, though mostly he was alone, and that was unbearable (he wrote). He did everything to avoid being alone, befriending strangers, tourists, other Americans (women?), and when months later he did finally come home (the exact date unknown to me), he moved immediately out of New York, back to Connecticut.

Letters. I had letters from all the places he went, letters that were not without words of love but which stated ever more firmly the sense of having done the right thing—"though it has taken all my strength, a strength I could find only by being far away from you."

You're not a bad man, Daddy, you're just weak. Of all Ann's taunts, this one may have cut deepest.

"Is it fair to ask you to understand? I thought if I made this one big sacrifice, perhaps in some way it would help Ann. And I thought perhaps in return, somehow, before I died, I'd be given the chance to make peace with her."

At long last, I marveled, a family resemblance! For those words sounded just like Ann.

"I hope one day, though I know it might take a very long time" (for him? for me?), "you and I might find our way back to each other again, as friends." In this letter, he gave a name and a phone number: someone, a lawyer I suppose (I did not keep that letter), whom I should not hesitate to contact if ever I found myself "in need."

How long would he have gone on writing if I hadn't stopped him? How long would he have gone on hoping we would see each other again if I had not crushed that hope?

The period that followed was terrible for me, like burning in hell.

Pure romantics do not believe a person can experience true love more than once. Though he or she may have many other loves in a lifetime, these are only shadows of the unique thing. I only know what happened to me, and I know it only now, looking back.

What is the taste of betrayal? For me, the taste of preserved lemon.

Sometimes you need to write something down before you can see it is false.

No one betrayed me.

Edie, you were right. Losing Turner could not destroy me. "Nobody dies of love, except in the movies" is a line from a very famous romantic French movie. (Though I think, in fact, people die of love all the time, just very slowly.) You saw me already at the next stage: tears dried, shoulders squared, getting on with life. You saw me marrying someone else. Sophie thought you'd make a good psychiatrist. Did you know psychiatrists do not believe in love at first sight? I told my psychiatrist-husband almost nothing about Turner. But if he'd known the whole story, I am sure he would have agreed with you, about the tangled father-daughter thing at the root of it.

I was no sooner out of the hospital than Solange began showing the usual signs. Now it was I who panicked at the sound of a busy signal. Solange was being threatened with eviction from her apartment because of noise. (She blasted music, she said, to try to drown out the noise in her head.) I should have known how unlikely it was she'd survive the loss of Drew intact. Their attempt to stay friends was not working. He had a new lover, new friends, a whole new life. It was only too clear: Solange would be left behind. It was all her fault, she was a worthless, stupid, hopeless, ugly, unlovable piece of shit; she was a freak, a madwoman, a burden: this was what the voices were saying, the voices she tried to drown out with rock.

Now comes the part where I meet my first husband. His is a new face among the familiar ones on Ten West. We cross paths often, but he is on duty, and there is no conversation between us until one day we happen to find each other in the cafeteria at the same time and we sit for five minutes with our coffees. The whole time, I am wondering whether he knows what the lunatics think of him. That he is kind but bungling. That he does not seem very bright. That he is the absentminded professor type. I wonder whether he knows that they call him "The Puppy." And I think how I would not want a doctor who seems as nervous as this one does just having coffee with a strange woman.

Even though she was not his patient, he waited until after Solange had been discharged from the hospital to call me. I was not surprised to hear from him, nor was I especially happy. He cleared his throat three times before asking me out. I'm not sure why I said yes.

I was not capable of enjoying myself again with any man yet, but Dr. Simon and I got along. On our fifth or sixth date we went to the ballet. The ballet was my idea, my balletomane phase having survived the disappearance of Turner. (The New York State Theater was always the one place I thought I might see Turner again, but this never happened. He had stopped going to the ballet, I think. Out of fear of running into me? Perhaps this was another sacrifice. After I learned he had remarried, I thought his new wife might not have liked the ballet, and he would not have gone without her. I did see the Holts again. I saw them more than once. They saw me, too, but either they did not remember me or they were pretending that this was the case.)

Jeremy would never be a fan of any kind of dance; he was more of a theater person, he said. But he was so pleased to be sitting next to me, to be doing something just to please me, and I could see this, and it was good to see.

It was a matinee, and afterward we went to visit his sister, who lived in one of the new high-rises that had gone up around Lincoln Center. His sister and her husband were some of the people for whom a sardonic new word had recently been coined, but if there was anything about being young, urban, and professional to be ashamed of, these two did not know it. From the first minute, they embraced me. They behaved as if I were not Jeremy's date, but his fiancée. Apparently the last woman in Jeremy's life had been a piece of work, and I gained many points just by being Not Nina. The wish on the part of Jeremy's family and friends to exorcise that red-haired she-devil was to become clear to me.

Later, the evening would seem to me almost staged for my benefit. The happy couple (for all that they, too, are divorced today) as tender and attentive to each other as newlyweds. Their professionally decorated but homey apartment. Their darling little girl who just happened to choose my lap to cuddle in (oh, the scent of a child's hair). The champagne brought out after dinner to toast the news of another child on the way.

Isn't it sweet? Isn't this what you want? If that writing had suddenly bled through the dining-room wall, I would not have been surprised. *What is the point in waiting?*

Because I believed that love was finished—that the kind of love I had known with Turner would not come my way again—and because Jeremy agreed we could start making a baby right away, I said yes when he *popped the question*. But I don't believe I would have said yes if I hadn't known about the other woman, from whom he had barely escaped alive, how he had writhed in the flames of her red, red hair, that love of his life about whom he never spoke, not before or after we were married.

So long as he understood there could be no wedding. I could never have pulled myself through a wedding, not even a small one. City Hall, that's all, was what I said. And that was fine with Jeremy. Weddings are never for the groom anyway, which is one of the things I don't like about them. But it was a mystery to others, a disappointment to his family, an outrage to his mother. What kind of woman doesn't want to be a bride? It increased the suspicion that already shaded her feelings toward me for not being Jewish.

Back in the days of Smash Monogamy, formal weddings had been condemned as pretentious and bourgeois and hypocritical (do women today even know what the white dress and veil are supposed to mean?). And no matter what it cost, an engagement ring could never be anything but tacky. The lone girl (some poor debutante) who sat in the college dining hall reading *Bride's* magazine was heaped with scorn. We would have spat in her food if we'd dared. Needless to say, most of the bride bashers ended up brides themselves. Some would wear white more than once. But for others there would always be that embarrassing, shameful, and hypocritical thing clinging to the institution of marriage.

I stopped keeping a journal long ago. But for many years of my life there have been periods when I did keep a journal, and those journals still exist. They can be found in the same cedar trunk with my other papers and documents. And yet I have never once taken them out. I have never had the desire to go open one of them, to check my memory against what is recorded there. In fact, I can't even remember the last time I opened one of my old journals, and I'm inclined to think I might never open one again. I wrote them, I kept them, but I have no curiosity, not the least interest in what they might tell me about the past today. Whatever happened, I prefer to re-create it. Even at the inevitable risk of getting some things wrong, I want this to be a work of pure memory and imagination. Instinct tells me that, in the end, what I'll have made will be closer to the truth.

Dear Edie, You were right, but you were evil.

*B*ad blood.

  I have my mother's disease. I am not surprised to have it. I have always known there is a genetic predisposition. But the doctors assure me my fate need not be the same as hers. To begin with, in my case, the disease has been caught early, there are drugs available for treatment that were not available in Mama's day, and, I am told, even more promising treatments are on the verge of appearing. I am healthier than Mama ever was, far more informed about the disease than she, conscientious about following medical advice. The prognosis, then, is quite good. Even if, in the end, the disease does get me, it is unlikely to do so as quickly as it did Mama, who had no treatment at all, who ignored her symptoms completely and was not even correctly diagnosed until she was nearly gone.

  Still, I have decided not to tell the children. I lie about the symptoms. A hundred other things could be causing them. I keep the pills out of sight.

The last year of my marriage to Val Strom was a strange one. Though we had little to do with each other at home, even eating and sleeping separately, we continued to work together at the magazine. *Caracara* was thriving. In its third year it had won a prestigious award for excellence in literary criticism. The award ceremony was held in a private club in Midtown, and I remember wondering how many people there noticed that Val and I did not exchange a word with each other all night. Not that this spoiled things for Val. The magazine was everything to him, he was deservedly proud of what his hard work had made of it, and that night he outbeamed the lights on the dais. Besides, without a word from me he knew I was proud of him. I was absolutely sure of that; less sure that he cared.

In spite of the ailing marriage, which I believed would resolve itself soon enough in divorce, this was a fairly quiet time for me. The children no longer came to me all day long with every little thing. They had reached that age when most children begin to be secretive with their parents, to be more likely to confide in strangers than in their own mother, and to have time only for their peers. And Solange, too, that moon child, needed me less. With a new doctor and changes in medication (and who can say what other, unknowable factors), she had entered a period of relative stability. Though she still drifted from job to job and never stayed long in any relationship, she was always working, she was usually with someone, and she was off the p-ward Frequent Flier list.

Val was often away that year. He would go off by himself for a

day or two or sometimes longer, sometimes leaving without any notice, barely filling me in on details. I minded less for myself than for
Jude, who could not be persuaded by mere words—not mine,
anyway—that although his father was a busy and important man,
of course he loved him. Val went off, to some conference somewhere, to give a talk or sit on a panel, to promote the journal, to
visit some author. So he said. He was still handsome, princely, sleek.
But having lost all desire for him myself, it was sometimes hard for
me to remember how attractive other women still found him.

I no longer recall the reason, or excuse, that took him to the
West Coast that December. I got the call in the early morning.
Somewhere on the road near Monterey, his car, or *her* car, actually,
had struck a pole. Although the car must have been going fast,
there had been no substance in Val's blood that might have im-
paired his driving. The night had been dry, the road clear. Had he
had an attack of some kind, heart or brain, as has been known to
happen? The girl, a student at Stanford, had been killed with him.
She was found completely naked, her clothing flung about the inside of the car. I was told this information would not be shared
with the public. I had to wonder why it was being shared with me.
I supposed there might have been legal reasons. I knew, but did not
share the information with anyone, that when they crashed, the
naked girl had been straddling Val's lap. For my husband had always been one to share his fantasies.

Many people would find it odd, but I let the children go to
school that morning without telling them. I needed to buy time.
The shock to Jude would be the greatest, and I wanted to talk with
him apart from Zoe.

I had meant to spend the day Christmas shopping with Solange.
Instead, she came over to the house, and while I made phone calls,
she took down the tree.

It was the end of *Caracara*. That was how Val wanted it. He had often said as much to me. In any case, under any other editor it would
not have been the same magazine. There would be one last issue,

which Val had almost finished putting together before he died. It would be longer than previous issues and would include several pieces in memoriam. It would also include a piece I had received several months earlier, which Val had rejected but which I held on to, stubbornly refusing to return it, as if somehow I knew its chance would come.

Part Seven

ORPHAN ANNIE AND THE HAND OF GOD

First time I see her she's got a black eye. More correctly I should say it's the first time I notice her, because I'm sure I must've seen her before that day she showed up on the chow line with one swollen, half-shut eye and three long red scratches down her cheek. Fresh blood. I figure she must've been jumped, and from the look of it, just a short while ago. Welcome to Maryville. Happened to me, too, the day after I arrived and many more times after that. But this is ancient history. You get older, you can count on being treated a little more gentle in this place, though you still got to deal with verbal abuse. But then everyone, including the COs, or should I say especially the COs, has got to deal with verbal abuse. Even the warden takes her fair share of mouth. Doesn't matter how many charge sheets you write up on them, these ladies are gonna have their say. But in prison it's no different from the street. The younger you are, the more likely you are to catch trouble, same as you're more likely to create it. When you get to be one of the grandmas, as they like to call us, whether we be truly grandmothers or not, you don't have to worry so much about assault. Except from the crazies, who you always better be worrying about. Most folks treat grandmas with respect and are even protective of us, though I got to admit this is starting to change, and it's getting to be more and more every bitch for herself. Ann, also known as Orphan Annie, says it's just a reflection of the world outside, the rotten legal system, racism, the gap between rich and poor. But Ann always talks like that. Same explanation for everything. I don't really have any explanation my-self. All I know is that, in the thirty-two years I've been here at Maryville, it has become a lot bigger, a lot more crowded, and a lot more mean.

Me and Ann were close to the same age when we began our sen-tences, but by the time she arrived I'd already served nine long years. (I am one of the few who can remember the Maryville Cor-rectional Facility when it was still Maryville Prison for Women.) And we both had the same distinction: in for murder, in for life. Except in my case "life" really means what it says, because I was sentenced with no hope of parole. Mine was a double homicide. I killed two people I knew only too well, one no-good motherfucker and one even more no-good whore, two people who deserved what they got and who I would kill again in a heartbeat, and that is all I intend to say about that.

I have grown old in prison and I will die here. And it's the ones like us, Orphan Annie and me, the ones who've been convicted of the worst crimes and are doing the most time, who end up being the role models. Outsiders may find this hard to understand, but it's a truth of prison life, and not just at Maryville. I try not to spend too much time thinking about how my life *might have been*, because that is only too likely to break my spirit. But I have often reflected on this interesting fact: no way outside these walls could my kind of person ever become a role model to anyone, let alone hundreds of folks. Such a thing could happen only behind bars.

By "hundreds," I don't believe I'm exaggerating. When I think of all the ones I've seen come and go. And come again, I am forced to add, for it's another fact of prison life that so many who are re-leased wind up right back, usually within just two or three years. Ann says whenever this happens she's not surprised, because all prison does is make it impossible for you to survive on the outside. So you go back to drugs, or hooking, or you commit some other crime even worse than your first. But me, I'm always surprised, be-cause I know for sure if it was me walking out that gate today there's no way I'd be back. I've heard from women after they've been released who confess they miss the place, and I know what this means. You make bonds here, like anywhere else, sometimes real deep, and for better or worse prison's not the kind of experience you can just walk away from. And then, bad as living behind bars might be, it can be an improvement over where some folks come from. Not having to hustle your ass on some freezing street, or face your pimp with a few dollars less than he's expecting—you can see why, for some, Maryville might even be a vacation. You see women coming back from their first appointment with a counselor or the shrink and they're in a daze. They can't believe someone actually sat there and listened to them. I remember feeling like that myself, and I can honestly say the best people I've ever known in my life have been people I've met on the inside. So I understand how someone could look back fondly on the place. But that's not the same as saying I'd want to come back. The people I understand best are the ones who say they'd rather kill themselves than go back to prison, and then find themselves a way to do it.

One time when I was still on the young side I was taken to a free-world hospital with a bad case of blood poisoning, and while I was recuperating I tried to slip past the guard outside my door. Didn't make it very far, but at least I tried. Wouldn't have had any respect for myself if I hadn't. On the other hand, I declined to take part in the only attempted breakout to occur during my time. That's because I knew it was doomed, a harebrained scheme hatched by a couple of true desperadoes. The idea was to start a fire in the dayroom and escape when the building was evacked. Supposedly, this had worked someplace else, in one of the men's state prisons, but I have my doubts. Here, all it got anyone was a long stretch in solitary, and the whole floor was punished by being without a dayroom, which meant no TV, for more than a year. When the ringleaders reappeared, you can be sure they soon wished they were back in the hole.

A bruised face is not exactly a blue moon around here, but that day in the mess hall, heads kept turning. What made Ann's black eye such a sight was that she was so pale. We were always saying

341

how she was the whitest person we ever saw. She was even whiter than Rabbit, the albino CO. She looked sickly, not just on account of her color, but because she was just skin and bones. I swear, if our cells had bars instead of sliding doors, that girl could've slipped out whenever she felt like it. The warden (I'm talking about the first one, Mrs. Lockhart) accused Ann of doing it on purpose, trying to make herself look like someone from one of those Jewish concentration camps. Why Ann would want to make herself look like that I don't know, but being skin and bones was just one of many things about her that Warden Lockhart could not tolerate.

But Ann always denied she was starving. She said a human being needs a lot less food than most folks eat, and she said look at the Asian people. At the time, the only Asian person we had to look at was Chinese Lucy (to tell her apart from this other Lucy, who was Puerto Rican, as if anyone ever even came close to mixing them up), and Chinese Lucy was this big fat girl with a full mustache who chowed down with the best of them.

Speaking of Chinese Lucy, who got paroled way back, here's a story. One day she mentioned something about how much she wished she could eat with chopsticks instead of a fork (no knives here, needless to say). She asked Administration if she could have chopsticks, but they said it was against the rules. This set the wheels in Ann's mind turning. How could this be? How many inmates before Chinese Lucy had even made such a request for there to be a *rule* about it? Next thing you know, she's got Chinese Lucy writing letters to this person and that one (actually, Ann wrote the letters herself, Chinese Lucy just signed them), and bingo, Chinese Lucy gets her chopsticks. And even though no harm ever came of those chopsticks, Mrs. Lockhart was so mad she could spit.

Anyway, this was the kind of thing Ann got to be famous for. She'd help anybody who needed it, say if they had hope of an appeal or were applying for clemency or filing a lawsuit. She said she had to do it because most of us didn't know shit about our own legal rights and because so many of us didn't have lawyers, or the lawyers we did have did not do a decent job by us. She said many inmates would never even be in jail if their lawyers had been half awake. She said somebody had to help all the inmates who couldn't read or write, and when the Hispanic population started growing and we got all these women who didn't speak English, she started learning Spanish.

As you might guess, Ann's free bilingual inmate consulting service did not just slip by under Administration's nose. Word came down that the one inmate she was probably *not* helping by such activities was herself. Nobody likes a rabble-rouser, is how a deputy warden put it. And Mrs. Lockhart herself had strong opinions on the matter. She charged Ann with "spreading propaganda that could lead to discontent and resentment and possibly incite inmates to riot or commit other disorder." Ann was told to stop conversing with inmates in Spanish, on the grounds that this discouraged them from learning English. For a time they took away her law library privileges, and COs could always find ways to harass her. So even though she was one of the least likely to possess contraband, on any given day hers was the cell most likely to be searched.

Now, you got to know that much of the bad feeling toward Ann on the part of the staff had to do with her crime. To a CO, an attack on a police officer is an attack on one of their own, even though it's common knowledge police officers look down on corrections officers. And take Mrs. Lockhart. She was the widow of a state trooper who'd been killed in a high-speed chase, and she had a son working for the FBI. To make things worse, Ann did not hide how she felt about authority, from Mrs. Lockhart on down. She would not show the proper respect or—what some of them really wanted to see— fear. She liked to point out the obvious, that just about every staff person was white (though this has changed some over the years) and just about every inmate wasn't. She said the whole American prison system was nothing but an extension of slavery. This got her a disciplinary hearing for attempting to cause a race riot, though I can tell you there was never any chance of any riot occurring over those words. Truth is, whenever Ann started running her mouth on

343

this subject, talking about slavery and racism, talking about blacks being stuck at the bottom of society, and how they lived so poor and how they filled up all the jails—the women of Maryville, most especially the black women of Maryville, turned a deaf ear. Never did understand how a person that smart could not tell right off how the women found that kind of talk insulting. And when she used the word *genocide* and started comparing black folks and Jewish folks—this above all the black women of Maryville did not want to hear.

In prison, you don't find many of Orphan Annie's kind, white, college-educated, and no criminal record, but the ones you do find tend to be real good about making sure that, whatever their true feelings might be, they always look like model inmates. Butter wouldn't melt in their mouth. At Maryville, we call them cupcakes. But Ann was no cupcake, and she took chances nobody wanting to look good to a parole board ever would. In fact, parole might've been one of the last things on Ann's mind. Four of the most popular words you hear behind bars are *when I get out*. Of course, I'd be most sensitive to this, so believe me when I say I never heard those four words come from Ann's mouth.

Ann says, "A person my size doesn't need more than a few ounces of food a day to stay alive," and I guess she proved that.

Now, the food you get served in prison is nasty, no two ways about it. But there are ways you can do better for yourself. You can buy groceries in the commissary, and you can have up to a certain amount brought to you every month from outside. And you don't have to eat in the mess hall. You can use one of the kitchens to cook in. But Ann never had food brought to her, and she never used the kitchen. Sometimes she'd skip a meal and stay in her cell, but most times she went to the mess hall. Not that this necessarily meant that she ate. Sometimes she took just a bite or two, sometimes she just moved stuff around on her plate. But if you were going to eat in the mess hall you were expected to *eat*. Ann's behavior could be seen as "uncooperative." She was accused of "trying to draw atten-

tion and sympathy to herself" and "making an exception of herself." Now, all this went in her file.

Ann said it was wrong for a person to eat unless he or she was
hungry. But that was just what we all wanted to know. How come
this girl didn't get hungry like everyone else? Because, you know,
being hungry was the only excuse we had for eating most of that
crap.

After I got to know Ann—which took a while, because I confess
for the longest time I didn't have much use for her kind—I got to
know how her mind worked. And I got to understand how, as long
as there were inmates who had no choice in the matter, Ann didn't
want to eat any better than them. I'm talking about those women
who didn't have anyone to bring food or deposit money in their
commissary accounts and had to eat whatever was thrown at them.
Which was true for most of the mental cases. Maybe Ann didn't
give a damn about food herself, but those times when we got so
disgusted we had to act (it was usually the maggots that did it)
she was always with the protesters. And she said her protesting
wouldn't mean nothing coming from someone who didn't eat in
the mess hall.

Anyway, around the same time Ann helped Chinese Lucy get
her chopsticks, she started agitating about the cockroaches. They
were everywhere, mostly in the kitchen, but also in our cells, in the
dayroom, even in the gym. In warm weather, some could be seen
taking the air with us out in the yard. They bothered everyone, of
course, but Ann more than everyone else put together. One time
she went to check on Carolee, who'd had a seizure that day, and
found her lying on her bed, too weak to brush off this roach that
had climbed on her face. Ann threw the kind of fit that lands you in
the hole, kicking and screaming all the way, and she came out of
there not mousy-quiet, like most do, but teeth bared, spoiling for a
fight.

Now, like the warden kept saying, there was no reason for Ann
to carry on about something needing to be done when something
was being done. This whole team of exterminators came to

Maryville once a month. But Ann kept saying that the stuff they used was probably doing more harm to us than to the roaches, who in any case were having no problem surviving it. She said she had a better idea, this natural pesticide she knew about that was safe and cheap and easy to use. Boric acid. Why not try it?

Ann put in a request to have boric acid powder stocked in the commissary and was turned down flat. Women might try to kill themselves by ingesting it, Administration said. Or they might try to poison someone else. In that case, Ann said, might as well ban laundry soap, bleach, deodorant, shampoo, disinfectant, and nail polish remover, since all these had been put to bad use at one time or another (not to mention baking soda and large quantities of salt). She said boric acid was a whole lot less toxic than some of these other products. We asked her then how it could kill roaches, and she said the roaches would ingest the powder when they cleaned themselves, which made them die of dehydration. You can see why no one took her seriously. A *natural* pesticide? Cockroaches *cleaning* themselves?

Then Ann asked to have some boric acid delivered to her so she could at least show how it worked. But again permission was denied. And denied and denied and denied. But after almost a year, in which the roach pop must've doubled, and Ann kept attaching to her requests more and more articles she found about the health hazards roach infestations could cause, Administration finally gave in. We figured at this point they just wanted to prove Ann really was out of her mind.

She started with the kitchen on our floor, sprinkling the white powder into every crack and corner, sweeping it under the fridge and behind the stove. Two, three days later the roaches were gone! Even more amazing, they stayed gone, for months. Not like before, when they'd come back soon as the exterminators' footsteps died away. Ann explained that roaches were smart and learned real fast how to steer clear of danger, so even if other parts of the prison were crawling, our area could remain roach free. How she got to be such an expert on cockroaches was a wonder to us. She said now that they were gone we shouldn't let our corridor get so filthy (a major problem throughout the compound). Ann cleaned her cell every day, and sometimes she cleaned the cells of some of her neighbors who were too depressed or mentally deficient, like Carolee, to do it themselves—yet another Rule Violation. How she found time to do this with all her other activities, like her regular job teaching in the prison school, I don't know. At night, when everyone else was asleep, she'd be up with a book. Wonder Woman. Didn't need no food, didn't need no sleep. Naturally, this got on some nerves.

Didn't matter that she was right. Administration just kept bringing in those useless exterminators.

I was the one who first called her Orphan Annie. Though she never talked much about her life before Maryville, no more than she ever talked about *when she got out*, we knew she was cut off from her kin, and we could see she didn't have many friends to visit. The more time she spent in prison, the less use she seemed to have for the world outside. I've seen this happen before, especially with lifers, and a lot of inmates discourage folks from visiting because it's just too stressful. But Ann's case was different. It was almost like she'd taken a vow, and this place was a convent instead of a prison. A place where you left the world behind and never looked back, where you gave up sex, starved yourself, worked like a mule, and devoted yourself to others. I remember thinking how she was even more like this than the real nuns working at Maryville. When I got to know her, I found out she'd been a touch like this even before she came here. If she'd ever seen the shrink, which she never desired to do, she'd have known he thought cutting yourself off from the world was the worst thing an inmate could do. But here was another link between her and the other "orphans," those women who never lined up to use the phones, never got letters or packages or any visitors at all. (In fact, Ann got more mail than anyone here, but it was mostly from strangers, and most of it, especially at the beginning, was unfriendly.)

You might think from what I've said so far that Ann was seen as a do-gooder at Maryville, and you'd be right. But if you thought this meant she was popular with the other inmates, you'd be way off. Nobody likes a rabble-rouser, said the authorities. And we said, Nobody likes a saint.

From the beginning, everybody, including me, found plenty not to like about Ann. *Who does she think she is* was what you heard all the time. The way I see it now, she was damned if she did, damned if she didn't. Nobody liked the fact that she came from an upper-class background, as far from most prisoners as you can get. But nobody liked it either that she wanted to be treated like she came from the bottom. She didn't understand that, by asking for this, she was actually putting herself above everyone. Who did she think she was?

If you know anything about inmate mentality, you'll know how it was possible for people to accept Ann's help while at the same time putting her down. ("Oh, now she got to learn herself Spanish. Like she always got to be showing off.") There were those who took her help for granted and didn't even say thanks, and then if things didn't turn out like they hoped, they'd curse her and accuse her of playing them. A few even assaulted her, and that's when the guards would rock back on their heels and shake their heads and say how Ann had brought it on herself.

But there was something about Ann that could rile people even when she was doing nothing. I have seen her jumped just for showing her face.

We're sitting in the dayroom, drunk on Winkie's moonshine, when Ann walks in.

"Uh-oh. You see what I see?"

"Holy shit. I see a ghost."

"Yeah, she scary."

"Do Caspar got a wife?"

"She whiter than a ghost, man."

"Yeah. She white as aspirin."

"White as a har'boiled egg."

"White as rice!"

"No, I got it! She white as Noxzema skin cream."

"Who invited her white ass in here, anyway?"

"I think we should call her Noxzema."

"Noxzema too nice a name for her."

"Is true. Noxzema a purty name."

"I don't care whats you call her. Just keep her away from me."

"She deaf, too."

"Bitch still standing there!"

"This a private party."

"Bitch lookin' to get it."

"Bitch, go find the white girls. Don't tell me you wasn't raised to stay away from niggers."

It was unfortunate that everyone knew about the money. Not that we're allowed to have money in here. But people would try to force Ann to get it to someone they knew on the outside. And more than one CO let her know how much nicer her life could be if she crossed their palms with silver. But you couldn't sweet-talk that money out of her, and you couldn't beat it out of her, either. Though that didn't stop folks from trying.

I like to say that, in many ways, time is as much a prisoner's friend as it is his or her enemy. Ann's luck changed as the population changed, and things got easier for her, as they did for me, after the first decade or so. And like I said, the smartest thing a person can do round here is grow older. As a grandma, Ann could expect less trouble, same as me or anyone else.

A big change came when we got ourselves a new warden. When Miss Harper took over—this was in '84—Maryville was in a bad way. The drugs-for-sex exchange between some guards and some inmates, long common knowledge round here, had become a major news story. There was the scandal itself, then there was the cover-up, and then there was the shake-up, with Mrs. Lockhart resigning and several officers losing their jobs.

As warden, Miss Harper was very different from Mrs. Lockhart (and from Mrs. DeFries, who came after). She had ideas about making Maryville a model prison, with special attention paid to problems specific to female inmates. First thing she did was give a big speech about all the things she wanted. She wanted more visiting days each month, including overnight visits with husbands and kids. She wanted marriage counseling and parenting classes and counseling for battered women. She wanted a bigger and better library and a writing program and more contact between inmates and the local community. She wanted every woman who got out of Maryville to be able to read and write English, and to be able to care for children (or at least not be a harm to them), and to know skills to help her find a job.

Some of the things Warden Harper wanted she got, some she didn't. Some she managed to get for a while before she was told that, for one reason or another, she couldn't have them anymore. Who knows how much she might've accomplished given more time. But Miss Harper, like so many of her own projects, did not last long at Maryville. But the years she was with us were a better time for Ann in particular. The two of them hit it off right away. Miss Harper treated Ann almost like an equal. It fact, it seemed to me she was a little in awe of Ann, maybe because of Ann's upper-class background. Anyhow, it was rare to see anyone take so quickly to Ann, and a lot of people didn't like seeing it. Some said that, except for the jumper, Ann could easily be mistaken by a visitor for an employee. Another complaint reached ears in Albany, something about "tea parties," referring I suppose to those times when the two of them sat in Miss Harper's office discussing school business. Maybe there was tea, maybe there wasn't.

I'm sure Miss Harper wished all the women at Maryville could be more like Orphan Annie. The two of them disapproved mightily of how most inmates spent their time. But you can't force these ladies to be productive if they don't want to be. Truth is, lots of them would be happy just to sleep or watch TV all day long. Miss Harper said we all needed more exercise. Junk food is plentiful in prison, and many inmates put on weight. But women just don't have the kind of motivation that drives male inmates to work out hour after hour in the gym. With the women, it's hour after hour of grooming instead, themselves or each other. Hair, nails, makeup, makeup, nails, hair. And lots of times a grooming session will turn into a make-out session, or even full sex.

It didn't matter that a lot of these women were working toward their certificates in beauty culture, Miss Harper still said too much time was being wasted in this way. And some of the worst fights broke out over the beauty samples donated to Maryville by one of the fashion mags. The samples were distributed by grab bag, and half the time the bag itself, one of those big plastic trash bags, ended up in shreds. And there was always screaming. "I don't need no fucking lipstick!" "I got mascara last time!" "I want some zit cream!" "This ain't my shade!"

Because we got the samples through Ann, who had some connection to the magazine that she never explained, she could've stopped them at any time, and more than once she threatened to do just that. But Miss Harper always talked her out of it. The women really looked forward to the grab bag, Miss Harper said, and it'd be a shame to take that pleasure away from them. Miss Harper understood better than Ann, I think, because she always wore makeup herself. She also wore jewelry, which, like makeup, is pretty important around here, since we can't do much about what we wear, which has to be either a state-issue jumper or clothing that's not all that different from it. Ann found it easier just to wear a jumper every day. No makeup for her, no jewelry. Far as I know, she never took beauty samples for herself, either. What would a nun like her do with any of that?

Speaking of which, the real nuns at Maryville and Orphan Annie didn't always see eye to eye. It wasn't the work the sisters did that she had trouble with. In fact, she and Sister Frances and Sister Clementine were all on the education committee and did projects together all the time. No, what Ann didn't like about the sisters was their religion. Ann didn't like religion. Said it was nothing but lies and superstition! She didn't believe in God, and she said the world would be a much better place if no one else believed in Him, either. She said there was no Father in Heaven guiding events according to His plan, only us human beings down here making a mess of it. There was no Heaven or Hell, no life after death, only this life and this here Earth full of pain and suffering and injustice. She said all religions were bad because they gave people a fake view of the world and oppressed the masses. She talked about how white Southerners argued against integration by saying if God wanted the races to mix, He wouldn't have created some people white and some black. She said we had to accept it was up to human beings to help one another and save the world from destruction. She said religion was like a drug, let the people have it and they'll look to the next life for salvation, instead of working for freedom and justice in this one. She talked about religious wars, and all the spilling of blood that was done in God's name. She talked about all the harm done to native peoples by missionaries, and she brought up genocide again and the Jews and the pope and how we Christians had covered ourselves with shame.

I don't know where Ann got all this from, but it certainly had an effect on the ladies. This is a place where a lot of praying goes on, and a lot of gospel singing, where people who never believed in God before find Him waiting for them. The Hispanic women in particular tend to be very religious. They always go to Mass, and most of them wear crosses or have crosses in their cells. They could get quite heated up when Ann said things like, If you're gonna pray to Jesus, you might just as well pray to the Easter Bunny. I was afraid we'd be seeing some more spilling of blood in God's name, in this very place that was named for His mother. I was glad when the chaplain decided to have a word with Ann. He reminded her that faith in God helped many inmates get through their time, and if they were to start doubting His existence now, they might fall into despair.

Fortunately, Ann took Father Walsh's point. Now and then you'd still hear her bitching about thieves, child abusers, and murderers describing themselves as religious while at the same time continuing to raise hell in jail. But she stopped trying to convert us all to atheism. Praise the Lord for that.

No, I didn't see myself ever befriending the likes of Orphan Annie. Who did she think she was, talking against religion like that? It gave me the same bad feeling about her as when her father died, and she didn't have the common decency to go to the funeral. Something about not wanting to have to see all these society folk. What kind of crazy reason is that?

I'm not proud of it, but I will say there were times when seeing her with another black eye gave me some satisfaction. And when Toy Babe come along, I could almost believe it was God's way of telling Ann that Hell existed, all right, and He had let this fiend out to prove it.

Two fiends: Toy Babe and Scarecrow. Scarecrow came first, but she was in another unit and though prone to fights not a meaningful threat to Ann till Toy Babe arrived. How those two managed to get permission for Scarecrow to be moved to our floor, and to a cell right next to Toy Babe's, whose own cell happened to be across from Ann's, was a mystery never explained. But looking back, I see the hand of God from beginning to end of this story.

Toy Babe could get Scarecrow to do most anything. At Toy Babe's command, Scarecrow set fire to Ann's cell, she snatched Ann's schoolbooks out of her hands and tore them to pieces. She was stupid, Scarecrow. She didn't seem to realize that, by getting someone else to do her dirty work, Toy Babe was protecting herself from charges that could earn her more time. Not that Toy Babe didn't do any mischief herself. But she was sharp and knew what she could get away with. And you'd be surprised how much you can get away with behind bars so long as you don't touch an officer, cause a riot, or destroy prison property.

We had Warden DeFries by then. She didn't hate Ann, like Mrs. Lockhart did, and she didn't love Ann, like Miss Harper did. For Mrs. DeFries, Ann was just another number. Meaning she wasn't about to lift a finger to help.

We didn't have real gangs at Maryville yet, but we had clubs, which was close. A club for white ladies, a club for Puerto Ricans, a couple of rival clubs for blacks. We had families, too, with parents called Mommy and Daddy, and Big Sister, Little Sister, and so on, though often there was just one Baby. We had some single-parent families, too, mostly mommies. And we had a few families, especially Hispanics, that got to be very big, and many families also belonged to clubs.

The trouble with belonging to any prison clan, gang, or club is that you end up forced to take sides you know are wrong or that you don't care about one way or the other, or you risk being punished as a traitor. My first days as an inmate—my "green time"—I didn't think I could make it on my own. But I soon learned the wisdom of resisting any kind of bond and staying independent. I've always had my friends, but I know how to mind my own business and keep a distance. Lifers are known to grow more solitary with age, and that's how it would be with me. I watched the same thing happen to Ann, though in a lot of ways she didn't have much choice but to be a loner. She'd never have joined any white club, nor would she have been welcome to. These were the days when Ann really had to watch her back. A rumor that got started in the reign of Miss Harper and refused to die was that those "tea parties" were in fact snitching sessions. I knew Ann was no snitch, and I also happened to know who the real snitch was. But like I say, what I knew best was how to mind my own business.

Ann was not Toy Babe's only victim, just her favorite. Ann tried to stay out of her way and not get caught alone with her or with Scarecrow or, worst of all, the two together. It's one thing to get beat. It's another thing to get held down and beat. A most dangerous place to get caught was in one of the stairwells. One time Ann was found unconscious at the bottom of a flight of stairs and had to be taken to the prison hospital.

It's the inmate's worst nightmare. To be a loner, with no protection, and singled out for regular assault and harassment. It's been enough to drive a prisoner to suicide. And some believed if homicide didn't get her first, this just might be the fate of Orphan Annie.

I was an eyewitness to the events that rewrote this story.

Chow time, and I'm sitting in the mess hall. From where I am I can see Ann, sitting with her back to me at a table across the aisle. I see Toy Babe and Scarecrow come up with their trays and make straight for two chairs directly across from her. Right away they start in. Not that I can actually hear them. There's always a racket in the mess hall, and the aisles are pretty wide. Fried chicken and mashed taters have drawn more of a crowd than usual, and there are plenty of guards around. Though fights do break out fairly often during meals, I figure Ann's not in physical danger from those two right now. No, they're just entertaining themselves (and surely others at their table) over lunch. Ann's ugly face, her skinny ass, how she looks like a ghost, what, is she deaf, is she fucking mute, where's the fucking money they told her to get them, and how she better dis and she better dat. I don't have to hear to know what they're saying, because I heard it all before.

Just that week Toy Babe started shaving her head, the big new fashion statement for the younger inmates, don't ask me why. She also got rid of her eyebrows and drew herself new ones, two dark diagonal stripes, like war paint, which made her look pissed off at all times. She was in the process of getting a tattoo, a spiderweb with a red heart trapped in it. Scarecrow had the exact same tattoo, between her shoulder blades. Toy Babe's was on her right upper arm, and it was about half done. Scarecrow was going to have "Toy Babe" tattooed somewhere on her body, or at least that was the word.

It just occurred to me that Scarecrow's name has probably given you the wrong idea about what she looked like. She was a tall, thin girl, with the longest arms and legs you ever saw. But the only scary thing about how she looked was how beautiful she was. If there was anything "crow" about her, it was her blue-black hair, which was long and straight and thick and came from having Seneca blood, through her mother. And here's a fact: Scarecrow's mother served time at Maryville and so did Toy Babe's mother, and they met when they were incarcerated together. So for them, visiting day was also a reunion. Not that inmates with relatives who've been at Maryville are all that special. The oldest staff members have watched three generations of the same families pass through, and a couple of inmates doing time now were born here.

Toy Babe was twenty-five years old and she had three sons, or rather two, because one got shot to death while she was awaiting trial. Scarecrow was two years younger, but she had six kids already. (Her mother had sixteen.) She also had the AIDS virus but didn't know it yet. She was a huge flirt and a favorite of the guards. I don't know where the name Scarecrow came from, but only inmates called her that. The guards called her Cleopatra.

Toy Babe had this ugly habit of talking and scarfing food at the same time. Every few seconds she'd throw back her head and laugh with her mouth all full. I stopped paying attention after a while, and when I looked back it was because I heard a crash. Toy Babe was on her feet. She'd jumped up from her chair so hard she knocked it over. You know how it is in a situation like this, how everyone freezes as if by magic spell. We all stared at Toy Babe standing there with her arms out from her sides, like she was about to sing a song or make an important announcement. Her mouth was open wide but no sound came. Her eyes were round and bulging. Seizures are common around here and so are asthma attacks, but I never knew Toy Babe to have either. I barely had time to finish this thought when I saw Ann come up behind her. I stood up for a better view and saw Ann wrap her arms around Toy Babe's waist in a kind of giant bear hug. It looked like she was trying to lift Toy Babe right off her feet. It would've been comical (Toy Babe had eight inches on Ann and outweighed her by some sixty pounds) if the expression on Toy Babe's face had not been so fearsome. Toy Babe pitched forward. Then she coughed and spat something into the air, and Ann let go. Toy Babe slumped to the floor. I saw Scarecrow squat down beside her, and then I couldn't see anything anymore, because there were too many people crowding round. Everyone was standing up now and some folks were climbing onto chairs and even tables, and the guards went into action, some of them streaming toward the scene and others turning this way and that, shouting at us to sit our asses back down *now*. Nothing freaks the COs out more than when there's some commotion and they don't know what's happening. It took a while for them to figure it out, and then the order came from a sergeant that we were all to leave the mess hall and return to our cells for the midday count, even though it wasn't quite time for that. Show's over, ladies, show's over, the guards kept saying. And so it was. A show so short you could've blinked your eyes and missed it, but what a show. I don't know if I'd have believed it if I hadn't seen it for myself. A person nearly choking to death with hundreds of people standing by watching. Little Orphan Annie saving Toy Babe's life!

Now you're probably thinking the next thing I'm gonna say is that from this moment on, Ann's troubles with Toy Babe were over. But if you are thinking that, you must be forgetting where this story takes place.

If anything, Toy Babe treated Ann even worse.

For shame, said Rabbit when we happened to strike up a conversation soon after all this took place. Rabbit was okay, for a CO. Not your best friend, needless to say, but not your enemy, either. When he retired, he'd be gifted with an afghan some inmates knitted for him, and he'd cry when he saw it. For shame, he said now. He'd worked at Attica before coming to Maryville, and though he acknowledged how Attica was a much rougher place, he said he preferred working there. This kind of thing, he said, wouldn't happen at Attica or any men's jail. It was bitch behavior, pure and simple. He said he had no idea how different guarding women was gonna be. With men, he said, you knew what was what. Men dealt with the world straight on. But women were devious. They didn't play fair. They were dirty fighters. And the way they turned on each other. "Make your skin crawl," he said. Even behind bars men were better than that, according to Rabbit. There was a code at Attica. But not Maryville. The women couldn't trust one another. No loyalty. Loyalty was king at Attica. There was a sense of honor that just did not exist among females. ("They ten times more likely to snitch.") And in their own way men, or at least the majority, he said, were more willing to abide by the rules.

"But here, you got these ladies always got to be challenging, challenging, testing your authority, seeing what they can get away with, seeing how much you'll take, needling you, grinding you, wearing you down. Drive a man to his grave."

Bad enough how ungrateful some women were for the legal help and tutoring and other things Ann was always doing for them. "But if you can't be grateful to the one that saved your life, who can you be grateful to?" Rabbit called what Ann had done to save Toy Babe's life "the Alzheimer maneuver." And after all Toy Babe had put her through! And two against one! And not one bitch standing up for her! No, women were bad, truly bad. Never happen in Attica.

*

Today it's my turn to mop the corridor, a job I hate and always put off as long as possible. In fact, any time I have extra cigarettes I use them to pay someone to do it for me—yet another Rule Violation. Today also happens to be graduation day. First I was planning to go, but I've already been to so many graduations, and no one I know is getting a diploma this time, so I figured might as well get the mopping over with.

I just set my pail down at the end of the corridor where the showers are when I hear a noise from one of the cells, way down near the dayroom. Which surprises me, because I figure everyone is at the graduation ceremony. The last person I expect to be around is Ann, because as a teacher she'd be at the ceremony for sure. But as I sneak down to investigate I hear the noise again, and it's definitely coming from Ann's cell. I stop short. She's not locked in, and she doesn't have her curtain drawn. From where I am, all I can see is her feet. She's sitting on her cot with her back against the wall, legs stretched out in front of her and her feet sticking off the edge of the mattress. She's not wearing any shoes or socks, and it hits me how small her bare feet are and how white they are, though the bottoms are a little darker, from dirt.

And she's crying.

You might think in prison you see folks crying all the time. But in fact inmates usually take care to hide their tears. No one has ever seen me cry except at sad movies, which is different because it's understood you're crying for the people in the movie and not anything to do with yourself. As for Ann, I saw her cry only once before, and that time we were watching TV. Some special program, I recall, a documentary about the past called "The Lost Dream" or "The Broken Dream," something like that. Time of Dr. King and Vietnam and demonstrations and street fighting. A couple of women said, Oh, I remember that, I seen that before. But most were too young to recall anything of those days. Me, I was already incarcerated for much of that time, and I didn't find the program all that interesting. Everyone was making fun of the clothes and the hairstyles. I looked round the room, and that's when I saw Ann crying. She caught me staring, and she got up and ducked out of the room. "Hey, where the hell she going?" "She the one signed up for this program!" "Fuck her. Let's change the channel."

And there was another time when I didn't actually see Ann cry but I saw her eyes get teary. Some of us wanted to watch a movie that night but the VCR was broken *again*, so we ended up just hanging out in our bathrobes, talking and smoking and eating the popcorn we made. I remember it was a specially relaxed and friendly atmosphere, one of those times when you can almost forget you're behind bars. Ann was there, too. All of a sudden her hands fly up to her cheeks and she goes, "My god, this is so weird! I feel exactly as if I were back in my college dorm." I thought she looked happy, but then her eyes got teary. It was one of the rare times anyone ever heard her mention that part of her life.

But now it's not like that. Now she's having herself one serious cry. I can't be mopping the corridor with her carrying on like that, so when I go back and start the job I make sure to rattle the pail to let her know someone's there. Maybe fifteen minutes later, when I'm at the place outside her cell where I was before, I peek in again and she hasn't moved. I can see her feet just like before. She's in the exact same position on the cot, with her feet sticking off the edge.

But this time her feet aren't quiet like before. They're twisting this way and that, and the toes are curling and uncurling, the kind of dance you expect from someone being tortured. But not a peep out of her.

I haven't been pushing the mop all that hard, but now I break into a sweat, and for a minute I think I'm having an asthma attack. I stare at those twisting, clenching feet and another pair of feet come into my mind. A pair of naked feet sticking off a bed just like that, twisting, toes curling and uncurling. Those feet are even smaller and they are black, but they are doing the same tortured dance. They belong to a time I recall as the worst in my life, a time when I knew either I had to kill or I had to die, and that is all I intend to say about that.

Another step, and I can see all of Ann. She's still crying hard as before, but she's got her pillow in her arms and she's hugging it and she's got one corner stuffed in her mouth. She's got her eyes shut, too, but when I walk into her cell she opens them wide, wide as they can go. I sit down on her lockbox, next to her cot.

I've never been inside that cell before. A lot of ladies here do whatever they can to make their cells more homey. They put up posters and pictures cut from magazines on the walls. They have family photos out, and they have rugs and stuffed animals and non-state bedding—whatever they can get away with, though the rules as to what is and what isn't contraband can change at any time, and you always got to be prepared for searches, when things might be damaged or confiscated (in some cases more like stolen) or even destroyed.

Ann's cell isn't bare. It's chock-full of books and papers, but still it's got an empty feel because there aren't any decorations, and whatever personal items she has must be under her cot, or under me, in the lock-box. There's nothing on the walls, but I remember some years back when she did have one photograph taped to the wall above her cot. It was a newspaper photo of the police officer she shot and killed. Actually, it was a photocopy of the photo, which she made in the library. When the COs saw it they went ape-shit and demanded she take it down. Ann refused, so they went in there and tore it down themselves. She made another copy and taped it to the wall, and again it was torn down. Ann filed a grievance, as I recall. She wasn't violating any rule that she knew of, she said. Maybe. But the COs won.

For a while we both just sit there. I don't know what the hell to say. It's not like this girl and I are friends. We haven't even always been neighbors, we just happen to be on the same floor at that time. In all the many years we've been together at Maryville, we've exchanged maybe fifty words, all short ones. I figure she's got to know I'm not all that fond of her, because I always make sure people I'm not fond of do know it. I'm feeling more and more uncomfortable. I'm trying to figure out what exactly I think I'm doing there. Just to say something, I ask how come she's not at the graduation. She takes the pillow away from her mouth and says, "I was on my way. Then all of a sudden, I don't know, something came over me. I started to cry and I couldn't stop." And as if this was a reminder, she starts to cry all over again.

This is an Ann I've never seen before, and it's an Ann I don't want to see. The only thing on my mind is to try and stop that damn crying. I reach out and take hold of one of her feet and give a little squeeze. She clutches the pillow to her chest and her eyes go wide again as I start gently massaging that foot. I think she's too shocked to move or speak, she may even be scared. She lets me massage one foot and then the other one. I look down at her matchstick legs and shake my head. Her ankles are smaller than my wrists. I put my fingers around her ankle to see if my thumb and middle finger meet. They do. Then I show her how those same two fingers don't meet when I put them around my own wrist. She's stopped crying, but she's still not saying anything. She looks mighty anxious about what's gonna happen next. I don't know myself. On impulse I start tickling her foot. Turns out she's ticklish, big time. She yelps and pulls her foot away. But I grab it back and hold it tight and keep tickling, while she thrashes and squeals for mercy and starts swatting me with the pillow. Then she jerks her leg so hard she yanks me right off the lockbox. I lose my balance and fall across the cot.

Neither of us heard the footsteps coming down the corridor. Now the CO is right there, staring in. It's Piggly-Wiggly, probably on his way to the kitchen to see what he can steal. He wasn't expecting to find anyone home, and he sure wasn't expecting to find us where *we* are. He stands there gawking, cheeks all red. He's so flustered, he can't speak. Finally he goes, "Now, now, ladies, none of that, none of that," and then hurries on his way. Ann and I look at each other and burst out laughing. We laugh a good long time, taking breaks just to catch our breath. We shake our fingers at each other. Now, now, ladies, none of that. *That*, of course, is another Rule Violation, and old Piggly-Wiggly isn't the only CO who prefers just to turn on his heel and run away from it.

If she hadn't done her crime, she wouldn't have gone to prison. If she hadn't gone to prison, she wouldn't have been there to save Toy Babe's life. If "something" hadn't come over her that day, she would've been at the graduation and not in her cell. If I hadn't decided to mop the corridor instead of going to the graduation myself, I wouldn't have found her crying. If I hadn't found her crying, I wouldn't have gone into her cell. If I hadn't gone into her cell, we wouldn't have become friends.

Oh, she could roll her eyes all she wanted when I said it. But I saw the hand of God in all this for sure.

One thing I didn't worry about was Toy Babe. To begin with, I'm not child-sized like Ann. I've always been big and fairly muscular, even though I don't work out. I had my share of fights when I was young, but not many folks looking for trouble would pick on me. Besides, I'd already killed two people and was doing life, meaning I didn't have a whole lot to lose. This in itself would stop most inmates from messing with me. Anyhow, I knew Toy Babe's type—the dirty fighter Rabbit was talking about—and that it takes more than shaving your head and picking on someone half your size with no street or survival skills or even common sense to make you a badass to be taken seriously, at least by me.

I didn't worry about the rumors either. Some figured Ann finally wised up and started paying for protection. Well, what they thought I might be doing with the money I don't know. When it was clear my lifestyle hadn't changed, there was no brand-new TV in my cell, no booze or other contraband being smuggled in by some bribed CO, and I was just as poor as I'd always been, the rumors would give way to the simple truth: I was hanging out with Orphan Annie because I wanted to.

But I'm not about to take all the credit for delivering Ann from her persecutors. There were other factors, too. (Hand of God.) For one thing, Toy Babe and Scarecrow now had a major distraction. This was YaYa, a flashy girl who tripped around in tight pants and platform heels, who took extra pains with her makeup and hair, and who owned some fine, almost definitely stolen pieces of jewelry which she flaunted, foolish and even dangerous though this might be. Envy is not an emotion any sensible prisoner wants to provoke, but many women here can't seem to resist. It came as a surprise to me when I first got to Maryville, how in an all-female pop so many women would still want to look their sexy best. I've had a lot of years to get over my shock at how many inmates want to look good to the male guards. And needless to say, many do look good to them, some irresistibly so. It's not supposed to happen, but COs have been known to fall for inmates, to carry on with them, and there have been cases of officers secretly taking up with inmates after their release. You wouldn't think prison was the most romantic setting in the world, but it isn't always romantic that turns people on. Anyhow, at any given time, you'll find every kind of love on display here at Maryville, from schoolgirl crush to the real, full-blown, undying thing.

YaYa and Scarecrow declared theirs to be the real thing and even went so far as to get "married," like others before them, in a special ceremony one June morning in the rec yard. The brides wore white—negligees someone sent them—and sunglasses, and they carried lollipops, and dandelions plucked from the rec yard cracks. It was such a sight, the guards, who are supposed to break up such ceremonies, stood by snapping pictures instead.

Toy Babe was beside herself and most certainly would've taken revenge if this had been any other time. But she had her appeal to think about. Toy Babe had a great lawyer, and her future was looking bright. Between now and her official release, she had to stay out of trouble. Her last days with us she was all but unrecognizable, holier than the chaplain himself.

YaYa and Scarecrow were both in for drugs, but YaYa had the shorter sentence and won parole first. She wasn't gone long before Scarecrow started getting sick and was transferred to the prison hospital, which was already full of AIDS patients. After a couple of months, though she'd only done about half her time, she got a compassionate release.

Not long after she learned she had AIDS, Scarecrow found Jesus. After her release, she wrote Ann a letter, apologizing for having hurt her. She was writing to all the people she'd ever done wrong, she said. Even if she didn't have an address for someone, or if someone had passed away, she'd still write a letter to that person and imagine them receiving and reading it. She was dying. She asked for Ann's forgiveness and that Ann show her forgiveness by praying for her. And she signed the letter with her real name, Yolande.

Ann said she forgave Scarecrow, but as an atheist she couldn't pray for anyone. I said you never know if something's going to work unless you give it a try. But she just rolled her eyes at me, like she did so often. There was no sign of it yet, but I kept hoping Ann would find Jesus herself one day.

Time—even hard time—flies, especially as you get older. On her forty-fifth birthday, I remember Ann saying, "Eighteen years! I can hardly believe it's been that long."

The inmate's handbook says the smartest thing you can do (after mind your own business) is keep yourself busy. I'm not one of them, but there are plenty of women here who think nothing of scrubbing and waxing their cell floors and washing down the walls not once but five or six times a week. There are also women, and I *am* one of *them*, who sign up for every course they're allowed to take. No one would believe I was once a big truant who failed everything in high school. I got my B.A. in 1973. (I feel shy even mentioning this, since I know how much it upsets some folks out there to think of me sitting here on my criminal ass with my criminal nose in *Hamlet*.) After that, I earned a certificate in paralegal studies, which led to my job in the law library, where you could say I found my niche. But over the years I've also learned how to cut hair, give manicures, knit, crochet, cook, plant trees, do carpentry, and make plumbing repairs. I've worked as a tutor, and as a secretary in the deputy warden's office. And now, through correspondence courses, I'm working toward a master's degree in writing.

I'm not sure of the exact time, but I'd say it was around then, when Ann turned forty-five, that she started to change. Like I say, as a prisoner gets older she usually keeps more to herself, and if she's lucky she may be able to lead a fairly peaceful life. Grandmas don't get harassed by officers the way new girls do, and they're not as likely to get written up or receive discipline as in the past. Often COs who've observed an inmate for years will decide she's paid her debt to society and been rehabilitated long before any parole board would agree, and they'll give her what freedom they can without getting themselves in trouble. Certain older prisoners who have their own TVs can become quite isolated. They stop socializing and instead of company keep the set on day and night, even while they're asleep.

Ann was not one to sit for hours in front of TV, and she didn't become any less busy than before. But she did change how she filled her time. She started devoting herself to a particular kind of inmate, the kind who needs help most. She still got involved with different projects and causes and such, but now she preferred working with inmates one on one. She'd always be on the education committee, but instead of teaching the most advanced levels like she'd been doing for years, she went after the hard cases, the ones with no English or with some kind of disability, the ones all the other teachers had given up on. And she started spending more time taking care of inmates with problems like Carolee's. Sad to say, at any given time, there's always a number who've suffered such neglect their whole lives they don't even know how to wash or groom themselves properly. Not to mention the retarded. I could tell you stories about the child they call Molasses, who's so slow she doesn't know which end to wipe. Ann took charge of such pitiful souls, she taught them how to wash, and in the one or two cases where the women couldn't be taught, she washed them herself. Yet another Rule Violation, but who was gonna stop her?

Ann tried befriending those women who everyone else avoided because they were such misfits or just so weird it was unpleasant or depressing to be around them. Like Misty, this teenage girl who never spoke and kept her arms wrapped round her head most of the time as if to protect it from a punch that could come any second from any direction. I was amazed at Ann's patience, since you could never tell if you were getting through to Misty, her mind was that far away. How the defense failed to prove her incompetent to stand trial was a genuine mystery. But over the years we have seen more and more of her kind. And more like Carolee, whose only crime besides being epileptic so far as I can tell was being homeless.

But what we are seeing the most of round here now is drug addicts and street women. When I first got to Maryville, there were about two hundred inmates. Now we got more than a thousand. They keep building new housing (there's talk now about adding a Death Row), but it never seems to be enough. Turns out the number of women going to jail is growing at an even faster rate than the men. Average age here is twenty-five, but we are seeing more and more in their teens. Most of the drug charges are for possession, and for lots of girls it's drugs *and* prostitution, the prostitution just about always being a means to the drugs. Ann calls these women POWs, meaning they wouldn't be here but for the War on

Drugs, which like she says has already taken millions of prisoners without winning any battles (except to get this or that politician elected on the promise to be tough on crime). Personally, in honor of former governor Nelson Rockefeller, I like to call these girls the Rockettes. As for teaching them a lesson, the two things that landed them here, drugs and prostitution, well, they don't have any problem whatsoever keeping up that lifestyle behind bars.

Having a large number of Rockettes has completely changed life at Maryville. Of all inmates, addicts tend to be the most troublesome. Ask anyone who knows prison life. Better to be thrown in with the killers than with the addicts. This might be another thing that will be hard for outsiders to believe, but I'm not just saying it to boast. Very often, your best-behaved, most respectable and hardworking prisoners will be long-termers with blood on their hands.

For a while I persuaded Ann to stop eating dinner in the mess hall, where the food never got any better and the atmosphere only got worse. She had to agree how much pleasanter it was for the two of us and maybe a few other women from our floor to cook something together and share it at the kitchen table. Ann wasn't eating much more than she ever did, but I was used to that. Eating disorders, like self-mutilation, were on the rise at Maryville, and some of those disorders made Ann's starvation diet look sane. But when a woman named Bharti found out Ann had a weakness for rice pudding, she kept trying to fatten her up with her homemade Indian variety. Only time I ever saw Ann come anything near to pigging out, with Bharti standing over her, grinning.

When some of us decided to join Oprah's Book Club, Ann suggested we ask the publishers to donate copies of the books. We did, and when the publishers agreed, we asked if they'd recommend other books and send them, too, so we could build up our library. Most of what we got was memoirs, people dishing the dirt on their families, spilling all kinds of beans, no matter how personal. We enjoyed these books and had lively discussions about them, but some found certain stories bewildering. "Her father did it to her just that one time, and she still crying about it?" "Why on earth would she walk out on a man who gave her such fine things?" "He says here he still made it to work every day. I don't call that enough jones to write a book about." There didn't seem to be many people writing about life behind bars, and that's when I first started thinking how, if I ever learned to write, I'd like to do that.

Ann didn't join the book club. She said she had too much else going on. In fact, I hardly ever saw her read just for fun anymore. There were heavy matters on my friend's mind.

AIDS. Nobody could say exactly how many had the virus, how many knew they had it and how many didn't, how many came into Maryville infected already and how many got infected after they arrived. Blind tests showed the infection rate was rising fast, and we could count for ourselves the growing number of sick and dying. (About those tests, last figure I heard—and I hope it was an exaggeration—was around forty percent.)

Ann was one of the volunteers who got together to help those with AIDS, and one of the things they did was visit patients in the prison hospital. There was much need for this, because the hospital was understaffed and because everyone was so afraid to have anything to do with people who were infected. In fact, just about everyone who knew they had the virus kept quiet about it. They didn't want to be treated like lepers, or maybe even assaulted, which happened to some. They didn't want to end up like HIV-positive inmates at other facilities who are forced to live in segregation.

But Ann said being just a volunteer was too frustrating. She thought she could do more if she had some training, so she enrolled in a program to become a nurse's aide. I thought this was going too far, and I said so. She was already spending way too much time in the hospital, I said, and I knew that because of the shortness of hands she was doing things that weren't really a nurse's aide's job. I knew you couldn't catch AIDS from someone like you catch the flu, and I believed Ann when she said she was always careful. But I also knew that hospitals were full of germs, and an overcrowded, understaffed prison hospital was a very dangerous place to be.

And in fact, she did come down with an infection, worst I ever saw, all over her face and neck and chest, and the glands under her arms swelled up so bad she had to hold her arms away from her. She had a fever, too. It took forever to get that infection under control, and at one point her fever spiked so high she started babbling. I was worried sick myself, and if Jesus didn't already know her name, trust me, He got to know it then.

While Ann was still convalescing, a Canadian woman doing research on American prisons was allowed to visit Maryville and observe inmates up close for a couple of weeks. One day, a CO brought this woman out to the yard where some of us were sitting on the grass, talking. She asked if she could join us, and when we nodded she sat down on the grass and took out a little tape recorder. We happened to be having what I thought was an interesting discussion. The question had come up, was it possible for a person ever to be truly happy while incarcerated, and we all agreed the answer was no, you could never be truly happy without being free. The most you could hope for was moments of happiness, but these moments could be powerful and you had to give thanks for them. We said we'd all known such moments and that we'd met with more kindness in prison than we ever thought possible. Bharti said that when she was sentenced she just figured she was going to be miserable every minute of every day till she got out, but in fact it wasn't like that. A new inmate named Kezia said how touched she was to discover how much singing went on at Maryville. And it's true. Every night, on almost every floor, there's at least one woman who can't settle down till she's belted out at least one song. The COs call these women nightingales, and when one is transferred or paroled out of her cage, some women on her floor may have trouble getting to sleep for weeks. And let me just add, we got some mighty fine dancers here, too.

Ann said it was after she came to prison that she realized she'd never been happy. And she didn't believe she would've found happiness if she'd remained free. The Canadian woman, who knew who Ann was and had talked to her before, alone, put a fresh cassette into her tape recorder and asked her please to say more.

Best if I copy what she said straight from the article the Canadian woman wrote, which I've got right here.

I don't believe I belong in prison. And I could say the same for many of the women I've met here. But unlike them, I'm not unhappy that I came to Maryville. For one thing, being here has given me a chance to do work that I know has been more urgent than probably any other work I might have ended up doing. Of course, you could say a person doesn't have to be incarcerated to do prison work. Take the sisters, for example. But it's different when you're actually sharing the life yourself. I'm not happy to be a prisoner in this increasingly dysfunctional institution, but I cherish what I've had—the privilege, as I consider it—to have experienced something that's given me so much insight into the human condition. And sometimes I think I may have found a greater— deeper—happiness here than I would have found outside. Because from what I can tell, all these years I've been secluded here, the world has changed for the worse. All you have to do is look at television to see how America has become even more plastic and consumerist than it was when I was young. The gap between the haves and the have-nots is even wider, and people seem to be getting greedier and more materialistic all the time. Yes, of course, I'd love to have my freedom back, but I don't know where my place would be in such a world, where the things I care about seem to have passed or are passing away.

Dostoevsky said you can judge a society by what goes on in its prisons. Take a look at the teenagers here and what shape they're in when they arrive, and you can see just how low our own society has sunk.

You can't hide from the world in prison, far from it. We see the worst of America, in the form of its worst victims. I hope while you're here you won't neglect to visit the hospital, especially the AIDS ward. American prisons are terrible places, and Maryville is no exception. But I'm not unhappy to be isolated from those who are responsible for it.

I remember how the Canadian woman stared at Ann like Ann had just grown a tail. But the rest of us had heard her say all this many times before. It was her own particular view, and she was always good at articulating it. It certainly wasn't a common one at Maryville. Most of the women, if they were honest, would've said they could never have too much money, and fancy clothes and jewelry would've been the first things they'd buy. In fact, most of what you hear these ladies talk about is the things they want and how they might be scheming to get them. Any nice thing someone else has, they are envious and dying to have it. And watch out they don't just take it. Even all the ones who've found Jesus, who praise the Lord for locking them up and saving them from the streets and from eternal damnation—that might be how they talk in Bible class, but other times it's a whole other story. It's all too obvious some people here miss shopping—or shoplifting, more likely—more than they miss their own kids. And being in prison only makes their greediness fiercer, so that the first thing many will do when they get out is get themselves rearrested, for stealing. And those who never could stomach Ann, both inmates and staff alike, found her kind of talk infuriating. Preaching the antimaterialist gospel to women who got nothing—who did she think she was? And they really did not respect a person who didn't appreciate the importance of money. To them, this wasn't any kind of virtue. Kissing it all goodbye, throwing her life away, like it seemed to so many she'd done—what a loser she was in their eyes. Only a fool would listen to her. Blowing away a cop, then sticking around to get caught—what did that prove? So she had a black boyfriend when she was young. So among her few visitors were two middle-aged black men—was this supposed to mean something? What did it mean?

But the thing that got me, now and other times when I listened to Ann talk about being in Maryville, was her blindness, her stubborn refusal to see the obvious. I am talking, of course, about the hand of God.

COP KILLER "HAPPY AT LAST" BEHIND BARS.

The headline appeared in an Albany newspaper. A story *about* the story the Canadian woman published in a magazine in Toronto. According to the Albany story, even after almost two decades behind bars, Dooley Ann Drayton had yet to show remorse for her crimes. Ann shrugged it off, like she shrugged off most media attention over the years. But because of both those articles, she got mail. Ann always got mail from strangers, but the amount went way up whenever something about her appeared in print. All incoming prisoner mail is opened by staff, so Ann asked them not to pass on the hate mail to her, or that they put it in a separate pile, which she could then throw out without reading. That still left a sizable pile, mostly from people promising to pray for her. Lots of folks out there seemed to be personally concerned for Ann's soul.

Soon as the doctor said it was okay, Ann went back to work at the hospital. By now she'd become very close with the patients, and while she was gone they'd missed her. Some—the sickest and most scared of dying—complained about being left alone too much, especially at night. They'd get frightened or they'd need something, and often there'd be no one to help them. Ann was upset when she heard that one patient had died during this time and how there was no one with that poor woman at the end. So she went storming into the hospital administrator's office, shouting about how a thing like that should never happen to any human being and must never be allowed to happen again. And was calmly told that it most likely would happen again, and there was nothing anyone could do about it. The hospital just didn't have enough staff.

That was when Ann requested permission to move onto the AIDS ward so she could be there twenty-four hours a day.

It was such a crazy request, so obviously impossible, such a big time Rule Violation, I knew I didn't have to worry. Warden gonna laugh you right out of the room, I told her, laughing myself. So when I saw her packing her things, I didn't know who to be more angry at, Ann or Warden DeFries. But what was I gonna do, write to the newspapers?

Wasn't our first argument, but I bet it was our loudest. It sounds weird, given what she was planning to do, but the word I kept throwing in her face was *selfish*. And I meant it. It beats the devil how that woman could never help some folks without always hurting someone else, usually herself. She was getting old now, she was sickly, she was all wore out. Since the fever, when she couldn't eat at all, she'd been living mostly on liquids and vitamins. Why don't you just stick an IV in your arm? I said. The way I saw it, she was killing herself, which seemed to me like the worst kind of self-ishness. What was she trying to prove? I kept shouting at her. You don't even believe in Heaven. What are you playing the saint for?

But Ann said she was just being practical. Away from the ward, all she did was worry about the patients, she said. So she might as well be with them. And she asked me to take her typewriter and keep it safe for her. Two other ones had already got stolen. I told her to go fuck herself.

"Oh, come on now," she said. "Cheer up! It's not like I'm being paroled!" Her idea of a joke. A joke that, I got to admit, struck me as funny. And a surprise, because Ann—well, Ann was a lot of things, but she wasn't funny. She didn't have a sense of humor, not really. You had to hold her down and tickle her to make her laugh out loud. I suppose that's why God made her ticklish. Now she wasn't laughing out loud but she was smiling. She was also saying something, but I don't remember what. Because I was concentrat-ing on that smile. I was telling myself to remember it. Remember that smile, I said to myself. Because sometimes you just know.

It was late one night, and Ann was checking on patients when she come across one who'd fallen out of bed. Ann could've got help from a guard, but this patient was just skin and bones. So Ann picked up the woman herself and got her back into bed. Then she noticed the woman's water pitcher was empty. Ann was on her way back with the full pitcher when she crashed to the floor.

Heart disease. Real common in prison. I've got some myself. And it was in Ann's family, too. That infection of hers had some-thing to do with it, so I heard. Like I heard that if you went too long without eating right, the heart would start to devour itself.

Anyway, the ambulance took her away that night and I didn't know anything about it till the next day. She was very bad and she was going to need an operation, but they had to wait till she was more stable or the operation could kill her. It was cruel not being in touch, not being able to have any contact with Ann. The sisters were a big help, but even they weren't allowed to visit her.

All I could do was pray, and I prayed for two things. One, that she would pull through, of course. And two, that she would've learned her lesson and start acting more sensible. She'd move off the AIDS ward and never go back. Our unit had just got word that, because of overcrowding, we'd have to start double-bunking soon, which was already the case in most other units. If two inmates here want, they can request to be cellmates, and if the inmates are grandmas, Administration is more likely to agree. And I thought how if that could happen it would be the greatest thing, because then I could keep a close eye on Ann.

Meanwhile, I was living with a corkscrew in my gut and seeing snake heads at night like when I was small. When I heard Ann got through her operation all right, I started to breathe more free. I couldn't wait for her to come home. But they said she was still pretty sick and she'd be staying in the hospital awhile, maybe even a couple more weeks. I couldn't go see her or even give her a call, but I made her a special get-well card (I don't think I've mentioned yet that I have a flair for drawing), and I had everyone on our floor sign it. And I put this card into a big envelope along with other cards, some bought in the commissary, some homemade like mine, from other folks, and we sent them all over to the hospital.

Next thing, Sister Clementine comes to our floor with the bad news. Ann isn't coming back to Maryville, she says, not now, not in a few weeks, not ever. She says soon as Ann is stable enough, she's going to be transferred to Eagleton Correctional Facility, downstate. I'm watching Sister's lips move, and I'm hearing her words as if through a thick wall or underwater. Something to do with Ann needing to be somewhere she could get better care, now that she had such a serious condition. Something about Eagleton being close to a famous cardiac center.

Later I heard this was really all about Administration getting the jitters. They didn't want someone as sick as Ann (like we didn't have plenty of other folks sick to death around here), they didn't want her dying on their hands and bringing attention to Maryville and to the hospital in particular. Because Ann was a magnet for publicity, and already it seemed at least one person had raised the question, what the hell she was doing living on the AIDS ward to begin with. And then I heard Ann was probably going to be released, like other inmates when their health care got to be so expensive the state didn't want to have to pay for it.

I didn't know which of all these rumors was true. All I knew was, not only was I never going to see my friend again, I was not even going to get to say goodbye.

Most times when an inmate is released or transferred out of Maryville, folks'll throw her a party. A bunch of us decided to throw one for Orphan Annie, too, even though the guest of honor couldn't be there. And we did it with style. There was music and dancing. There were speeches, and there was Bharti's famous rice pudding. And of course there was plenty of weeping. Toward the end, Misty wanders in, and like usual she can't tell what's going on. She stands there with her arms wrapped round her head, twisting this way and that, saying, *Who dead? Who dead?* Ruining the party. So finally I go to my cell and get a Polaroid snap of Ann I had up on my wall. I show it to Misty and she grabs it and brings it up close to her face and she starts howling. I grab it back but Misty won't stop. She keeps howling, her voice rising and rising, without even breaking for air—just like this dog that lived next door when I was a child, that got trapped one night in a fire.

✳

"Write about a person you met in prison whom you admire."

It was my counselor who talked me into taking the writing class. This was just after I got out of solitary. I'd taken a swing at

Headless Chicken. It didn't matter that I was too drunk to connect. I was still charged with assaulting a guard, a major crime around here. Thirty days: I got off easy. Mainly because I'd never assaulted anyone before. Or call it grandma time.

My counselor these days is a nice young fellow named Alex. He looks like an Alex. He's got big bright teeth and round wire-rimmed glasses, and he wears suspenders, which someone told him can prevent backache. I've noticed he blushes easy. He blushes when I can't for the life of me see what there is for him to blush about. But it seems to me anyone with that particular trait is probably a decent character. Wish I could say this for all the counselors.

I am required to see Alex from time to time. After I got released from segregation, he told me we had to find a better way for me to deal with problems than trying to drown them in moonshine. Let me say, nothing is easier to come by behind bars than moonshine. Routine searches always turn up a couple of batches per unit. My friend Winkie brews hers out of Hawaiian punch and potatoes. She's been caught a couple of times, but she always goes back to making more. She hawks her best stuff as Hawaiian Kayo. "Two cups and you out for the count, baby." But I never could hold much liquor, and it didn't take more than one cup to get me drunk. And from there it was just another sip to disorderly.

I don't even remember swinging at Headless Chicken, let alone why. I also don't remember much about the days leading up to that event. I'd just been assigned to Alex, and he sent me to the shrink, who was either deaf or forgetful, because he just kept asking me the same questions over and over, was I having suicidal thoughts, was I hearing voices, and so on. Funny, he never asked me was I praying. I was. More than ever. But I knew the thing I was praying for was wrong, wrong as could be, a prayer the Lord would never answer and that could even bring down His wrath. So praying wasn't the same comfort to me like it used to be.

I had to see the regular doctor, too, round this time, and he said my blood pressure was too high and I had to take medication. Soon after that my heart started acting up. My chest felt like I had a pitchfork stuck in it. If I so much as sighed too deep, there was pain, and when I had asthma the pain got so bad either I threw up or passed out or both.

The doctor gave me other pills and my heart settled down. In body I was better, but in spirit, oh my, oh my. Crying. Crying all the time, over nothing. Scared. Waking up at night in a sweat. Dreams I would not tell you about, dreams of a motherless child. It got so I was afraid to go to sleep, and I asked permission to leave a light on. I got permission with the help of the shrink, and then a month or so later along comes some son-of-a-bitch-of-a-sergeant to say *Can't do that*.

Is it any surprise I turned to Winkie?

The writing class was new. Back in the day, Maryville had a regular writing program and even a little magazine, but funding for all this had been cut. Now some foundation came up with a grant, and a teacher from the state college was hired to come teach three classes a week, beginning, intermediate, and advanced. Anyone with a college degree wishing to participate was automatically put in advanced.

I told Alex I wasn't interested in any writing class. But I was even less interested in group therapy, which would've been his choice. My taking the writing class was our compromise. Alex said I needed to do something, as he put it, to take me out of myself. I said I could think of better ways to accomplish that, and he blushed as deep and mysterious as ever.

First time I set eyes on the teacher I was disappointed. Not that he was ugly, but he was so bland, a dry-toast-no-butter kind of person. You couldn't tell his age. He might've been thirty or he might've been fifty. Lightbulb-shaped head, wispy hair, bumpy skin, wrinkled shirt, squeaky little voice. Another easy blusher!

I wasn't sure just what we'd be doing, but at least I knew more than some. First day, Kezia raises her hand and says, "Wait a minute. You mean *we* do the writing in this class?" But that's nothing. You wouldn't believe what some folks here don't know. I once heard two cellmates fighting. "New York ain't no *state*, stupid,

New York is a *city*." When I worked in the kitchen and asked this other woman working there to get me some parsley, she said, "Do it come in a can or a jar?" Another time this same woman said, "A tree can grow out of the ground without somebody plant it?" There are those who don't know how to read, and those who don't know how to drive, and I bet less than one percent can swim.

The teacher said to call him Neal. Neal was nervous that first day and for quite some time after. There was no guard in the room, and I don't think Neal was prepared for some of the things he was gonna hear. ("I always think, If only I didn't happen to have that chair leg in my hand . . .") Neal gave us exercises out of a book called *In Writing Is Healing*. "Write about an experience that made you feel special." "Write a letter to someone you think did you wrong." People would read what they wrote out loud, and then everyone was expected to say something.

One day Neal wrote this on the blackboard: "Three things in human life are important. The first is to be kind. The second is to be kind. And the third is to be kind—Henry James." Well, I didn't know if I agreed with all that, but I wasn't about to say so. Neal said we had to make everyone in the class feel safe. He meant for opening up and telling their stories, but he could've been thinking about something else, too, especially after a fight broke out during the second or third class. No big deal, the rest of us were able to stop it right off, but I could tell Neal was shook up, and I even wondered if he'd quit. I also wondered if he was going to report the fight, like he was required to do. He did neither.

He was kind, and he was kind, and he was kind. And when the grant money ran out, he stayed on as a volunteer. Couldn't leave my ladies, he said. And then he explained it was really for selfish reasons he was doing it. Because *he* got so much from *us*.

"Write about someone you met in prison whom you admire."

It started as a couple of pages and then, like magic, grew and grew. Ann's magic typewriter helped make it grow. (I came to believe there was a spell on that machine, because it never got stolen.

And by the way: whoever stole those other two, you can bet it wasn't any inmate.)

Even after the course was over, I was still working on that assignment. At first I told Neal I didn't think I could do it. I didn't think I could write about Ann. But I wanted to, I kept trying to, I kept trying to do like Neal said. "You have to find the right tone," he said. "If you find the right tone, you can write about anything."

All fine and good, but how do you find the right tone?

"Well, that can be hard," Neal said. "But try this. Write as if you were writing for someone you know will understand. A friend, say. Someone you trust. Someone who already knows a lot about you."

I sat down and began writing for Jesus.

Dear Mrs. Strom,

Many thanks for your letter. After such a long time, I'd pretty much given up hope of hearing from you. To answer your first question, I picked you to send my essay to because you are one of the magazine editors who have kindly donated a subscription to Maryville, and I thought you might be a friendly reader. I cannot say how happy I am that this has turned out to be so.

Of course I understand how you might want to make some changes. (You should know that, to protect certain individuals, innocent or guilty as the case may be, I have changed some things myself.) I know my writing is far from perfect and expect you'll find plenty of spelling and grammar mistakes needing to be fixed. But if you don't mind, I want to say that I would not want anything to be done that would change the tone. I want the tone to stay like it is.

As for my name, I see no reason anyone has to know what my real name is. If you don't want to call me by my prison number, which I understand, you could just call me Anonymous. Or if you prefer, you could invent a nice name for me . . .

✳

I chose the name "Olympia Underwood."

✳

Dear Mrs. Strom,

Many thanks for the copies of Caracara *which arrived today. I cannot say how proud I am to see "Orphan Annie and the Hand of God" included in such a fine magazine.*

I was very sorry to learn of your husband's passing and wish to express my deepest sympathy. It must be a comfort to you to have the words of so many people who clearly loved and admired him gathered together in these pages.

Thank you also for offering to send a copy to Ann Drayton. I thought you might want to know that she is back in the hospital. She says it's just some kind of relapse and not anything to worry about. When inmates from different facilities want to be in touch, they have to apply for special permission. We just got ours a couple of weeks ago and are only now catching up. In the beginning, Ann tried to fight the transfer to Eagleton. Now she says she's trying to make the best of things, as has always been her way.

If you wish, I will keep you informed how she's doing. Meanwhile, I think we should all do some praying for her . . .

It's always who you know.

Three phone calls, each to some person I had met through Val, got me permission to see her. But only for five minutes. (Doctor's, not jailer's, orders.)

The guard at her door searched me with an air of annoyance before returning to his *TV Guide*. The door was half open. Almost the first thing I saw was the shackles.

There is a genetic disorder called progeria, which causes premature aging in children. Of all the patients he saw in the course of his medical training, Jeremy once told me, none distressed him more than those stooped, wizened, palsied boys and girls, doddering about the ward like octogenarians. That is what the person lying in bed looked like to me. Hair so white and face so pinched, the head of an old woman, a very sick old woman. But the flat body under the sheet might have been a child's. The thin, smooth arms exposed on top of the sheet were like a child's arms. And the eyes that watched me as I pulled up a chair were the naked, wondering eyes of a child.

Leg shackles. She was gravely ill, with barely enough strength to turn her head. Had she made it as far as the door, the guard could have blown her back to bed with a puff. But just recently I'd read that it was not uncommon to make hospitalized prisoners wear shackles even while giving birth.

I could not recall ever having seen her sick before.

"Are they treating you well?" I said. "Do you have everything you need?"

She forced a smile. "I'm in the best of hands." Ironic. "Of course, if I wasn't who I am, I wouldn't even be here. They'd never have transferred me. They'd have let me die back there."

To find her at least this much her old self brought me comfort.

I had to bend forward to hear her. The words came out whistling, as if the air had to pass through some kind of grate. Her breath was foul. I had smelled that kind of breath before, at other sickbeds. I knew it was often caused not by illness, but by an empty stomach. Even healthy people on fasts could have such bad breath.

Five minutes. I saw there was to be no word about the past, nothing about our quarrel, no attempt to explain or patch things up. All these thoughts I had fretted obsessively about on the drive up from the city.

I had brought pictures of Zoe and Jude, but the moment would never come for me to take them out. I had also brought a copy of *Caracara*, which I would leave on the bedside table when it was time for me to go.

Because she asked what I was doing now, I told her I'd been invited by some people who'd worked at the magazine to join them in starting a bookstore. But probably I'd say no. "It's impossible to make an independent bookstore work these days."

And at this my old friend rallied—to scold. "You always begin by thinking it can't be done. That's always been your biggest problem, George.

"What do you keep looking at?" she asked. And I realized she didn't know. She had never had the strength to sit up and look around the room. It was a Catholic hospital. High on the wall above her bed was a crucifix. But I only shook my head. I would not have been able to speak in any case.

Suddenly she closed her eyes. Sunk into pain, or fatigue, or perhaps even sleep. It occurred to me that of course she must be sedated.

Forgive me. During the minutes that remained, though I held her hand, though I looked at her face, I thought not of Ann but of Turner. Never to see him again. Not to have been able to see him even one last time. Not even to have known of his death when it happened.

"I knew you'd cry." Her hand stirred in mine, and I realized in agony she wanted to reach up and touch my face, but she was too weak. I lifted her hand and pressed it to my cheek.

Not to be able to speak of him now. So wrong to tell her; so wrong for her not to know.

Just before she faded again, she said, "If I had more time, I would have. I needed more time. I'm sorry. I'm so sorry." But I did not know what she meant. Time to be my friend? Time to save humanity?

A nurse appeared in the doorway and raised her eyebrows at me.

When I bent to kiss Ann, I caught the smell again, and I bore it away with me, inseparable from the notion of decay, of a wasted body devouring its own heart.

*

A burning question: Why did Ann put up a photograph of Thomas Sargente on the wall of her cell?

The last time I saw my friend Cleo, I asked her what she thought about this. Neither the passing of time nor Ann's suffering had done much to soften Cleo's judgment. "As far as I know, in prison, when an inmate puts up a picture of a murder victim, it is generally regarded as a trophy. Why else do you think the guards got so upset?"

I knew she was right. I had heard the same thing. But I refused to believe Ann was capable of this.

So the question remains: Why?

Perhaps she was trying to understand. Perhaps she was trying to change. Perhaps the photograph was meant to be a daily reminder. By meditating on it, she would uncover those feelings of remorse that had so far eluded her. Or perhaps the hanging of the photograph was itself a sign of remorse.

But where was the evidence for this? Cleo wanted to know. Ann had never uttered a word of remorse.

I don't know. It is true that had her feelings changed, she would not likely have kept silent about them. Perhaps, in the end, she was never able to separate remorse for what she had done from betrayal of Kwame. I cannot know this for sure, but it would be in keeping with her nature: her strictness and her purity, her diamond hardness, her terrifying honesty.

✳

I have gone to visit Gansevoort Street several times. I have stood outside the building and looked up at the second-story window, where the shades are always drawn. The place now seems to be some sort of office for the meatpacking center below it. The air on that street reeks of carcasses, and at certain hours the gutter runs red.

✳

I want to know about a certain speck of time: between the moment the first shots were fired at Sargente, and before Kwame was shot by Heffernan. This would have been the time when Kwame turned around to look up at the window. He and Ann would have been looking into each other's eyes at the very moment the bullet struck Kwame in the back. In that moment, he would have understood what she had done, and why. I want to know what was in Kwame's eyes ("His *beautiful* eyes, don't you mean?"). Disbelief? Reproach? Forgiveness? Love? How often must that moment have come back to Ann. And her famous words: *If Thomas Sargente had said* nigger *one less time, he might not be dead.* And: *If it weren't for that crazy fool, my brother would still be alive.* How she lived with all this, I don't know.

✳

The Great Gatsby.

Ann had read the book before I did, in high school. "We were taught that it was *the* American novel, all about the American dream and the American spirit of hope and possibility." For Ann it was a troubling proposition that, for Americans, idealism is inseparable from materialism. And for all that the book was said to be an

385

indictment of a certain element of the aristocracy, the decadent rich, there was no mistaking how much the author himself was attracted to glamour and the power of money.

"He writes so gorgeously about the beautiful people and their beautiful things, he makes the reader want those things, too." True. The cars. The clothes. The mansion. "Most Americans would give anything to be at one of Gatsby's parties."

Ann hated the way Fitzgerald had represented the working class: the hopelessly worn, emasculated George Wilson and his desperate wife, Myrtle, to whom Fitzgerald is so cruel.

My problem with the book was different.

The book is full of ideas, two of them named Jay Gatsby and Daisy Buchanan, but no real characters . . . We are meant to see Gatsby as a romantic hero holding fast to his dreams. But it is hard to believe any such person ever existed. I did not accept much about his improbable life, least of all his love for Daisy. I did not for one minute believe that he would have kept his illusions and his innocence through years of social climbing and the getting of money through sordid means and his connections to organized crime. I did not believe that he would not have known at this point in his carefully constructed career that San Francisco was not part of the Middle West. I did not believe his description of Daisy's golden voice, that it was "full of money"—just as I did not believe the description of Gatsby's smile: "it understood you just so far as you wanted to be understood, believed in you as you would like to believe in yourself"—because that is not how human beings hear or see one another . . . The book is filled with overstatements like these, which sound deep and clever and golden themselves, but strike them and they ring untrue . . . The description of Gatsby "balancing himself on the dashboard of his car with that resourcefulness of movement that is so peculiarly American" is another example. That is not a man balancing on that dashboard, but a myth . . .

The story line has many weaknesses, beginning with Daisy's ignorance that Jay Gatsby is living nearby . . . It strains belief that Gatsby would invite Nick Carraway to come along when he shows Daisy his mansion for the first time. The only reason the narrator is invited along is so that he can describe everything to the reader. And why would a man think to woo a woman born to wealth, a debutante, with a husband rich enough to own a string of polo ponies, by flinging about his expensive shirts?

Are we seriously meant to believe that the rich are more careless than the poor?

The pathetic showing at Gatsby's funeral is cloyingly sentimental, and how likely is it that, out of the "hundreds" who attended his parties, there would not be at least dozens who would also attend his funeral, albeit some more out of curiosity than respect . . .

So that was my problem with *The Great Gatsby*. I did not believe a word of it.

Perhaps the most jarring and inexplicable detail of all is this: Why do the two men who rush to where Myrtle lies in the road after being struck by Gatsby's car immediately tear open her shirt? When they do, they discover her nearly severed left breast, which is what the author wants us to see. But who, rushing to the aid of a blood-soaked accident victim, begins by unbuttoning her clothes?

"But, Mom," says Zoe. "You were *high* when you wrote this."

We are in the living room of my new apartment. I have finally moved to the neighborhood where I used to dream of living, when I first came to New York. The building is not too far from Gansevoort Street, not far from Bank Street, where Nicole and Whit Bishop once lived. Not that any of this was taken into account when I was apartment hunting. I was simply looking for a smaller place.

Zoe and Jude are both with me tonight; we have just eaten supper and are getting ready to go meet Solange.

Now that she has read *The Great Gatsby* herself, Zoe has fished out that old term paper of mine that she first came across when she was helping me pack.

To her, it is a perfect novel. She does not understand my view at all, though mine is the one more in keeping with the book's reception, in 1925. ("No more than a glorified anecdote"—H. L. Mencken.) Fitzgerald himself thought the book failed to sell because it lacked any "important woman character." True. And quite a statement, when you consider the character of Daisy was based partly on his first love and partly on his wife.

"How can you not see that it's a great love story?"

"Oh, I don't know. I guess I just like my love stories to include some important woman character."

"You are so totally wrong about this book."

Now she is reading *Tender Is the Night*. Fitzgerald, never one of mine, has become her favorite writer.

She says, "You don't like him because you're so unromantic."

"Did you know that he said all women over thirty-five should be murdered?"

"Well, that isn't *me*."

"I hope she'll be a fool," says Daisy of her newborn daughter. "That's the best thing a girl can be in this world, a beautiful little fool."

Jude, who has also read *The Great Gatsby* in school, says, "I think Gatsby is gay." Lately he has taken to saying this about so many men and boys, I have begun to think he is trying to tell me something.

But my daughter will not be diverted. "Gatsby dies for his dreams. He makes the ultimate sacrifice for the woman he loves, and that's awesome."

"Enough about that book," I say, sensing the threat of a more serious argument.

Love. Children. Sacrifice. For your *children*, yes, you would throw yourself without hesitation in the path of a train. And when the train passed, they would step right over you.

"Mom, I think you should reread it."

I have reread it. And to my own surprise, I felt almost exactly the same way about it. This time, though, there was something always in the back of my mind to make Gatsby a touch more plausible. For hadn't Ann done it—held on to her purity and her dreams and illusions all those years? Hadn't they both remained faithful to an ideal vision of themselves formed when they were still in their teens? The change of name, the dedication to the creation of a new self, the fierce determination to escape what they were born, the passionate belief in unselfish devotion. The *heart*.

And this time, when I came to the famous part about careless people smashing up things and letting other people clean up the mess, I heard Cleo's words: *"I know her kind. These spoiled rich kids . . . these rich white girls who end up making a big fucking mess and destroying other people's lives . . ."*

I remember assemblies in grade school, how the principal would end every address with the words, "And remember, boys and girls, you are an American. You can be anything in the whole world you want to be! So dream *big*."

I think it is significant that *The Great Gatsby*'s reputation as the greatest masterpiece of twentieth-century American literature did not blossom until the fifties, and that those most responsible for that reputation have been schoolteachers. It is such an easy book to teach. Short, clear, safe. What makes Gatsby "great"? How does Gatsby represent the American dream? What does the green light symbolize? What does the valley of ashes symbolize? What do the eyes of Dr. Eckleburg symbolize? Compare and contrast: East Egg / West Egg. Jay Gatsby / Tom Buchanan. New York / The Middle West.

"We're going to be late," says Jude. And we all rush downstairs to catch a cab. Then we have to wait while Jude rushes back upstairs, because we have forgotten the champagne.

As always, the children are looking forward to seeing their Aunt Crash. "She is such a hoot!" Riding uptown—she lives in Washington Heights now—they keep interrupting each other with "Remember the time she—"

It was Jude's twelfth or thirteenth birthday. Solange wanted to give him something very special, she said, waggling the card behind her back. She wanted to give him something she had received from me, something she had treasured for years. Jude regarded the scrap with complete bafflement. "Who's Mick Jagger?"

Sir Mick, now.

Remember the time she—

It was only recently that they told me how she had turned them both on to pot when they were still in grade school, and how another time, when they were not much older, she gave them orange juice spiked with LSD ("just a touch"). And though it was many years ago, and they were not harmed in any way that I could see, I was very angry, I am still angry, I will always be angry that my own sister did this to me.

But tonight we are all smiles. Tonight we are having a celebration. Solange has published another book, a book of poems this time. It is called *Dating the Exterminator*, and it has just won a literary prize.

Riding uptown, I get the feeling I often get riding through the city in the back of a cab: a feeling of serenity, almost of fulfillment. I am happy tonight because I have the children with me. But mostly this feeling I am talking about has to do with sheer love of the streets and the life of the streets, and the sense of that love being shared by millions of others, and how it grows more haunting and piercing, now that there is the ever-present threat that the city might, perhaps even soon, be destroyed.

Solange's book has an epigraph, from Rilke: "Rich in memory are those places from the past that can never be revisited." In my case, the house where I grew up. The town library (burned). The handsome prewar building on Madison Avenue where *Visage* had its offices was torn down a few years after the magazine died, and was replaced, seemingly overnight, by a tower block three times as high. Where Bonwit Teller stood now stands Trump Tower.

Here are more lines from *The Great Gatsby*.

I liked to walk up Fifth Avenue and pick out romantic women from the crowd and imagine that in a few minutes I was going to enter into their lives, and no one would ever know or disapprove.

I like to remember when I was one of them, or to pretend that I am one of them still, sensing that restless man at my back and half turning, no, turning all the way, open-armed, saying, *Pick me, pick me.*